Gods From the Machine

ANDREW LY

ISBN-10: 0991444701
ISBN-13: 9780991444700

For the girl who sparked my imagination

Gods From the Machine

ACKNOWLEDGEMENTS

Storytelling at a glance seems to be an easy task, but it's truly harder than it looks, especially when you don't have support. Thankfully I did. As a self-published author, I've had hurdles thrown at me, but luckily I was able to carry on. Here I'd like to personally thank everyone for their pivotal roles in helping me finish my novel.

Thanks to my parents, for having faith in my decision to pursue my dream. Words cannot describe how grateful I am to their years of loving guidance and support. To have utter devotion and making sacrifices for their only son is something that I wish to repay. Hopefully this is a start.

Thanks to my sister, Katharine, for her input and support throughout the entire writing process. The best sister a guy could ask for.

Thanks to my editor, Cindy, whose services helped shaped my story to the best it could possibly be.

Thanks to my best friends, the Peter's Crew, who kept me grounded and for being at my side when the stakes really mattered. Love you guys.

Thanks to my friends and family members who instilled invaluable confidence and positivity in my efforts to produce something beautiful.

Thanks to the readers at andrewjly.com

And of course, thanks again to the girl who sparked my imagination. Without you, this would have been impossible.

1

THE BEGINNING OF THE END

Nick made sure his parachute was secure on his back one last time before he pulled open the side hatch on the plane, exposing them to the outside world. A whistling gust of air hit him in the face like a brick, chilling and effectively breathing energy back into his body. The strong wind took care of his sweaty palms, leaving only the nervousness in the pit of his stomach.

The pilot flipped on the flashing red lights overhead that signaled their arrival, "Parachutes on, boys. Get ready to deploy."

"Ready?" Matt shouted. His voice was almost lost against the wind.

"Let's find out." Nick took one more deep breath before he leapt into the darkness.

He fell faster and faster, gaining full speed, but it became difficult to keep his eyes open. He couldn't risk closing them, however, or he'd easily wind up crashing face-first into the ground or impaled on a sharp branch. A line of trees approached quickly. Nick pulled the parachute open and gently glided down. When branches tugged at his clothes he unbuckled his chute and dropped the last ten feet, using his shoulders as a cushion to hit the ground and roll to absorb the impact. The execution was successful—almost perfect. Peter himself would be proud.

Nick straightened out and peered around the brush for Matt. He'd jumped out right after him so he should have landed somewhere nearby.

"Over here," Matt called.

Nick glanced up just as Matt dropped a few feet in front of him. He stood there in his full knight uniform: a long, white and gold trimmed coat whose hem ended just above his feet; leather black gloves and boots as well as a blue armband to mark his particular field of expertise. His personalized long sword hung at his waist. The Glenhaven Garrison's symbols, a shield with two wings were sewn on both his shoulders. He looked magnificently heroic.

Becoming a knight was a high honor, and had been held in that regard ever since the beginning of the Great Demon War over a century ago. Ever since, the world had been separated into three groups: civilians, demons, and Garrison knights.

The Garrisons themselves were elite military academies set around the world. Their purpose was to produce knights trained in the art of demon slaying. The candidates usually came from wealthy families and were chosen at the age of six because their bodies needed to be molded and developed to perfection. Knights needed to be in peak physical fitness in order to combat demons effectively. This wasn't the case for Nick, an orphan who lived within the Garrison walls long before he could say his first words.

"You were quiet the entire ride. Are you sure you can do this? If you want, I'll be fine going alone. I can call the pilot to pick you up and I'll tell the old man we were both there," Matt said.

"No. Peter assigned this to both of us specifically. He had to have his reasons." The possibility that he might finally get his hands dirty would be a welcome change. It won't be like before, no, it'd be different this time. No way was he going down in history as the screw-up of the entire Glenhaven Garrison. Not Nick Emberson. Not ever again.

"Whatever you say, man, but try to look more alive! I know you can be more enthusiastic than this!" Matt spun around with his arms open. "We're in demon territory! You should be thrilled to be outside the shield!"

Nick nodded solemnly. Of course it would be easy for Matt to take this mission lightly. Everything in life seemed to come easier for him anyway. Nick glanced at him, his light, messy brown hair and hazel eyes complemented his round face, which made him conventionally attractive, but it was his charming disposition and sense of humor that made it easy for people to like him. He was also few inches taller than Nick, with the broad shoulders and muscular build of a finely tuned athlete. It was no wonder he became a knight so quickly, but then again, being the sole heir in the prestigious Cunningham family meant he had the added pressure of upholding a long line of established warriors. However, despite the reputation of his lineage, he never let it go to his head. He was the kindest and humblest person Nick knew, as well as his best friend.

Unlike his friend, Nick was just a soldier. Instead of wearing white and gold, he was supposed to wear the traditional and bland olive jumpsuit that classified soldiers. However, he took great pride in his appearance, and went with a more distinguished ensemble: a grey t-shirt, black mesh pants, and the standard black combat boots were all he needed on assignments. He also wore a custom black jacket of his own design, which was both stab-resistant and waterproof. It ended at his thighs, and all other unnecessary frills were cut out in order to be more efficient. It wasn't as fancy as the knight uniform, but in his opinion it was more tactically intelligent.

For the most part, Nick considered himself quite plain looking, aside from having a nearly perfectly symmetrical face and a narrow, pointed nose. His thick hair was a very dark shade of brown, combed neatly to the side. He had auburn eyes and an angular facial structure with a prominent, square jawline. His already-light complexion was paler than usual and he had lost some muscle tone as a result of his poor living habits. It wasn't his fault he had little desire to eat or sleep; everything was riding on this mission to be a success, which meant he had no room for mistakes. The anxiety it gave him was fuel enough to keep him going until he was finished.

"According to the coordinates, Sir Marcus, along with his secret treasure, should be buried somewhere over there." Matt pointed straight ahead, beyond the brush and swamp.

"It's too quiet. I was expecting a surprise," Nick said.

Matt shook his head in disbelief. "Let me get this straight, you're unhappy because we aren't getting ambushed? What did you expect, a greeting from a bunch of Hellbeasts? Or would a group of Dreadknights be better?"

"I'm not looking to find trouble, I just didn't think it would be this quiet." Truth be told, Nick was more disappointed with the fact that he always stuck with the plain and simple assignments. For once he'd like to be challenged. Was that such an odd request? Ever since the disastrous incident in Fyria, Peter had been extra careful in selecting assignments for him, making sure they were so simple that even a toddler could handle them without much difficulty. It was almost insulting.

Matt shrugged. "Well, it beats being in Glenhaven."

Glenhaven was the city where they lived and was known as the "center of the world," but other than housing their Garrison, it was a rural and forgettable place. The quiet town saw very few visitors, and for most of its inhabitants, it was a place for retirement or seclusion. It was boring and lonely, but sometimes Nick envied the people who were allowed to live normal lives. Part of him wished he could have just been born as a regular kid, instead of flying miles outside his hometown in search for buried treasure in a dead knight's tomb. But then again, he realized, those kids probably dreamed about leaving their safe little city and finding adventure. This used to be impossible because of the demons, but as technology and time progressed, it soon became a reality.

During the Second Coming, the last major war twenty years ago, a Garrison from a different country had developed a protective barrier known as the Holy Shield that warded demons. Though the shield restored some semblance of civility and normalcy, a part of Nick feared for the day that the demons would break through and rise again.

They walked for a while, trekking through mud and shallow swamp before finally reaching a small clearing covered in roots. Not just ordinary roots, but those that appeared as if they've been growing here for years. They looked to be a type of demonic plant by the way they expanded and compressed, as if sucking the oxygen around them. They were easily over four feet in width and ran rampantly, blocking the entrance to the tomb a couple meters further down the path.

"My wolf was starving the whole way here. I think maybe we should let him feast." Matt grinned, brandishing his sword. His "wolf" was actually short for *Wolfsbane*, a custom-made long sword crafted by one the finest whitesmiths of their Garrison and imbued with holy properties. It was a beautiful blade, passed down from generations of Cunninghams. At the bottom of the hilt, a molded grey wolf's head bared its ferocious fangs. Each knight, from whichever class they chose to study, was given a standard weapon as a token upon completion of their training. However, for those who had achieved knight status, like Matt, they were given the special honor of choosing any weapon they wanted. Nick was never allowed to even touch a sword before, so the conflict of choosing between different weapons never came up.

Matt stepped back and, with a grunt, cleaved the thick root into two like a knife splitting butter. The plant let out a high-pitched screech. It flailed in the air a few moments before falling dead, oozing dark green liquid. His nose flared and he recoiled in disgust. Nick held his breath and covered his mouth. The last time he took a whiff of a demonic plant's blood his stomach churned for days.

"Cursed vines. I knew this plant looked too wild. The demons must have placed it here to stop us from reaching the tomb," Nick said.

"Well, they're not doing a very good job." Matt slashed on through with ease. "If they wanted to keep us out they should have put something with more bite instead of bark."

Nick couldn't help but chuckle at the lame joke. Eventually Matt's cutting efforts opened a path leading to the entrance of the tomb.

"Okay, so the plan is to go inside, open the chest, grab whatever is in there and get out. No mistakes. Got it?" Matt said.

"Of course." Nick brushed stray foliage and thorns off his jacket. It was the same when they discussed it at headquarters and it was the same on the plane. They walked through the entrance to find a single lit torch clung close to the right wall, ripe for grabbing. How long the flame had been lit troubled Nick. He didn't like the idea that there could have been other visitors before them.

"So what do you think the Supreme Commander would want with an old relic?" Matt asked as they walked down the narrow stone path.

"I don't know, and I don't care. Orders are orders and I plan to stick to them," Nick said.

Matt laughed. "I guess, but it's just like old Pete to make us jump through unnecessary hoops to teach a lesson. Seriously though, why now? Why not just leave this thing to collect dust?" Before Nick could reply, he extended his arm over Nick's chest, and pointed a distance in front of them. "Speak of Ozarael, I think we've found it."

In plain view sat a large chest covered in layers of dust. Behind it was a giant tombstone marked with the words *Sir Marcus, the Orator.* It was a befitting name from all the tales

Nick had heard of him, the legendary knight who was said to have stood fearless before every demon, never cowering even in the face of impossible odds. It was said that during the final struggle, many knights had lost their morale, but his passionate words alone gave hope to thousands of soldiers, guiding them through several successful battles and turning the tides to victory. Unfortunately, he died just before the Second Coming ended, never able to realize his contribution to mankind's survival.

Matt saluted proudly. "One of the greatest knights in Garrison history." He whipped out an old key he was given for this mission and opened the chest. At the very bottom was a golden cloth wrapped around some objects. Matt shook it open; two shiny pieces of metal tumbled out. It was a sword—no, a broken sword. He lifted the hilt piece in the air. "This is it? We came all this way for this?"

"Just grab it and let's get out of here." Nick sighed. He couldn't even hide his disappointment. It was too good to be true. After he screwed up the last mission he knew there would be consequences, but to get assigned to something like this was the worst thing imaginable. It was actually degrading how he had become nothing more than a glorified errand boy. As they were halfway along the corridor, a small rumbling shook the ground. Dirt poured on them from the ceiling like sand trickling down an hourglass. Stone bricks followed shortly, pounding the earth like cracks of thunder. The tomb was collapsing on itself! A trap placed for unwanted visitors.

They sprinted towards the exit. Matt tripped. The sword pieces flew from his hands and clattered against the wall.

"The sword Nick! The sword!" Matt cried, as the stream of dirt was catching up to them.

Nick snatched up the sword pieces. As his fingers wrapped around them, the pieces began to glow white-hot. He turned back to help his companion back to his feet and they dashed towards safety. Nick bit down hard on his lip to hold back from screaming, making sure he kept his vision straight enough to cross through the entrance before the brown earth caved and buried everything.

Outside, he heaved the sword pieces to the ground. His hands were charred and smelled like an overcooked steak. They stood in a small clearing, on a grassy knoll next to the pile of rubble that was once the tomb.

"Your hands!" Matt gasped. He tapped the signal button on his tracking device. "We need to get you a medic, fast!"

In less than an hour, a Garrison jet arrived. With no room to land, medics dropped a rope ladder with an attached stretcher. Matt helped Nick onto a stretcher and they reeled both of them to safety. All he could think about the whole ride back to base was the fact that he had managed to get hurt by nothing. Not a single run-in with a demon. Nothing. Alone, he managed to burn himself badly enough to warrant an ambulance ride. What a joke. No wonder Peter had so little faith in him. As he lay staring out into the night sky through the tiny pair of windows in the back, he could only imagine what the others would think when he returned. He could already see the snide look on Paul Evans' face as he was hauled into the infirmary for a measly hand wound.

Once he was treated and bandaged up, he was given a summons note by the nurse. Peter had arranged for a talk and it was urgent. What he wanted to discuss was a mystery, but it was convenient timing because there was much Nick needed to get off his chest.

Nick walked through the long corridor and down the spiral staircase towards Peter's office. Surprisingly the stinging pain in his hands had faded, though it still hurt to curl it into a fist. Two guards holding spears stood like statues on both sides of the doors, staring blankly ahead. Nick paused to allow them to scan him and ask for the purpose of his visit, before granting him entrance.

He found the illustrious Supreme Commander of their organization sitting behind his giant mahogany desk with the Glenhaven seal etched square in the center. Thick, hardcover books stacked from the floor up decorated the walls around them. Two ladders set on both sides to give access to them all. Nick glanced at the golden cane resting on the edge of the table and couldn't help but see the irony.

Despite his advanced age, Peter Masters sparred regularly with the other knights as if he was still in his youth. Nick knew this firsthand. As an orphan, he had the privilege of being personally trained by the Supreme Commander of their organization. It was an honor given only to those who had shown the most potential or displayed an extremely high skill level. Unfortunately at the same time, this meant Peter was a difficult taskmaster, as his methods were harsher than others and his expectations were far more demanding. Even now, with plenty of wrinkles around his eyes and mouth, a receding silver hairline, as well as a grey beard, the man showed no signs of slowing down.

"You wished to see me, Supreme Commander?" Nick knelt before him. The old man's displeasure was reflected on the white marble floor. This wouldn't be a pleasant conversation.

"Rise, boy," Peter said, gruffly.

Nick obeyed, and stood facing him. The old man was dressed in his gold cloak. Nearby in a glass display, was a knight uniform decorated with various medals to commemorate his impressive track record. Their eyes did not meet as Peter was too busy looking through stacks of paperwork sprawled across his desk. "I want you to think for a moment about the best punishment you see fit for yourself."

"Punishment?" Nick took a few moments to register what he said. "We did exactly what you wanted—we got the sword! The mission was a flawless success!"

Peter moved his eyes from the desk to Nick's, his gaze piercing, "Flawless? Look at your hands and tell me that again. You were deliberately told not to handle the sword. Those orders were given to Matthew Cunningham, and believe me he will be punished as well."

"Like it even matters," Nick muttered.

"What was that?"

"Punishing me is no worse than what I've already been doing around here. I run back and forth with petty assignments that contribute nothing. Frankly, I'm tired of it. In fact, it seems like I'm just sitting around playing soldier behind these walls. What's the point of keeping me here if you have no plans to send me into real combat? I can't even use a sword. I'm the only one here who hasn't been trained to use any weapon. I only know hand-to-hand combat. It's clear by now that I'll never become a knight, so tell me, what other menial tasks do you have left to humiliate me with?" Nick said.

"Watch yourself, boy," Peter growled.

"You're right, there is no need for an explanation because all I get are excuses anyway. Tell me why I should even bother fighting for this cause anymore because in my eyes, I'm just a waste of space here."

Peter gave him an unnerving stare for the longest time before finally letting out a sigh. He tented his fingers. "Do you know what is special about tomorrow night, boy?"

Nick was taken aback by such an odd attempt to redirect the flow of conversation. "The New Year's Cotillion."

"Do you know what the significance is about the day after?" Peter asked.

Nick shrugged. "A drunken morning of regret? Vomit stains on the fine linen? Overall embarassment? Anything goes during the Cotillion."

Peter laughed heartily. "I see you're not as vain as you look. But I've never known anyone to forget their own birthday! When the clock strikes twelve tomorrow night you turn eighteen and take the final step from adolescence into adulthood!"

So it was, but his birthday was of little importance. Maybe for others it signified a milestone in their lives, but for him it was just another number. Not once in all his life spent living at the Garrison, had they been known to celebrate birthdays. He had always assumed it was to keep personal relationships from interfering with work.

"Eighteen doesn't mean the same thing to me as it does to the others." Nick folded his arms. "What can I do this year that I couldn't do before? It's not like I've got a life outside these walls. I'm not a civilian. And since I'm not getting a chance at the trials, I'm not going to be a knight either. I'm sitting exactly where I was six years ago."

"That's not true. In these past six years you've grown much wiser, you just don't realize it yet. Metamorphosis is the difference between a worm and a butterfly as well as the difference between finding success and constant failure. I cannot explain the situation to you right now, but give it a little time and you'll notice the changes in yourself. I promise you'll understand soon enough. In light of the fact that tomorrow night is the New Year's Cotillion, you and Cunningham will have your punishments put off indefinitely. Consider it an early birthday gift."

"Thank you, Supreme Commander." Nick bowed.

"Now go on." Peter gave a flick of his wrist.

Nick left feeling very confused. He found Matt outside pacing around the two guard sentries, looking quite flustered. He glanced up at the sound of the door shutting, and ran up to Nick.

"What happened? I can't believe we screwed this one up! What did he do to you? What's he going to do to me?" Matt looked as if he was about pass out.

"Nothing." Nick was surprised to hear the answer come from his own mouth.

"Nothing?" Matt repeated.

"Nothing."

Matt let out a breath of relief. "Really? I talked to Joni earlier and she said we were definitely being punished. She heard it from Gabriel and everything. But if that isn't the case then I can still take her to the Cotillion."

Joni Bliss was one of Matt's oldest friends, and had the distinction of also being his girlfriend. She was a nice girl, but was much too timid for her own good. She found the prospect of killing anything—even a demon too mentally taxing. So instead of joining the frontlines, she decided her services would be better spent in a field that best suited her kind nature and became a cleric.

"Well I hope you have fun, because I'm not going," Nick said.

The New Year's Cotillion was an extravagant, formal ball thrown by the Garrison at the end of each year to commemorate the services of soldiers and knights. It began in the evening and would go on through the next day. This was a symbol and a reminder to everyone to begin their lives with joy, and to carry on this merriment until the next year. But for most kids of this generation, it was the night to let loose of all other obligations and party until the wee hours of the morning.

"Seriously?" Matt asked. His eyes were wide in disbelief. "Peter let us off in time for the biggest bash of the year and you're staying in?"

"Seems that way. I don't even have a date so there's really no point."

"You got to stop being the stick-in-the-mud. Can't you find the blessing in all of this?" Matt put his hand on Nick's shoulder. "We are going to party hard tomorrow tonight, bud. And not just because of Cotillion. Think about it, it's your birthday and a New Year's extravaganza all wrapped in one!"

Nick forced his best smile. He hated formal dances or parties with groups of over ten people. Not because he was an anti-social person, but because every party always seemed to come down to a physical altercation between him and a couple of unruly knights of the Garrison. Thanks to years of hand-to-hand combat experience, he'd always come out on top, but the gratification wasn't worth the punishment for it afterwards.

They parted ways, with Matt taking this chance to rest up before the big ball tomorrow evening. Before that, he advised Nick to relax after their successful mission, but of course Nick wouldn't, or couldn't. Instead, he decided to go to the library to brush up on some of the Glenhaven Garrison history. Why did the Supreme Commander choose him particularly for this mission, and why was he so specific about the little details? He was so busy ranting earlier that he had forgotten to ask.

Nick pulled several books about prominent knights in history off the shelves and sat at a table with a single desk lamp. He needed to find out exactly why Peter was so interested in Sir Marcus and his sword. Several tomes had nothing about the orator or his blade. There was no mention of the sword until he came across one of the older textbooks and discovered something interesting.

There was only a single page dedicated to the deceased swordsman: a hand-drawn portrait of Sir Marcus standing very regally on a boulder overlooking the sea with his sword slung at his hip. A small inscription below the picture read:

> *"My life has forever been intertwined in servitude, but I have no regrets for a cause that is just. With the knowledge that the coming dawn will be my last, I vow to fight until my dying breath. Bravery, Justice, Wisdom, and Peace are the core that lay in the hearts of the men who stand with me. My brothers and I can never surrender no matter the obstacle, for the day man loses the will to fight, that day will mark the end of life itself."*
>
> *-Sir Marcus Kinsley*
> *The Second Coming*

Nick sank into his chair. The Second Coming was the most recent demon war. It occurred to him at that point that something wasn't right. For years the sword had remained buried within the grave of this fallen knight, yet retrieving now was suddenly of great importance. Why now? And why was it so imperative that he not touch it? Peter was a great mentor and one he respected, but at the same time, he was a man with many secrets. What would he have to hide?

The sound of soft footsteps took Nick's attention from the page. Joni walked casually into the room, but she was too wrapped up in her thoughts to notice him. She was a slender girl of small stature, and an oval face that was pleasant to look upon. She had dark brown eyes and jet black hair cut in a jaw-level bob. She wore the standard female knight uniform, which was much more form-fitting than the male counterpart. The jacket was also cut shorter to the waist and the boots ran much longer up the leg.

She finally noticed him sitting there, gasped, and pressed her hand to her chest, dropping the plastic bags filled with streamers and the other decorations to the floor.

"You nearly gave me a heart attack! What are you doing in the library at this hour?"

"I was having trouble sleeping. Thought I could read a book and maybe the boredom would put me out. What are you doing here so late?" Nick said.

Joni scooped up the bags. "I was helping the decorating committee with some last minute banners for Cotillion and I needed to find the exact design for the Glenhaven Seal as a reference."

"Isn't it just a shield with a feather across it? Not that it matters because I don't think anyone going to Cotillion will pay attention to some banners."

Joni laughed. "It's actually a kite shield with an angel wing on both sides. And for your information I'm an artist. I can't just slap on anything and pretend it's fine because I'll know the difference." She pointed at the stack of books next to him. "Mind if I take a look?"

"Help yourself." Nick closed the book and slid it across the table to her. Joni took a seat across from him and began skimming through the pages.

"You know, I was talking to Matt and he said you were planning on skipping the Cotillion. I have to say, it'd be a real waste of Peter's generosity if you stayed inside."

"That's easy for you to say. You and Matt are like the ideal couple, so you're going to have fun regardless. Besides, you both know I hate dancing."

"I think the real problem is that you don't have a date." Joni pulled a pen from one of the bags.

Nick shrugged.

She wagged her index finger at him. "Look Nick, you're pretty easy on the eyes. You could have had a date if you planned ahead. Now all the good girls are taken."

"So you can see my dilemma," Nick said.

"What about Rebecca Ryder? She's cute and I don't think anyone asked her yet."

"She's going with Paul Evans."

"That must be salt to the wound." Joni grimaced. "Then again, he *is* the president's son. I'm sure no girl would say no to him."

Nick raised a brow. "Are you telling me you'd say yes to him too?"

"Spare me, he's a creep." Joni sketched the insignia. "But at least he's going to the Cotillion."

"So he's a socially active creep."

Joni rolled her eyes. "That's not the point. You never go to any events, Nick. Maybe if you were a little more open-minded you'd be more popular with the other knights."

"That's not the real reason everyone hates me and you know it. By the way, I don't get why you're defending him. You're my best friend's girlfriend, that should put you on my side by default."

"Of course I'm on your side. I'm just saying you should just let loose once in a while. You're too young to be so tense all the time. So what's it going to be? I want to celebrate your birthday with you and it won't be the same if you're not in the room when it happens." She capped her pen and tossed the book back to Nick.

"Fine, I'll go." Nick reclined back in his chair. "Tell Matt thanks for going through such lengths just to convince me."

Joni smiled. "I'll let him know it was a success. And remember, it's open invitation, so at least you'll get the chance to mingle with some of the civilian girls." Joni picked up her bags, and left him in the library alone again.

She was right, why should he miss out on this opportunity? Why should everyone else get to have fun while he was sulking in the library? He would go and try his best to enjoy it, or at the very least, meet some people who weren't already poisoned by hate for him. He was feeling optimistic for tomorrow night, but little did he know that it was just the beginning of terrible things to come.

2

MY FAIR VALENTINE

The New Year's Cotillion met Nick's expectations in the worst way possible. The theme this year was "Moonlight Romance," and so the venue was hosted at an elegant, two-story ballroom with an outdoor garden and several balconies for private mingling. There was a small lake outside with small boats for rentals, as well as a lit stone path for lovers who wanted to take a casual stroll. Nick wore his Garrison formal clothing: a silver tunic over a white dress shirt with matching slacks.

With drink in hand, he waded awkwardly around the center deck of the second floor for almost an hour, watching couples dance below. It was uncomfortable to be so out of place, surrounded by so many people, but isolated from everything at the same time. Nobody there he could relate to: no friends other than Matt and Joni, and they were busy dancing with each other. Members outside the Garrison were not usually allowed to partake in social gatherings, but for special events like the Cotillion, everyone was welcome. So far, he didn't meet any new people, just the same old unfriendly faces. What a waste of time. Perhaps he shouldn't have come at all.

The double doors swung open. Almost immediately everyone stopped and turned their attention to the newest civilian guests: a sea of blondes and brunettes, but in the crowd a single red headed girl caught his eye. Unfortunately her face was obscured by everyone else in front. Nick felt a bit strange that he had such an intense desire to see this person up close, but something told him she was worth taking a second to discover. What was the harm with a little curiosity anyway? It wasn't like he was preoccupied with anyone or anything else at the moment.

Nick made his way across the bridge, but there was no sign of her in the pack of girls. Perhaps she'd made her way to the first floor. He shuffled through a raucous group of Garrison soldiers, walked down the stairs and into the crowd of dancers.

As he pushed and squeezed between sweaty couples, he realized she was probably invited as a date by one of the other knights. Like most everything in his life, it was too good to be true. Nick gave up, and turned to walk upstairs and back into his own private bubble. It was then that a melodic voice drew in his ears.

"I'm looking for Matthew Cunningham. Have you seen him?"

Nick found himself staring into the face of the red headed stranger. It was dark and the lighting was very inconsistent due to the flickering strobe lights, but even then he could tell she was strikingly beautiful. Nick let his eyes drop quickly to the floor and rise back up, doing a double-take on every feature of this mysterious girl. He tried his best not to stare, fearing it would make her feel uncomfortable, but he couldn't help it. She was a complete knock-out.

"Excuse me?" Nick had never felt more dumbstruck in his life.

"I'm looking for a boy named Matthew Cunningham. He invited me to this dance, and I don't know anybody else that showed up from my school. I wanted to thank him for the invitation. Have you seen him?"

"Matt? Well, last time I checked…" Nick looked around the room. Matt was nowhere to be seen. "He was dancing with his girlfriend."

She smiled politely, sticking out her hand formally. "You look familiar. Have we met before? I'm Quinn Valentine. What's your name?"

"I don't think so. I definitely would have remembered you." He took her hand and shook it. "I'm Nick. Nick Emberson." She had a pretty firm handshake for someone who appeared so delicate.

"Well, it was nice meeting you, Nick Emberson. Maybe I'll see you around." As she walked away, Nick was at a complete loss for words. He must have stood still for at least five minutes with a dumb look slapped across his face before he was snapped back into reality by a hand tugging his shoulder.

Matt waved a hand in his face. "You okay there buddy? I just saw what happened."

"Y-yeah, sorry I just got a little bit distracted," Nick said.

He laughed deviously and nudged Nick suggestively. "I could only see the back of her head from where I was standing, but from your dopey expression I could tell she was something. Do us all a favor and wipe the drool off your face before you ask her to dance."

"Matt." Nick's heart thumped against his chest like an out-of-control jackhammer. "This girl literally just took my breath away. I barely had time to say anything, but there's just something about her."

Matt's eyes lit up. He grabbed Nick shoulders and turned his body to face him. "What's her name? Where is she? This is big Nick! I'm telling you, we have to catch the perpetrator before she strikes again!"

Nick chuckled lightly. "Very funny, but unfortunately I think she's interested in you. Her name was Quinn, and she was actually looking for you. Should Joni be worried?"

"Quinn. Quinn..." Matt repeated the name as he tried to remember. His eyes grew wide upon realization and he snapped his fingers. "You mean Quinn Valentine? Sorry, that's been such a popular name since the Great War. Leave it to celebrity heroines, right? Anyway, I met her when I went in town to invite some civilians. Apparently she just transferred to Glenhaven High. She's never been to a Garrison Cotillion before so to be nice I invited her. I didn't think she'd actually show up, but I guess it worked out in your favor, didn't it?"

Nick struggled to keep his face from heating up. Thankfully, the darkness concealed how red he must have appeared. He had dated many girls in the past that were considered to be very beautiful, so why was he feeling so strange now? Why did knots tie up in his stomach and his heart palpitate so quickly?

Matt laughed loudly. "So Nick, what do you think? Should I work the good old Cunningham charm?"

"What do you mean?" Nick asked, still not fully recovered from the encounter.

"Where did she go?" Matt scanned the room. He flashed a devious grin. "You're about to owe me big time. You're so lucky we're best friends, Nick."

Before Nick could stop him, Matt patted him on the shoulder and hurried in the other direction. He disappeared into a crowd of dresses and formal wear, leaving Nick standing there like a sailor stranded out at sea. If Matt was thinking about doing what he thought he was doing... No, Matt wouldn't set him up, would he? He was always looking out for his best interests, but Matt also knew Nick was not very good with confrontation. What was he trying to pull? Before long, Matt reentered the room with Quinn trailing closely.

"So I hear you've met my best friend Nick," Matt said.

Quinn smiled warmly. "Yeah, he was the cutest knight I've met tonight."

Nick felt himself turn as red as a tomato.

He couldn't stop smiling as Matt continued, "So Nick, having gotten better acquainted with Quinn here I found out that she also happens to be very interested in Garrison weaponry."

Nick was catching on. Matt had a certain reputation for his knack with women, before settling down with Joni. A natural-born smooth talker, he was an absolute genius when it came to the art of flirty banter.

"Here's an idea, buddy. How about you show her the *Wolfsbane*? It's hanging on one of the chairs over there." Matt pointed to the dinner table where he had been sitting. He turned back to her for approval. "What do you guys say?"

"Sure, I'd love to see what you got." Quinn smoothed her hair with a slender hand and flashed her smile once again.

Nick couldn't decide whether he should be pleased or mortified. This was going to be a challenge for sure. He had to admit, he was rusty when it came to the dating scene, but he wasn't letting this opportunity slip by. Time to play it aloof. A girl like this was probably used to being the center of attention and he had to try to avoid all the common pitfalls of the guys before him.

"So it's settled then," Matthew said. "Listen, I'd join you both, but Joni wants to dance." Right on cue he snapped his fingers, pretending he had just come up with a new option. "Here's an idea, how about you guys go up to one of the balconies. It's a nice night, so the moonlight should do it more justice." He took quick glances to his sides. "Now I got to get back before she gets mad. Have fun guys." He moved quickly out of their circle and got lost in the crowd.

"Um, shall we?" Nick asked.

"Lead the way," Quinn replied.

Nick found the *Wolfsbane* on the chair and laid it gently into her hands. He led her up the stairs and outside to a vacant balcony. The night air was colder than before, much to his pleasure. However, she didn't share his reaction: she wrapped her arms around herself and her face scrunched up in a very uncomfortable looking manner.

"Cold?" Nick teased.

"Is it that obvious?"

"Here." Nick pulled off his tunic and draped it around her perfectly sculpted body. He felt the goose bumps along her arms as he helped her slip it on.

"Thanks, but what about you?" Quinn asked. "That shirt you have on can't possibly be thick enough to keep you warm."

"It's nothing. I happen to like cold weather. Winter is the only season that doesn't irritate me."

"You must be a robot then, because it's like twenty below right now." Quinn breathed warm air into her hands.

They grew silent and took in the night sky. The moon had the perfect ambience for a situation like this, so cliché and obviously romantic, but perfect nonetheless. As Quinn was busy examining the blade, Nick snuck a better look at her in her natural state, without the shoddy lighting, and realized why he was justified in being so taken by her in the first place.

She looked even more beautiful out here. In the room, it was hard to distinguish her dark hair color, which he could see now, was clearly a rich, fiery red. It was medium length and just touched her shoulders. Her face was devoid of imperfections and had the classic features of a true beauty, with high cheekbones and a cute, button nose. The way she carried herself seemed to be both self-assured and independent. However, these traits probably came across as arrogance, which threatened other girls. Her milky complexion seemed to radiate in the moonlight, giving a distinct contrast to her hair. She had big, deep green eyes, which were accented further by her black dress that was simple in design, medium in length, with spaghetti straps. The dress hugged her figure in a way that blew his mind. The word "perfection" seemed to be the only way to describe her. Built like a supermodel, it was as if she walked straight off a billboard and into reality. She was very feminine, but also had a slight seriousness that indicated that she wasn't meek, like the average civilian. Beneath her cool exterior, she carried a very powerful personality as well, one that should not be trifled with.

"What do you think?"

"It's beautiful," Quinn murmured, feeling the intricate details and patterns on the surface. She brushed her fingers along the fangs of the hilt. "Thornish steel. It possesses a herringbone pattern down the middle of the blade. The angular waves give off almost a mesmerizing effect, don't you think? Such impressive craftsmanship. It has to be a late Avon. I wonder how Matthew got hold of something this rare."

Nick raised a brow. "I'm pretty surprised you could tell just by looking. Not many civilians know much about our weapons, much less the famous whitesmiths that craft them. Do you know a lot of whitesmiths where you're from?"

"Sort of, I just believe when you're living in a crazy world like ours, it pays to stay a little informed, right? But where I'm from the people—even civilians—eat and breathe this stuff. I guess you can say it's in our blood."

"Then I take it you're from Thorne," Nick said. Thorne was the city with the largest, most powerful Garrison in the world. It was also the first Garrison established as well as the battlegrounds for the Great War's final showdown.

"Very close. I lived in a small town outside of it, but I guess when you live so close to such a holy ground it becomes hard to avoid its history," she said.

As Nick watched her, he couldn't help but become completely and utterly fascinated with her. There was something about her presence or the way she spoke that was just so enamoring, entrancing the way she seemed to call to him as if putting him under a spell. He'd never felt like this before, not with any other girl.

"So Quinn…"

"Hmm?" she responded, her attention still wrapped up in the brilliance of the sword.

"We should be getting back inside," he said.

She took her gaze off the blade for a moment and tilted her head to face him. "Right." Quinn smiled. "We should probably take it back to Matthew, just in case right?"

He placed his hand on her lower back, guiding her outside the room as he closed the door. As they walked down the stairs, the loud and obnoxious music shifted into a soft, slow song. The crowd of people that had been shaking wildly to the beat now broke into pairs, and swayed gently against the smooth vocals of some teenage pop sensation.

"Would you like to dance?" Quinn asked. Her tapping foot and bright eyes beckoned him.

"I'm not very graceful on my feet," Nick admitted.

She laughed heartily. "I thought members of the Garrison were trained in everything. Don't tell me that doesn't include dancing?"

"We are, but trust me you don't want to see me on the dance floor," Nick said.

Quinn put out her hand. "Try me."

She didn't wait for his response and pulled him onto the floor. It was weird for a girl to be so forward and in control, but soon he found himself actually enjoying being led by her. As they swayed side to side, he became lost in the motions. The personality she displayed this far, had been light and breezy, playful, with no sign of seriousness at all. Nick was mystified. Never before had he dealt with someone he could not read. Trying to unravel her, trying to break her down was like solving a riddle wrapped in an enigma.

"Your friend Matt did a good job trying to covering it up," Quinn said.

"What do you mean?" Nick asked.

"Don't worry, I thought that whole balcony set-up was cute," Quinn said.

"Much like my dancing, I'm not usually very good at this kind of thing," Nick said sheepishly, playing it off as best he could.

"You're very honest. I find that attractive."

Nick was taken aback once again as he twirled her with the music. It was at this point he thanked the Heralds for making dance training a required course.

"You're the first person to say that. I mean, I'm sure you can see how everyone feels about me," Nick said. There was a very distinct space of separation between them and the other dancers.

Quinn laughed. "They hate you, is that it? Look, when I first met you I had this feeling about you. It screamed different, as if there was something not quite right about you. If I was anything like one of these girls here, I probably would have stayed away." She leaned in close, so close he could almost feel her lips on his ear. "But I'm not like all the other girls."

Nick couldn't help but grin. "I've never met a girl like you before. You *have* to know how intimidating you are."

"Intimidating? Really, I don't think so." Quinn smiled innocently. "I think I give tests though, to root out the boys from the men." She had to be kidding. There was no way she couldn't see the effect she had on people. The way everyone looked at her, the way she could part the room with just the flick of her hair. This fair maiden could send a soldier into battle armed with the strength of her smile alone.

"Did I pass?" Nick said.

"I think so. You intrigue me, Nick Emberson. Usually all guys I meet I can tell what their intentions are from the start, but you took a little more work. It's almost like there are two sides to you."

"Most guys would have a hard time talking to a girl with such confidence. Not many people are like you, they can't just open themselves up like a book and get the same results," Nick said.

"Life's too short to always beat around the bush. I find I enjoy things more when I get to be myself," Quinn said.

"That's a good answer."

"My turn. Why is a guy like you hanging around a bunch of over-privileged snobs? You obviously must know how out of place you look around them," Quinn said.

"Well I wouldn't if I had a choice, but I promised Matt I would celebrate my birthday with him."

"It's your birthday? Well, happy birthday."

"Thanks, but it's tomorrow actually," Nick said.

"Wow, what are the chances? Being born on the New Year has to be some kind of good luck," Quinn said.

"It must be good luck because I got the chance to meet you tonight."

"You're getting better at this," Quinn said.

Their eyes locked and Nick realized his cheeks were blazing hot. He must look like chili pepper at this point. He could never hide his feelings very well, but Quinn kept her brilliant white smile on him, as if she didn't notice at all. At that exact moment everyone was staring at the clock, chanting as the countdown began.

Ten…

What to do? They're already doing the New Year's countdown and he was aching to kiss her, but maybe now wasn't the time. When was there ever a time for these things? Situations like this only come once in a lifetime. The best time would be now!

Nine…

She brushed her hair behind her ear. Obviously, if he was going to make a move, it had to be now. No holding back!

Eight...

Her arms wrapped around his neck as he was being pulled closer into her space.

Seven...

"Wha-what are you doing?" Nick stammered.

Six...

"You talk too much sometimes," Quinn whispered as she pressed her index finger to his lips. His heart was racing wildly.

Five...

"Poor Nick, everyone deserves a present on their birthday," she cooed.

Four...

"Having just met you, I'm not really sure what you like..."

Three...

Nick was practically on fire.

Two...

"I hope this'll do..."

One...

She pressed her lips into his the same time the party poppers and horns blared around them. Screams of excitement echoed in the large room. Nick wrapped his arms around her waist and put forth every emotion he was feeling into his lips. It was everything he imagined it would be and more, like kissing a goddess. The sound of cheers seemed to drown out, as if the whole purpose of his life was fixated on this one moment. When they finally stopped, Nick was left in a daze.

Quinn smiled. "Happy birthday, Mister Emberson."

"That was some present," Nick replied.

Holding her in his arms in the center of that dance floor, Nick felt that nothing else mattered at that moment. This girl he just met seemed to erase every bad feeling he felt in his entire eighteen years of living. It wasn't like him to fall so hard so fast. He barely even knew her, and yet he already knew that letting her go would be the biggest mistake of his life.

3

ANGEL FEATHER

The celebration died down after that. The ballroom that was once packed with lively, obnoxious kids was now almost cleared. Everyone was partied out, and either retired for the night or left to roam the city. The floor was littered with color-ful party favors and confetti like it was painted a multifaceted rainbow. However, the night was still young, and Nick was in no mood for sleep.

"What would you like to do now?" Nick asked once they were outside. "Do you have a curfew or anything?"

Quinn shook her head. "Let's go somewhere! it's still too early to call it a night."

Nick gave her a curious look. "Anywhere you had in mind?"

She thought for a split second. "Heaven's Peak! I've heard people talk about it. It sounds magical."

Nick nodded. "Sure." Thankfully, he had borrowed one of the more durable Garrison vehicles.

Nick had lived in Glenhaven his entire life. Heaven's Peak was the tallest mountain in the city. It was a famous landmark and a natural monument that helped the city attract the bulk of its tourism. Since it was a rite of passage, everyone who lived here had visited Heaven's Peak at least once in their lives. In his case, it was also like a second home—a quiet place where he went to think, where he could enjoy the stillness of nature that hadn't been touched by growing industrial renovations.

During the drive up, he remembered Peter once told him of a legend surrounding the peak when he was very young, but like all kids, he wasn't really interested in listening to what he said, and just let it go through one ear and out the other. Now that Quinn suggested going, it was a missed opportunity he could have used to impress her.

As they approached the peak, snow began to fall. Traveling deeper and deeper, the combined darkness and stillness made the forest seem eerie. Nick looked from the corner of his eye at Quinn, but she seemed enthralled. They passed a small lake, up a singular road leading to places higher along the mountain. The trees seemed to grow in groups as they crept silently uphill, as if they were traveling into an endless wood.

At the peak, there was a big clearing but it was hard to see anything in front of them due to the snowfall. Nick parked under a tree. When they got out, they were quickly enveloped by a veil of light snow.

"It makes sense now doesn't it?" Quinn said.

"What does?" Nick asked.

"The name Heaven's Peak, I mean. We're up so high it's almost as if we can touch the sky itself."

"Yeah, I can barely see a thing though."

No response. Nick squinted over the hood of the car to the passenger side. She was nowhere to be found. What just happened, he thought, worried at the same time. She couldn't have traveled too far. Could she have fallen off?

"Um, Quinn?" Nick asked loudly, "Where are you? I can't see you at all." He waved his arms in front of him, hoping to reach out to her.

"I'm right here." Quinn emerged from behind him. She looked like a goddess molded by the Heralds above.

"You're doing that again," she said.

"What?"

"Gawking." She laughed.

"I wasn't gawking. I just couldn't find you, that's all. I thought you got lost, or worse."

She laughed. "Oh is that right? There's nothing to be afraid of, I'm right here."

Her hand reached over and clasped his, interlocking to form a tight bond. Her soft hands were warm as she led him through the snowy trail, further until they reached a side of the peak where the snowfall couldn't reach.

There, Nick could see the foliage and massive rocks at the foot of the cliff and the bright city lights in the distance. The edge of the cliff was the perfect spot for a view of everything this town had to offer, and it was breathtaking.

"It's so beautiful…" Quinn whispered.

"It's amazing at night. To be honest I haven't been here in such a long time. When Matt and I first found this place,

I thought that it would change into one of those spots where kids came to make out."

"What's wrong with that?" Quinn asked with a flirty grin.

"Nothing," Nick said a bit too quickly. He cleared his throat. "I think a piece of nature as beautiful as this should be given the proper respect."

"I can understand that."

They became silent for a while and when Nick glanced at her, she seemed to be wrapped up into her own world. "Is something the matter?"

"No, nothing." She smiled faintly. "Just something I remembered. An old story."

"What is it?" Nick asked, curious as to what she was thinking. He had so many questions for her, so much more he wanted to know.

"This was the site where a great battle was once fought, one that caused the loss of many lives. I'm sure you know what I'm talking about. The Frozen Fifty Incident?"

"The Frozen Fifty Incident is the reason why it snows all year round here," Nick said.

"That's one reason. It's also because of that incident that Orichalon ore was formed here, the same ore whitesmiths use to coat Garrison weapons," Quinn said.

Orichalon ore were small, uniform white stones that were shaped like water droplets. They formed on high mountainous regions where the temperatures were low. These stones were especially valuable to the Garrison because they contained holy properties. They were very versatile and could be crushed into powder, melted into liquid, or used to brew potions. One of the main reasons why a Garrison was built in Glenhaven was due to its close proximity to one of their most prized resources.

"What exactly happened during the battle here?" Nick said.

"Well, the story goes that during the Great War, a demon known as Bergice slayed fifty of the most elite knights single-handedly. He was cornered at this exact spot where we're sitting now, and with his power to control ice, he froze fifty soldiers, smashed them into pieces and spread their remains to cover this mountain to mark this as his territory. Because of this, the temperature of Heaven's Peak remains the same year around as a testament to the cold way they were so brutally massacred.

"The worst part is that he's still out there, hiding some-where like a coward with his demon brethren," Quinn contin-ued. "The whole world tries to forget about what those demon monsters have done to us and they think that they won't reach us behind this barrier. But even with a Holy Shield protecting us, it would be foolish to pretend like none of this happened. I feel when doing so we also forget a part of ourselves. For a brief time the Great War erased our identities. Every city, every landmark, and everything that made us who we are were taken from us during their reign. For those years that our forefathers stood in servitude of demons, there was a time where we could have lost everything."

"I can't remember a time when there weren't any Garrisons," Nick said. "But that's just the way the world works. We have to move on and learn from our past."

"Have we really learned anything? Quite frankly all we've learned from our past is fear. That's why we live the way we do. If it wasn't for the fear they've brought upon twice now, then there wouldn't be a need for Garrisons."

"You seem to forget that Garrisons also brought back hope to those who are scared and defenseless. Humans are more capable than you give them credit for," Nick said. "Judging from your tone, I think you believe that having a military dedicated to demon extermination isn't necessary at all. But if there weren't knights to fight for justice then during the Great War or the Second Coming, you could have just as easily kissed those thoughts goodbye."

"I guess you're right," she said.

"That being said, I think it's funny that you managed to overlook one of the key details to that very well-known story," Nick said.

Quinn looked at him, offended. "What did I miss?"

"You forgot about the Angel's Feather. The legend also says that because the angels viewed this atrocity with unbearable sadness, they shed tears from Sanctuary that would eventually become what we know as Orichalon. However, hidden among them is an even rarer stone that forms with ten times the strength of regular Orichalon. The Angel's Feather. Like this one." Nick randomly dug his hand into the icy floor and pulled up a large white rock in the shape of a feather.

"How did you do that? The odds of finding one are a thousand to one!" Quinn grabbed the stone from his hand.

Nick's eyes widened as he realized he held the precious stone in his hand. "Wow. That was done entirely by luck. I've never thought I'd get the chance to see one in real life!"

"An Angel's Feather," Quinn said to herself, lost in its beauty. "It also has a very unique story behind it that you may not have heard before. In fact, it's a story that people from Thorne believe in."

"Keep it." Nick smiled.

"Thanks." Quinn held the stone above her head, looking at it with one eye closed as if examining it through a microscope. "Normally, Angel's Feathers are said to be impossible to find.

They say if you happen to come across one and you break the stone in half and give one piece to your true love, then your lives become intertwined forever. Something like a soul mate, you know? And nothing, not even death, can keep them apart."

"I didn't think you were such a firm believer in love," Nick said.

Quinn laughed. "I'm a believer in a lot of things, Nick, but love isn't one of them. It just doesn't exist."

"Well, not with that attitude," Nick said, surprised by her cynicism.

"Look, it's a charming fairytale to be sure, but that's just it—it only happens in a make-believe story you read to children. Nothing more. Otherwise, how can anyone account for the numbers of people who are separated today? Or for couples, who were once so close, ending up resenting each other after taking their vows?" Quinn said.

Nick chuckled to himself.

"What?"

"I never expected to find a girl who was so down on that concept. A part of me thinks you're just bitter. Jaded by something that happened to you, am I right?"

Quinn had a sad, bittersweet look. "Does it have to be one or the other? Okay, love doctor, what's your take on it?"

"I believe in it now."

Quinn raised a brow, flashing a grin. "Trying to flatter me now? Aren't you afraid of coming on too strong?"

"No, I'm just not afraid of taking chances. I used to be a nonbeliever, just like you," Nick admitted. "Up until recently."

"What changed your mind?"

Nick shrugged. "One day it just happened."

"What was her name?" Quinn asked.

Nick shook his head. "It had nothing to do with me. I was on a mission delivering a special antidote for a small town midway to Hyperion. This woman's husband was dying after being infected by a cursed plant. The curse put him in a coma and was corrupting him, which caused his body to rapidly deteriorate. There was an extremely high chance he wouldn't survive. When I had to break the news to her, all she did was nod and hold his hand."

"Then what happened?" Quinn asked.

"I got there late. I was sure the man was already dead. Nevertheless, I made the trip to their home in the off chance that maybe it wasn't too late. To my surprise the man had wakened and was just fine. The doctors were stunned to see he recovered. As I stood there, I overheard his wife ask him how he survived. And he replied, 'I had to come back to you.' That's when I knew that maybe it wasn't just a fantasy. The power of love could actually heal."

"That's a nice story, but how often does it happen in real life?" Quinn said.

"Not often enough."

"Anyway, it's getting late. I have an early morning tomorrow. Can you take me home?"

"Sure," Nick said, "I should be getting back too."

Quinn was quiet for the ride through the forest. Her attention was focused on the special Orichalon he gave her. It wasn't until they reached the city streets that she spoke.

"Turn here," she said, as they passed a streetlight. They drove until they arrived into a desolate side of town, where the houses were all torn down and there was no sign of any other residences. "Make a right there."

Nick turned into a neighborhood with only one house down at the end of the cul-de-sac. It stood ominously in the dark and he couldn't shake the irrational belief that it could be haunted. He pulled up to the small cottage, which was probably decades old. Though it was hard to see, he made out the stone-like structure that made up the bulk of the home. Its roof and the sides were all moldy and discolored, which he could distinguish even in the dead of night. However, he saw a blue truck parked perfectly in the center of the driveway. It seemed to fit. Old house, old car.

"This one?" Nick couldn't possibly believe anyone lived in this rundown shack. There were some bushes in the front, which probably gave the place some personality during the day, but the huge walls that wrapped around the perimeter made it appear to be almost like a penitentiary or prison of some sort.

"It looks like a total dump, but it's actually very nice inside. I'll give you the grand tour one of these days." Quinn pulled off her seatbelt. She didn't budge, but merely glanced at her house from the car.

"Quinn…"

"Yes?"

She tilted her head in a curious fashion, and he knew what he had to do—what he wanted to do. She had kissed him first, but now it was his turn to take control and be the man. He leaned in, the scent of her hair invited him closer, but before he could make his move, his body swelled with heat.

"Nick what's wrong?"

"I feel strange…" Nick said.

Quinn was speaking quickly, her voice growing fainter until he could hear her no more. Minutes seemed like hours and the feeling intensified until Nick could barely see or sit straight. It was as if his body was shifting, and the center of gravity was lost. The image of her face blurred, the surroundings became fuzzy and distorted. Nick needed air. He managed to open the latch on the door and step out onto the empty street. He took a few steps, and everything seemed like it was shaking violently. He couldn't keep his balance; his eyes were getting watery. His throat was parched, inhibiting his ability to speak. His senses were quickly failing him. Nick gasped for air as the last feeling faded from his body. Then he blacked out.

Nick opened his eyes. "Where am I?" He was standing upright now in an unfamiliar room, surrounded by people he did not know. He was dreaming—he was sure of it. He had been here before, lost in this exact same place. The people all wore black cloaks that covered everything except the lower part of the face. Everyone was silent. There was only the rhythmic sound of a beating drum.

"What's going on? Who are you guys?" Nick asked.

No response. Not even a second glance. It was as if he didn't exist.

Nick smelled burning in the air: the thick choking scent of ash seeped into his lungs yet it was strangely invigorating. The cloaked figures walked around, carrying flaming torches. They set their torches down to reveal a red carpet that led into another room. He followed the carpet and found more cloaked people chanting, bowing their heads in a prayer to some deity.

What followed was something he could not believe, but on the wall was a giant framed picture of him wearing a similar cloak without a hood. Under it was a porcelain bowl with water on a pedestal.

They were chanting now: "Agrian! Agrian! Agrian!" over and over again. He walked further to examine the bowl and its contents, only to discover his own reflection in the clear water. His eyes were red, burning like a wildfire. They were demon eyes, filled with evil and hatred staring back at him.

He knocked the bowl onto the floor in shock, shattering it into millions of pieces. The water burst into flames, creating a wall around him, trapping him. The entire congregation rose to their feet in perfect sync. They removed their cloaks, revealing their faces. They were all him! Mirror images, with the same burning crimson eyes that bore into him like daggers! Without another word they converged upon him. Nick could not fight back or resist, only watch as they swallowed him whole, taking him into the deepest recesses of darkness.

4

THE CROWNED PRINCES

Nick awoke in a cold sweat. He was back in his room under his soft sheets. His face was faintly warm as he rubbed his eyes open.

"What happened?" he muttered.

He had many recurring dreams, and this one was no exception. However in this particular dream, he always woke up before it progressed too far. It wasn't until now that he found out who was under the black hood. This time, the hood was removed to reveal that it was actually him, surrounded by mirror images who called him "Agrian," a name he had never heard before.

"You tell me, bud. When we found you, you were about to burst into flames, or at least something close to it," Matt said. Nick lurched forward to find his friend in his room, leaning against the doorframe. "We had medics in and out of here trying to find out what was happening to you and they all chalked it up to be one big freak fever. They said it was a fever of two hundred degrees to be exact. You scared the hell out of everyone including me. I thought for sure you were going to die. If it wasn't for Quinn bringing you back, I don't know what would have happened."

"Where is she?" Nick asked.

"Quinn? You know the rules about civilians on base grounds. I sent her home right after she dropped you off. The look on her face though, said she was scared and confused. I take it the date didn't exactly end as expected?" Matt said.

"Whatever gave you that impression?" Nick said sarcastically, rolling onto his stomach. "I had another nightmare. It was different from the ones I have of Susan. This one caused me to flip out…on a date no less. It isn't normal."

"For what it's worth, at least you're safe. But now it's back to reality, bud. We got to pay our dues to the new transfers from the Fyria Garrison. Peter wants all the troops there in formation and looking our best, so hurry up and get changed." Matt was already dressed in full knight uniform. His usually messy hair was combed back, looking extra well-groomed for the occasion. This meant they were most likely going to be broken into their respective fields of expertise.

Garrisons were broken into five subdivisions based after the four Heralds of Creation and the general soldier class. They each had different requirements and functions that worked cohesively together to keep a Garrison running smoothly.

The Brave Unit, named after Zelios, consisted of knights fighting in the frontlines. These knights had to be physically promising as well as having mastered all aspects of a single type of weapon in the Garrison arsenal. This was the hardest unit to gain entry to because the training was very rigorous. It was also the most dangerous, and yielded the highest casualty rate. However, many of those with claims to fame received it from their impressive streak on the battlefield. Those associated with this unit had red patches of the Glenhaven sigil stitched to their combat gear.

The Justice Unit was created for those who proved that they possessed high fighting potential, but to a lesser extent than those from the Brave Unit. They were similarly trained in most aspects, but were only required to master one weapon of their choosing. Most of their training was in the usage of the holy machines like aircraft, ships, and cannons. They were distinguished by the Glenhaven sigil on a blue patch that represented Yuriel. As a naturally gifted pilot, this was the obvious unit for Matt.

The Wisdom Unit knights displayed higher learning potential than fighting prowess. They were trained for combat, but focused on training knights towards betterment in academia. They were required to pass a series of tests that were an extremely mental challenge. Their ranks consisted of: whitesmiths, historians, researchers, scholars, alchemists, and engineers. These knights were the foundation to the Garrison and were provided with the latest in technological advances and were forging the equipment. This unit was named after Mecurius; the color of their patch was gold.

The Peace Unit was the final section. It was the only all-female unit. Like the other units they were also trained in combat, but were more focused on acting as support for the Brave and Justice Units. Since Joni had an aversion to killing, this unit suited her strengths nicely. Those involved were trained to become medics, nurses, clerics, healers, and diplomats. Strangely, the name of the Herald involved with the Peace Unit was lost in history long ago, but everyone knew his color symbol was lavender.

The general soldier class consisted of people who were either too young, too unskilled, or did not fit as a knight in any of the other classes. The responsibility of this position was doing grunt work like cleaning, cooking, and general errands. They wore olive green uniforms to signify their ineptitude. This was where Nick was ranked.

"Forget it. I'm not in the mood. I'm going to stay right here." Nick pulled the sheets over his face. It wasn't worth the embarrassment of wearing the uniform.

"You've been sleeping for the past five days. People are starting to talk," Matt said. "They say it's that's why you're still a soldier. They say you're not frontline material."

"I don't give a damn what the other knights think."

"Obviously, but I worry about you, bud. I'm pretty sure Quinn's worried too. Who knows, maybe you made a better impression than you thought," Matt said.

"You're my best friend, but you don't have to say that. I know I messed up. That was hands-down the worst way to end the night. I don't know why she would ever want to speak to me again. Not when I'm like a walking time bomb."

"Fine, if that's how you feel then I won't give you the number she left for you." Matt grinned. Nick pulled the blanket off and waving in front of his face was a thin white sheet of paper folded in half. Just before he could snatch it out of his hands, Matt slipped it back into his pocket. "Told you it went better than expected."

Nick sighed in defeat, leaned over and grabbed his black jacket that was hung over his chair. Matt made a coughing sound of disapproval.

"What?"

"No casual wear today. Not even your signature jacket. Supreme Commander made it very specific that we all had to wear our official uniforms—said it was important we look like a professional organization. Get ready, and I'll meet you in the Grand Hall before the speech."

Nick groaned and grunted as his friend left. He allowed himself a few more minutes of peace, thinking about Quinn as he stared at the ceiling. He couldn't stop from grinning however, elated by the surprisingly good news.

Eventually he got out of bed and went to his closet. He dusted off the shoulder pads and gave it a few swings to air out the olive green uniform before putting it on. It had been ages since he'd actually worn the traditional garb, so it fit kind of snug on his thighs and upper torso. He didn't realize that he gained quite a bit of muscle since the last time there was a formal event. After he was done squeezing the last button on, he made his way to the Grand Hall.

The Grand Hall was the meeting point for the soldiers and knights, also serving as the prime location for most of the indoor group activities. It was also the largest room in the Garrison, and today it was filled with people. Rows and rows of soldiers and knights stood in block sections at the front of their unit's color-coded banners, facing the central platform where their leader sat behind a podium. Next to Supreme Commander Peter were five chairs, two of them occupied by his archangels: Sir Lucius and Sir Bartholomew. Sir Gabriel wasn't present at the moment.

Archangels were the second-in-command after the Supreme Commander. They were in charge of leading the troops into combat. The archangels of this Garrison were known collectively as the Trifecta, and the most fearsome knights in all of Glenhaven. They gained their reputations through their uncanny expertise in their fields and affinity with their angelic ancestors. It was because of their skills that they were granted access to the most coveted holy abilities and secrets.

Sir Gabriel entered the hall; he gave Nick a nod and took his seat among his peers. Gabriel was the only archangel he knew on a personal level, and was also the one most favored by the Supreme Commander. It was never stated as fact, but everyone knew this because he and Peter were always together. Even when missions did not require his assistance, Peter welcomed his opinion. Gabriel had shoulder length black hair that he wore in a ponytail. Despite his hair, he had very masculine features, angular and well-proportioned. He was built like a tank, and carried all the traits of a great warrior. Because of this, Gabriel was arguably the best archangel of the Brave Unit.

Nick found Matt in one of the many rows of the Justice section and got into the space he reserved next to him. He watched and waited patiently for Peter's announcements. The horn blared, and the last of the remaining knights loitering outside were finally corralled into their formation positions.

"Hopefully Pete won't notice you standing out of section. It looks like they're about to announce them. Are you excited?" Matt whispered.

"Not really. I'd rather be training than wasting time here. So, about that number?"

"Oh right." Matt slapped the paper in his hand. "She seems like a keeper, she called at least twice every day to make sure you were okay."

Peter approached the podium, tapped on the microphone a few times to make sure the signal was fine, and cleared his throat to gather everyone's attention.

"Members of my esteemed Garrison, welcome all for this momentous occasion." Peter smiled. Nick had never seen the old man bare so many teeth before in his life. "Last year was an exceptional year for us all, and once again our city is kept liberated of demons, in part due to the combined efforts of you all. I wish to extend a thank you to each and every one of you for all your skills and services."

Applause erupted and cheers from the troops echoed throughout the room.

Peter waited a few moments for them to settle down before he continued. "However, the New Year would not be new without a few changes, now would it? I want to present to you all, the two new arrivals from our brothers from Fyria. The first, being Daniel Swift!"

A small boy stepped from the Brave Unit section of knights and walked to the platform. He had curly, sandy blond hair and a baby face that supported big, round cheeks. Across the bridge of his nose was a group of tiny freckles. Nick couldn't believe it, this kid was a knight! His cheerful demeanor and dimpled smile suggested he was untarnished by the perils of war. He gave a friendly wave at the crowd, before taking one of the two vacant seats next to the archangels.

"He has been chosen by one of our resident archangels, Sir Lucius Crescent, to be his new apprentice!" Peter said. "The first apprentice chosen in over a decade!"

The applause was scattered this time around, many of the soldiers were bitter by his selection.

Sir Lucius Crescent smiled broadly and his blue eyes gleamed with pride in the lights overhead. With his cropped spiked, white blond hair and perfect tan, the man clapped approvingly. Though he was sitting at the moment, it was clear Lucius was a tall and very handsome man. No wonder he was a popular topic among the female knights. Nick had never personally spoken a word to him, but from what Joni had told him, Lucius was a charismatic and charming person who was head of the Wisdom Unit. Not only that, but his uniform was decorated with a multitude of medals, signifying his position as an archangel was well deserved.

"Are you serious? I should be apprentice before that guy!" Matt muttered loudly. A few other groans echoed his same sentiments throughout the hall, and soon spurred the room into an angry mob.

"That little runt can't be the next apprentice!"

"He's not even old enough to drive!"

"He hasn't even gone through puberty yet!"

The disgruntled crowd was not very subtle with their displeasure, but they had every right to act unruly. This entire ceremony was an unorthodox and unnecessary way to gather knights who had dreamed of being an apprentice and effectively slapping them in the face with rejection.

Apprenticeship was a selective honor bestowed by an archangel of a Garrison to a knight who had shown great promise as both a disciple and on the battlefield. The archangel would mentor them personally, molding them into their future replacements. Judging by his first impression, Daniel had no special qualities; in fact, he seemed much too timid to take on such a role. To the other knights he was the stranger from a different Garrison who usurped their chances at glory. Maybe he had some hidden talents that only the archangels knew about.

"QUIET!" a booming voice commanded and the clamoring room became silent.

Nick glanced at the archangel called Sir Bartholomew "The Fist" Irons, whose intimidating visage and powerful voice quelled the knights in one word. He was known as "The Fist" because his weapon of choice was a giant silver gauntlet made of Thornish steel, which was grafted onto his arm and also functioned as a prosthetic right hand. Like Nick, he was a master of hand-to-hand combat and was said to have crushed the skulls of a thousand demons. He had a thick, square goatee that wrapped around his equally square mouth, but that was the only hair on his body. Scars covered most of his face; combined with his gigantic size it created a figure of pure intimidation. He was known to be the brute of the Trifecta, the physical force behind the two other archangels. Whereas Gabriel was Nick's ideal image of a knight, Bartholomew carried notoriety as the Brave Unit's most merciless knight. He was also the only one who did not choose an apprentice, but this didn't surprise Nick because Bartholomew was not one to work well with others. He stood back, his arms folded, with a permanent scowl on his face.

"Thank you, Bartholomew. Today I would like to announce the arrival of my granddaughter, Alyssa Masters! She will be staying in Glenhaven as a knight of our Garrison. Though she won't make an appearance, I'd like you all to know that I'm in very high spirits about her arrival. A huge feast will be held in her honor," Peter said. It was odd, but kind of nice to know the old man had a softer side, considering he was always brooding in his office or dispensing punishment.

After it was all over and he had dismissed everyone, the soldiers and knights went to tend to their usual business. On the way back to his dormitory, Nick was aching to call Quinn when he was suddenly pulled aside by Gabriel, who looked serious.

"Nick, the old man wants to see you. There's something very important that we need to discuss," Gabriel said.

He only had enough time to exchange a quick confused look with Matt before he was pulled through the current of other soldiers and into the briefing room where everyone— including the archangels and their apprentices—was already waiting for him.

Gabriel's apprentice, Paul Evans, was there. He was the only knight Nick could honestly say he hated. He had white-blond hair like Lucius, but styled it in a short, buzz-cut. He had a similar build and height as Nick, but he was definitely more toned. His sky blue eyes were complemented by a pointed chin and thin nose, just like his father, President Evans. The corners of his lips were always raised, giving the impression that he had a perpetual sneer on his face. Much worse was his off-putting personality, which he used to its fullest potential when bullying other knights.

Nick knew that Peter needed to talk to him, and his ongoing feud with Paul had to be put on hold. The vibe of the room gave him a bad feeling about this entire meeting, especially since everyone was looking at him with grim expressions. He took a seat at the opposite end of the table.

"Nicholas, I'm glad you got a chance to join us," Peter said. The smile he wore in the Grand Hall was gone.

"What is it you wish to discuss, Supreme Commander?" Nick asked.

"An unidentified group of demons has launched several systematic attacks in the west at small towns around the country of Fyria. The safety of my granddaughter in that Garrison has been compromised. This has forced my hand. Everything these demons touched had been picked apart, and now we are facing a threat that's moving faster than we had ever predicted. If we don't stop it soon, there's a chance this could lead into the next war," Peter said.

Nick's heart beat faster. "This is the first I've heard about any type of threat. How many of the others are prepared for war?"

"They're not. Only the people in this room know about this attack," Lucius said. "The Fyrians are proud people. They refuse to accept help from anybody. If not for their strong ties with our Garrison, we wouldn't have even known this was going on."

"Why are we sitting here talking when we could send a force there and stop them? They must to be punished for this!" Nick said.

"No. Alerting everyone now would needlessly cause a mass panic, and that isn't exactly the smartest thing to do. However, before we can retaliate, we need to get a clear idea on who was behind all of this. We believe it is a small faction. A group of unruly demons supporters, but nothing to get worried about," Gabriel said.

"There's more than that." Daniel shook his head. The poor guy looked absolutely desolate, as if he was on the brink of tears. "There have always been rogue demons, but, how could they get by the Holy Shield? What demon has that kind of power?"

Lucius glanced to Peter. "Supreme Commander, perhaps it is time to explain the true reason for this meeting."

"Yes, it's time. There have been a myriad of powerful demons in history, but by far the most dangerous are the Crowned Princes. They went into hiding after the Second Coming, but the emergence of Agrian the Inferno Bearer signals their return," Peter said.

"Agrian…that was the name I heard in my dream," Nick said.

Bartholomew exchanged a look with Gabriel.

"Astonishing, just like you had predicted Supreme Commander!" Lucius said.

"Predicted?" Nick said.

"I always knew there was some incredible quality about you boy," Peter said. "And as you grew older I became more and more convinced of the truth about your past. You are living proof that it has come to this. The reason you never knew your parents, the recurring dreams that plague you, that night that you came down with such a high fever! These were no mere accidents, but a prophecy of things to come! You are Agrian, the Inferno Bearer!"

"Wait, you all think I'm a demon?" Hearing it said aloud sounded absolutely ridiculous.

"We didn't just drum all of this up, Nick. We knew. We have always known. Believe me, we were skeptical at first, but over time we saw more and more of the Inferno Bearer in you each day. The day you were found was the exact date when Agrian seemingly went into slumber. Those strange dreams you've had—they're all happening because Agrian is desperately trying to break free from the shackles of your mind," Gabriel said.

"That's not true, I have them because of what happened in Fyria." Nick looked to Peter. "I'm not a demon. Don't you think I would know if I was? I'm a soldier, a flesh and blood human! I have nightmares because of issues that I can't deal with! Supreme Commander, tell them!"

Peter shook his head. "I'm afraid there is no use in denying this, my boy. It has been clear ever since I found you all those years ago."

"Getting burned for touching Sir Marcus' holy blade just confirmed what we already knew," Gabriel said.

Nick was at a loss for words now.

"I can see this is very confusing for you, but listen and I promise you will understand everything after this is through." Peter cleared his throat, so that all eyes were on him. He tented his hands and closed his eyes, as if channeling the memories of the past.

"Many, many years ago, the world was just a vast land created by the Heralds of Creation and their infinite power. These perfect angels decided to create human life in order to see how people could live with flaws. The Heralds created Ozarael, the first human. That was their first and final mistake. Because he was human he was denied entry into Sanctuary, the floating palace where the Heralds reigned and was instead sent to live on the land below. They did not see that loneliness and hate slowly filled his heart, and he devised a plan to corrupt those around him in his quest to mold a world in his own vision. Tired of his meaningless existence, he craved to be stronger, to be better, and to prove that he was superior to his creators. For this to happen he needed his own army. So he divided his most powerful sins into five demons: Bergice the Prince of Fear, Elzodeus the Prince of Greed, Tempyst the Prince of Pain, Durenth the

Prince of Sorrow, and Agrian the Prince of Rage. However, he kept the most powerful sin and hid it deep within himself, never letting anyone know his true motives. With that he crowned himself king and sent his princes on a path of destruction. With their terrible influence, they helped him corrupt and cultivate an army that invaded and destroyed the heavenly essence of Sanctuary. Without their holy fortress, the angels were forced to flee to battle on the land below them. Their home torn asunder, the angels could no longer survive, and in time they would die. But a slow death wasn't good enough for Ozarael. He wanted them to suffer.

"In his mind, the final act of vengeance would take place on the land where he was exiled, with him as the crown ruler over humans and demons. By this time the human race had grown to quite a large population. A human man by the name of Victor Masters took it upon himself to find a solution of dealing with the demons. Conventional weapons were all but useless against them. In one of his travels he met the dying Herald of Wisdom, Mecurius. Mecurius sensed that Victor was a wise and good-natured soldier. With his last breath he blessed him with the code of angels—ancient texts that held the secrets to access the power of angels. It was a gift for the humans to use as their last defense against the demonic forces of evil. With this newfound knowledge, he trained and imbued his soldiers with angelic powers and holy weapons. His leadership quickly gathered many supporters and disciples who soon helped him form the first Garrison in the city of Thorne.

"Victor and his holy knights went on to defeat hordes of demons and became legendary figures for their aid during mankind's darkest hour. However, over their many victories they had not yet seen battle with any of the Crowned Princes, and thus were unable to truly stop the sources of the demons. By mere chance, Victor was able to find one of the six demons, the one with power of flames and challenged him to a one-on-one showdown. This demon was none other than Agrian, the Prince of Rage—a demon renowned for his terrible and wicked might. After a grueling battle, Victor eventually fell to Agrian's might and succumbed to death in front of his men and his only daughter, Quinn.

"Fueled by revenge over her father's death, Quinn sought to personally end Agrian's life with her own hands. Posing as one of the many enslaved human she snuck into his private empire. She feigned loyalty and affection towards him in an attempt to gain his trust. The ruse paid off; she became his most trusted confidant and lover. Then one night when everyone was asleep, she went into his chambers, brandishing her father's sword in order to slay him in his most vulnerable state. However, as she drew the sword closer to his neck for the killing blow, the moonlit sky shone upon his face, and she couldn't do it. She realized throughout her stay she had fallen in love with the demon. Despite the despicable acts and pain Agrian had caused her, she saw the innocence of a child reflected in his slumber and spared his life.

"The next day, Quinn confessed to Agrian her entire plot, expecting certain death for her betrayal. But instead, Agrian revealed he had also fall deeply in love with her. In order to be with her, he was ready to do anything to repent for his horrible deeds, including turning on his own brethren. Agrian joined the remaining holy knights in their crusades against his brothers. With his aid, they killed the demon prince, Durenth, which brought them one step closer to victory. As the war dragged on, it appeared as if the humans would be victorious against the demons. However, Ozarael, the most cunning of them, deduced that Quinn was the source of Agrian's change. In an attempt to turn Agrian, Ozarael revealed an unsettling truth: to demons, the passage of time meant nothing because they could live for eternity, however, Quinn was a human and was incapable doing the same. With those final words Ozarael swore vengeance against Agrian and disappeared. Without their king, the lesser demons had no choice but to flee as well.

"But nothing could stop what would happen next. Saddened by the truth, Agrian searched the ends of the world for an answer that could keep the lovers together. The journey ended in vain because there was no way for a mortal to cheat death. However, Yuriel, the Herald of Justice descended upon them and as the final gift for their aid, granted them each a wish that was within his power. Quinn wanted to save Agrian from becoming a monster, and to let him know the beauty of the world unburdened by evil. So she sacrificed her life in order to bless Agrian with a soul and with that, humanity. It was then Agrian made a pact with Yuriel, on which he vowed that he would forever serve Quinn's final wish until the day the demons were all eliminated. Only when the world would no longer require his service could he finally be with his love."

It was quiet after Peter had finished telling the story. All attention shifted back onto Nick. Even Daniel, who was twiddling his thumbs for most of the speech, was now watching Nick intently.

"This, my boy, is the story of your life," Peter said. "You were reborn with the soul of Agrian the Inferno Bearer, the Prince of Rage. You are destined to engage in one final showdown with Ozarael, to decide the fate of the free world. Now that you are back, the Crowned Princes have been alerted and will be no doubt hunting for you."

Nick couldn't react, but just sat there and trying to absorb it all. He was Agrian, the Prince of Rage this whole time? It was absolutely mindboggling how much he never knew. Though he tried to think of inconsistencies, ways to poke holes in their story, he couldn't do it. Everything made sense. Why he was never allowed to learn swordplay; why they always babied him with easy assignments—it was all because they couldn't let anything happen to him. Before he'd always wondered why he was different, but now he wished he never knew.

"You are the key to unraveling their plans. It was said that only the Inferno Bearer's unique power could bring peace back to our fragmented world. They want you dead for your betrayal and will do anything to find you, which is why you will have to strike them first," Lucius said.

"Me?" Nick said.

"Ozarael and his Crowned Princes are the beginning and the end to demons. Kill them, and our demon problem will finally come to an end," Gabriel said.

"However, this presents an issue because my granddaughter can no longer reside here under my protection," Peter said.

"Why?"

"Agrian was meant to fall in love with Quinn. Alyssa, my granddaughter, carries the same blood as Quinn which means you both are bonded by the same sacrifice she made those many years ago. If the Crowned Princes were to discover the connection, both your lives would be in jeopardy. Only by separating you two can I ensure that our ultimate goal can be reached and that you both remain safe."

"I understand completely."

"Well, I'm guessing that means the feast has to be cancelled as well," Lucius said.

"No, we'll carry on as if everything is normal. We promised a feast and they will receive one. I trust everyone here can be discreet about this meeting? Good. Meeting adjourned, except for you, boy." Peter pointed at Nick.

As everyone else trickled out of the room, their faces expressed a combination of both pity and sorrow as they passed him. Alone, except for Peter and Gabriel, he sank in his chair, still dazed as Peter hobbled toward him on his cane.

"I know this is much for you to take in boy, but be certain it was all for the best. We had to protect you from your true identity so that no wind of your existence could reach outside the Garrison."

Nick shook his head. "But it doesn't matter now, does it? In order to destroy them, I have to reveal myself. The rest of the Crowned Princes will find out I came from Glenhaven and that will put everyone in danger."

Peter put his hand on his shoulder. "You need not worry about that quite yet. The last place they'd look for you is behind our walls. When the time comes I promise you'll be prepared. Just remember, you are now one of the most important assets to our organization. Now go rest. Tomorrow will be a big day for you."

"What's happening tomorrow?" Nick asked.

"The trials, my boy. You're becoming a full-fledged knight," Peter said. "Don't tell me you didn't see this coming? It was only a matter of time."

"According to your skillset, we're placing you on course for the Brave Unit," Gabriel said.

Nick couldn't believe it. He never dreamed this day would come. Every year when a soldier came of age they were allowed the test for knighthood. However, since most of those soldiers already had vast combat experience as well as weapon proficiency tests, he thought he would be ruled out. This was more than he could take.

"A-a knight?" Nick stood from his chair and bowed. "Supreme Commander, you have no idea how much this means to me!"

"But I do. Just because demon blood courses through your veins doesn't mean I see you as anything less than the fine soldier you've become. Of course, even though you haven't killed before…that doesn't mean we'll take it lightly on you."

"Thank you Supreme Commander."

"Good. Now go. I'm sure Cunningham would be glad to hear the news you have," Peter said.

Nick bowed once more, feeling elated as he went looking for Matt.

He searched the halls and the several facilities before finding him in the training room working up a sweat with a wooden practice sword as he delivered what would have be the killing blow on one of the other soldiers.

"Nice try, but you left yourself open for that one." Matt helped the poor kid up before sending him away, humbled. He flashed a grin at Nick. "Looking to spar? I'm in the zone right now and I want to get a quick one in before our feast."

"You know you can't beat me when it comes to a fist fight. I have some good news though," Nick said.

"What is it?" Matt took off his training gear, and tossed it into a nearby laundry bin. "You're only getting punished for a month instead of two?"

"I'm getting a chance at the trials."

Matt's eyes bulged; he wrapped Nick a giant bear hug. "I can't believe it! That is great news! Is that what they wanted to talk to you about earlier?"

Nick was about the mention Agrian and the Crowned Princes, he bit down on his lip before the words could escape. Matt was his best friend and they never kept any secrets from each other. It was against Peter's wishes to tell anyone outside the meeting. It would be hard, but he had to respect it.

"Yeah, that's it," Nick said. As they walked to the feast, new thoughts flooded his mind. What was going to happen next?

"Please tell me Peter's giving you a chance at the Justice Unit?" Matt said, hopefully. "We could finally do all the traveling we've been waiting for! We could take a jet and visit Coros!"

"I wouldn't want to risk losing my knighthood by suddenly taking a vacation, Matt. Besides, they're putting me in the Brave Unit."

Matt frowned. "The physical requirements are a lot more demanding than any other unit. Not to mention, you'll have to work along with Paul and all his cronies."

That didn't sound appealing, but the more obvious strain on him was being a demon and keeping his cover in an academy where there were eyes in every corner. Not only that, but he had to be careful with the changes occurring in his body. What being a demon actually meant, and how it would affect him and others around him was another concern. How could someone cope with knowledge such as this? How did someone cope with realizing they had become a monster?

5

A KNIGHT'S TRIAL

Nick splashed cool water on his face, letting it trickle down his chin and into the sink like a broken faucet. He had another terrible dream the night before. He thought that he could alleviate some tension through his usual morning routine. Today he paid particular attention to some of the new changes that occurred to him physically. Color returned to his complexion, and he had regained lost weight, a fact he realized was due to Agrian. He also felt different inside and the way he carried himself around others had changed as well. Assertive was the only way to describe it. Where he used to have self-doubt and shyness before, he now bore a sense of reassurance and pride. They were subtle changes, but he actually felt like he was becoming a different person.

The attention he commanded from his peers had also changed. Whereas they still hated him, his physical prowess garnered the envy of the other knights. Weight lifting, pushups, pull ups—he could do it all, and more of them than anyone else. Even as he was taking his daily run with Matt around the track, the gazes of the others burned into him from the sidelines, watching and wondering how Nick Emberson, Peter's skinny errand boy could have changed so drastically.

"You have to tell me how you did it." Matt huffed and puffed to catch his breath. They were sitting on the grassy part beside open track field after a five mile run. "In all the years I've known you, you've never beaten me in a race. How do you still have energy to go on?"

Nick got to his feet and hopped around in a boxer's stance, throwing a flurry of combination punches in the air. "I don't know why, but lately I feel like I can take on the world!"

Matt chuckled. "I take it you've spoken to the lovely lady? How you can focus on training is beyond me. I don't know about you, but girls rule my world. Put demons and damsels together and I'd always go for the latter. That's the only way Matthew Cunningham operates!"

"I spoke to her, but I haven't exactly set up a real date yet," Nick admitted. It was frustrating since he wanted to see her so badly, but at the same time he couldn't afford any distractions that could ruin his chances at knighthood. He had to keep his eyes on the prize.

"Smart thinking. Wait until after it's all said and done and you get knighted," Matt said.

"Don't jinx it," Nick said, "I don't need any bad omens going my way. The pressure is running high and I can't fail in front of the others, even if they expect me to."

"You won't. But since when did you ever care what the other knights thought? Last time I checked Nick Emberson was fine being a loner. In fact, he seemed to prefer it," Matt said.

"I don't and I do, but I can't look like a loser in front of Paul. The guy has been pushing my buttons my entire life, and the sooner I prove that I'm not such a screw up the sooner I get a chance to personally slap that arrogant look off his face," Nick said.

"Wouldn't we all love to see that? But let's be honest, you're a long way from being on his level. Even I won't get to his level the way things have been going," Matt said. "Thanks to Gabriel's wise decision, that sociopathic brat is going to be the next archangel in a couple more years and we'll have to start taking orders from him. Just thinking about it is enough to make someone want to transfer to a different Garrison."

Nick dropped his hands to his sides, letting his shoulders slump. The realization that he would never be an archangel was a great disappointment. He had the qualifications to become a knight, but that was the extent of his growth. He could never be an archangel like Lucius or Bartholomew because no sane knight would follow a demon's orders. It went against all their rules and teachings. What bothered him most was the idea that Peter was the only reason he wasn't immediately expelled. The others only tolerated him now because of the Supreme Commander's wishes. How would they react if they knew about his demon heritage? Would they still see him the same way after Peter was gone? The thought of his mentor one day dying made Nick's disappointment topple into sadness.

After the light weight training with Matt, Nick took a quick shower and returned back to the dormitory to study for his exam. He knew everything by heart, all the codes, history, techniques—he had them down pat. The only thing left was to regurgitate it onto paper and hope for the best. As he read over various texts, he was startled by a knock on his door. Who could be visiting? He opened it to find Gabriel, dressed in full armor, like he was about to be deployed into battle.

"How are you holding up, kiddo? Nervous?" Gabriel said.

"I really don't know what to expect. Being a knight has always been my dream, but being considered for the Brave Unit was an even bigger surprise."

"Why do you say that? Don't tell me you forgot how the units function?" Gabriel said.

"Of course not, every knight-to-be knows about the units."

"Then what seems to be the problem?" Gabriel said.

"I've only ever gotten training in hand-to-hand combat," Nick said. "No other weapons."

"As Agrian, your fists *are* your primary weapons."

Nick ran his fingers through his hair. "I guess I feel unprepared you know? I mean one minute I was picking up packages and now I'm going to be a knight! Everything is happening so fast."

"After sparring with Lucius earlier I remembered something Peter told me when I was your age before I took the test. Maybe I could give you some last minute coaching before the big show. You interested?" Gabriel said.

Nick nodded; any information from an archangel would be beneficial, especially if it came from the Supreme Commander's right hand man and the general of the Brave Unit. Gabriel took a seat on the single chair in his room, while Nick sat on the corner of his bed. With all the scratches and markings on his armor, one had to wonder how many intense fights he had been through in his life.

"You're a smart guy so the written test will be a breeze for you, but what I want to talk to you about is the fight itself," Gabriel said. "Everyone going into the trials thinks it's going to be exactly what they expect, but it's not. It will surprise you and it will make you question yourself and your abilities, but don't let it. The only thing you can do is carry on and fight smart. If you stick to this, you'll pass with success."

"Will I know who my opponent will be?" Nick asked.

"No, it's all selected randomly right at the beginning of the match. They don't want anyone to have an unfair advantage. I can tell you that all fighting will be hand-to-hand, which will work to your advantage," Gabriel said.

"So what do I do?" Nick asked.

"Like I said, use your head to your advantage and not just your body. Forget the fact that you have more experience in this particular set of skills than the others and instead humble yourself. Overconfidence is the most common pitfall for first timers attempting the trials. Don't let it work against you," Gabriel said.

Gabriel's advice was comforting, but it still remained that his repertoire of fighting abilities were vastly limited to most others. Nick had only mastered hand-to-hand techniques, but in only staged scenarios. In this instance, he had to envision the trials to be a fight for survival. The losers of the trials were forced to embarrassingly spend another two years retaking courses before they were given another shot. Nick did not want to be twenty and still competing for this this rite of passage. Losing was not an option.

"Now I'll leave you back to your studies," Gabriel said. "See you on the field in a few hours."

After the pep talk Nick waited anxiously until he was summoned for the written exam. It took place in the middle of the Grand Hall. About fifty other students would be there, all with the same purpose. Once every pencil was dispensed they were allowed to begin.

He finished first and with plenty of time to spare. Like Gabriel promised, the written test was a piece of cake. However, he couldn't say the same for some of the others. A few soldiers struggled, erasing harshly on the paper or having what appeared to be a mental breakdown. One person even banged their head on the table in frustration. Nick was pleased with himself. With a spring in his step he took a last look at his paper before he turned it into the elderly administrator. She had a scowl upon her face as he walked off, probably a bit insulted that he completed the first hurdle so quickly.

He was escorted outside to wait for the results. He sat alone on the bench until all the other test takers were finished. One by one they joined him. Still, he sat alone however, as they conversed amongst themselves, each exclaiming how well they had done. It wasn't until the final test taker emerged did they finally begin to sweat. It only took ten minutes before the test results were finished. The elderly administrator walked out and pasted the scores on the wall, leaving quickly before she was run over by the sea of excited soldiers.

Nick waited as they came and left either rejoicing in joy, or holding their heads low in disappointment. Once they were all done and gone, he approached the pinned up paper. It was a list of names in alphabetical order, and had either "pass" or "fail" written next to them. Nick took a deep breath and scanned for his name. Pass! He passed! He felt instant relief, despite knowing he could not fail the written portion. A note at the bottom of the page redirected those who had passed to the training grounds, where the next portion of the test would occur. Now the true test awaited.

Nick entered the training grounds next to the track and field, a giant coliseum with spectator stands surrounding it. He knew he was late because it was filled by people cheering or booing a fight currently taking place. On the scoreboard was the list of people fighting for knighthood and their opponents. They were on fight number four by the time he arrived, with the first three challengers successfully passing. Lucky them, they didn't have the anxiety to wait for what was about to come. Nick's picture placed prominently next to the number nine, and there was a question mark over his opponent's face. Just like Gabriel said, it would be a surprise.

Peter and his archangels sat near the scoreboard next to the announcer who was fervently describing the match in complete detail through an overhead microphone. Peter and the archangels were talking among themselves and pointing fingers, most likely giving their opinions on matchups. Nick followed along the sidelines and into the waiting pits, taking the seat labeled nine. Time passed on as five more matches went by, the final one before his. It ended in disaster however, as a poor girl was mercilessly pummeled by a brawny, pig-faced boy. Her dreams of knighthood shattered, like her ribcage. Her opponent was an arrogant prick, a knight by the name of Cyrus Cavil and one of Paul Evans' close friends.

It made no difference to Nick that the matchup ended in his favor, but for Cavil to flaunt his victory annoyed Nick to no ends. Paul, with his cronies sat in the stands laughing raucously. He clenched his hand into a fist. Disgusting. Bullying was something Nick never tolerated. Seeing it in action and especially when it was to a girl made his blood boil. Paul would get it one day, and he hoped he would be the one to dish it out.

"Now. Number nine, Nick Emberson! Please take center circle!" the announcer said. Nick tossed his jacket on his chair and stepped into the field as directed. There was no applause except for a couple of whistles and a "whoo" from Matt. He was the only one moving in the stone-faced crowd, pumping his fists in the air for support. Nick stopped in the center circle and waited for the name of his opponent. "And here to do combat with him for the honor of knighthood is none other than resident knight, Henry Wales!"

Another of Paul's goons stood up. The crowd erupted into cheer. Nick was pleased with the choice. He'd have an easy time projecting his rage onto someone so similar to Paul. If he squinted hard enough, he could imagine Paul's face on his body. But before the guy could leap from the stand and onto the battlefield, Peter tapped the announcer's shoulder and whispered something into his ear.

"It appears there's been a change of plans," the announcer said. "In a rare change as ordered by our Supreme Commander, Daniel Swift will replace Henry Wales in this fight! I repeat, Daniel Swift, the apprentice to Sir Lucius shall be taking on Nick Emberson! This will be a hand-to-hand fight, with the winner chosen by knockout!"

The crowd went wild. They haven't seen a straight, serious blow-to-blow fight all day and they were craving bloodshed. This was an unorthodox decision by Peter to be sure—to have an archangel's apprentice enlisted in a bout. Fighting another soldier facing the trials was one thing, but an apprentice? It had never been done before. Did Peter have that much faith in him to do battle with someone who was regarded as superior than a knight? Something was strange about this arrangement, but Nick was never one to back down from a challenge. The crowd was already excited and he himself was curious about what would ensue. He felt it inside himself, the bloodlust and desire to fight. Was this how Matt or Peter felt when they were fighting? It was entirely new to him, this kind of thirst. But one thing was for sure, the energy from the crowd and the promise of a challenge brought out a different side to him.

Nick waited as Daniel approached the center ring. He towered over the kid. Daniel's chipper smile made it hard to believe this matchup would be worthwhile to see. Any way he saw it, it was one-sided, and would end with Daniel lying face down in a puddle of his own teeth. However, he remembered what Gabriel had told him. Underestimating his opponent could spell out disaster. To pass this trial, he couldn't afford give up any type of advantage.

"It's a real honor to have a match with the legendary Agrian," Daniel said happily. "I hope I can deliver a good fight!"

Nick couldn't hold his laughter anymore. He regretted it instantly once he saw the look on his opponent's face.

"What's so funny?" Daniel asked. "Was it something I said?"

"Sorry, it's just I don't know whether to be insulted or not. No offense, but you're the smallest knight I've ever seen."

Daniel's eyes narrowed. Just like that, his cheery disposition vanished and he was a completely different person. "If I were you, I'd worry less about my size and wonder more about how I became an apprentice."

"Hey look, I—"

Nick's apology was cut off by the sound of the bell.

Almost immediately it seemed as if Daniel had teleported from right in front of his eyes. He made his appearance by delivering a clean punch to Nick's face, causing him to stagger backwards out of the circle.

"Watch out!" Matt called, but his warning came too late.

Nick took a swing at his chest, amazed at his own speed in his new body. Daniel barely evaded it, dancing around the blow and moving to the side. The kid was fast, faster than even Matt. Another blow to back of the head by the small warrior, and Nick nearly fell on his knees. He turned, but Daniel had disappeared again.

Nick was getting frustrated. His insides heated up with anger. How could this little runt be giving him so much trouble?

"Nick! Fight back!" Matt yelled from the sidelines. "He's just pummeling the crap out of you!"

Nick swung again, only to catch air in his fists once more. His failed strike went punished with a kick to the ribs. As Nick used one free arm to shield his side, another punch met his face and knocked him on the ground.

He hated being put on the defensive and he was getting even madder, but how could he stop the assault? He got back up but was immediately forced into a defensive position. He was trying his best to bide time. Daniel was faster, but weaker compared to other soldiers in his previous fights. Even still, Nick knew he wouldn't last much longer if he didn't have a chance to retaliate. Eventually, the small hits would accumulate and he'd be left as a bloody stain on the floor.

He swung at Daniel but missed again, leaving himself open to another clean shot to his face. His left eye was swelling. The small apprentice was the most agile person he'd faced yet.

Nick was running out of options, and he was losing, but for some reason, as the fight dragged on, he no longer seemed to care. Instead he felt wonderful. Being in the position he was in, and getting knocked around gave him a strange sense of pleasure. He couldn't explain it, but he felt like a masochist, or someone who got sick thrills from getting beaten. The entire time his heart was pounding against his chest and he was excited, physically exhilarated. A voice spoke softly inside his head, telling him to push on through, assuring him that victory was within his grasp. He had to win. That was the bottom line; there was no other option. No matter what he had to do, he had to win.

As these thoughts poured into his head, Daniel kept the pace, steadily whittling down Nick's defenses. The pressure was piling on, and Nick was getting tired, but he wouldn't give up. He would never give up.

"Had enough?" Daniel taunted, continuing the assault.

"Stop the fight!" Matt shouted in the midst of the loud audience. "He can barely defend himself!"

However, no one intervened. Nick looked from the corner of his eye and saw Peter and the archangels watching intently, not saying a word. They were studying him, waiting for something to happen. Then he realized that they knew something. He had the power to win all along. Now was it time to use it. Agrian, the Lord of Rage was at his doorstep, waiting to be unleashed. He didn't want to admit it, but a part of him knew that this was why Daniel was chosen. They needed someone with enough skill to free the beast within him. They needed to challenge Agrian in a way that would spurn his desire to prove himself. They got their wish.

At the same time, the voice inside his head grew louder and deeper. It was Agrian saying telling him that the time had come. The Lord of Rage could no longer be ignored.

Something surged in his body: his heart palpitated violently against his chest, until he felt like it would explode. He screamed at the top of his lungs and as he did, his arms burst with flames, the power of his transformation pushed Daniel a few feet back.

Nick's arms became a dark crimson color—spikey, scaly appendages protruded from them like demonic gauntlets. They seemed to be a cross between his human hands and reptilian claws. Fire burned at a constant and controlled rate around his arms, glowing brightly with his desire. Strangely, it didn't hurt him at all. His heart returned to normal, the pain in his chest disappeared. He only felt relief, like the built up pressure valve was finally released. Not only that, but he felt stronger as well. His senses were seemingly enhanced and all the damage Daniel inflicted was nothing. This was the power of the legendary demon. This was the power of the Inferno Bearer.

In the stands behind him he heard Peter say to his disciples, "His eyes…look at his eyes…" Nick turned his head, and saw the shock on their faces at the drastic change in appearance. Everyone was silent now.

"They're red!" Somebody gasped. "His eyes are red! Crimson red!"

"He's not human!" a girl cried.

"He's a demon!"

"A monster!"

The audience became a mix of emotions. They were afraid. They were angry. They were anything but pleased with this turn of events.

"There's nothing to fear! Everyone remain in their seats, this is an exercise!" Lucius shouted, trying to assure everyone in the stands. But even his silver tongue was impossible to quell their horror now. Soon everyone fled in panic at what they had witnessed.

Peter retained a calm disposition. "Nick, try to control Agrian. Remember who you are despite all the anger you feel."

"He loses more control as the fight drags on, until he will stop at nothing to destroy Daniel," Gabriel said. He too was monitoring Nick's behavior very carefully. "It is in his nature."

The nature of all demons was destruction. Fitting, considering all he wanted to do now was to scorch the earth and send everything around him to fiery ashes.

Meanwhile, Daniel, who was caught off guard by a punch, refocused himself and attempted to attack Nick once more, but he was stopped abruptly by Nick's vice grip. His reflexes were astounding, his speed now surpassing the archangel's apprentice.

"Wh-what are you?" Daniel's eyes reflected pure horror as Nick clenched his fist over his adversary's hand, increasing the pressure. He felt joy watching Daniel crumple to his knees, the pain stricken all over his face gave him a rush of excitement.

"Had enough?" Nick asked mockingly.

Nick could hear his voice clearly now. It surprised him at first, as it sounded as if there was another person standing next to him speaking the exact same words at the exact same time, echoing him. One voice he distinguished as his own, but the other was deeper and gravelly. With that, he punched the baby-faced knight in the stomach, sending him reeling, before delivering a swift kick to his jaw. The force took him across the field, crashing through the opposite stands and into a wall. When the dust settled, he was sitting unconscious, caved into the wall like a mounted trophy.

Around him the audience was all but gone now. Only a few brave spectators and the ones who already knew his secret were left. Matt was among the few who had stayed, and he was looking on with shock and awe. Nick's secret was out. Now the whole world could see he was a demon. Good, there was no use hiding the truth anymore. If they wanted to see his powers, then he would oblige.

"You all wanted to see a show? I'll give you something to stare at!" Out of instinct Nick produced a fireball in his hand and hurled it into the stands. Metallic chunks hit the ground with harsh clangs, leaving the arena lit with smoldering debris.

The burning inferno that came from his onslaught was pure ecstasy. Nick grinned and threw another fireball at the opposite stand. As the fire raged on, so did his desire to watch it all burn. He created a whirl of flames around him, a barrier between himself and the rest of the world. They could try to drag him out, but it wouldn't be easy. The voice that came from his mouth was the same one in his head, telling him to continue, fueling his anger. He had to engulf this arena. Behind the fire stood a single figure—it was Matt!

"Nick, you have to stop this!" he said, coughing and hacking from the smoke. His face was pale as a ghost. "You're destroying everything!" Seeing his friend and the fearful look on his face reminded him of the night with Quinn. The same look she had right before he passed out the morning of his birthday. For a second he was back in control.

"Matt, h-help me!" Nick gripped his head. It was painful trying to resist. It felt like he was stuck between two chain-linked ropes pulling at him from his sides, ripping his entire body in half. "I can see what I'm doing...but I can't stop myself. I'm having terrible thoughts, and I can't get them out of my head! Agrian is inside me!" He screamed at the top of his lungs, trying to expel the demon with this moment of clarity. By the end, his voice was hoarse and he dropped to his knees. He was himself again.

A gust overhead blew the smoke and flames away and there, standing before him was Gabriel. His white angel wings were fully extended as he glided down in front of them. The archangel looked as Nick imagined a Herald would appear like. The large, feathery wings cast a shadow that blotted the sky. He looked absolutely majestic, a strikingly awesome figure as he held his sword out in defense. Nick had heard stories of the archangels taking flight, but he had never witnessed it until now.

"This trial is over. You've won, Nick. There is no reason for you to continue. I suggest you surrender and gracefully take your punishment for damaging base property," Gabriel said.

Even as he heard the words coming from Gabriel, and the solution to his discretion given to him plainly, Nick's grasp on humanity quickly slipped away again. Overconfidence just like he was warned. The demon inside was not one to compromise.

"I refuse," Nick said his other voice added steel to his words as he got to his feet. "The fight is over when I say it is!"

"Nick, stop!" Matt said, but it was of no avail. Nick's eyes were burning crimson as his desires were still unsatisfied. Daniel was merely a small morsel of an opponent; taking on Gabriel would be the main course. He relished the thought of besting Glenhaven's champion knight. To defeat their greatest warrior was too tempting an opportunity for his inner demon to pass up.

"Matthew, don't get any closer! That is not Nick!" Gabriel shouted. "He's possessed, now move back before you get hurt! That's an order!" Matt reluctantly obeyed, walking back to what was left of the stands next to Peter and the others.

"Good, I didn't want him to get in the way," Nick said.

Gabriel did not budge. "Arrogance and ruthlessness are traits of a demon. Are you going to stand by the very ideals of those you wish to vanquish? You are a member of our Garrison, it's time you prove it!"

Nick shook his head, stepping closer to him, "I'm not fighting for any demon. I'm fighting for myself!"

"Wrong! You are not the same person you were before!" Gabriel shouted. His words stopped Nick in his tracks. "The Nick Emberson I know would never let his emotions control his actions! You are letting Agrian control you!"

"Silence fool!" Nick snarled. His voice was darker and deeper than ever, the fire on his demon hands was blazing fiercely. "Agrian is what I was missing my entire life. And now that we are reunited, I am whole again. I am complete!"

Gabriel sheathed his sword back at his side, "Then I will not fight you, Agrian. Not like this, when you are acting like nothing more than a petulant child."

"Child?" Nick screeched. "Then tell me how it feels to have your heart ripped out by one!" He lunged forward, aiming for a swift kill by piercing him through the heart with his claws.

Before he could reach him, Paul intervened with his broadsword, parrying the attack and pushing Nick back. "If you won't face him, then I will, Gabriel. I won't let this demon tarnish the reputation of our Garrison. The holy knights exist to exterminate vermin like him."

Peter looked to Nick, who glared back. With some reluctance he finally nodded. "It appears we've yet to see Agrian's strength at its fullest. Perhaps it would be suitable for Nick to fight someone with much greater experience. But if only if he battles according to our rules."

"I accept this challenge," Nick said.

Excellent. Forget Gabriel, what he really wanted was a shot at Paul. Now with Agrian at his side, he couldn't lose. He smiled malevolently and walked to the center of the circle. The original announcer had fled. It was Bartholomew who would call the battle.

Bartholomew waited until they were both ready and situated in the arena and that everyone else who wasn't involved was safely behind the lines of combat. Paul looked as smug as ever with a mocking grin on his face as he stared Nick down.

"This duel shall be hand-to-hand. Winner will be chosen by knockout. No time limit. Go," Bartholomew said.

Nick was the first to strike. He drove forward and delivered an upward kick. He was still getting used to this type of law-defying fighting. It was time to test out his limits.

Paul blocked with both hands, grabbed Nick's free leg and swung him across the field. As he sailed, Nick dug his hands into the ground, clawing into the dirt to slow his speed and then used the force to lift himself into a back flip, landing perfectly on his feet.

However, Paul was already in range and delivered an upper-cut aimed straight for his chin. Nick leaned to the side, narrowly avoiding the punch. He countered with a quick to sweep from below.

Paul easily jumped over the kick and grabbed Nick's arm, pulling him in for a clean shot to the face. The shot was much more powerful than anything Daniel had thrown. Nick jumped back, allowing his arms to burst into flames as he threw a fireball at Paul.

Paul ducked and spun to a kick into his chest. The force lifted Nick in the air, defenseless. Paul gave a smirk as Nick fell closer to the ground and into range.

Nick smiled back, as he straightened his body, and extended his fist, allowing the flames to mold around his body into a flaming arrow that was aimed down on his foe. He became more aerodynamic and felt himself speed up significantly.

Paul's eyes widened with surprise as the force of the drop collided with him, and a cluster of dust and debris filled the air. As the smoke cleared, they were both at a standstill, locked into a fierce grapple. Nick and Paul glared at each other with great ferocity, neither letting up.

"You do realize you don't stand a chance against me, don't you?" Paul said. "I've killed over a hundred demons while you were playing messenger!"

"Didn't anyone ever tell you, if you played with fire, you'd get burned?" Nick's hands blasted fire into Paul's, burning his hands and knocking him over. Sounds of shock echoed in the audience at the sight of the second apprentice to fall that day. Nick had just won.

Paul howled with pain, rolling over, much to Nick's delight. But the thrill was short lived, as Paul was back on his feet almost instantly.

"That was the best you could do, wasn't it demon?" he huffed.

His hands were deeply charred. He whispered some words, and a bright light covered his hands. The luminous glow was painful to look at, forcing Nick to raise his arms and shield his eyes. When the light finally disappeared, the burn wounds were gone. Paul's hands had completely recovered. It was then that Nick realized he had used, an angelic healing technique, to speed the recovery of wounds. The perks of being an apprentice.

"Nice trick, try mine," Paul said with a smirk. His hands began to glow with the incandescent light once more, but this time Nick knew at once he was about to fire the Luxilight: a projectile beam of light. It was one of the most powerful techniques passed down by the angels in order to combat demons. Enough skill in this technique could take down even the most resilient demons. Most knights struggled to master this advanced move, but Paul wasn't the type to fake his strength. He unleashed a pillar-like beam that Nick tried to block with his hands, only to find that they pierced his flesh like razorblades. It went past and into his chest, inflicting cuts all over his body.

Now it was Nick's turn to crumble to the floor. The agonizing pain in his arms and chest was like getting hit by the full force of a train—that blast was unbearable. What did he just do? He was bleeding profusely all over the dirt, there were several large cuts dispersed on his scaly flesh.

Paul walked casually to Nick, raising his arms in preparation for the finishing blow, "That was just a preview. Allow me to give you a full demonstration!"

Nick was as good as finished, but he was in too much pain to care at this point. Before any more fighting could continue, Gabriel shouted from the sidelines. "That's enough Paul!"

Paul hesitated slightly before finally dropping his arms back to his sides. He scoffed at Nick, obviously frustrated that he couldn't finish the job. He stared down at Nick, with intense expression of utmost contempt. Paul looked back at the remaining spectators and bowed politely, delighted by his victory.

"The fight is over. Paul wins," Bartholomew said.

Nick looked at the aftermath weakly, turning his head to see Lucius pull Daniel from the wreckage and help him onto a stretcher. He felt terrible now that Agrian was out of his head. It was like all sense of morality was repressed when he tapped into his demon powers, as if he had no conscience. But now that it was over, he felt the full force of the consequences. The coliseum was in shambles, he had frightened off everyone, and he lost to Paul all in a single afternoon. He was on the ground, but he couldn't feel much lower than he did now.

"You okay, bud?" Matt asked, as he came over. "Paul messed you up pretty badly." Nick was a bloody mess as he struggled to sit up before falling flat again on his back.

"I'm fine." Nick turned his head away from him. His pride was shattered.

"I don't want you bleeding to death out here. I'll be right back, I'll go to the infirmary and get someone out here," Matt said.

Nick waited. He had finally learned that the true extent of his demon powers was wrapped inside an angry and uncontrollable part of him. The more he gave in the more he became further intertwined with the evil side lurking deep beneath his soul, a side so evil it could even hurt the people he cared about. It had him thinking about how he wanted to fight Daniel so badly, that he'd go through anyone. At that time, Gabriel was just an inconvenience that he was willing to kill just to satisfy his own desire. What if Matt had pushed his buttons, or worse, what if Quinn had been there? Could he distinguish the difference between friend and foe? To what lengths was the demon inside him willing to go? He shuddered at those thoughts. From this trial alone Nick understood how little control he had on his own actions when he was using his powers, and it frightened him.

6

TOWER OF GRAVES

Guilt was all Nick could feel the next couple of days. Being holed up in his room for a few days was his official punishment, but he didn't think it was nearly severe enough for what he had done. He'd been violent, disrespectful, and openly antagonistic towards his peers and his superiors. For that, he deserved much more than a few privileges revoked and solitary confinement. However, today was his last day, and now that he just about finished serving his time, he was about to embark on his first mission as a knight.

Beating Daniel garnered him his knight title, but doing so in the manner that he did was something that was unforgivable. He made his way to the strategy room to find the people he offended and only hoped his sincerest apologies would be accepted. As he walked passed some of his fellow knights they made sure he acknowledged their opinions with sounds of disgust or fear, and some had a mixture of both. Those who disliked him before because of rumored favoritism and past follies now had a genuine reason to hate him. It was unnerving to say the least, but it was to be expected. He was a demon, the enemy.

On the bright side, his hands made a full recovery within the night. He now had a better threshold for pain and increased durability thanks to Agrian, but he wasn't quite invincible. That much was proven in his bout with Paul. The way he looked at him during their match, it was almost as if he intended to kill him.

He arrived in front of the closed doors, he took a deep breath before pushing it in. In a stroke of either luck or misfortune, everyone was inside discussing a new mission. Peter, Matt, Paul, and the archangels were all together except for Daniel, and they were talking among themselves when he entered. Then it suddenly became quiet.

"I'm glad you guys are all here," Nick said. He made sure he gathered all their attention's before he continued. "I just wanted to apologize for my actions before. It wasn't able to control Agrian and I hope this won't affect our team dynamic." His eyes slowly rose to meet Peter's who was sitting in his usual spot.

Peter's solemn expression transformed into a smile and then he was suddenly laughing. The rest of them followed and erupted in laughter. "No need to get sentimental, boy. We all know you feel bad. Now stop blubbering like a baby and take a seat."

"Yeah, it wasn't your fault." Gabriel was taking everything in stride, despite the exchange they had before. "You're adjusting to being a demon. Everyone already knew the risks. We just didn't expect things to escalate so quickly like it did. Besides, you passed the exams and you beat your opponent fair and square."

"How is he?" Nick asked.

"Daniel still needs time to recover, but he's taking it all in good humor. I must say, you did quite a toll on the little guy. Then again, he must have known he had it coming to him. He admitted he exchanged less than friendly banter throughout the match," Lucius said.

"I'm just surprised you didn't tell me," Matt said. "I mean, it makes sense now. There's no way you could you have beaten me in a race without any supernatural help."

It was Nick's turn to laugh. Even knowing he was a demon didn't change Matt's opinion of him one bit, and he was grateful. Everyone else also seemed to have forgiven him, which alleviated some feelings of guilt. He had been afraid he could never face them again, but apparently it took a lot more than hospitalizing another soldier to fall from their good graces. The only person in the room who didn't seem amused was Paul, who left abruptly as the laughter subsided, making sure that Nick caught his glare as he passed him by.

Matt made a mock shudder just as the door closed behind him. "Is it just me, or did a cold draft just blow through here?"

Gabriel waved a hand of dismissal. "Let him be. He's a little mad because he thinks you got off easy. You wouldn't believe how he wanted us to punish you, Nick. I never thought I could meet someone as brutal as Bart!"

Bartholomew growled with annoyance.

Nick couldn't help but feel it was a bit justified. But he was glad he was getting the silent treatment from Paul because he wouldn't have to try to rebuild a relationship with somebody he hated.

"Now that this whole debacle is over, let's get on to new business. Pete? What is the run down for our newest knight?" Gabriel said.

"Are you boys up for a mission?" Peter asked.

Nick and Matt nodded at the same time.

"Excellent. Your task is to bring the sword shards you collected from Sir Marcus' tomb to Garreth Graves in Hyperion. Only he has the knowledge and skill to restore it. Time is ticking. We need to act fast so we can strike first. The tremendous power of that blade alone is enough to slay a Crowned Prince," Peter said.

"Strike first? I thought you didn't want to cause a widespread panic by keeping things under wraps," Nick said.

"That was our original intention, but with the explosive combat trials that showcased one of our own as a fire wielding maniac, people were starting to ask questions," Lucius replied. "And so during your little isolation punishment, we took the liberty to host an assembly where we divulged everything and officially announced the attacks in Fyria."

"It was better received than we expected. Most of the kids were more pumped to fight than anything else," Gabriel said. "We sort of lucked out with the generation of today. Zero fear because you guys weren't born during their reign. A blessing because if any of you had only seen some of the atrocities we saw…well, you wouldn't have this death wish."

"Over time, Nicholas' cultivation of skills will be a huge asset," Peter said. "However, right now we need to press every advantage we can get. We need to fix that sword immediately."

"I'm sorry, I still don't understand why we need Garreth. We have plenty of great whitesmiths here in our own Garrison," Matt said. "Last time I checked, Garreth left because he hated us."

Nick knew very little about whitesmiths other than they were a part of the Wisdom Unit. As far as he knew whitesmiths were weapon forgers that specialized in blessing weapons for the Garrison armory. Every soldier and knight had their weapons crafted and imbued with holy magic because it was the most potent weapon at their disposal to vanquish demons. However, very few people chose to spend their lives training to be a whitesmith because it seldom offered glory. Also, many considered spending hours or days crafting equipment for other people to be boring. Then there was also a strict policy for whitesmiths to work in the confines and the safety of the Garrison, which outwardly made them appear as cowards.

"Unfortunately there is no one remotely as skilled as a whitesmith as Garreth Graves. Though it's true he left our Garrison for his own personal reasons, it has become both your responsibilities to convince him to make an exception for this one instance. Every member of Sir Marcus' family has long since been deceased. We can't turn to anybody else," Peter said. "I trust this request is simple enough for two knights to handle?"

Nick nodded. "Of course."

"Good. We'll have vehicular transportation available for you both in thirty minutes. Take this time to properly equip yourselves before you leave," Peter said. He adjourned the meeting and Nick and Matt left to get prepared.

Even though he had a new uniform, Nick was more comfortable in his own attire. He put on a simple, white V-neck shirt with black pants, combat boots, and his signature jacket had the Glenhaven sigil sewn on the left arm, with a red Brave Unit patch on his right. He strapped on leg holsters and fitted them with knives. There would probably be no battle with Graves, but it never hurt to be prepared for the trip.

As he finished, Matt walked into his room, wearing his full uniform as usual. His sword, *Wolfsbane* was sheathed at his waist.

"Let's get this show on the road," Matt said.

They went to the garage facility where all the cars were located. Every car ever manufactured could be requested or delivered for use to their Garrison. However, they all had to be painted in a variation of the same white and gold color scheme with their Glenhaven crest located somewhere so that people could identify them. Nick passed over some of the fancier cars because he already had his choice in mind.

"The usual?" Matt said.

Nick nodded as they jumped into his favorite silver sports car and sped along to the industrial city of Hyperion. However, an idea suddenly crossed Nick's mind.

"We're going to make a quick pit stop somewhere," Nick said.

"Where would this be exactly? You know Peter wouldn't like it if you brought someone along, especially a civilian," Matt said.

"Since when are you the voice of reason?" Nick said.

Matt chuckled. "You know I don't care about bending some of the old man's archaic rules. I just don't think he'd be happy with you taking some girl for a joy ride around town."

"She's not just some girl, Matt."

His time was well spent into solitary confinement, as his punishment allowed his relationship with Quinn to blossom with daily call transmissions. He told her the good news and about the events that occurred in between, but omitted the details about his demonic side. It was a nice treat to hear her voice, but he longed to see her in person. Now that he was promoted, what better reward than to spend a day with her on his first mission?

The sound of his engine was loud enough to alert her of his arrival. She came out just as Nick pulled up to her driveway. She looked absolutely stunning in a simple black tank top with a red patterned flannel over it and jean shorts. He stepped out to embrace her as Matt took the liberty to switch to a seat in the back. Once they were all settled in, they headed on their way to Hyperion.

"I was beginning to think we were never going to see each other again," Quinn said.

"It really has been too long Quinn," Matt agreed. "I think Nick here feels the same way. Poor guy just can't stop talking about you."

"Really, Emberson? You've missed me that much?" Quinn teased. Her green eyes seemed to brighten as she smiled her dazzling smile.

"Just a little bit," Nick said. It was an understatement however, as seeing her in the flesh reminded him exactly how much he missed her, especially the little things, like way she always called him Emberson.

"So where are we off to?" Quinn fumbled with the radio, looking for a station. "I mean, why are we going to Hyperion? It's a civilian city, nothing but concrete jungle. What business would two knights have there?"

"Our mission is to find some guy to help us rebuild this sword." Matt unveiled the shimmering blade pieces from the gold bag it came in. Nick blinked a few times as he caught the reflection of the blade. He gripped the steering wheel, remembering the painful experience the night he made the mistake of handling the blade. As a demon, he was extremely sensitive to holy weapons. This one in particular was seemingly more dangerous to him than others.

"So you guys are going to a whitesmith?"

"That's right…" Matt nodded, as he exchanged a look with Nick in the rearview mirror. "I'm pretty impressed. I never knew civilians knew about whitesmiths. In fact, I didn't think it was very common knowledge."

"It's not," Quinn laughed, "But I'm not a stranger to what happens around the world, as Nick has probably told you. I've moved around my whole life, meeting people and learning new things."

Nick raised a brow. He had no doubt she was well educated and worldly, but curiously, Quinn was very well researched when it came to Garrison. Considering everything on base was sworn to secrecy, how did she know so much?

"That's good, but it's best to keep that information to yourself. You never know who might hear, and if somebody found out, it could spell a lot of trouble for you and us," Nick said. "Garrisons have many enemies in the shadows. Namely demons, but there are also a great number of human supporters."

"Lighten up," Matt said, "you'll scare the poor girl! Besides, does she look like she's one to tell?

Nick glanced at her, the wind blowing gently through her fiery red hair as she brushed it away from her face. She was no longer listening. She was lost in her own world, gazing out the window in the distance at the grand scenery surrounding them. She was absolutely breathtaking. Whether or not Matt was right or wrong, he'd like to believe that this perfect vision was a reflection of her true self.

"No, I guess you're right."

As soon as they arrived within city, they found Graves Tower rather easily. It stood out as the tallest and most recognizable building. Garreth's family spent no expense to set themselves apart from the competition. At the very top was a structure shaped like a capital G which was also a light fixture that shone brightly. The Graves were an illustrious family, renowned for discovering the formula and device that created the Holy Shield. However, Garreth's parents had passed away during the Second Coming, leaving their only son a hefty inheritance and a multimillion empire to run alone.

"Wait, what are we doing at Graves Tower?" Quinn asked nervously as they parked in the underground structure.

"I thought we told you, Garrison business." Matt turned to Nick. "You got to tell your girlfriend to listen to the stories because I hate repeating myself."

"I think you guys should just go on ahead without me," Quinn said.

"Because?" Nick asked.

"It's not important, really," she said.

"Well then, just tell us," Matt said.

"Everything I know about whitesmiths?" Quinn pointed up to the top of the building. "That's how."

"So what, you knew Garreth Graves," Matt said. "He's a pretty well-known person in general. You'd have to be living under a rock to not know the name behind the creation of the Holy Shield."

"Actually, we used to date."

"Oh."

Though he didn't let it show, those four words hit Nick harder than Paul's Luxilight beam times a hundred.

"Come again?" Nick said.

"That's how I know about whitesmiths and the Garrison. We used to date, but it was a long time ago. I wonder if he still remembers me."

Quinn was speaking so nonchalantly Nick wasn't sure whether he should be concerned or relieved. He knew she wasn't shallow like most girls, but to have dated a man of his stature and vast riches was a little daunting for him. Needless to say, it felt like the boots he needed to fill as a boyfriend suddenly grew twice as big.

"Well if you put it that way, maybe it's not such a good idea that you come in with us. We don't want to open up old wounds," Matt said. "What do you think, Nick?"

"Up to her." Nick tried to maintain a level of coyness. He didn't want to admit that he was slightly jealous.

"Just don't take too long, okay?" Quinn said as she climbed back into the car.

Nick and Matt went straight to the elevator and rode it to the first floor. To his surprise, Matt didn't mention a word about Garreth and Quinn. He must have already known how it made him feel.

As the elevator doors parted, they found themselves in a beautifully decorated room. The floor and everything else was seemingly made of marble. There was some simple furniture, with a few couches set out for people to wait and couple plants placed randomly. At the center was a single square desk, with a receptionist sitting with a phone to her ear.

Nick and Matt made their way to the front desk, just as she finished her call.

"Hello, and welcome to Graves Tower," she said cheerfully. "What can I do for you today?"

Her nametag read Abigail. She had shoulder length brown hair, curled at the ends like a doll. She wore a light grey blazer and matching pants. What made Nick feel a bit uneasy was what seemed to be permanent smile on her face, as if putting up a pleasant facade for so long had ruined her ability to express her emotions naturally.

"We're looking for Garreth," Nick said. "We need to speak to him. It's very important."

"*Everyone* is, honey," she said, with that same forced smile, "but I'm afraid Mr. Graves is quite busy this afternoon. Maybe you can schedule an appointment for the next available time." She opened a notebook and flipped through a couple of pages. "How about the fifteenth of this month, let's say around, next year?"

"Next year?" Matt groaned loudly. "We drove all this way for nothing!"

Nick wasn't about to allow a pesky receptionist stop him from completing his first mission. "Tell him it's official Garrison business from Glenhaven and he needs to speak to us immediately. If he refuses, then we will continue to stand here until he does."

Abigail gave a look of discontent. "Very well," she said, trying to maintain the perky attitude, "I'll try to get through to him."

She pressed a series of numbers on the phone pad on her desk and waited for it to ring a couple of times before someone on the other line picked up. She placed the call on speaker for them all to hear.

"Yes, what is it now, Abigail?"

"Mr. Graves," Abigail said cheerfully. "We have a couple knights here who want to meet with you right now. They say it's very urgent."

Garreth sighed over the line. "Abigail, you know I'm busy right now. Please just schedule them for an appointment, and I'll meet with them the—"

Nick leaned into the speaker. "My name is Nick Emberson and I've come here on behalf of the Glenhaven Garrison to talk to you."

"We also have a package for you as well," Matt added. He jangled the bag he was carrying for good measure.

"The Glenhaven Garrison?" Garreth asked incredulously, his tone was suddenly pleasant, almost jovial. "Send them up at once. Hold all my other calls."

"At once sir," Abigail said with surprise as the phone clicked off. "That is so strange… Mr. Graves never takes personal visits without appointments. You may take the elevator to the fiftieth floor." She pointed them to the far left.

"Thanks." Without a second thought Matt skipped to the elevator on the right and pushed the button. Before he could enter Nick heard chair legs screech across the marble floor behind them.

Abigail was on her feet. "Excuse me, but that elevator leads to the basement level. It is reserved only for Mr. Graves and individuals with special clearance. Please use the *left* elevator." Nick rolled his eyes. Of course there were two elevators built in, just having one was not impressive enough.

This time they took the left elevator to the fiftieth floor, which was also the very highest level. In no time at all the door opened and they were inside a big office. They walked in and were immersed with Pailean inspired artwork and furniture around the room. In the center, was a big glass table where someone was sitting their feet resting up. Nick couldn't see the person's face because he was holding a newspaper, but it had to be Garreth.

He was shaking in his seat, apparently laughing to himself, crinkling the sides of the newspaper in his hands as they approached him.

"Garreth Graves," Matt said with a grin.

He dropped the newspaper on the table and sat up. Garreth looked a lot different than what Nick had envisioned. For one, he looked nothing like a knight in the traditional sense. Just by reputation and the way others had described him in the past, Garreth had to have gone through years of training, but the man in front of them looked like he hadn't picked up training weights in his life, much less any sword. He was as skinny as a twig, short in stature, with big, square framed glasses that took most of the room on his face. Not that there was much room left as his medium length black hair took the rest of it. He wore clothing befitting a multimillionaire: a crisp, white suit jacket with a dark blue dress shirt underneath, black dress slacks, and an argyle tie that matched the pants and shirt.

"Matthew Cunningham you old dog!" Garreth walked to him with his hand out, which Matt shook with his free hand. "It's been far too long!" Another difference Nick noticed was that he seemed to have a more sociable personality, despite his reputation for holding long term grudges.

"You must be the man called Nick Emberson." Garreth flashed a warm smile and extended a hand to him. "It is certainly nice to meet you."

Nick nodded and shook his hand.

"Please, have a seat." Garreth gestured to the two chairs in front of his desk. "Would you guys like a drink?" He picked up the half empty glass on his desk and took a sip. From the look of the brownish color, it wasn't something a person should be drinking at this time of day, especially one whose responsibility was to run a successful company.

"No thank you, we should just get right down to business," Nick said.

"Very well." He leaned back in his large leather chair. "I'm sure the reason has to do with what's inside that bag, right?"

"Yes, we've recently found the sword that belonged to Sir Marcus and we need your help in restoring it to its former glory," Matt said.

"So you've found his legendary blade huh?" Garreth leaned forward to refill his drink. Nick could smell the contents from the bottle. It didn't help that his enhanced senses seemed to work against him at this point because he could practically taste the alcohol. It made him feel queasy. "I can understand why you decided to bring it to me, but artifacts like that don't interest anybody here in Hyperion. We're a diplomatic city you see, one that does not look too kindly upon those associated with the Garrisons."

Matt nodded. "There's another reason we brought it back. Fyria has been attacked by demons and Peter believes it to be a sign of an impending war."

"You didn't mention a specific name, so I'll assume this is a renegade demon group. I'm sure as Fyria's allies you can handle it," Garreth said.

"Not if the Crowned Princes step in. And believe me, they will," Matt said.

Garreth laughed as if it was the most ridiculous thing in the world. "That's impossible. The Crowned Prince's return can only be marked by the Inferno Bearer's reappearance. Every soldier and knight knows that."

"Well, it's true, and he's sitting right in front of you," Matt said.

Garreth almost fell out of his chair as the realization struck him. "Him? But how can this be?"

"If I didn't see myself shooting fire from my hands with my own eyes then I wouldn't believe it either," Nick said.

Garreth's facial expression did not change. He nodded slowly, as if translating the message once more. "So what? Half the world is populated by demons. What's so scary about a few more?"

"I don't think you understand the gravity of the situation," Nick said. "Millions of lives are at stake if they regain power. You've heard the legends. You know the stories. We need Sir Marcus's sword back in our arsenal if we are to prevent a disaster from happening."

"You mean did I understand the fact that the Crowned Princes returning are a surefire sign of an apocalypse?" Garreth asked. "Or how ridiculous it is that you think restoring a dead knight's antique can help you win a war?"

"According to Peter it can," Nick said.

"You're the best whitesmith we've got, man," Matt said. "Your hands are pure magic when it comes to crafting equipment and we need you to help us. You know you can do it, you're the only one who can."

"If you haven't noticed, I don't work under any Garrison anymore. I'm running a successful business and I answer only to the president now. Not to Peter and certainly to neither of you. I don't need to be involved in this anymore. It simply doesn't interest me."

"You're not seriously saying sitting here and pushing papers all day long is as fulfilling as saving lives?" Nick asked. "At least take a look at the sword."

Matt placed the gold bag on the table and slid it towards former knight. Garreth glanced at them both briefly, curiosity in his eyes. He adjusted his glasses and shook the contents out. Sure enough, a fragment of metal and a hilt decorated by jewels laid in front of them. This was the first time Nick had a chance to look at the sword in proper lighting. Truth be told, ever since it burned him he was a bit hesitant to handle it again. It was simply magnificent and at the same time, rather peculiar. It had a unique design he'd never seen before. The bladed portion was undulating instead of straight, like a tongue of flame.

"Truly beautiful craftsmanship," Garreth said as he inspected them in his hands. "It's a shame it's been reduced to this."

Garreth scoured through the small bag as if looking for something more, only to end up disappointed. He dropped the sword pieces back on the table, and leaned into his chair, clasping the bottom of his chin with his fingers in deep thought.

"What do you think?" Nick asked.

"From what I see it can be done, but it would require some research on my part. However, *will* I partake in its restoration is another question. Like I said before, I'm not interested in running around with swords and playing hero anymore," Garreth said.

"Then I guess Paul was right about you," Nick said.

"Paul Evans?" Garreth scoffed, his eyes narrowing. "He's already stolen what was rightfully meant to be mine. I was supposed to be the next archangel. I bet Blondie still brags about being Gabriel's apprentice, doesn't he? I bet he keeps rubbing it in people's faces even now. The smug prick." He took a sip from his beverage and slammed the cup on the table.

"Was that the reason you left?" Matt said.

"It was the final straw in a long line of constant betrayals." Garreth grew rigid in his seat, as if the question managed to unnerve him. "If you ask me, both of you should cut your losses and leave as soon as you can because once Peter's done using you, you'll be discarded like yesterday's trash."

But Nick wasn't in the mood; he could feel his temperature rise as his anger grew. The room became quiet, as they sat and looked around to each other, with no one saying a word until Garreth spoke again.

"If looks could kill Nick, I'd say you'd like to see me dead Why? Does my disdain for Garrisons make you upset?"

"No, but I'd definitely like to punch you in the face right now," Nick said. His hands gripped tightly onto the arms of the chair to prevent the demon within from lunging at him.

"Calm down, Nick. Garreth, there has to be something more to this than you not wanting anything to do with us. Forget Paul, Peter, and whatever problems you had in the past, and try to see the bigger picture," Matt said.

"I've seen the picture and I don't care," Garreth said.

"Just like that, huh? So what was the point of seeing us when you were just going to blow off the idea anyway? You knew who we were and what we wanted, but you really had no intention of ever helping us, did you?" Nick said.

"No I did not. I just wanted to see you Garrison lapdogs come groveling on hands and knees. I wanted to see you all fall off your damn high horses just once, and realize that the world isn't here to serve the order of your angels anymore. I'm not some kind of magical genie that can be summoned with a snap of Peter's fingers. Things have changed. I've changed. And there's nothing you can do that will make me reconsider," Garreth said.

Garreth had a prominent history with the knights, so he had to have been briefed about the importance of the sword. With all the knowledge he had, he must know how much leverage could be gained on their side if he helped. Why did he have such a grudge against the knights? What happened between him and the others at the Garrison that drove him to put the world at stake?

Garreth adjusted his glasses. "Anything else? As you know I'm a very busy man, so if you please." He stood up, prepared to show them out.

Nick, sitting complacently in his seat, had just about given up on their mission. It was futile to convince the multimillionaire to help when he obviously detested anything related to the holy knights or the Garrison. Suddenly Nick's eyes became fixated upon an object in the back: a black katana on the mantle directly behind Garreth, and in between two Pailean-styled paintings. The sword looked much different than anything else in the room, but the real reason it stood out was because the scabbard was worn and old, something that wouldn't normally catch the interest of someone with Garreth's stature.

"That's an impressive sword." Nick pointed to the rack. "I've never seen something like that before. Where did you get it?"

"Pailo, like everything else in this room." Garreth rose out from his seat to better look at the sword. "It's called *Rosewind*. It was the original katana I used during my days as a knight. Better than the old regulation rapiers, don't you think?" He gave a resigned sigh. "I've always enjoyed Pailean culture and among the choices of weapons, their swords are by far my favorite design. Such elegance, such grace is the katana."

"I've only seen them in pictures," Matt said. "But if you ask me, they seem a little flimsy for my taste."

"I'm sure that was the reason Peter never incorporated them." Garreth drew the sword off the stand, cradling it as if it were the most delicate object in the world. He sighed softly. "Such a long time ago, wasn't it?"

Matt nodded. "Yeah, you were a great swordsman. One of the best we had."

"I was, wasn't I?" Garreth placed his hand on the dingy katana sheath. His mouth curled into a frown as he dropped his hand from the scabbard and turned back around. The sweet sentiment from his face had been replaced with bitterness.

"Unfortunately, like everything else in this world it changed, for the worse. No matter what you do the Crowned Princes cannot be defeated, not even with the power of the Inferno Bearer. It would take years before you could even begin to master his skill in combat. By then it would be too late."

Nick slammed his fists into the chair's arm support breaking both sides into wood chips. "You got to let go of the past," he said, his voice hard as steel. "I don't know what happened to you, and I don't want to sit here and listen to a sob story. This isn't a therapy session. This is about war. It's about lives on the line. We came here for the purpose of resurrecting the broken sword that could help, but you're turning us away for your own selfish reasons. Fyria won't be the first casualty. The world will sink into despair and it won't be long before Hyperion does too. So you can either sit there sulking about the past or you can let go of your hatred for the knights and help us make a stand in defending our future."

Garreth walked to the window and gazed outside. He seemed to be struggling with inner turmoil, muttering silently to himself. After a back and forth exchange with himself, he spoke, but only to serve disappointment.

"I expected more from him." Garreth stared out the window, his arms crossed behind his back. "I expected him to acknowledge my potential and see me in his footsteps, but I was wrong." He turned around now, his teeth seething with rage. "I fought and bled, but I was never good enough, no matter how hard I worked or how strong I became! I would have given my life for Peter's Garrison—for some shard of his approval! But in the end my service meant nothing. And now, after years of silence they decide they need me again. Well you can forget it! You'll receive no help from me."

"Garreth…" Matt said.

"You've already insulted me enough. Now leave now before I call security," Garreth warned.

"Come on man there's no need to—" Matt began.

"LEAVE NOW!"

Matt was stunned, but Nick knew that at this point they were just wasting their time. Garreth Graves had left everything in Glenhaven for a different life in Hyperion, for an escape from the knights and be free to make his own choices. The thought of that alone made Nick envy Garreth. It wasn't enough that he was richer than Matt, or probably more successful than the president, but he also had the choice to do whatever he wanted. He wasn't forced to live out a destiny, to have his whole life planned beforehand. It was something Nick would never be able to do, and it made him angry to think about it. He had the option to deny them. And as great as the Garrison was, it was still a system Nick was attached to. It was prison despite its noblest intentions to be anything otherwise.

"Forget it." Nick stormed off to the elevator. "He's not going to help us." He stabbed at the button with his finger to go down.

"Just wait a second, I think he'll come around." Matt followed him with the bag of sword pieces jangling in his hand. The door chimed and opened before them. They shuffled into the elevator just as they heard footsteps. Matt held the door for a split second, awaiting Garreth to appear. But he never did.

There was only the sound of another bottle opening. The smell of alcohol filled the air as its contents were poured into a fresh cool glass.

Outside they met with Quinn, who was leaning on the side of the car. She tilted her sunglasses upwards, "Something tells me things didn't go out as well as planned."

"You think?" Nick said, as they climbed into the car.

"So what now?" Quinn said.

"We have to report my first mission was a complete failure," Nick said.

The whole way back to Glenhaven he kept thinking about their conversation with Garreth, replaying it over and over in his head. The whitesmith who had served loyally for several years now regarded his past with such contempt. Nick couldn't blame him; on the contrary, he felt sorry for him. He'd gone to Hyperion looking for help from the knight, but the man he found wasn't a knight at all, just a shell of a man consumed by his own hatred.

7

DOCTOR NUMEROUS

A few weeks later Nick was eating alone one afternoon in the community cafeteria when Matt joined him. Today he looked more energetic than usual, with his bright smile and the strange, sparkle in his eyes he usually had when there was interesting news to be told.

"The word on the street is that despite our unsuccessful mission, Peter hasn't revoked your spot at the frontlines. What do you think about that?" Matt said.

"That seems really unlikely," Nick tossed the last piece of sandwich into his mouth. Since their last mission was a failure, he wasn't exactly in the mood to be discussing the next one.

Matt frowned. "I expected a better reaction than this. What's wrong? Are you still mad about what Garreth said? Forget him. He's just bitter about everything."

Nick nodded across the room to Daniel whom he had been watching for some time. He was sitting by himself, wrapped head to toe in bandages. Being hospitalized was bad, but having virtually everyone shun him for losing was such a pathetic sight to behold. Every member of the Garrison was at the knight initiation and they all saw what had happened, but no one came by to ask how he was doing or bother to help him when struggled to carry his lunch tray. No one offered to sign one of his various casts. Not a single person cared. They all just went about their business, passing him by as if he didn't exist at all.

"Some warm welcome," Nick muttered.

"You mean that Daniel kid?" Matt asked. "You know, if you put the two of you together, you look sort of similar, like he could be your long-lost cousin."

"Doubtful."

It was true that he had the same sad slouch Nick had the first couple of years as a soldier. Other than that, no way he bore any similarities to the bright-eyed apprentice. He may have had Matt as a support system through all the rough times, but there was no way this light hazing could compare to the constant rejection Nick had to endure for years.

Daniel was the new guy; he was the transfer. This was normal and after a few months, it would eventually stop. However, as far as he knew Daniel was also the youngest apprentice in the Garrison history, which meant he was currently resented by all other envious older knights who deemed they were cheated out of the position. Earlier Nick saw him wave at Paul, only to be rebuffed and earn the jeering laughter of the other knights. If a fellow apprentice like Paul and his goons seemed to despise him, it was more than likely because he didn't consider Daniel an equal for his crushing defeat at the trials. Strength was the only way to become popular among warriors, and he had pretty much ruined his chances the day he lost.

Worst of all though: Nick knew that he was the cause of Daniel's misfortune. It was his lack of control that put Daniel on a stretcher and alienated him from his peers. Knowing this, how could he be excited to go into war when he could potentially be dangerous among his own soldiers? He couldn't control his crazy rage when he became Agrian.

"I should go talk to him," Nick said. "I mean, after all I did I should at least attempt to make things right."

"You did set back the Garrison budget by blowing him through a wall, but trying to patch things up is going to be social suicide," Matt warned. "He's an apprentice who not only publically lost, but lost to a *demon*. Get it? His reputation is as good as gone. None of the other knights will ever accept him now. Everyone already sees you as an outcast. Do you really want to jump into the deep end by adopting that kid?"

"My reputation never stopped you from being my friend." Nick stood up. "Now are you going to come with me, or not?"

Matt grinned. "You know, I think Peter got the wrong guy. You're way too soft to be a blood lusted demon. Fine, let's bring the welcome wagon to the little guy." They moved their trays a couple tables over next to the sad-eyed knight.

"It's good to see you're doing much better, Daniel." Nick took on of the many empty seats next to the boy. He was rewrapping the loose bandages around his arm. Somehow he still retained the goofy smile on his puffy face even after being so battered.

"I must look better than I feel." Daniel's mouth drooped sadly. "For an apprentice to lose, especially during the knight trials, is just embarrassing. Maybe Lucius was wrong to have chosen me."

"I say look at the positives. Doesn't it make you feel better knowing Nick here was actually part demon?" Matt sat on his other side. "And not just any demon, but the Prince of Rage! I mean, getting the stuffing knocked out of you by a demon that high on the food chain is what would have happened to anybody."

"It didn't happen to Paul," Daniel said.

"To be fair, Paul's been an apprentice for a long time. Gabriel's worked him hard too, making sure he would be the best. So far he's proven to be the best fighter here aside from archangels," Matt said.

"That's true…" Daniel's face brightened a little. "But it wouldn't hurt as much if the whole Garrison didn't seem to hate me."

"Get used to it. It'll only get worse if you let them get to you," Nick said. "If anyone causes you any trouble, you can always count on me or Matt. And to be honest, you were a great challenge during my trial. I mean, you had to be in order to unleash Agrian right?"

Daniel scratched his face. "Thanks Nick, you're a really cool guy. You know, what I can't understand is why everyone seems to hate you. Even before they found out you were a demon, they never liked you. No offense, of course."

Matt glanced at Nick. "That's actually a long story, and I don't think it needs to be said, but let's just say he's been through his fair share of problems."

"It wouldn't interest you anyway," Nick said.

Daniel nodded, but winced at the pain of moving his head so quickly.

Suddenly static crackled from a loudspeaker. Bartholomew's voice boomed through the microphones requesting the presence of Nick, Matt, Daniel, and Paul to the briefing room. They cut their lunch short and walked to the room. Paul was already there, waiting silently as he pretended not to see them walk inside. Nick and the others took a seat in their usual spots just as Lucius approached the stand with a manila folder in his hand.

"Do any of these people look familiar?" Lucius was quick to get down to business. He pulled several photographs from the folder and slid it towards them. They gathered around the pictures like a campfire, examining and scrutinizing every detail. "We sent a member of the Justice Unit sent out there for reconnaissance a few weeks ago. It was taken two hours ago around the wreckage at Fyria." Lucius threw the bloody stub of a finger on the table. "This is all that's left of him."

Daniel took one glance before he turned away in disgust. Everyone else stared on in stunned silence.

Nick picked up the picture and took a good long look at the faces. Wait. He recognized a burly man with a very closely shaven head and a broad chest. He wasn't wearing much clothing, appearing only to have on a tight, black sleeveless shirt to accent his physique and matching pants.

"That's Astaroth. He's hiding in his human form, but it's definitely him," Nick said.

"Good eye, but take a closer look. What can you tell me about the man next to him?" Lucius said.

Beside Astaroth was another large man in a lab coat and an eye patch. He had a thick beard and slicked-back hair. Judging only by looks, he appeared to be a composite image of all the stereotypical mad scientists portrayed in films.

"I don't know…" Nick frowned, shaking his head. "I've never seen that man before in my life. Who is he?"

"That, my friend is Doctor Numerous, and the root of all our trouble. He's the one who betrayed us to the remaining Crowned Princes during the Second Coming," Lucius said.

Nick focused on the image, memorizing the face of the man responsible for his transformation. "A lot has changed since his departure, and it turns out he has much bigger plans for Fyria than we ever imagined."

"Doctor Numerous…Wait, that sounds familiar." Matt rubbed his chin in thought. "Which Garrison is he from? Coros?"

"No, Doctor Numerous was part of the Garrison in Fyria up until he fell from grace," Paul said. "He was an alchemist who made a very worthwhile contribution when he pioneered the famous, Light Prison. But that is the extent of my knowledge."

"You all may have heard stories, but I knew that man back when his name was Frank Barrett." Daniel's his face looked ages older when he got serious. He stared blankly into space with an intensity Nick had not known he was capable of show-ing. "Yes, he was a brilliant alchemist and scholar, as well as the first person to master the art of trapping demons in beams of light. But behind his achievements was a terribly troubled man. No one knows why, but his craving for knowledge eventually turned his sights onto the study of demons. He became cor-rupted by his lust for power and got into contact with Ozarael himself. Before he could be executed for his crimes, he escaped and has been in hiding with demons ever since. It is because he was allowed to live that everything has taken a turn for the worse."

"This is the reason we believe Fyria is under siege," Peter said. "However, what we do not know is why he would come out of hiding now. As a single entity, Doctor Numerous is just a nuisance compared to his superiors."

"Speaking of the Crowned Princes, why would they try to recruit Doctor Numerous? He's human. They would slit their own throats before ever trusting a human," Nick said.

"Desperation creates opportunity. Even the Crowned Princes needed help at the time and he was the one to give them information. Interestingly enough, his strength had also been sufficient to secure a position as one of the Crowned Princes's Infernals. He's rising through their ranks meteorically," Gabriel said.

"Infernals?" Matt said.

"Do you kids even pay attention to the lectures we give you?" Lucius sighed.

Matt shrugged. "Must have slipped our minds."

"The Infernals, better known as the Infernal Four, are comprised of four demon generals who serve directly below the Crowned Princes. The members include: War, Pestilence, Famine, and Death. Only four can exist at any given time, which means Doctor Numerous had to have taken his position by force. By doing so, he has gained one of their unique and extraordinary demonic powers, though the extent of their powers is still unknown," Lucius said.

"Where do we come in?" Paul asked. "Member of the Infernal Four or not, I will bring his head back on a silver platter."

"Settle down, son. The archangels and I have decided it would be more beneficial to our cause if we can successfully capture Numerous. Having his knowledge would better serve us if he was alive," Peter said.

Paul folded his arms in disgust. "Mercy for a traitor? He deserves nothing less than death. We're too soft on our enemies and we forgive them too easily."

Gabriel threw him a warning glance. "If everything works in your favor, you'll get the chance to administer it, Paul. But our Supreme Commander is right. If we have a chance to prevent anyone else from getting hurt, we should take it. It won't be as glorious, but having one of their Infernals as a captive would give us a good insight on their goals."

Paul bowed apologetically. "Excuse my indiscretion, Gabriel. My apologies Supreme Commander, I was out of line." He turned to leave.

Nick shook his head; the guy was as bloodthirsty as a demon. Yet he was an archangel in training while Nick was the one with the monster vying for sole ownership of his very soul.

"I'm guessing this will be my next assignment," Nick said.

"I thought you already heard. Usually news travels quickly around here, especially the bad kind," Gabriel said. "We'll be charging in full-force with both the Brave and Justice Units. This means you and Matt will be with us when we attack the settlements the demons have in Fyria."

"They've already formed settlements?" Matt asked.

"We have to make that assumption," Gabriel said. "Numerous would not have made such a bold move in that territory if he wasn't willing to stay for the long haul."

"We know Numerous well enough to know how he thinks and operates. He's methodical. And that means he's going to be there a while, searching for any remains of research they had in their Garrison. Then they're most likely going to turn it into a demon stronghold. A single Garrison is more or less designed to be impregnable, and is heavily armed to defend against any land, sea, or air based assault. Numerous will not give up this footing without a fight," Lucius said.

"Fortunately there is still some time before this happens, but the idea is still the same. We need to move quickly before it's too late," Peter said.

"The problem is the guy's been spotted all around the world, and that means that he's being guided by at least one of the Princes," Gabriel said, "And if they somehow manage to take Fyria and disrupt the delicate balance we have among the Garrisons, then everything will fall into chaos."

"Got it." Nick stood up from his seat. "Are we done here?"

"Yes, you both may leave," Peter said with a wave of his hand. Nick and Matt bowed and left.

Nick stomped out of the briefing room in a hurry, but was stopped abruptly as Matt grabbed his shoulder. "Hey man, what's going on? And what's with the hot and cold routine? You're getting me a little worried." The hallways were running rampant with soldiers out of training or on their way to their respective missions.

"Nothing."

"It's Doctor Numerous, isn't it?" Matt said. "Don't tell me he's got you all riled up. I don't want you to do anything stupid because you're mad at the traitor."

"Nothing. I'm the Inferno Bearer, right? I'm some omnipotent warrior reincarnated in order to fulfill the prophecy. I'm supposed to be all these great things, this salvation for the world, but it just doesn't matter to me." Nick hated to admit this out loud, but it was true and it had been boiling inside him for some time now.

"Why not? You know, you've been acting a little strange since that day we spent in Hyperion," Matt said. "Don't tell me you let Garreth get to you?"

"Garreth was right! We're just lapdogs anyway, and the worst part is, I'm a lapdog that has no future. Anything and everything I'll ever want will always be out of my reach. Do you know how unfair that is? We're stuck in this rat hole of a Garrison for the rest of our lives and the only thing I can do is serve people who hate me until I drop dead! And now they're scared of me? All of them think I'm a damn psycho! So explain to me why I should even care?"

"You're forgetting the cardinal rule of our job, bud. Glory or fame is second to the safety of the people. Creating a world that is safer for the generations of tomorrow is the reason any of us stay on board. That's the reason we take the lectures and the punishments. That's the only reason that matters. Now tell me the truth, something else is bothering you, isn't it?"

As usual Matt saw right through him, through the shallow veil of irritation was the true reason. Something else had been bothering him. It was because of a conversation he had in Hyperion that he had finally seen the truth. After getting chastised for their failure to finish such a simple task of enlisting the esteemed Garreth Graves' help, Nick had become despondent. He was shaken to his core, and it greatly diminished his drive. Deep down inside it all had to do with her.

"You're right. It's something I've been thinking about ever since we left Hyperion," Nick said.

"What is it?" Matt asked.

"When Garreth was talking about how badly he was treated, it got me thinking about what my stake was for the Garrison. I'm not exactly loved around here and if it wasn't for my powers I'd be disposable. I mean, if someone like Garreth was tossed aside like that, what chance do I have? I can't give up everything to be left with nothing to show for it," Nick said.

"Nothing left to show for it? Don't you know that—" Matt stopped, finally understanding what was truly at stake. "—It's not about Garreth at all. It's about your life without her, isn't it?"

Nick nodded.

"Her? And here I thought you weren't interested in girls," Paul said.

They turned to see him coming around the corner looking as smug as ever. How long had he been standing there? "Garreth blames his failure on others when in fact he was just too prideful to admit I was the better candidate. He couldn't stand Gabriel choosing me. It was absolutely humiliating for him. If I were a loser I would feel the same way."

"Don't you have an assignment to get to, Paul? Or an appointment to kiss Gabriel's butt?" Matt said.

Paul was clearly not amused. "No. Unlike you buffoons, I'm privileged to the most confidential secrets of the Garrison. I'm on the way to do my own reconnaissance."

"You're going to Fyria—alone?" Nick asked, skeptically.

"I would if Gabriel gave me permission. I'm not scared of Doctor Numerous, even if everyone else seems to be. He's lucky I'm not hunting because if I did happen to cross him, you can be sure I would be the last knight he'd ever see," Paul said.

"Were you in the same meeting as us? You couldn't kill him if you wanted to because they want him for questioning. Those were direct orders from the Supreme Commander," Nick said.

Paul smirked. "Look at the demon boy trying to sound official. Maybe it would be best if you didn't lecture me, Nicholas. The last time you ran your mouth I had to put you in the dirt where you belong, and I wouldn't mind doing it again." Paul tapped the polished hilt of his broadsword in a thinly veiled threat. "Now run along little girls, class is starting soon. I'm sure you don't want to be late." He laughed snidely as he walked away.

"As much as I want to punch that guy in the face, I have to admit that would probably be the only shot I'd get in. Damn him and his combat skills," Matt said.

"You're talking to the guy who was his personal punching bag. I'd like to tear his head off one day." Nick felt his face heat with anger.

"Relax. He's the Garrison golden boy. Of course they'll let him get away with practically murder." Matt looked at his watch. "But that doesn't work for us. It looks like we're going to be late for training no matter how fast we run. I'd rather ditch than get Bart's wrath. You know how mad he gets when people interrupt his lessons halfway."

"I'm really not in the mood to listen to lecture today anyway," Nick agreed. Bartholomew's lessons were always so tense because everyone was always so intimidated by him. "Right now I'm being pulled back and forth."

"You need a second opinion. You should talk to Joni," Matt said. "She's the best at this kind of stuff. Girl talk, and all that other junk. I told her about Quinn and she didn't think it was a good idea."

"You already told her? That was supposed to be a secret!" Nick said.

"Look, Joni and I don't keep secrets from each other, but you can always trust her to keep one for a friend. If you ask me, she has always given me the best advice. She has that maternal instinct, you know? That certain quality that allows her to empathize with anything," Matt said.

"I guess I will, but it has to wait. I have to pick up Quinn from school," Nick said.

"Visiting a civilian school should be interesting," Matt said.

The two friends parted ways. Nick had never been to a civilian school, and he was quite surprised to see the differences. He parked at the end of a packed loading zone just as the kids were dismissed. It was weird to not see any weapons in clear sight or matching uniforms. They all seemed carefree, talking and laughing in their peer groups. It was a lot different than life at the Garrison.

As he pulled to the front of the line, he saw the looks of the many who longed to be part of the Garrison. Their faces were glowing with a mix of both admiration and envy. It was these moments in which Nick felt the sense of pride for what he did. Then there were the other days when he wished to be part of the normal world, to be one of them just for a day, not have to wake up knowing that they narrowly avoided an apocalypse from completely wiping them from existence.

Just then Quinn came out of a classroom, carrying her books and looking strikingly beautiful as always. She didn't belong here, not among people so plain and ordinary. Her hair especially made her stick out like a sore thumb. He waited for her eyes to find him. When they did, she smiled her perfect smile and walked towards him. Nick made a note of some boys ogling her from the sides. He chuckled to himself as their brokenhearted faces descended into despair as she stepped into his sports car, courtesy of belonging to an esteemed military academy.

"I'm hungry." Quinn gave Nick a peck on the cheek. "I was late and haven't eaten a single thing all day. Can we get some food, Emberson?"

"Where would you like to go, Red?" Nick turned out onto the open road.

She looked at him inquisitively. "Red? That's a first." Quinn gave a sly smile. "Where'd you come up with that?"

Nick shrugged. "I like that you gave me a nickname, so I figured why not come up with one for you? And it just popped in my head. Do you like it?"

"I love it! It fits perfectly for me." She tossed her fiery locks over her shoulder.

"So what would you like to eat, Red?"

"I could really go for a good burger right now. Any recommendations for a girl with an appetite?" Quinn said.

"How about Hank's Hamburgers? It's an old joint by The Pier, but I've never had a better burger. They're made fresh every day, I think you'd like them," Nick said.

"Sure, I'm always up to try something new."

Aside from Heaven's Peak, The Pier was the only good site for most of the fun in Glenhaven. It was originally built as a docking harbor for the Garrison's Justice Unit and was big enough to house a fleet of ships. However, at the last minute they changed their minds and moved the fleet to a different location, leaving their finished work to the city. Glenhaven had no use for it and renovated it into a giant shopping center for fun activities and their leisure lifestyle. There was a Ferris wheel, carnival games, and restaurants selling fast food and desserts. Unlike other recreational centers, every attraction was floated on the water, which added a certain uniqueness that gave way to many tourists.

"This place is amazing," Quinn said, as they walked hand in hand to the burger stand. He was happy to have impressed her. Outside the restaurant, chubby old Hank himself was handing out heart-shaped coupon flyers to those who passed by. She grabbed one and read it aloud, "Buy a meal for two, get a free romantic ride on the Ferris wheel."

"What do you think, my friend? Does your lovely companion want a romantic ride for two?" Hank shot them a big goofy grin. He rubbed his greasy beard with his hand. "It's a limited time offer, so you better grab this while you can."

"Can we, Nick? Can we?" Quinn used her puppy-dog face to its fullest potential. It had a devastating effect on him.

"Sure, why not?" Nick knew full well that this "limited time" offer was a marketing ploy used by old Hank on unsuspecting tourists.

They ate their cheeseburgers and shared an order of fries in a hurry because Quinn had her eyes on a huge teddy bear at a nearby ring-toss game. After about twenty tries he got the hang of carnival games and began winning at each station they played. Of course, they opted for mostly "couple" games, like knocking down bottles with a rubber ball or throwing darts at balloons, winning prize after prize until they had more stuffed animals than a toy factory. They gave away most of their winnings to sad, empty-handed kids, only keeping the big teddy bear he won at the first game. After they were done and had their fill they went to the Ferris wheel for a ride, where they did a couple of full rotations before the ride conductor decided to mix things up, stopping them at the very top.

Old Hank may have lied about the time availability of his deals, but the promise of romance was real. The view was absolutely gorgeous, much more beautiful than Nick ever cared to notice. The orange setting sun meant the daily fireworks show was soon to come, putting a perfect end to a perfect day.

Quinn tugged on his shirt. "This was the best idea ever. I think it even tops our first date."

"I don't know, I think finding rocks pretty much tops any date I've ever been on," Nick said with a smile.

Quinn slapped him gently on the shoulder. "Emberson, you're so ridiculous. Look at the view. Glenhaven is so pretty in the daylight. It's much better than from Heaven's Peak."

"I was meaning to ask you, what did you do with the Angel's Feather that we found?" Nick asked.

Quinn winked. "It's a surprise! I'll show you tomorrow after you pick me up from school and we go to our spot. I think you'll like it." She played with his fingers. Their "spot" was Heaven's Peak because that was where they first realized their feelings for each other.

"Wow, when you say it like that it makes me even more curious. Can't you give me a tiny hint?"

"Nope. Live with it," Quinn smiled playfully. "Patience is a virtue. Besides, don't you have to get back to your knight friends soon?"

Nick sighed. "Yeah, if I'm out too long people will get suspicious. Matt can only make up so many excuses before they catch on, and if they found out I was seeing a girl outside the walls they'd ship me a thousand miles away."

"Then I'd never see you again." She frowned. "Go on then, I don't want to get you into any more trouble."

"I'd like to think trouble and you go hand in hand. And I think it's all worth it."

They stayed on the Ferris wheel until the spectacular fireworks show was over. Afterwards he took Quinn back home and jetted to the Garrison. He prayed he didn't miss anything important all the way back.

Battle cries and the clanging of metal echoed through the walls. Nick wandered down the halls and outside to the recently destroyed coliseum to find Gabriel and Bartholomew battling it out in a training bout. Matt and Joni sat among others on the bleachers watching and cheering. Archangels trained on many occasions, but it was always a spectacle that never failed to draw crowds. Members of different troops were chanting and shouting out the names of the commanding officers they supported. It was a common occurrence, and one that always fueled the rivalry over the long contested "strongest archangel" debate.

Between the two currently fighting, Nick believed Bartholomew to be the physically stronger, and Gabriel the more well-rounded and versatile. He had never seen Lucius in a bout, as the archangel preferred to keep his matches private. This led to many rumors about Lucius discovering a secret technique. But no matter what, any match between archangels promised no one would leave unscathed.

Today appeared to be a weapons test, a tame exercise that forced knights to adapt to different styles of combat. Each of their sides had an arsenal rack with weapons that both catered to, or challenged their style of fighting. Nick walked in just when both sides had exhausted most of their weapon choices. Gabriel's side was left with long swords, spears, and maces to match his proficiency in swift, quick strikes. On the other side, Bartholomew's rack consisted of giant axes, broadswords, and poleaxes.

They picked up weapons, striking and parrying each other until their weapons were either broken or unable to be used effectively in that situation. Gabriel was much faster than Bart, delivering a flurry of high frequency jabs with his spear. However, Bart's endurance and iron fist were equally impressive, as he was able to block them and counter with a swing from his giant axe.

"It's like watching living art...if art was a badass battle to the death!" Matt exclaimed. He laughed to himself. "I seriously can't believe you challenged Gabriel. I know you were out of control at the time, but if he actually *tried* to fight you—you'd be a stain, no doubt in my mind at all."

"On the bright side, at least it wasn't against Bart," Joni said.

In the arena, the hulking giant caught a spear thrown at him, then crumpled it with one hand like a twig. That silver arm of his was deadly. Nick's throat dried up at the thought of being choked in that armored grip. It would be like squishing a tomato.

"Yeah, if it wasn't for Peter, Bart wouldn't hesitate to put you in the infirmary. I can't wait for the day when he decides to pick as an apprentice—if he ever does. They're going to have an interesting time together," Matt said.

"Times like this I'm glad I'm part of the Peace Unit," Joni said.

Daniel walked up to them. "What are you guys talking about?" He took a seat next to Nick, smiling and cheerful as usual.

"We're talking about how badly Nick would lose in a fight against an archangel," Joni said. "I'm sure you'd know about that better than the both of us."

Matt nodded. "What is it like, getting to train with Lucius? Like, did he teach you any secret tactics? Did he show you how to get wings?"

Daniel shrugged. "Lucius has been a very good mentor. He's taught me so much already. I'm trying my best, but sometimes I think he expects too much. I don't even know why he chose me, it's not like I'm any different from any of the other knights."

"You can say that again," Matt muttered. Nick jabbed him in the side with his elbow. "You know it's unfair! He even admits it!"

"Lucius is one of our most respected knights and an archangel to boot. If he sees some potential in Daniel then it's probably well deserved. But I'm curious too, what is the trick to getting wings?" Nick said.

Daniel shook his head. "I have no idea. I'm still a long way from learning such a coveted ability."

That was no surprise. Only four individuals at the Glenhaven Garrison had them. Receiving those beautiful white wings was the symbol of a knight's full potential. It was granted to only the Supreme Commanders and archangels who would then pass on that knowledge to their disciples. Having wings also gave the ability to touch the sky itself, a feeling Nick knew would never be his as it required a pure soul. Nick was a bit envious, knowing he could never understand that feeling. Seeing the world in that perspective must be breathtaking.

"You are so lucky! To be a descendant of angels means you will actually be able fly someday!" Joni spread her arms and flapped them like a soaring bird.

"I guess so. But Nick is luckier. Everyone says they dream of flying, but who can say they have a role in saving the entire world? After all is said and done Nick's going down in history as a legend!" Daniel's eyes brightened and he threw his arms in the air. "The Inferno Bearer! Just hearing that title is way cooler than sprouting wings, don't you think? I can't wait to see the looks on those demon faces when we go to Fyria."

"Fyria. That's right," Nick said softly.

"Three months we're going to be stuck doing cleanup," Matt said. "At least I get to do it with my girl by my side." He took her hand into his and kissed it gently and Joni giggled.

"Maybe even longer," Daniel said. "But I'm so excited to finally experience field work firsthand. What about you, Nick?"

Nick was watching Matt and Joni flirt. The two lovebirds had something he could never have with Quinn—a normal relationship. The looks on their faces could not have spelt it more clearly. Three months in another country without Quinn? By then she would have moved on. Trying to juggle his priorities would be hard, but things were made even more difficult with the fact that he couldn't tell her he was a demon. Not only that, but he had an obligation to go into war, which meant he didn't even know if he would return.

This is what Garreth must have felt and what he wanted to tell Matt. There were no more words left to say. Venting his frustration to Joni was just going to be an opportunity for him to validate his relationship. But he was Agrian, Lord of Rage, and he was on the list as one of their most dangerous enemies. If they were hunting him, they would eventually find out about her. What then? He knew what he had to do. He had to end it.

8

A COMPROMISE

"Do you know what it feels like to chase something, but in the end find out it doesn't even matter?" Quinn asked as they were sitting on the edge of Heaven's Peak.

They were at a spot overlooking the city and watching all the tiny people intermingle in their daily lives. Nick loved that she always asked deep questions because they always led to learning more about her. He just couldn't get enough. Whenever he trained he thought of her, whenever he slept he dreamt of her. Everything was Quinn. He ate, drank, and breathed her. There was something about her he couldn't describe, the type of lightness he felt whenever she was around. It kept him at peace, especially lately when he was at war within himself.

It was the day after his epiphany and he dreaded what was coming next.

They made plans to meet at their special spot today, but now their day to spend freely was brought down by a terrible new circumstance: this would be the final time he saw her before they would be separated. His assignment was in Fyria, a city far in the west. It would take a week to get there then he would spend three months, miles apart and without any communication with the outside world. He knew this was just a prelude of things to come. Eventually he would be shipped to all corners of the world until the demons were eliminated for good. This was his ultimate purpose. He couldn't ask her to stay with him, knowing full well that they wouldn't be able spend time together like normal couples. It wasn't fair to someone as amazing as Quinn. Once everything was said and done, how could they be a normal couple when he was actually a demon?

Breaking up was the only right thing to do, to end things before she felt as deeply for him as he had come to feel for her. Because in the end she deserved the best, she deserved a chance at happiness.

"I'm actually finding that out the hard way," Nick muttered. His hands were shaking as he spoke. All this thinking had taken a toll on him physically.

"What do you mean?"

"I'm going to cut to the chase right now because I think it's the only way before any of us gets hurt. Something has happened recently...and I—I can't afford to be with somebody right now. I can't go into the details about it, but it's for the best," Nick said.

"You're breaking up with me?" she asked.

Nick heard the hurt in her voice.

"Yes."

"And you thought telling me meant that I wouldn't be hurt?" Quinn's voice was rising. "Well it's too late for that, and what's worse is you won't even tell me why."

"I wish I could, believe me I wish I could," Nick said.

"This is because you're a knight now, isn't it?" Quinn said.

Nick only nodded.

"I see," she said.

Nick sensed the sudden mood shift, and he felt inclined to ease the tension. "Before I met you, I always felt empty. Whatever I did or any type of happiness I was chasing seemed always out of reach. I thought becoming a knight closed that gap, but I now know it was you. And now that I'm right here with you, I can't see why I ever wanted to be one in the first place." He gazed into her beautiful green eyes. "It all feels like a big mistake now."

"I guess you never counted on being happy, did you?" Quinn touched his cheek. Nick shook his head sadly. "That's the problem with working for a Garrison. Everyone has to play by their rules."

"Well up until this point, my life had been one train wreck after the other," Nick said. "I never thought I would feel this way about anybody. I never had anything else to live for. I figured fighting for the world was something I had to do alone. I convinced myself that I could never find a reason to leave this all behind."

Quinn sighed sadly. "Now look where we are."

Nick took her hand. "Look, I don't want to do this, but the truth is it's the best for the both of us. I've taken an oath as a Glenhaven knight, and that means I now have enemies all over the world trying their best to hurt me and those I love. If anything were to happen to you I wouldn't be able to live with myself knowing I was responsible."

"I'm a big girl, Emberson. I can take care of myself just fine," Quinn said.

"No you can't. You have no training, and you live outside with the rest of the world. If anyone ever found out about me—about us—they would come for you."

"What exactly makes you so special? What makes you different from the hundreds of other knights watching over us every day?"

Nick wanted to tell her everything right then and there. He wanted to tell her that he was linked by fate to a struggle that was beyond his control. He wanted so desperately to let her know, but he couldn't.

"I can't tell you any of the details but there is a crisis happening now, and the Garrisons need knights more than ever," was all he could say.

"Fine. I get it, I don't need a chaperone. I'm not a little kid, but there's no reason to lie to me."

"You know that's not what I mean, but it's the truth." Nick looked into her sad face. "Even if I could protect you always, I still have to keep my promise to the Garrison and to my Supreme Commander."

"Why? What does he have to do with this?"

Nick dropped his gaze to the floor, "Peter's been like a father to me. He raised me, gave me a home. I can't disrespect him by breaking the rules he set for us."

"Sometimes rules are made to be broken."

"You don't give up, do you?" Nick smiled sadly.

"No, but it's kind of disappointing that you are." Quinn pulled her hand away. "I've been through this before with

Garreth and he chose being a knight. It hurt, but I knew deep down it was because we never truly belonged together. But with you…I know how much better we are together. We both feel something we've never felt before, but you want to throw it away? Because of someone else's rules? Because you're scared? If I knew that was the Nick Emberson I met on New Year's Eve I would have steered clear."

"You know it's not what I want, but—"

"But what? What do *you* want? Honestly you've been talking about your servitude and what Peter wants, but what's so hard? If you want to stop seeing me then don't try to pin it on your stupid Garrison. You alone have a choice to make, and if it's not going to be me then I guess we don't have anything more to say," Quinn said. She stood up, and turned to leave.

Nick sighed. Someday she would understand that he only did what he had to do out of love. But then the lovesick eighteen year old in him kicked in, and before he could stop himself Nick grabbed her arm.

"Wait. Sit down," he said.

"Why should I? You made yourself very clear. Don't try to sugarcoat this, Nick. Just don't. I'm not going to sit here and listen to more reasons why we shouldn't be together." Quinn tried to pull away.

"Just stay please." Nick held on tight. "I'm not finished yet."

Quinn finally relented and took a seat next to him, but she wasn't speaking any longer. She was listening while avoiding his gaze. He couldn't blame her for any of this. She had every right to be upset. But it wasn't as if he wanted to do this, Peter's granddaughter was almost murdered because the Crowned Princes wanted her dead before she could have any influence on their success. What lengths would they go if they found out about Quinn? She would be the next target. And what then? Could they just run from it? It was asking for trouble.

Deep down, he knew he couldn't let go of the best thing that happened to him. Was it selfish? Maybe. But he couldn't bear to live without her now—she had become so integral to everything in his life. His world revolved around her now.

"Forget Glenhaven," Nick finally said.

She looked up at him, flustered. "What?"

"Forget them all. I don't want to be a part of anything that doesn't let me live the life I want. I'm going to tell Peter I'm through."

"What about your oath? You were chosen for a reason. You can't honestly expect them to succeed without your help," Quinn said.

"I have no doubt they'll take away my knighthood. If they banish me too, then so be it. I don't want to be part of anything if I have to give you up," Nick said.

"That's sweet, but leaving the Garrison after pledging your oath is treason. I'm being selfish. I can't ask you to turn your back on your country; they'll brand you as a criminal. Besides, there's a crisis, which means the Glenhaven needs a knight like you. I know you, and if they need someone to help hold the world together from falling to pieces, then it'd be you."

"Why does this have to be so hard? I don't want to leave… not without knowing that I could come back to you. But I can't leave them either! There's nothing I can think of!" Nick said, frustrated by the circles he was running around in.

"Let's just put it as a goal, the day they don't need you any-more. I promise that day will come," Quinn said. "Until then, we'll keep everything a secret. How does that sound?"

"A secret?"

"Better than the alternative don't you think?"

Nick leaned in and kissed her.

"Here, I want to give you something," Quinn drew a simple black necklace with a white pendant attached to it. The pendant was carved to look like a small feather. "I made it from the Angel's Feather we found the first time we came here. I thought it'd be best to give it to you at the exact spot where I found it."

"You carved it into an actual angel's feather." Nick marveled at the detail and professional craftsmanship.

She draped it over his neck. "It symbolizes us. Angels born from Sanctuary are considered the epitome of perfection. Aside from god-like powers, what every angel has are wings. Every angel needs two wings to be complete or they can't fly. They're incomplete. Kind of like you and me, we need each other if we want to soar. Separated, we're just two flawed people, but together we're perfect."

"But there's only one," he said.

Quinn pulled her hair back and lifted the feather pendant tucked under her shirt.

Nick smiled as he took her hand and squeezed it. It was the single most thoughtful gift he had ever received. Though she'd never know it, he needed something like this, a token that would remind him he was still human inside.

"Some might see this as a declaration of love." He felt the intricate design in his hand. "I thought you didn't believe in love?"

"I think I'm starting to." Quinn smiled.

9

THE CALL

By the time Nick strolled in a large group of soldiers had gathered around the big screen monitor in the Grand Hall. Wearing a grin on his face, he was still elated from finding a suitable compromise to his dilemma. He joined Matt in viewing the video projection that captured the attention of everyone in the room. The projection showed people running out of a collapsing building, their faces filled with fear and hopelessness. The strangest part was that the buildings, as well as its surroundings, were covered in ice. Cars, trees, nothing was spared. The screen switched to close up shots of several people who were frozen into statues. It was an absolutely terror to behold.

His feelings of joy were suddenly sapped. "What is this?" Nick said.

"Fyria. We thought Doctor Numerous was our only problem. We were wrong. It's far worse," Matt said.

"He's just torturing them now, and putting them all in this big show," Paul said. "He's creating irrational fear, breaking down whatever hope they have left." He punched a nearby wall. "Damn him!"

The emergency distress signal blared loudly, echoing throughout the stations. It relayed the messages from nearby cities and Garrisons currently in danger and in need of assistance. The red lights that accompanied the sound were also flashing wildly, indicating the level of the threat. Nick had never seen it at red before. Nor had he witnessed an emergency call that gathered such a large assembly of soldiers and knights at one time. This was the first time he had ever heard the distinct sound, the only other times he had known it to be used was when older knights regaled tales of the Second Coming.

"Why is everyone standing around? It's a distress call. We should answer it!" Nick shouted, outraged by everyone's calmness.

"We have," Daniel said. "We've responded to them hours ago. But, they still keep calling. They must be in really bad shape over there."

"Why haven't any troops been dispatched? We have to hit the threat right now and hit them hard. They're one of us! They're our brothers and sisters! And yet everyone is standing around doing nothing!" Nick shouted.

"While you were busy wasting time doing who knows what, the archangels and our Supreme Commander have been going over a plan of attack. We're on standby until they give us our orders to proceed. Until then, we sit tight," Paul said.

At a nearby table, Lucius and Bartholomew stood as the only two people not watching the horrors on the projected screen. They loomed over the map of Fyria, speaking in hushed whispers, moving around miniature scaled objects they placed over it, testing out positions. Where were Gabriel and Peter in all of this?

Gabriel entered the room. He made sure he had everyone's attention before he spoke. "Plans have changed. We've made preparations to go to leave their tonight." As usual, he was in his full uniform with his sword slung over his back. He glanced around the room and pointed at Nick. "I was looking for you. You are no longer part of this mission, kid. Peter's orders."

"Why?" Nick said.

"Our sources have identified and confirmed that one of the Crowned Princes has been seen with Doctor Numerous. Considering the lack of training you have had ever since your powers emerged, it has been decided you will do us better a service if you stayed behind," Gabriel said.

"Which Crowned Prince is behind this?" Nick glanced at the screen and saw the icy wasteland and realized he answered his own question. It was Bergice the Blizzard, the fearsome manipulator of ice who was responsible. But the fact that his mere presence was unnerving for everyone was a testament to the strength of this member of the Crowned Princes. How could such a powerful entity be defeated?

"Bergice, the Lord of Fear. He's not to be taken lightly, even against our army and archangels," Gabriel said.

Nick had heard stories about the one known as Bergice, the demon involved in the infamous Frozen Fifty incident. There wasn't much information to study him by, as was the case with most of the Crowned Princes due to their elusiveness. However, there were always the same common characteristics people used to describe him. He was regarded as an unstoppable killing machine known for his brutal and merciless tactics. Every encounter with him had ended in death. Despite knowing all this, Nick was still determined to go. If the prophecy was right then he would have to face him eventually. What better time than now when they needed him most?

"Why fill my head with delusions of grandeur just to have me stay home? I can help—I want to help!" Nick said.

"You will, in time. For now it's still too soon. You haven't even had a chance to properly fight your first real demon yet," Gabriel said. "You'll have your chance soon enough and when you do, you'll be glad we left you behind."

"I've been training for this. I know I messed up before, but I can control it now. I've beaten one of the Crowned Princes before, right? That means I can beat the others," Nick argued.

"Flawless logic, but you have to remember that what happened in the past doesn't mean the same outcome will occur again. The person standing before me and the person in the past are two very different people. The Agrian that killed Durenth was a full-blooded demon. You are a man with a demon's soul," Gabriel said.

"I think you're being unreasonable right now. You don't have faith in me," Nick said. "None of you do!"

"Is that what you think? Fine. I'll let you come, but on one condition." Gabriel folded his arms.

Nick raised an eyebrow.

"I want you think about what you just said. Think real hard and be completely honest with me. Do you really believe what you've said? Do you really think you've been able to control Agrian the way you want to? You think you've truly mastered the demon inside? If you have no doubt that your transformation won't end up putting yourself or those around you in danger then you can come along," Gabriel said.

Nick didn't want to think about it. He didn't want to search for the answer because deep down he knew Gabriel was right. He wasn't ready. This was just having another relapse from the demon within. Like a constant addiction, he was drawn to bloodshed and destruction. Since the trials, Agrian was starving for battle and it was affecting the way he perceived things. The loss he suffered created an insatiable desire to seek redemption.

"No," Nick said finally.

"Alright then." Gabriel patted Nick on the shoulder. "Don't be so disappointed, kiddo. You'll have your time to shine. Fate has already determined that. But by that time, you'll be wishing you didn't." He walked off, lugging the sack of weaponry over his shoulder.

At this point Nick did rounds throughout the halls checking for people. Empty. Everyone had gone. He went to the briefing room to find only Peter, who was gathering some documents into his briefcase.

"Supreme Commander, I need to talk to you," Nick said.

"I assumed Gabriel explained my reasoning for taking you off this mission," Peter said.

"Please reconsider. I have to go back for her sake."

"That's precisely why you can't. Going back will tear at the seams of your already fragile soul. You've been carrying that burden for quite some time, but you've never learned to let go. If you want to honor what Susan Stillwell stood for, then you will obey my wishes," Peter said.

"Who is going to run things while you're gone? Who will the people here turn to?" Nick said.

"I can't expect to have the support of the Garrison if their own leader isn't willing to stand at the frontlines with them in battle," Peter said. "Bergice is Ozarael's right hand, and without question the second most dangerous demon in existence. Doctor Numerous is also with him, and the only human who possesses intimate knowledge of the inner workings of their demon hierarchy. If we hope to prevent a full-scale war, then we must stop Bergice and capture Numerous. With the elusive alchemist in our custody, we could pinpoint the location of Ozarael and put down any chance of a demon uprising. We cannot pass up this opportunity."

Nick couldn't argue with that reasoning.

But was Peter up to leading his army? His Supreme Commander was using his cane more often than before. Even though Peter was powerful in his old age, it still didn't change the fact that it would be more risky to go into live combat. None of this eased Nick's mind.

"So what am I going to do all alone here?" Nick had always been chaperoned at one point or another by someone in the Garrison. Being on his own was a very new concept.

"Don't worry you'll have company. I've assigned Matthew and Daniel here as well as Paul in the event something should happen," Peter said.

"I can understand Matt and Daniel, but Paul? I hate the guy. I don't care if he is the president's son, I refuse to follow the orders of some sociopath while you're gone."

"I am aware of the ongoing conflict between you two, but we need a more seasoned knight here, one who knows the protocols and Paul fits the bill. Even though President Evans requested him to stay, I firmly believe he's a good influence on you. Despite his somewhat questionable nature at times, you'll see, this will be a good experience for the both of you," Peter said.

Nick could almost feel the vomit almost burst through his mouth. The words "good influence" and Paul Evans were two concepts that did not work together in a sentence, let alone real life. Opposite attraction only worked between people who had redeemable qualities. There was nothing redeeming about the pompous, privileged Sir Evans. The fact that Peter believed there was a possibility they could learn to like each other when they could barely be together in the same room was laughable.

"Right." Nick decided to at least humor the old man's request before he left.

"There's also something I wanted to talk to you about before I take my leave." A knowing smile broke through Peter's stern visage. "I know why your mind's been scattered the last couple of months. You've been seeing a girl outside the Garrison, haven't you?"

"What are you talking about?" Nick tried to keep his composure.

"A little birdie has brought to my attention the conflict you have between your duties," he said. Peter walked to a file cabinet nearby and skimmed through the manila folders. "Was I lied to?"

"That depends who told you," Nick said.

Peter laughed, and he gave Nick a paternal look. "Do you believe Paul was the one to inform me? Can you believe he wanted me to punish you? I don't know why you kids try to keep these things from me. I was young once too, if you can believe it. I can see it in your face. You're happy, a lot happier than you've been these last couple of years. You've obviously fallen in deep with this young woman, and I'm glad you've learned to share yourself with another person, but I don't have to remind you about the repercussions your actions can have, do I?"

Nick nodded. "Knights aren't allowed to fall in love, unless it is with another member of a Garrison. Their lives are dedicated to the safety of the people they've sworn to protect. I know. I know all about the strings attached."

"It's only for the best, my boy. Especially since you're now the most wanted man in the world, you can only bring danger to this girl's life." Peter sighed.

"Well anything that was there is now gone." It was a blatant lie, and Nick felt guilty for saying it, especially when it came to Peter—he couldn't even look at the old man right now.

"I'm sorry to hear that, but it was for the best. If this girl feels the same for you, think about how much strain you'd put on her if she knew you were risking your life as Agrian," Peter said.

"I understand."

"I thought you'd be more upset. I'm surprised. You're taking all of this rather well."

"I kept my distance so she doesn't know about my past. My real past. It figured it would be better this way, right?" Nick said.

Peter raised a brow. "Yes, you mustn't let anyone outside these walls know the truth about your heritage. They wouldn't understand. How could they? Humans were taught to despise your kind. Even though we don't feel the same here, history has made it impossible for them to see it any other way."

"I know that. Did you think I wanted her to find out I'm a monster?" Nick said.

"Sadly, I can say it's worse for my own granddaughter. Unlike you who can run with our Garrison, she must live in exile for she is considered a threat to the Crowned Princes. I think about how she feels sometimes, always living life behind a glass prison." Peter sighed. "I hate myself for putting her in that position, but it's for her own good, even if she doesn't believe it."

"She was brought to Glenhaven after the first attack on Fyria, wasn't she?" Nick said.

"Yes, but I relocated her once more. Poor child, always on the run, never able to stay put for very long. It's terrible isn't it? She's never had any real friends all because she had the curse of being born in this family."

"At least she has a grandfather who loves her deeply and is willing to do anything for her," Nick said.

"I appreciate that, my boy. I don't know, sometimes I think I'm making all these mistakes. I've never had to raise someone so rebellious," Peter said.

"That's not true, you had to raise me."

The old man chuckled, and a smile crossed his wrinkled face.

"Most humans are narrow-minded creatures in that they only see what they've been taught to see. You know you've always been a son to me, Nick. No matter what anyone says, you're not a monster," Peter said.

Nick nodded. "Alyssa was her name, right? Alyssa Masters. It has a nice ring to it. I'm sorry I never got the chance to meet her."

"I'm damn glad you didn't," Peter said, "You're crazy if you think I'm going to let her near a punk like you."

Nick couldn't contain his urge to laugh, and soon they were both laughing raucously. Even in the most serious circumstances, Peter could always change the flow of the conversation and make things easier.

"Will you be coming back on schedule?" Nick asked after their laughter settled.

"Fyria is very far and it will be even longer because we've decided to take an alternate route to avoid an unwanted confrontation. Bartholomew thinks it will be approximately three months we're expecting to be stationed there. Should any problems arise in my absence, you can always contact us," Peter said.

"Bergice…I still can't believe it. Once he's taken care of, it'll only time be a matter of time before the other two remaining members reveal themselves," Nick said.

"Hopefully not too soon…for our sakes."

Two senior knights came into the room, and helped Peter carry his supplies, with the exception of the long sword lying on the table. It was Peter's most prized weapon. He picked it up with one arm and slung it behind his back.

"Promise you'll be on your best behavior, boy. If anything happens, I want a full report as soon as possible, understand?" Peter said.

Nick bowed. "Yes, Supreme Commander. Have a safe journey." With that, Peter was gone.

He gazed over Peter's desk as he walked around, only the sound of his boots squeaking across the marble floor. Three months without Peter. The knights on their way to Fyria would be tested and pushed to their limits in combat, all while he sat safely behind the veil of the Holy Shield, behind an impenetrable fortress. The protection this stronghold offered was unparalleled. They said no demon could breach these walls. That was proven false when Doctor Numerous broke through and led an army and a Crowned Prince to siege Fyria.

Nick went to his room and pulled his suitcase from his closet. He emptied his drawers for the bare essentials and packed them all away. He had to leave before Matt, Daniel, or Paul returned. If he was going to Fyria, he had to go without their help or knowledge.

Maybe he wasn't ready, but maybe he was. If he hadn't killed a demon yet it was because he was always hiding behind in the comfort of the Garrison base and never venturing out and doing what needed to be done. He was going to find Doctor Numerous and Bergice and kill them personally, just like the prophecy predicted. But before he made the journey, he had to visit Quinn one last time.

He drove to her house and knocked. No sooner did she open the door did she leap into his arms and embrace him in a warm hug. When they separated he noticed she was wearing an apron. Over her shoulder, he saw freshly cooked vegetables and meats on the table. Her face was red and her eyes were puffy. She must have been crying for some time.

"What's wrong Red?"

"I just saw the news announcement," she sniffed. "I thought you would have been gone by now."

"No, not yet. I wanted to say goodbye," Nick said.

"But the news said everyone already left. Don't tell me you're planning on going alone?"

"I have to."

"Then I'm going with you," Quinn said.

"Don't be ridiculous."

"Because I'm acting impulsive like you? Sleep on it tonight, and if you still feel the same way tomorrow then I won't stop you."

"Alright."

After the meal Nick was left with dread in the pit of his stomach, unable to sleep with all these thoughts rushing through his brain. Quinn was sleeping soundly with her head nuzzled comfortably on his lap. He thought about just taking off, but he didn't want to go without at least saying goodbye.

How were the others doing? Paul and Daniel were probably going off the deep end, wondering where he had gone. Paul probably put Matt through a line of questioning for his whereabouts and he probably reasoned that he left to visit Quinn for the night, thinking nothing else of it. It would all come to a shock when he didn't return in a few a days. Nick imagined the looks on their faces when they found he had disabled the vehicle tracking device.

Nick wasn't looking for a companion on this trip. In fact, the less people involved the better. If he was alone no one would ever get hurt.

He woke up covered in drool, unaware that he even fell asleep. Quinn was nowhere in sight. She must have relented. Nick crept out quietly, only to find to her sitting in the passenger seat of the car.

"Quinn…"

"I said I wouldn't stop you, but I never said I wasn't coming along. So let's get going, Emberson. We don't have all day."

Nick shook his head and smiled. He got into the driver's seat, started the engine, and without another word they were on their way.

10

DOLERE FLOS

Passing through Hyperion was a bit of a sidetrack to Fyria. And though it wasn't exactly the fastest route, the roads between the cities were protected by powerful holy magic, which made it the safest. Driving down the long strip of road, Nick saw different Hellbeasts trying to break through the invisible holy wall that acted as a barrier between certain death and destruction.

Inside the city walls, they needed to grab some supplies for both food and shelter for the long journey. Nick stopped at a busy downtown market.

Having Quinn would actually be quite beneficial to this journey. Her strong knowledge in demon history from living nearby Thorne for so many years could provide great insight on enemies he either forgot or had never heard about. Her cooking skills were vastly superior to his, and having someone to talk to would keep his mind sharp. To top it off, he got to spend time with her, which was the main reason why he was hesitant to leave in the first place.

They walked around the markets hand in hand, stocking up on tents and toiletries. Afterward, they found a boutique for stylish female clothing, and finally a supermarket where they could pick up fresh groceries. When they couldn't find the necessary ingredients for a special dish Quinn had in mind, they explored other shops until they did.

The whole time Nick couldn't help but notice that downtown Hyperion was very different from Glenhaven. People were always on the move, walking in and out of stores and along the streets, never slowing to appreciate the beautiful scenery. This was typical behavior for city people since there weren't any familiar faces or "usual" customers, and everyone seemed to go about their own business. Hyperion itself felt hollow, as if it lacked a heart or warmth which gave the city an almost foreboding impression.

However, the biggest difference between these people and the Glenhaven residents was the people here seemed to hold an intense grudge against Garrisons, and were quite vocal about their dislike of knights. He couldn't walk past a single person without hearing a rude remark or chides against his way of life. It angered him, but he kept his emotions in check to avoid causing an unwanted commotion. Luckily, he made it a habit to never wear his official uniform and could just blend in anywhere.

"Why does everyone here hate us?" Nick asked quietly, as they past another obnoxious anti-Garrison couple to enter a supermarket.

"There are a lot of reasons," Quinn said. "They think having such a strong military power can infringe upon their freedom. You know, if you think about it, it's kind of justified too. I mean, protection is nice, but at what cost? Also, many people here had family members who lost their live during service in the wars. That's why people enjoy living in cities that are strictly civilian—they prefer to live without the reminder of bloodshed."

"They wouldn't be talking that way if this place didn't have a Holy Shield. If you ask me, they complain because they have it too easy. They've never had to ward off a demon attack or been put through the psychological trauma of taking a life," Nick replied.

"That may be true, but I also want peace. What better way than by becoming a living example?" Quinn picked up a small shopping basket.

"I think you would fit right in here with Garreth," Nick said.

"Oh right, bring up the ex-boyfriend just because he lives down the road." Quinn tossed a few cans of soup into the bin.

"Well, as the current boyfriend, don't you think I'm entitled to ask some questions? Unless you're too afraid to answer them…" Nick said.

"Go ahead, ask away." Quinn put a few packs of potato chips in the basket.

"Okay, what ever happened to him to make him hate the Garrison so much? I've never seen such resentment."

"That's easy. Unlike the people here, Garreth was originally a part of a Garrison and loved everything about the holy knights. He was in the Wisdom Unit, and a genius whitesmith. His parents were also the ones who invented the Holy Shield. When the time came, and an archangel named Gabriel had to choose an apprentice, he was supposedly the prime candidate.

But unfortunately for him, the Supreme Commander of the Glenhaven Garrison advised Gabriel against it. Garreth lost his dreams, and the rest is history."

"Yeah, he told us the last time we visited. To be rejected like that…it must have crushed him," Nick said.

"It was worse because Gabriel is his older brother. Being turned away in favor of Paul broke his heart. He was never the same person."

Nick was at a loss for words. Gabriel was Garreth's brother? In all his years, Nick found it strange that he had never heard the archangel mention a sibling of any kind. Then again, it was easy for him to hide it, considering most members of the Garrison were discouraged from divulging too much personal information in the event they got captured and demons could use that information against them. Even still, it was almost cruel to not acknowledge you had a brother.

"Any more questions?" Quinn dumped the basket of meats and vegetables on the cashier's counter.

Nick shook his head. "No that's all the information I need for one day." They purchased the groceries and walked back to the car to load everything.

Once they were back on the road, Nick rolled down his windows and turned up the mood music, letting it blare on his way out of the plaza. As soon as he pulled back onto the road the Fyria, however, he was caught in a major traffic jam. He slammed on the brakes, bringing it to a screeching halt. All the cars were at a complete stop and people were leaving in droves in all directions. From up ahead came roars that sounded like animals. Screams echoed downtown, with groups of people rushing out the doors of stores and buildings, their faces gripped with fear.

"Demons!" they cried.

"Help us! Please!"

"Someone call the Garrison!"

Nick peered through the windshield. There they were: Hellbeasts. They appeared to be wolves and they looked hungry. But how could they have broken through the shield?

He turned to Quinn. "Stay here. Roll up the windows. Lock the doors."

"There's too many for you, you can't go alone!"

"It's my responsibility to make sure these people get away safely. Just stay here and don't make and sudden movements."

Nick stepped out of his car before she could protest further. Leaving it parked in the intersection along with all the other abandoned vehicles, he ran into mass of fleeing people and came across the beasts—ten of them—combing the streets, searching for their prey. They weren't wolves, but hounds. The difference was insignificant. They were still carnivorous demons.

These beasts looked absolutely disgusting. Three times bigger than normal hounds, roughly equivalent to the size of a car, their fur coats appeared as if they had been eaten alive, like rotten corpses. Overly grown fangs protruded from their mouths. Their eyes were red, mirroring his own as a demon. He could see by the way their mouths were dripping with saliva that they were thirsty. What could he do? Calling for help was out of the question. Judging from their expressions, they were keen to strike at any given moment. He knew what he had to do.

"Over here!" Nick waved his hands, trying to draw their attention. But it was of no avail. They were too fixated on the grand feast of screaming people up and down the street to bother with him. Maybe there was a way around that. Quinn and the others were far enough away to see him now and with the ensuing mayhem keeping everyone busy he was free to become what he was meant to be. He lit his hands into flames, and immediately reunited with Agrian. With a demon back in the driver's seat he could cut loose and make short work of these beasts.

As soon as he transformed, the hounds stopped their assault on the humans, and tilted their heads at Nick, looking at him with an odd curiosity. Have they never seen the Inferno Bearer before? Perhaps his status as one of the Crowned Princes of demons meant he had some control over these mutts.

Wishful thinking. As soon as the thought entered his mind they snarled and snapped at him. Several long and black, spider-like tendrils emerged from their backs, making them look even more monstrous. The tendrils whipped the air antagonistically. A confrontation was imminent.

It was time to show what hours and practice controlling his fire abilities in the training room could do in a life or death situation. From getting started to using them efficiently, they were all linked to his current state of mind. He had to produce the negative emotion of rage and use it as fuel for powering Agrian. It made sense when he figured it out, considering his title was the Lord of Rage. However, to keep things in control, he started off small. Minor spurts of anger or annoyances were the stepping points he used before they snowballed into stronger feelings of frustration, which eventually made him resentful, which in turn created a festering ball of fury. He kept this frame of thought and built on these emotions until it reached its peak and evolved into the strongest negative feeling of all, the uninhibited animalistic desire for destruction.

It worked like a charm.

The pack flew at him, but the distance between them gave him more than enough time to react. He caught the leader of the pack by the jaws and flung him into a vacant car. Two others darted at him on both sides, but he dove forward into a somersault, narrowly escaping getting ripped in half by their sharp jaws. But he was careless, and ended up in range of another dog. It took a huge bite into his arm, gnawing deep as Nick spun to shake him off, slamming it into another hound.

His right sleeve was torn, revealing his bleeding arm. Rookie mistake. A real knight would never have been so easily thrown off guard. A real knight would be able to tear through these beasts with his sword, like scissors cutting paper. He didn't have a sword, but he was a knight and now was time to prove it. He baited them to come at him in a group before igniting a flaming wall, which burned the eager two to ashes. Three to go. He leapt through the fire and caught one of the dogs by the neck. The tendrils from its body whipped at him, but wilted after Nick snapped its neck in his arms. The cracking sound of bones alerted the remaining two who were hesitant now, whimpering in fear. Perhaps if he wasn't so enraged, he'd have shown some mercy. But Nick was so far away from mercy now. He punched one of them as hard as he could with a flaming knuckle, sending its burning carcass down the street. The leader of the pack and last one remaining, pounced at him, but he dodged and grabbed the creature from behind. The tendrils latched around his neck, attempting to choke him, but one swift fiery punch to the side of the animal forced it to relinquish its grip. The Hellbeast staggered a few steps before it toppled over, blood escaping from its torso. It finally died with a raspy gurgle.

Behind him the fire wall he created still roared with life, but with his powers he extinguished the flames as fast as he created them. The training he had paid off, and he was pleased with how much control he had developed just a few short months. However, it was too soon to be counting his progress as he still had other duties to fulfill. Like where were the other five of the pack?

As Nick walked around the abandoned shopping center, his priority was looking for any survivors left behind. He didn't want to leave anything to chance. He cleared out every store, finding either nothing or the bodies of the already deceased. Eventually he stumbled upon an old mom and pop establishment that had its windows shattered. He walked in, the bell chime sounding his arrival. Nick heard someone groaning and walked to the counter.

The shopkeeper, an elderly gentleman with glasses lay motionless, giant horizontal slash wounds across his chest. They appeared to be four fingered claw marks, with a width much wider than the wolves.

"Sir, let me get you to a hospital," Nick said.

When Nick knelt to help him up, the man groaned. "Get out here, kid…"

Upon closer inspection of the man's body, his dark red stained clothes indicated he had suffered much blood loss. It was sending him into a state of shock. He had to take the man to the hospital quickly, but judging by how long much time had elapsed, the man was almost out of time.

The man was growing paler and shaking as he looked at Nick, pointing behind him and muttering nonsensically. Whatever did this to him broke him beyond mental repair. Nick lifted the man's shirt to inspect the wound. The Hellbeasts in this area couldn't have delivered such a clean slash; there would be signs of smaller claw marks or bite wounds. The thing that did this was very precise and had claws that were much larger.

Nick waited with the man for the few minutes he had left to live. Having Hellbeasts so close to their headquarters was a bad sign. Doctor Numerous and Bergice were in Fyria, which meant that they were definitely out of the question. So then, what else could have gotten through?

He stood up, pulled out his communicator, and dialed Matt. He didn't care if he would get into trouble for leaving, this required immediate answer from someone with more experience. As the communicator rang once, the wall closest to him crashed down. Before he could react, a giant black claw lurched through, grabbed him by the throat and jerked him through to the other side. At some point, Nick dropped his device.

Now in the back alleyway, he came face to face with a large humanoid demon. It pulled him against his nose, mouth inches away. Its foul breath almost made Nick vomit. The creature took a few long sniffs then tossed Nick to the floor.

"I thought I recognized this scent...but this—this cannot be!" the demon exclaimed. "This is the scent of the traitor, Lord Agrian!"

Nick wiped the dirt off his jacket and stood up. The demon was at least twice his size. Its entire body was pitch black, and had a gooey texture, as if it dripping with wet paint. It had two curved horns that protruded out of its head with a menacingly large mouth with rows and rows of razor sharp teeth. Instantly Nick recognized him.

"You must be Astaroth."

He chuckled. "It seems you've stumbled upon our little raid. How long have you known?"

"That depends. How did you manage to break through the Holy Shield?" Nick said.

"A gift from Doctor Numerous."

"All those people...dead," Nick muttered.

"Vermin compared to us. What a surprise, I had come to this city under the orders of Doctor Numerous. Little did I know, I would end up meeting the infamous Inferno Bearer. It is high time you've rejoined our cause, my lord."

"If I refuse?" Nick gauged his foe, trying to find any discernible weakness or any advantage he could press.

"The humans pushed us out into the wilderness. They've treated us like animals! Twice now we had to suffer the humiliation of being crushed by their kind. It is time we rise again!" Astaroth snarled.

"I am a knight of the Garrison. It is my sworn duty to protect the people of this city."

"Then the rumors are true, you are no Lord of Rage, but merely a pathetic mortal with his power," Astaroth said.

"It's best not insult me, I'm not exactly the most forgiving person. But I'll take the highroad and let you off easy this time if you give me a clue as to what Doctor Numerous has in store."

Astaroth laughed. "What makes you think I'll obey such a demand?"

"This."

Nick threw a fireball at the behemoth, blasting him backwards. He recoiled in pain. Nick jumped up to strike with a blazed punch only to be caught within one of Astaroth's tendrils. Some more coiled around his arms and legs, snaring him in place.

"Too easy." Astaroth laughed. "You are no Inferno Bearer, you are nothing. Now go to the eternal sleep!" he hissed, as he brought down his claws for a full swipe.

Nick ignited his arms, tearing through the tendrils. He flung them off and tackled the dazed Astaroth into the open streets. It'd be easier this way. More room to move.

"For that, I will drink your blood!" Astaroth hissed.

Astaroth wasn't going down easily. He was already on his feet once more. He anticipated Nick's plans and outstretched his tendrils into long ropes. The tips shaped themselves into blades. He swung them at Nick, keeping him at bay and forcing him on the defensive.

"You cannot hit me if you cannot reach me!" Astaroth jeered.

With the blades moving so quickly, cutting up chunks of cement, Nick knew they would shred him to pieces. Close combat would be impossible now. However, Astaroth didn't know he was holding back. Nick summoned a wall of fire from behind the demon. His entire backside caught the force of the blaze and the demon screeched in pain. Astaroth retracted his tendrils in an attempt to extinguish the fire, but it only fanned the flames more brightly. Nick used Astaroth's distraction to his advantage to move up the side of the building. Then he leapt over Astaroth, stamping him square on the back of the head with both feet. The momentum shoved him forward and slammed his face into the concrete. Nick took this opportunity to send a fiery blow straight through his back, tearing through the soft flesh into the other side. The pain forced him to return to his human form. He was naked, vulnerable like the day he was born.

"It can't be..." Blood dripped from Astaroth's lips. "You were supposed to be weak! How could you have beaten me?"

"Easily. Quite easily. Think of it as payback for the old man you murdered."

"You dare mock me! I am Astaroth the Annihilator!"

Nick stepped hard on the hole in his back. Astaroth screeched in pain. "I disagree. From up here it's pretty clear you're dead."

"You think you've won? You have no idea what we have in store for you. Doctor Numerous has a plan and now the Crowned Princes have returned, whether you fools like it or not! This city will be the first sacrificial lamb in the name of all demons!" Astaroth said.

Nick grabbed him by the head, pulling his face from the ground. He stared the demon in the eyes. "Tell me what Doctor Numerous is planning or I swear I'll—"

"You'll what, kill me? I'm already dead!" Astaroth laughed.

Nick shook his head. "No, not yet."

He flipped him over to face him and pummeled him repeatedly in the face and into the ground. Specks of dirt and stone bounced around as he was mashed deeper and deeper. It wasn't until there was a hole about a foot deep where Astaroth's head used to be before he stopped.

He reverted back to his full human form and returned to the car, feeling satisfied with his victory. This feeling was short lived when he found that Quinn was gone! The passenger door hung wide open. He looked around in a panic, but before he could imagine all the terrible situations, he found her emerging from one of the abandoned stores.

"Why did you leave? You could have been killed!" Nick said.

"Relax, Emberson. I helped some old folks out of the buildings, there wasn't any sign of trouble at all," Quinn said.

"We better leave soon. I'm sure everyone has evacuated by now but at least five Hellbeasts got away."

"They're dead," she said.

"How can you sure?" Nick asked.

"Follow me," Quinn said.

They walked to the border of the city and forest area where the demons must have broken in. There was a distinguishable break in the shield at this area. Several paw tracks marked the ground. At the entrance there was a pile of five other hounds. "I saw them running this way. I figured they were retreating so I went back to find you. I think someone must be helping us."

"Glad to know there's someone else here that isn't completely helpless," Nick said. "But what are we going to do about the break? If we leave it, then the demons are just going to keep coming in but I can't guard this post all day."

A sound of rustling came from the trees. Quinn grabbed Nick's hand. "What's that?"

A figure emerged from the forest shadows. It was Daniel. He was dragging a sword with one hand; he had cuts and bruises across his face and body. His clothes were tattered and torn and he appeared as if he was on the verge of collapsing at any second. What was he doing here? Paul would never let the newest member of their organization travel this far alone.

"N-Nick…we found you." A smile of relief broke on his face as he reeled towards them. "Sir Marcus's sword was stolen."

Nick caught him just before he dropped to the ground. His breathing was slow and labored. "Daniel what's wrong?"

"They're in the Den of Pain," Daniel murmured. "Hounds took the sword. Garreth…" He passed out cold.

"He's been poisoned!" Nick revealed the large thorns poking out from his ribcage. He plucked them out and threw them aside. He had dealt with enough cases of poisonings to know one at a glance. "The Dolere Flos did this to him. I'm sure of it."

"The Dolere Flos?" Quinn said.

"The Dolere Flos are plants that produce toxic thorns and are indigenous to the Den of Pain. It is also the only place where the antidote exists. If the others are inside then they could be seriously hurt," Nick said.

"Be careful. It won't help if you get poisoned too," Quinn said.

"Make sure he doesn't die until I get back."

Nick sprinted through the tall brush and followed the trail Daniel's sword left straight to the entrance of the den. Legends have provided many stories as to how the Den of Pain received its name, but no one truly knows for sure. Some say it was used to be a chamber for gruesome torture. Others believe it was because it was the prime breeding location for demons. Or perhaps it was because of the poisonous plants that thrive in the cold and dark environment. However, one thing was certain—no one who ever ventured inside returned alive.

He peered into the darkness and set his arms ablaze. As much as he disliked how his arms appeared, having portable torches was convenient for traveling. He found a clump of the poisonous plant on the ground near the entrance. They pitched and snapped violently at his presence, trying to prick at his legs to send him into a state similar as Daniel. Luckily, his pants were too thick to puncture. He bent and, avoiding the thorns, ripped out the root and stuffed it into his jacket pocket. Brewing the root into a soup would be able to cure Daniel. The first part was easy enough, but now it was time to find Matt, Paul and for whatever reason, Garreth.

He walked down the main pathway for a while, surprised to see few signs of demonic activity. They must have all been taken care of back in Hyperion. He continued further until the ground felt slightly off, squishy like wet dirt. The faint scent of fertilizer was in the air. Nick knelt and picked up some soft dirt and sniffed it—just as he suspected, it was a type of fertilizer, probably used for growing plants in the dark. It was strange since no farmer would dare grow anything outside the Holy

Shield where their crops would be unprotected from demons and the inhospitable environment. Not to mention the fact that, without sunlight, it was impossible to grow anything worthwhile in this dark, dreary place.

Someone shouted Matt's name. He stood tall and listened. The voice was muffled, but familiar. It had to be Paul. He followed the sound to a small clearing surrounding a small pond. Around it, dozens of dead hounds decorated on the moss covered ground. There were large cuts zigzagged their bodies, Matt and the others must have been able to take care of themselves. However, there was no sign of his friends. Was it just his imagination?

"Hey!"

Nick spun into a combat-ready position only to find himself face to face with a weary looking Paul carrying an unconscious Garreth Graves.

"No need to get startled. It's me," Paul said.

"Daniel's been poisoned. What are you guys doing down here?" Nick said.

"Poisoned? Poor fool." Paul shook his head. "Garreth had a particularly bad run-in with some Hellbeasts, but he'll live. It's quite apparent that his sword skills have taken a drastic decline since his falling out."

Paul dropped the millionaire owner of Grave Tower on the floor like a sack of potatoes. "As the one in charge, I made the decision to search for you after I found out you removed the tracker from your vehicle. We traced your last known location the other day to your girlfriend's house and the trail went cold. We were then contacted by the president about the attack in Hyperion. We found the Hellbeasts and trailed them to the break in the Holy Shield, which subsequently led us to this den. Together we investigated and it turns out Astaroth had been living in this cave for a few months. However the demon was nowhere to be found. At the same time we had found Garreth also answered the call to action and we were ambushed," Paul said. "As you can see, we have it under control. Now answer my question: Why did you leave the Garrison when Peter had explicitly told you to stay in Glenhaven?"

"I needed a break from my solitude. Now where's Matt?" Nick said.

"He was on the heels of a hound, looking for a chance to redeem his previous failure." Paul pointed behind at a giant rock that covered another path.

Nick squeezed through the small opening and found Matt on his knees, cursing over a puddle of water. The room was different than the others. There were shovels, buckets and bags and bags of fertilizer. It was like a hidden gardening shed. At the top, a large opening let the sun shine brightly, illuminating the room with natural light.

Matt turned around. His face was dirty and defeated. "They took the sword, Nick. I can't believe I screwed up so badly. All I had to do was keep it safe, and I messed it up."

"I'm just glad you're safe." Nick could already hear Peter's gruff voice, chastising them for being so careless.

"I can't believe I let this happen," Matt said.

"Tell me everything," Nick said.

"I dropped it in here. During the scramble I decided it would be better to bring the sword pieces with us rather than leave them to get stolen. Stupid. We followed the trail to the break in the shield and found the den. After we went inside to investigate, we wound up trapped by a legion of Hellbeasts and it gets snatched from me. We kill almost all of them, but the last one managed to escape before I could get it," Matt said.

"Was there was somebody else in here? Someone human?" Nick said. "I just took care of Astaroth, but could he have broken through by himself? He said it was a 'gift' from Doctor Numerous, but the story doesn't add up."

Matt shook his head. "No it couldn't have been Doctor Numerous. I think Astaroth might be working with someone else."

"Another?"

"I couldn't get a good look at the guy with all the hounds trying to rip my head off, but there was another man here, and he was carrying a foreign sword, like the Pailean katana Garreth owns," Matt said.

"Any clues that could give us some idea of what we're dealing with?" Nick said.

"The only thing I noticed was that he dripping wet." Matt motioned to the large puddle of water on ground, which had already begun to evaporate.

"A Pailean knight, here? We have to inform Peter or the others if there's a possibility that this demon uprising affected another Garrison," Nick said.

Matt's eyebrows furrowed. "We can't. The communicator signal was blocked shortly after they entered Fyria. We can't send or receive calls while they're inside the city."

"I don't like this. It's like we stumbled upon something big, but we have no idea how to approach it," Nick said.

"But if that's the case, are we too early or too late?" Matt said.

There was an eerie silence as they stared at each other. In his quest to get to Fyria he had been blinded by operations within his own neighboring city. Then again, how could anyone have suspected foul play in a peaceful city? This was an unpredictable and highly questionable turn of events. Nick was hit by the sting of regret. Astaroth, the personal bodyguard of Doctor Numerous, had been killed. Their only lead had run dry. Was it possible Numerous had enlisted the help of another fallen knight? But what other knight had the intellect to break down the shield?

"I don't think we'll going to find anything else here. Although I did come across some journals Astaroth had kept. Who knows, maybe they contains some answers.

"We should take it back and have it analyzed thoroughly before we make our next move. But first we have to get Daniel the antidote." Nick remembered the roots he pulled earlier.

Matt's eyes widened. "He was poisoned by the Dolere Flos? How long has it been? We have to go before it's too late!"

They met with Paul and rushed back to entrance, the whole way Nick's heart didn't stop pounding. If Daniel died then it would be his fault. Everything was always his fault. Normally he would have brought the cure back as soon as possible, but this time he neglected to help in favor of finding more Hellbeasts. How could he have been so callous? A friend was dying and he didn't even think twice. He realized then that Agrian was seeping further and further into him, causing him to become more ruthless and uncaring.

Nick rushed through the trees. His heart stopped when he saw Quinn and Daniel sitting up. He looked to be his same cheerful self.

"Daniel, you're all right!" Matt exclaimed.

"I don't know what happened, but I woke up feeling a lot better." Daniel shrugged. "I swear, for a minute it was as if an angel was looking down upon me."

"A miracle." Quinn turned to Nick. "Took you guys long enough. He's lucky to be alive."

Paul stepped forward, lugging Garreth in his arms.

"Garreth!" Quinn shouted.

Paul dropped him at her feet. "I've already stopped the blood loss and bandaged him where he needed it. All he needs now is rest and he'll be fine."

Garreth woke briefly at the sound of the voices and peered into Quinn's face. "Alyssa, is that you?"

Matt glanced to Nick and then back to her. "Alyssa?"

11

NIGHT TERRORS

"Did he just call you Alyssa?" Matt said.

"I heard him say that," Daniel said.

She turned away in the other direction. Suddenly all the pieces of the puzzle clicked into place and Nick reached an epiphany.

"As in Alyssa Masters. You're Peter's granddaughter!" Nick said.

"What kind of deception is this?" Paul he drew his sword. "Supreme Commander Peter's granddaughter is a long way from here. You must be an impostor! A demon in disguise!"

She backed away with her hands up. "Wait a second. Quinn is my middle name and Valentine was my mother's maiden name. I used them as an alias to protect myself. But yes, my true name is Alyssa Masters."

"Why should we trust you?" Paul said. "You could be making this all up. In fact, you're probably behind all of this!"

Nick looked into her eyes and there was no doubt in his mind now.

"Put your sword down." Nick stood between them, the sword pointed at his face.

"Why am I not surprised? You were a fool when Peter picked you up as a child, and you're a fool now. For all we know she could have infiltrated our organization by deceiving you! I won't let the opportunity to exterminate a demon escape me," Paul said.

"Are you blind or just stupid? Garreth obviously knows her, which proves she is who she says she is. Now put down your sword!" Nick said.

"Supreme Commander wouldn't be pleased if he found out you cut down an innocent civilian based on a hunch," Matt warned. Paul gave him a look of disdain and huffed angrily, before sliding the sword back into its sheath.

With the threat of death gone, Nick approached her with a question that was burning inside of him. "Of all people…why would you keep this from me?"

"I had to lie. I had to escape it all. Even if it meant risking my life by exposing myself—it wouldn't have mattered anyway. I spent my whole life hiding in a bubble created by my grandfather. If I didn't leave then I was as good as dead," Alyssa said.

"What about us—was that just another part of the plan to escape?" Nick said.

"Of course not," she said.

"This is bad, this is really bad." Nick paced around, raking his hands harshly through his hair. The one time he met a girl he liked and it turned out to be Peter's granddaughter, the same granddaughter the Crowned Princes wanted dead. "I can't believe this is happening. This is too twisted."

"You're freaking me out, Emberson."

"Okay. Before things spiral more out of control, let's put this whole thing on pause right now because it looks like we should put Garreth in a hospital," Matt said.

"Where should we take him? Civilian hospitals can't treat a wound like this," Daniel said.

"Bringing him back to his office won't do either. We should take him to his house, it's not very far." Alyssa pointed at the large loft a couple of streets down. "We need someone to take care of the break in the shield in case something else tries to come through."

"Paul and I will stay behind and repair it," Matt said. "We'll meet you all back at Garreth's place after we're done cleaning up here." Paul gave a stiff nod, looking quite regretful for his earlier behavior.

Nick carried Garreth's body back to the car with both Daniel and Alyssa following slowly behind. His mind was making a million connections a second. Everything suddenly made sense, how she met Garreth, how she knew so much about the Garrisons, and especially her name! The surname of Valentine had great historical significance; it would be impossible for someone to make a mistake. Was he just that stupid then, to go along so blindly without putting the obvious together? Or perhaps he didn't want to face the facts—the truth that he was lying to her about who he was as well.

They arrived at the three-story building she'd indicated. It was unusually grandiose in design compared to the others around it, taking the curvy shapes and colors from Pailo. Dark red and tan were the main color palettes used to accent and separate it from this otherwise plain looking city. It was extravagant to no end, everything he expected from the boy millionaire.

Nick followed Alyssa with Garreth slung over his shoulder. She punched in the security code at the doorway. It chirped, signaling that the code was accepted and they found an elevator, which they took to the next floor. There they were immediately bombarded by more Pailean influences such as the décor in his living room, with little wood dolls and low tables with sitting mats. Nick propped Garreth on his bed in the master bedroom and returned to the living room.

Nick glanced at Daniel, who seemed to sense the vibe of the room. "Uh—I'm going to help the others. Did you guys need anything while I'm out?"

Alyssa didn't say a word nor did she look at him.

"Okay...I'll be right back." Daniel closed the door softly behind him as he left.

Nick was grateful to Matt for stepping in, as it gave him a chance to collect his thoughts and become more rational.

"Can we talk?" Alyssa asked finally. "I know this is a little hard to take in, but let's just try to be adults. Let's be honest with each other right now and just say what we're thinking."

"Do you have any idea how bad this is?" Nick asked. "Of all the people in the world, why do you have to be *his* granddaughter?"

"What does my grandpa have to do with any of this?"

"Look," Nick said, pacing around the room, "I also have a confession to make. If you are Peter's granddaughter then you must know all there is to know about demons."

"I have extensive knowledge on that subject. What's your point?" Alyssa said.

"Then you know about the Crowned Princes," Nick said.

"I don't understand where you're going with this."

"Do you know the story of Agrian and Quinn? The love that helped save the world from being enslaved by demons? Do you know what happened to those two?"

"Of course, Quinn gave her life in order for Agrian to be reborn with a soul, and he pledged his life to honor her final wish by searching for peace for all humanity," Alyssa said.

"That's not all. Before the remaining Crowned Princes went into hiding, Ozarael vowed they would make him pay. They promised they would destroy everything he held dear as punishment for his betrayal. The only thing that Agrian ever cared about more than himself was Quinn."

"I don't understand. Why are you telling me this?"

"Because I *am* Agrian!"

Alyssa fell back onto the couch in disbelief. "That's impossible. My grandfather made me spend my whole life hiding so this wouldn't happen!"

"I guess dodging fate isn't as easy as I thought. I've broken my promise to Peter and now look where we are. To top it off, there's something strange going on in this city," Nick said.

"You're right. This is all happening really fast. I just need some time to think," Alyssa stood up and walked briskly past Nick. "I'm going to check up on Garreth." She closed the bedroom door.

Nick sat alone until the others came back from repairing the break in the seal. For the rest of the day Alyssa stayed in the room. Perhaps she wanted to avoid him. If that was the case, he felt he should give her the time to let everything sink in—he needed it as well.

For the time being, they would be settled down here in order to dig up clues about Astaroth's sudden appearance, and his reasons for using the Den of Pain as a base. Luckily Garreth's loft was quite large, with three guest bedrooms—more than enough to accommodate their stay. Alyssa had a room, Nick had one, Paul and Daniel shared a room, while Matt volunteered to sleep on the pullout couch.

Nick made the choice to close himself off from the rest of the world, only coming in and out for lonely meals. Deep down he wanted so badly to talk to her and resolve everything, but he couldn't. It wasn't the fact that they both lied—that was never the issue—but the fact that he couldn't face the truth about his own past. How could she reciprocate feelings for a monster? The fact that he was betraying Peter's trust by lying to his face was one thing, but to find out that he was also putting his granddaughter's life in the same jeopardy Agrian did years ago was too much of a burden. Because of his hasty actions all the consequences were toppling over like a row of dominos. What of his battle with Astaroth? He destroyed the only link to vital information because he was so hotheaded. And though no one placed any blame on him, he wished to be punished somehow, to be disciplined, and reprimanded so he could find solace.

After that incident, Paul went on the prowl for clues about Astaroth's involvement and the other unidentified "wet warrior." Nick had never seen such dedication from a single person. Night and day he was be out for extended periods of time, only coming back for a few hours of rest before resuming his quest with extreme zeal. He was relentless. The trail was still fresh.

Patrolling an unfamiliar city must have been his way of finding redemption for not being there to stop him from losing their precious sword. Even now, in the dead of the night, he was on the hunt. Nick could only wonder what would happen if he actually found the root cause of all this.

Matt and Daniel were doing more or less the same, but were making rounds posed as normal citizens to find more clues, always coming up empty-handed. Perhaps this individual knew they were trying to find him, perhaps he knew better than to make another appearance. He had to have been a demon though, since there was no way an average person could outmaneuver Matt.

Nick confined himself in his room for the majority of the day, thinking about what he'd done. He chose to live this way, avoiding everyone for a while. He knew what they probably thought, and looking them in the eye was very difficult right now. It was twelve in the morning. Everyone would be either sleeping or preoccupied with something else. It would be easy to sneak past them.

He walked by Alyssa's room, and wondered what she was up to. He resisted the urge to pay her a visit and went to the rooftop instead. It was a nice night to train. Being high above the other complexes meant he could use his fire powers without drawing curious viewers.

Nick spent plenty of time honing his demon powers. Transforming his arms was easy now, just like breathing. He could do it by sheer will, the only drawback being the fact that he still wasn't able to control the shift in attitude that came with the intense emotional rollercoaster of harboring two conflicting souls. It was a double-edged sword since the more he gave in to Agrian, the more he was able to access the power, which amplified his abilities and senses to supernatural heights. But the demon within him was more than willing to look past his natural moral compass. He would have to eventually figure out a way to stop that from happening, before he got out of control and potentially hurt innocent people.

To begin his training, Nick transformed into Agrian. Easy enough. He would hold onto this form until he felt bloodlust or any uneasy thoughts began to take hold, which then would be his cue to revert back. During these trials he became fascinated with ideas that could extend and create better uses for his fire powers. Though it wasn't perfect yet, he had developed the ability to conjure various shapes and weapons out of the flames. After he was done with that, he'd try more precision-based attacks. He would set up targets on other buildings and strike them with small, but concentrated bursts of flame.

After all was done, Nick went back to the loft and took a quick shower. He was feeling hungry after such an intense workout and decided that he earned himself a snack. He went to the kitchen, feeling his way in the dark. He found some canned chicken soup in one of the cupboards, poured it into a pot and placed it on the stove, letting it heat under a small flame before he noticed an occasional flash of dim light at the bottom crack of Garreth's room door. He turned the knob and peeked in to see that Garreth was sitting on the floor, polishing his sword while the television was playing infomercials on mute. He was sitting so close to the television the images of the people in the advertisements reflected off his glasses.

"I'm surprised you're not asleep yet." Nick turned on the ceiling lights and illuminated the room. "After all that's happened lately, I would have expected you to be more tired than anyone else."

"I never sleep when I'm stressed." Garreth blinked a few times to readjust himself to the sudden brightness.

His eyes were bloodshot; he continued staring blankly at the screen. "I'm used to running a high profile company that usually keeps me up till the break of dawn. But now that the demon problem has made its way into my city, there's a lot more on my mind. I can't do a thing about either right now, so this seemed like the best way to pass the time." He pointed at the television.

"I can imagine." Nick yawned loudly. Apparently being a millionaire bachelor still meant you still had a lot of responsibilities in order to maintain such a luxurious lifestyle. Go figure. He'd always thought prancing around in suits and looking important was work enough. Maybe he had misjudged Garreth. "It's good to see Alyssa was able to help you recover."

"She's one of a kind, that one. Even if she wasn't trained as a medic you'd have trouble telling her apart from the real thing." Garreth paused to turn to face Nick. "I feel terrible that I caused this tension between you two. It wasn't any of my business. Had I been in a better state of mind, I wouldn't have said anything. But just so we're clear, everything between me and her are over."

"No agenda?" Nick said.

"None at all, I promise."

"I appreciate that. Don't worry, I'm not holding what happened against you."

Garreth rubbed his eyes. "So then, what's keeping you up at night?"

"The burden of being me." Nick heard the sounds of rattling and went to check on the pot, which was boiling now. He poured the contents into a bowl. "Soup? I made extra," he offered as he reentered the room.

"No thank you." Garreth went back to cleaning his sword. It was already spotless as far as Nick could tell, yet he continued to polish it at the same spot in the same constant motion, like an obsessive compulsive disorder.

"Paul still hasn't found a clue yet, has he?" Nick asked.

"Not one. It's quite remarkable actually. He's always been so good at tracking down demons. He's had the best reputation for it, at least ever since I can remember. I guess times have changed."

"Unless, maybe he's having trouble because he's not after a demon at all." Nick drank his soup. It was delicious on this cool evening.

"Are you talking about that sighting in the Den of Pain?" Garreth asked.

"The way he looked and the dressed...do you think it could have been a Pailean knight?" Nick asked.

"Matt's description was odd. Since I wasn't conscious at the time, it all seems more than odd. I can't imagine anyone striking me as 'wet warrior' when I visited Pailo. Besides, that Garrison has no business in Glenhaven or Fyria. The location is too far in the east to even know about the problems we have here. I think it was all in his imagination, a compilation of the stress from fending off a horde of Hellbeasts."

"What about the fact that he blames himself for losing the sword?" Nick said.

Garreth blinked a few times. "I'm sorry it fell into the wrong hands. If only I had repaired it before then it would be safely tucked behind the Garrison walls."

"It's in the past. But something else bothers me. I thought demons couldn't touch weapons imbued with holy magic, but I thought that only applied to it being used offensively. Last time I barely touched a piece and it nearly burned through my hands."

"A great whitesmith can forge a weapon based upon their level of skills. Perhaps Sir Marcus found a whitesmith capable of crafting a weapon with so much Orichalon that it could repel demons by mere touch," Garreth said.

"Then how do you explain the Hellbeasts that stole it? Shouldn't it have warded them off as well?"

"That I can't answer. Even with my talents, I have never been able to create something like what you describe."

"I would think being related to one of the greatest archangels of our time would give you some exposure to a few famous whitesmiths," Nick said.

"So Alyssa told you. Gabriel's no brother of mine. Not after what he did."

"Some say that it nearly drove you insane," Nick said.

"Emotions are difficult to predict because they can be controlled and manipulated. That's why most Garrisons are very careful about who they allow into their forces. Demons can easily corrupt the weak-minded. But they have not been able to turn me," Garreth said.

"Doctor Numerous was a wise man as well. From what I know he was also a brilliant academic, just like you," Nick said.

"Yes, the similarities are uncanny." Garreth put down his sword for the first time. "Everyone, no matter who you are, possesses a certain light and darkness inside of them. Sometimes if you're unstable, it's hard to distinguish what is supposed to be good or bad. Demons like to find knights at these crossroads, exploiting their vulnerabilities, and bringing out the worst in them to create fallen knights. What's even worse is that these emotions eventually create a void in you. And you desperately search for some peace, or some way to ease the frustration and the isolation. You eventually turn your back on the people you once cared for and eventually lose sight of who you truly are."

"I've been trying to deal with some inner demons myself," Nick said.

"Is that why you've been hiding out in your room? Alyssa's been worried about you. She's wondering why she's barely seen you the past couple of days. Would you care to elaborate?"

"Just some personal issues I have to deal with on my own."

"Well, she waited up for you earlier." Garreth picked up his sword went back to his routine. "She said if I happened to bump into you, to say she'd like to see you."

Nick cleaned his empty bowl and headed to her room.

Alyssa was sleeping quite peacefully. It had been a tiring day, especially for him. Looking at her though, in her absolute perfection, made him feel a lot better. She stirred slightly. Nick didn't want to disturb her now. He could talk to her in the morning. As he was about to leave, she spoke.

"Stop…" she mumbled. Her expression was suddenly distraught. Her body tensed up as she grabbed the sheets with both her hands. "Help…somebody help! Help me!"

Nick didn't know how to react, except for reflexively rushing to her bedside.

"Stay away from me!" she screamed, thrashing around. It looked like she was trying to lift this invisible weight in front of her as she struggled. "Help! Help!" She tossed and turned until her fear appeared to have finally peaked, and she shook herself awake. She leapt into his arms.

Nick held her tightly, cradling her head into his chest. "It's okay, it's okay. Everything's going to be fine, I'm right here," he said softly. "You just had a bad dream."

"I-I couldn't." She sobbed incoherently. Nick brushed his hand through her tangled hair. Warm tears soaked through his shirt as she continued to cry while burying her face deeper into his chest. "I was so scared, Nick."

"Tell me what happened." He rubbed her back gently and rocked her back and forth. "What did you see?"

"I was so helpless," Alyssa sniffed. "I couldn't run. I couldn't do anything. Only watch."

"Did you see demons?" Nick asked.

"I don't know. It was standing over me but I couldn't see what it was." She pulled her head back slightly, to look at him now. "That was the scariest part. I can't even describe what it was. All I know was that something was trying to take me away from you, and no matter how much I struggled I couldn't fight it."

"Whatever it was, it won't get to you now. I'm here, and nothing's going to take you. I'm going to get you a glass of water, okay?"

Alyssa grabbed his hand. "No don't. Don't leave me alone right now. Please Nick." She was absolutely terrified, trembling as she spoke. "I don't want to be alone right now."

"It'll just be a sec—"

"No! Please Nick, I need you to stay right here with me." Her eyes were puffy and red. She could start all over again if he left. Nick knew couldn't bring himself to leave now.

"Of course," Nick said.

Alyssa pulled up the sheets and Nick climbed in with her. "Promise you won't leave." She made herself comfortable on his arm as a pillow.

"I promise." Nick wrapped his arms around her waist. He could feel her heart pounding quickly against him.

"I hate sleeping, Nick. I hate it so much," Alyssa said softly. "The night terrors never seem to stop no matter how hard I try."

Nick lay perfectly still by her side waiting for her to drift back into sleep. It happened rather quickly, and soon her heartbeat returned to a normal pace. He didn't want to move away now, in the chance that he would wake her, so he waited until morning. Before long, he drifted away.

He woke the next day with her still in his arms. It was the most pleasant sleep he had in a while, and he felt refreshed. He stretched feeling back into his arms, which had gone numb through the night, trying his best not to move so much as to wake her, but it was too late.

Alyssa turned into him. "You're awake?" She rubbed her eyes. "What time is it?"

Nick glanced at the clock in the room. "It's three in the afternoon. We slept almost half a day."

Alyssa shrugged, wrapped snuggly in the blanket. "Are you saying spending the night with me wasn't productive?"

"Actually, it was the best sleep I've had in a while." Nick stood up. He yawned loudly as he reached for the ceiling.

"Where are you going, mister?" Alyssa asked, still half asleep. "You're not planning on leaving me are you?"

"I'm going to make us some breakfast, err—lunch." Nick couldn't tell if she was really paying attention because she responded in a half sleep language which Nick took for consent, and he went to the kitchen. On the way he checked all the rooms and found that the loft was empty. Where could the others have gone?

Nick was too lazy to make anything extravagant, and since breakfast was the least appetizing meal of the day, he decided to cook something simple. He settled in making waffles, eggs, and toast, the staples to a nutritious meal. After making enough for two equal portions, he distributed them onto separate plates and set them at the table. The sweet aroma from the cooking must have woken her up, as she was at the foot of the stairs just he finished pouring the last drops of orange juice into a cup.

"Smells wonderful," Alyssa said. She planted a quick kiss on Nick's cheek. "My very own bed and breakfast. Remind me to give you a good tip later." She took a seat at the circular dining table. She was quite happy, seemingly oblivious to the awkward conversation they had a couple days before. Or perhaps she wanted to continue on with their lives as if none of it ever happened. It was a welcome change, one Nick didn't want to ruin by opening his mouth about the past.

"I'm holding you to that." Nick sat opposite her. They swallowed up the food hungrily, with every piece seemingly disappearing in a matter of minutes.

"That was delicious." Alyssa glanced around the empty room. "It's pretty quiet around here. I wonder where everyone is."

"If I had to guess I think they're doing recon. We should join them."

"Right. Give me a minute to get ready!" She went to her room, and came back changed into a white, sundress with a green ribbon in her hair to match her eyes.

Nick smiled. "Let me grab my jacket."

They went up and down the streets looking for any clues to the "wet warrior" and found only dead ends. Every person they asked led to different areas of the city. Eventually they were led to the park that was adjacent to the Garreth's building complex. From the numerous testimonies, there had been several sightings of a man who wore Pailean clothing standing suspiciously by the pond at various hours of the day. They could not pass up the smallest chance to finding a lead.

According to the big stone sign, the park was called Paradise Pond. It was a spacious area with a large, clear pond in the center. The place was crowded with people running with dogs on leashes, old folks on benches by the pond feeding the ducks, and kids playing on the swings and the sandbox. Alyssa and Nick walked hand in hand to a more secluded side of the park and sat on the grass in the shade of a giant willow. Its branches loomed over and touched the surface of the pond.

"This seems like the most inconspicuous place to wait for this guy," Alyssa said.

"I've missed you." Nick held her in his arms. "I've missed this. Listen, there's a lot I want to say—"

Alyssa put a finger to his lips. "Let's enjoy what we have for what it is. The past is behind us now." Her eyes lit up suddenly. "How about a reintroduction? Tell me a little about yourself—I mean the demon part of your life."

"Well, there's an evil demon that occupies my body and occasionally we like to work together and kill other demons in order to keep the world from being enslaved. But on the plus side, I have a wonderful girlfriend to keep me sane."

"Yikes. So it's kind of like being a coin that's always flipped isn't it? You never know when you're good or bad," Alyssa teased.

"No one likes predictability. I guess you could say it's kind of a quirk I have. Some might find it charming."

Alyssa smiled. "Your girlfriend must be real special to put up with that kind of charm."

"She's the best thing that's ever happened to me. It doesn't scare you though? Knowing what you know about him?" Nick asked.

"Quite the opposite. I was worried that I would have scared him."

"Why would he have any reason to be?"

"I think playing with fate can have adverse effects on people. One day you think you've met the perfect person, but then it turns out that in the grand scheme of things, it was always meant to be," Alyssa said.

"Fate brings people together, but it doesn't guarantee a happy ever after."

Nick leaned in and kissed her deeply. When their lips parted, she took in a deep breath, exhaling euphorically as the wind gently pushed through her hair. The natural atmosphere was exquisite, but no beauty could come close to matching hers. Like an intricate work of art, Nick could just sit there and watch her for hours.

"I love this…it's perfect," Alyssa said. "Just living in the moment, you know? Something as simple as a day in the park is really all there is to it."

Nick smiled at her. "Serenity is all around us."

Alyssa eyes closed her eyes, soaking everything in. "It reminds me of my parents. Every weekend we'd have a little picnic in our backyard, and play games. We had a giant willow tree just like this one, and my dad had built a swing on it for me. At the end of every picnic, I'd swing on it until the sun went down. It was my favorite part of the week, just being with family."

"Your parents sound amazing," Nick said.

"They were the best. And I'm grateful to still have their memories. What about you? What do you remember from your childhood?"

"Nothing I say can top that." Nick felt the tension in his chest as he plucked some grass off the ground.

"You've got to be more specific. Come on, I know you're adopted, but I hardly know anything about young Nick Emberson's time in the Garrison."

"You really don't want to know," Nick said.

"Try me."

When it was evident that only a proper answer would satisfy her curiosity, Nick gave in.

"If you insist." Nick cleared his throat. "Growing up in the Garrison I was treated differently. I never knew my parents and I didn't come from wealth, so naturally everyone who saw me had a weird reaction—like I was a poison to avoid. Peter tried his best, but he couldn't always protect me. They wouldn't tell me outright, but I instinctively knew they saw me as something less than what they were, and it hurt me to the point that…that I couldn't look at myself in the mirror because I started to see what they saw. Peter reassured me, kept telling me that I was 'special,' but the truth was, I didn't want to be 'special,' I just wanted to belong.

"Eventually I gave up. I grew distant from people because I thought that trusting them would only end up hurting me. Then I met Matt, the first person other than Peter who looked at me as a person and not just some 'thing' to put up with. We've been best friends ever since."

"I'm sorry that happened to you. People can be so cruel," Alyssa said. He could have just let that be the end of the story, but something urged him to continue, to release the valve that had been wound so tightly for so long.

"I deserved all of it." Suddenly Nick was short on breath and his heart was racing.

"What do you mean? Is everything okay, Nick?"

"There's another reason I was treated the way I was and why Peter never allowed me to get my hands dirty." Nick had a hard time mustering the strength to say it, but he had to tell her. "I-I killed someone. Susan Stillwell."

"Susan Stillwell—the legendary cleric?" Alyssa said with surprise. "But that's not possible. She died in a fire."

He felt queasy just hearing the name said aloud. The memories poured into his head and he once again relived the pain.

Nick nodded. "It was because of me that she died."

"This must be eating you up inside."

"Peter tried to cover the whole story in order to protect me, but people talk. It wasn't as if it'd make a difference. Nothing could get rid of the images in my head. Like you and the night terrors, there are things I'm afraid of—things I can't explain, but they torture me. Unlike them I know exactly what keeps me up at night. For years, every time I closed my eyes I saw her there, suffering because of me. I can't even count the nights that scene played over and over…the agonizing pain she felt as I watched her die."

"Tell me." Alyssa rested her hand on his arm.

"It's funny, I think on some level I knew I was a monster even before Peter told me the truth. No matter how much I tried to believe differently, the looks on the people's faces never let me forget. No matter how much Peter tried to conceal, the looks of disgust from those who remember is too much to bear."

Alyssa gazed into his eyes. "Let me help you, the way you helped me."

Nick had all this pent-up inside for such a long time. Would it be so bad to let her—the girl who he'd fallen so madly in love with—into his world? Before he wished to take this secret to the grave, let the burden die with him. But she cared for him and he could see that she wanted to help him, and he so desperately wanted to tell her everything.

"I'm here for you no matter what Nick." She squeezed his hand. "If you're not ready to tell me, then don't, and I'll understand. But I just can't stand by and watch you suffer like this."

"No, if I had to tell anyone it would be you," Nick said. "Let me find a place to begin." Where to start? Where did it all begin? Nick thought hard, and a rush of memories resurfaced. Like always, he didn't like backtracking through his mind, but it was time he did for himself.

"Six years ago, when I was twelve, I was sent with Matt and a group of others to stop a disturbance in Fyria. The city was under siege in what was one of the biggest assaults in recent history. Our commanding officer at the time was Susan Stillwell." Nick paused to clear his throat. It was getting harder to speak.

"During the attack, Susan broke away from the other soldiers to find and kill a group of five or six renegade demons that were fleeing. We followed them into the abandoned offshore oil-rig.

"When we finally cornered them, it turned out that had been led straight into a horde. Susan fought bravely, but she wasn't equipped to defend herself against a small army. She told me to run, but I panicked and dropped the lantern I was carrying. A fire started, and the building came down between us, which trapped the demons and Susan. She was crushed by the ceiling, barely alive. I was too scared to run. I watched as demons tear her apart and the entire building engulfed in flames. I was only saved when Matt and the others got there." Nick turned away; he couldn't face her now. He had to let her know the truth, but couldn't bear to see the look of disgust.

But to his surprise, he was taken into a warm embrace. "Nick…I never knew. I never knew how much you had to bear alone. It must have killed you."

"Wh-what are you doing? I'm a terrible person. I deserved to die that day, and instead I was given a full pardon by Peter."

She shook her head, and her fragrant hair tickled his nose. "My grandpa saw the good in you, just like I do. You're not a terrible person, and it's not your fault. You can't blame yourself for something like that, something out of your control. Susan Stillwell's death wasn't vain. In saving you, she gave the world a chance at survival."

Nick wrapped his arms around her. Instead of being scorned, or treated with contempt, she'd accepted him. Without judgment and without hatred. He held this in for so long; he never knew how great it felt to share a piece of himself to someone.

"I promise I'm never going to let anything happen to you," Nick said on the brink of tears. "I swear I'll protect you always."

"I trust you. And when you said you didn't deserve any-body…well that's just not true. You're good enough for me."

When the sun set they realized that the "wet warrior" wouldn't to make an appearance. They went back to the loft and found a full house. Garreth isolated himself away in his office; while Paul was eating a small meal alone at the dining table; Daniel and Matt were watching television on the couch. They all looked exhausted.

"Where have you two been all day?" Daniel asked.

"Searching for leads," Alyssa said. Nick exchanged a know-ing glance and he tightened his hand over hers.

"Right." Matt turned off the television. "We also went clue searching today. Me and Daniel decided to go back to the

Den of Pain. We found bags of Dolere Flos stuffed in boxes. It looked like Astaroth was planning to ship them somewhere. We combed the place over but found no sign of the sword, which means it's probably long gone."

"What would anyone want with the Dolere Flos?" Daniel asked.

Paul put his plate in the sink. "I couldn't find the warrior Cunningham was talking about, but I went downtown. Nobody has seen that knight, but there's talk about a strange man with an eye patch. They say he's farmer and he had been coming back and forth the last few months buying fertilizer and bags to store crops for shipment." He pulled out the picture Lucius left them and waved it in the air. "I showed them this picture and they agreed that it was match. Turns out the traitor found a new hobby."

"What would Doctor Numerous be doing in Hyperion?" Nick said.

"I don't know, but this proves he has had a hand in the attacks. Astaroth's presence and the break to the shield spell it out plainly enough," Paul said.

"Guys, you have to check this out!" Garreth called from the other room. Everyone hurried in. His computer monitor was a collection of pictures with times and dates labeled in the corners. "I hacked the security cameras of every farm supply store within a two hundred mile radius and used facial recognition to match Numerous' face. He hasn't just been in Hyperion. He's been in just about every store at every civilian city in any country you can name: Glenhaven, Thorne, Fyria, Pailo—you name it. All were visited by a one-eyed farmer."

"But look at the time stamps. These areas are miles apart, yet he's been at all these locations within minutes of each other," Paul said. "How can this be? How can anyone travel this fast?"

"Teleportation isn't a demon ability…is it?" Daniel asked.

Matt shook his head. "None that I ever heard of. He's a wanted man. There's no way this guy can be moving across the country and still get under the radar of every Garrison. There has to be something wrong with the facial recognition, or it must not be working correctly."

"I developed the system myself. It's state of the art," Garreth said.

"We have to warn my grandpa somehow," Alyssa said.

"Where was his most recent appearance?" Nick asked.

Garreth typed a series of keys and another screen popped up with a list.

"Downtown Hyperion, like Paul said." Garreth scrunched his face. "Come to think of it, most of his appearances have been sighted nearby here."

Nick glanced around at them all. "I was told once that he was methodical, a perfectionist when it came to everything he did. After all that's happened these last couple of days, I have a feeling that whatever he's planning will come into fruition soon."

12

BLACKOUT

The weather reports that morning said it was to be the hottest day of the month with a high of a hundred and ten degrees. The sun was at its peak and beating down hard on the citizens of Hyperion. Blazing, when applied to normal standards, but perfectly comfortable for Nick. He was awake, but lying with his eyes closed under the shade of a tree at Paradise Pond with his head nestled in Alyssa's lap. She was reading a book in one hand, while playing with his hair with the other.

The gentle breeze carried her familiar fragrance and he took a deep breath. He loved the way she smelled. It was the same perfume she wore ever since they first met; a lightly scented combination of irises and jasmine. Like a trusty bloodhound, he had memorized this perfect scent and associated it to the comfort it gave him, the way a parent's heartbeat gave ease to a frightened child.

It was funny, with her presence around him he felt so much more human, so much more capable in every way. Despite the problems they'd faced in the past, their bond had grown even stronger as a result. But even though his nightmares were over, there was something else that kept him tossing and turning at night. The issue at hand was one they had yet to identify, but had to be dealt with quickly before the consequences spiraled out of control. Unfortunately, all they could do was wait for signs of the culprit's return.

It had been just a little over a week since they had deduced Doctor Numerous as the instigator behind the demon activity in Hyperion. Looking back, Nick wasn't sure why they didn't figure it out sooner. Doctor Numerous was human which allowed him to move from city to city and get under the Holy Shield without much trouble. His longstanding time with the Garrison as an alchemist would explain why he would have a particular vendetta. Still, taking a sword enchanted by holy properties would do little to help the demons.

But that wasn't Nick's main concern. Even now that they knew of his involvement, how could they hope to stop him? Nick knew how to combat demons and knights, but how could they battle someone who had mastered both sides of the spectrum? Doctor Numerous had a genius intellect and experience well beyond them under his belt. Challenging him would be even more difficult considering he had been recently become one of the Infernals, the group of powerful demon warlords that served directly under the Crowned Princes. Nick already had trouble defeating his subordinate and a few hounds, how could he hope to stop someone who was in a completely different league?

He felt a slight thud as she dropped her novel onto the grass and let out a short, exasperated sigh.

Nick opened his eyes. "What's wrong?"

"I haven't spoken to my grandpa since he left. I can't shake the feeling that something has happened to him," Alyssa said.

Their quest to Fyria had certainly hit a roadblock, and Nick had all but forgotten about his original goal to come to Peter's aid. He felt guilty that he was content with lounging around in Hyperion while the others were off in battle.

"You don't give the old man enough credit. I'm sure there's nothing wrong. He's a fighter, and one of three men to ever become a Supreme Commander. And he has the support of the best archangels I know," Nick said.

"I guess I'm just being paranoid, aren't I?"

Nick sat up and wrapped his arm over her shoulder, "No, you're just being cautious. I know a little about paranoia, and if you let it just sit inside you, it'll just make you crazy. Let's try contacting him again and I'll prove he's just fine."

"There's no Garrison here, so we can't to make any calls in Hyperion," she said.

"Maybe we should try back in Glenhaven? I mean, it's been a while and our guest has yet to show himself." He pulled her up and they walked back to Garreth's loft hand in hand. The city always had an abnormally large amount of traffic, but people left in droves after a sudden power outage the night before. The streets were curiously empty today. Rumors sprang around that the city was the next demon target in line. The same citizens who chastised and hated the Garrison now needed their help more than ever.

Consequently, Hyperion became a ghost town, an apocalyptic wasteland set seemingly several years into the future. Silence filled the air through the tall buildings and skyscrapers.

There were no lights on in any of the shops; the once thriving metropolitan was dead.

Back inside the loft, Paul and Garreth were slamming buttons frantically on the computers in his office.

"Listen, Alyssa and I are going back to Glenhaven. If we can make contact with Peter then maybe he can give us a sense of direction," Nick said.

"I'm afraid that's not an option right now." Garreth typed without looking up.

"What's going here?" Alyssa asked.

"Glad of you to finally join us," Paul said snidely. "Are you done having your little picnic or would you be needing some more time to go pick wildflowers and frolicking in the woods?"

"Don't talk to her that way," Nick snapped.

Paul glared at him. "I was referring to you, demon. I would never accuse Lady Alyssa of behaving like the animal you are. It's because of you and your poor judgment that we're in this predicament in the first place."

Nick stepped forward defiantly, but Alyssa grabbed his arm, holding him back before the situation escalated too far.

"The last thing we need is you two to fight. We've got bigger problems here. This wasn't just a freak power loss. The electricity in the city has been officially cut off, and we have no idea who could have done it. We're in a widespread blackout," Garreth said. "The only reason why everything is still functioning here in this loft is because of the backup power supply that I installed myself."

"The entire city is blacked out?" Alyssa said.

"Yes, but this presents a bigger problem," Garreth said. "The Holy Shield generator was designed to last for a while without power, but it can only last for so long without a constant energy source. If we don't bring power back soon, the shield will lose its effect and the barrier protecting us will fade away, leaving us wide open for a full-fledged demon assault."

"That must be why everyone fled." Paul looked out the window. "Then again, with a coward as their president I'm not very surprised."

"Is there any way to stop this from happening?" Nick said.

"There is one method that surely won't fail," Garreth said.

"That was what the Holy Shield promised, wasn't it? Look how great that turned out," Paul said sarcastically.

Garreth threw him a look of contempt. "Don't mock my family's legacy. If it wasn't for the Holy Shield, people would still be living in fear and hiding their entire lives."

"What exactly do you think they're doing right now?" Paul shot back. He was getting increasingly closer to him, as if goading Garreth into a fight.

A flash of anger brought Garreth out of his chair, with his eyes glowering down on Paul. His usual calm and professional demeanor was gone.

"Enough!" Alyssa shouted. Thankfully she was there because they needed a voice of reason to reel them back in to civility.

"How long will the backup generators last?" Nick asked. "And what's this about a foolproof solution to the problem?"

"We have about forty-eight hours." Garreth sat back in his seat. "Normally that's not enough time to bring the power plant back into use. However, before the development of modern electricity, this city used the river's hydroelectric power at the dam. I've sent Matt to Griffon River to check out the situation, but he's yet to report back."

"I hate standing around here as if we're just waiting for doom to take us," Paul said. "The fools who abandoned this city should perish for their own weakness."

"Don't look at it that way. Right now we're the last line of defense. And not just for this city, but for every city in the world," Alyssa said.

Garreth nodded. "Hyperion is my home. I won't abandon it now in its greatest hour of need. If I'm going to preserve it, I'll need all the help I can get."

"Where's Daniel?" Nick asked.

"I haven't seen him all day. He needs to be here for this too," Alyssa said.

"Daniel went to scout for stragglers and to get them to safety," Paul said.

"We'll go help him," Alyssa said.

"That won't be necessary since we've come across another roadblock," Paul said.

Nick let out an exasperated sigh. "What is it now?"

"I was assisting on the ground level as well and I came across the part of town where Graves Tower was located and I could go no further," Paul said. "Then I realized everything was frozen solid. The entrance. The windows. Every inch of the fifty stories of that building was covered in layers and layers of ice."

"Could this have been done by Bergice?" Alyssa said.

"Impossible, he's in Fyria. If someone else has the ability to manipulate ice, it should be investigated later. Right now we need to generate power to keep this city safe. The only chance we have now is to use the dam," Garreth said.

"Right, then we'll go make sure everything is fine with Matt," Alyssa said. "Let's go, Emberson."

Griffon River was just a few miles outside the city. Thankfully, it was untouched by the ice, though the weather was noticeably cooler as they moved further and further from the city. They drove down the single strip of empty paved road—the only route to the river—to the dam. Nick remembered visiting this river a few times when he was younger with Matt on one of their missions. They were delivering a personal parcel to President Evans, and had accidentally dropped it into the water. He dove into the freezing water to retrieve it, unaware that he had never learned to swim and nearly drowned. Matt rescued him of course, but he had gotten in trouble for damaging the package and hated large bodies of water ever since. Since then he had learned to swim, but to this day, the sounds of rushing water never failed to instill fear inside him.

Nick parked next to the only other vehicle in the lot. Usually the area would have been filled by tourists who wanted to see the majestic river, but today it was deserted. They walked down the dirt path and found Matt easily enough, as he was the only person on the edge of the bank wearing the white signature Garrison clothing.

"Brings back memories, doesn't it, bud?" Matt said as Nick and Alyssa approached him. He picked up a rock from the mound next to him and tossed the small stone into the rapid moving river.

"Were you able to find out the problem?" Nick asked.

Matt nodded. "As you can see the river is running fine as it should, but I guess someone had an extreme dislike for hydropower." He pointed at the dams, all of which were torn apart. The wooden wheels that were supposed to be churned by the rushing river were dismantled into very even pieces. "Look at the precise cuts in the wood. Whoever did this was skilled with a blade." He gestured at a wet piece of the wreckage.

Alyssa picked up the wood and rubbed her finger along the smooth edge. "No roughness at all. It's safe to say that this wasn't the work of Doctor Numerous, since we know he doesn't use swords."

"Then maybe Astaroth before you killed him?" Matt shrugged.

"Astaroth didn't use a sword either," Nick said. "He relied solely on his demon powers. Even with bladed tendrils there's no way he could have cut this uniformly. I sense a third party."

"Those are the only two demons that with a motive for doing this, but since this wasn't their handiwork then I'm at a loss," Matt said.

"We figured the possibility of a third demon in this little operation. Paul went to Graves Tower and found that every entrance was frozen shut. Do you know what could have caused that?" Alyssa said.

"When you mention frozen, I just think about him." Matt's eyes darted to Nick and back to Alyssa.

"I know what you're thinking, but that can't be true. The Lord of Fear is miles away," Nick said.

"Then something else got in. We have no idea how long that break in the shield was open," Matt said.

"Well there's nothing we can do here now, so we might as well cut our losses and try a new plan," Alyssa said.

As they turned to go back, Nick stopped and became rigid. Goosebumps erupted on his arms and striking chills ran up and down his spine. The bright, clear sky became grey and gloomy. Before him cascaded a single snowflake. He caught it with his palm and watched it melt in his hand. Soon after, the clouds covered the sun and everything around him took a darker shade. The warm air disappeared, transforming into an unforgiving cold wind. For the first time in his life, he felt the sensation of cold attack his skin, making him quiver and shake. Suddenly, more snow trickled from the sky, slowly at first, then in a matter of minutes the green grass and paved roads—everything around them was covered in white.

The snowfall was unrelenting, coating the tops of the trees and buildings. Standing still, they were also feeling the effects of the weather change. Nick shook his head, causing the light flakes to flutter to the ground.

The river had stopped running, and was now frozen solid.

"I have a bad feeling about this," Matt said.

"Me too," Nick muttered.

A loud rumble shook the ground, nearly knocking them off their feet. A giant ice wall shot up from the snow, blocking their entrance back onto the road. Three more ice walls shot up, boxing them in at all sides. The height of these walls seemed to stretch miles high, too high for them to leap over. They were trapped.

Nick wanted to kick himself for being so absentminded. After all the strange occurrences in this city he still let his guard down. He should have known that they were vulnerable to an attack. But who was behind this? The wet warrior?

"Desperation. Isolation. Unforgiving cold. These are the embodiments of fear and ice," a voice said. A man was speaking, but there was something off about the way he spoke. It was mechanical, almost synthetic in that there was a lack of emotion.

"Show yourself!" Nick yelled. He pulled Alyssa behind him and transformed into his demon form, readying himself for any surprises that would appear.

"As you wish."

Suddenly a man dropped, seemingly from the sky, landing in a kneeling position with his head hung. He rose slowly, revealing more of his features until he was standing tall.

His complexion was very pale, almost as if his skin had been made from the snow beneath his feet. He had sleek, silver hair that was neatly combed back. He was dressed in traditional Pailean clothing, with a pristine dark blue vest over black dress shirt and matching slacks. He had a katana in a white scabbard slung at the right side of his waist. But the most distinguished feature was his striking blue, emotionless eyes that seemed to penetrate right into a person's soul, the effect of which made Nick uncomfortable. It was like staring into an empty abyss, into the eyes of pure evil.

"That's not Doctor Numerous…" Matt said, his voice trembling.

Was it the cold? No, Nick thought. There was something more sinister afoot, something else that drained the color from his friend's face.

"You…you're behind all of this," Nick said slowly, his mouth at a loss for any more words and his throat dry. Something came over him, another sensation he had never felt before and he couldn't react. His spine was tingling, his breath short. He felt fear.

"All while providing an excellent distraction for us to have some time for ourselves," the man said.

"What do you want?" Alyssa asked.

Among the three she was the only one who didn't seem affected by this man. How could she remain so aloof at a time like this? It made Nick feel a little silly, but there was no mistake, he was certainly frightened of this man.

"You presume that you possess any traits to capture my interest. I don't want a knight or any mere mortal. I require the Inferno Bearer." the man pointed a thin pale finger at Nick.

"Who are you?" Nick asked.

"Don't you recognize me, Agrian? Or has time taken such a toll on your memory that you no longer remember your own brother?"

"The Lord of Fear," Matt managed to utter.

Bergice the Blizzard, one of the Crowned Princes stood before them. He was the demon known for such cruel and unusual atrocities like the Frozen Fifty Incident. Nick hoped he would have more time to prepare before he would face a threat this large in scale. However, fate works in mysterious ways, and in this instance it had worked against his favor.

"Why are you working with Doctor Numerous? You didn't need him to take over Fyria," Nick said.

"He was the gatekeeper into this realm of paradise that you've been holding out from us. I'm surprised you figured out our little operation. I'd forgotten you're quite astute when you want to be. Doctor Numerous has been working for us for some time now. In fact, he's here—in that building, actually." Bergice pointed to Graves Tower. "Conducting one of the greatest experiments of all time. If he should succeed, the world will once again be plunged into fear."

"What happened to your hatred towards mankind, why would you allow him to join your side? Nick said.

"Before I answer that question, first tell me this, how does it feel to be ostracized from the ones you consider allies? Frustrating to no end, I'd assume," Bergice said.

"Not as frustrating as it is to know I used to be one of you," Nick said.

A pang of real anger flashed itself across the ice demon's expressionless face. Had he struck a nerve?

"I know all about you, Bergice. I've known all about your kind my entire life. They kill the defenseless. Oppress the weak. Force them to live in constant fear. I know injustice when I see it," Nick said.

Bergice laughed. "Even when these mortals castrated you, you still managed to keep that silver tongue of yours. But there is a reason why I am called the Lord of Fear. My sole purpose in this world is to plunge mortals into absolute terror."

"So what happens now, are you going to try to take me to Ozarael? Or do we finish it right here?" Nick said.

"Don't be in such a hurry to die. I'm more curious to see if living in that host body dampened your fighting ability. What do you say to a small exhibition? I want to see how far you've come along training underneath the Garrison. Surely you must have learned some new tricks."

"Maybe you could ask one of your other demon lackeys that tried bringing me in like Astaroth? Wait, no, he's dead," Nick said.

"True, his endeavor to kill you was comical at best. But I'm a whole different game from him. Death dealt by my hand requires more precision and calculation, all of which will happen in due time. For instance, the first step to punishing you requires that I kill your two friends over there." Bergice pointed at Alyssa and Matt. "I know you inside and out, and I know that bringing out your rage is the only way to put you in your natural state."

"This guy's insane! We got to get out of here!" Matt said.

"Nick—the walls!" Alyssa said.

Nick spun around and hurled a fireball at the icy barrier. An explosion of white gas filled the air at the spot he struck, but there was no other discernible effect once the smoke cleared. The walls remained unfazed; they were still trapped.

"Your attempts are futile. Truly, are you the Inferno Bearer?" Bergice said.

"How did you find us?" Nick said.

"Ah yes." Bergice stepped forward. "I suppose my presence has caused great confusion. I'm here to finish my business with Doctor Numerous. I helped him stage a full scale war in Fyria in order to distract everyone from our real plan."

"Then there's no war," Alyssa said.

"The war your companions are fighting is real, but neither Doctor Numerous or I are involved at the moment. In fact, I was on my way to visit him during the final stages of his project before I stumbled upon you." Bergice sprang forward suddenly. However, he leapt past them and knelt down to gather snow into his hands. "I wish the whole world could be this beautiful," he said, lost in his own world. "A scene devoid of all life. Just endless black and white. Perfection."

"Quite the act Bergice," Matt said. "We know Nick's the only reason you're back. But you're not taking him!"

"Stop calling him that. That is a terrible name for the Inferno Bearer," Bergice said. "Agrian fits you much better, brother. It's the true reflection of your demon heritage."

"I'm nothing like you!" Nick yelled back, much to the surprise of the others.

Bergice shot Nick a curious look, and Nick found himself fuming with unrepressed anger. The Crowned Princes were responsible for killing hundreds of thousands for their own pleasure, like some sick sport. Nick didn't want to be categorized into something like that. He didn't want to be known for something so despicable.

"You reject us again?" Bergice growled. "What makes you believe the humans will ever truly accept demons like us? One day they'll turn their backs on you."

Nick shook his head. "No, I'm not going to pretend I wasn't born a monster. But make no mistake, I'm nothing like you. I'm fighting for something different, so don't call me brother."

"Then tell me how you felt when you killed Astaroth in cold blood." Bergice paced around them casually.

How he felt? Nick stiffened, and the memories of that day filled his head. He could flashback to that day now, the regret he felt now that all was said and done.

"You parade around like you've achieved humanity by siding with the humans, living alongside them, and adopting their practices when deep down you know that we are one and the same. Don't bother answering. I know exactly how you felt that day. No matter how much you try to deny it, Astaroth's bloodstains are on your hands and you enjoyed every second of it, beating the life out of that demon. Admit it—you yourself are the epitome of evil. Denying otherwise would just be another lie. Even now you try to hold yourself back, but refuting your baser instincts won't do you good because Agrian will find a way to escape."

A splitting headache forced Nick to grip his face with both his hands. Bergice was pushing his buttons, and it was working. Agrian was trying to break free. The throbbing shots of pain in his head caused him to double over. The demon inside was desperately trying to take control. Nick couldn't let that happen—not around Alyssa.

"Of course you can try to fight it, but it will not work. You must unleash the demon in you that's been dying to escape from that vessel. Bring your fury upon me! You have no other choice!" Bergice said.

"Leave him alone! You're messing with his head!" Matt shouted. "Don't listen to him, Nick. I don't know why he wants to get you riled up, but it's obvious he has something up his sleeve."

"Matt's right, he's just trying to manipulate you," Alyssa said.

Agrian's urging pulsated through every inch of Nick's body. It got worse until he found himself on his knees, burying his face in the snow to numb the pain. He needed to transform, to find that air of relief before he went insane.

At that moment, the angel feather pendant jumped out from under his shirt and landed on the snow with a light thud. He looked down at the white stone and the detailed carving took his mind off the agony, away from Bergice's mind games. Just like that, Agrian's voice became softer and softer until it faded away. He was himself again. He could think clearly, the rhythmic throbbing dissipated. Nick brushed the snow off and got back to his feet.

"You're right. Thanks guys, I almost lost it for a second."

Bergice's face dropped. "What? What are you doing?"

"I'm choosing another option. I'm choosing not to fight you. I won't be a puppet to your game, Bergice," Nick said.

Bergice merely shook his head in amusement. "Clever tactic, but ultimately useless. Going against your nature is a coward's solution." A cruel smile broke across his face. "If you won't fight me, who will stop me from killing your friends?"

Nick's heart sank as he realized that this was true. Little did they know they were welcoming their deaths with open arms, with only their unwavering loyalty towards him. But it was pointless. They were no match for a Crowned Prince. As Nick turned to face Bergice, the ice demon's blue eyes were gleaming with an insatiable hunger. Nothing would stop his bloodlust until he satisfied his appetite for killing in a bloodbath.

"I will bring out the true Agrian even if it is against your will." Bergice drew his katana. The blade was blue tinted and had been sharpened very thinly, to only the width of a piece of paper. He held it out in a stance, ready to kill. "Let's see how well you can keep your human facade when you watch your friends slain before you. How many heads must I lay before you until you decide to fight back?"

"Don't you dare." Nick's body heated up as he got into his battle stance. The flames on his arms intensified reflexively.

Nick was shaking uncontrollably now. The words that came from his mouth were binding, as if they were law itself. Because every scenario and every story he had heard involving Bergice the Blizzard, had him always come out the victor. The Prince of Fear would not let his victory come without a trophy because it was his nature.

Alyssa and Matt stood at his defense, but Nick felt far from relieved. In fact, he was absolutely terrified. He hadn't experienced a fear like this in such a long time, but the dread had seeped into his body and he was trembling. With his girlfriend and best friend in the presence of Bergice, how would they come out alive?

Matt had his *Wolfsbane* at the ready. "You forget that us weak humans still have the ability to fight."

"So confident," Bergice said. "But I feel the fear that dwells within your heart. Even so, you still face me with unwavering determination. What is your name young knight?"

"Matthew Cunningham, and in the name of the Heralds and all that is true, I will not let you leave here alive!"

Bergice chuckled lightly. "You can't even begin to fathom the number of times someone has threatened me. It's always the same: light banter, insults, and then a battle to the death. In every instance I always let them believe they have a chance..." His cold eyes became daggers. "It makes it much more satisfying seeing them die with that self-righteous look on their faces."

"You don't scare us," Alyssa said. "As long as there are people who believe in our cause, then demons will never win."

"You have an invincible spirit. But unlike your spirit, your mortal bodies are flesh and blood. You can be broken!" Bergice said.

"Leave them out of this, Bergice," Nick said. "Your fight is with me. I'm the one you want."

"I'm afraid there isn't much you can do to persuade me, Agrian. I had given them the chance to leave with their lives but instead your companions have challenged me to do battle and my honor dictates that I comply.

"And you," Bergice glowered at Alyssa. "Agrian's one true love. The prophecy rang true just like Lord Ozarael said. It pains me to see what a pitiful state you've been reduced to, brother. This role you've been placed in, acting as a puppet following the orders of these pathetic crusaders, all in the name of love. It sickens me."

Bergice turned his gaze upon Matt next. "I've grown tired of all this talking. Your friends want to protect you, let them try." His eyes darted back to Nick. "Let them try to their hardest. Victory can't settle for anything less."

As one, Matt and Alyssa jumped in front of Nick. Nick wanted to argue but he didn't have anything to say to that. He was the key to the salvation of their world. Putting himself into danger wouldn't help their cause, but letting them pay the ultimate sacrifice with their lives wasn't the answer either. There had to be another way. But what else could he do?

Alyssa grabbed Nick's arm and pulled him behind her, to the sidelines. "Go! Get out of here!"

"Our orders are to protect you at all costs," Matt said.

However, Nick would not budge. He couldn't bring himself to leave them, not like this.

Bergice's blue eyes turned crimson. "None of you are leaving until I say so."

With a wave of his hand the walls of ice moved outwards, opening their constricted box to a much larger space. Now they were among trees and Griffon River, but still trapped with nowhere to run. Nick looked on with uncertainty.

"This arena will serve as the perfect backdrop for your demise. Come forward, brave knights. Come meet your greatest fears."

13

RAGE VERSUS FEAR

Things escalated quickly. Two of his friends were ready to welcome death with open arms. If he was to save them both, he had to act fast. But even if there wasn't a wall of solid ice blocking their path, how far could they hope to run? How could anyone escape from the Prince of Fear? From his reputation alone Nick knew he was in a league of his own. Over the years he had slaughtered some of the most fearsome knights and always emerged as the victor.

Bergice had complete mastery over his ice elemental powers. They were like two sides of the coin: he was cool and collected, while the burning sensation of rage intensified in Nick's head. Nick looked to Alyssa and Matt for some direction, but from their expressions it seemed that they were also exhausted of ideas. In the face of fear itself, they weren't searching for a way out of this situation. They remained at his side as true knights, ever vigilant and unwavering against the impossible odds.

Bergice chuckled. "How you knights do enjoy doing that don't you? You enjoy preaching about equality and righteousness, yet always work in numbers like flies picking the remains of dead a carcass. There's no honor in that." He paused, his face serious this time. "But then, two bothersome insects can be easily crushed with one strike."

A troubled thought struck Nick as he realized that Alyssa was unarmed. Even after she had revealed her true identity, she had never once mentioned proficiency in combat. She had training from the Fyria Garrison, but Peter was very protective of her. Why would he allow them to mold the last person in his bloodline to become a warrior? If anything she would have been put through medical training instead, which worried Nick more than anything else now. Without a third weapon in their arsenal, they were at an extreme disadvantage.

Matt echoed his sentiments as he held his sword steadily in position. "Somehow I don't think you can take him with your bare hands, Alyssa. But I guess we're not in any position to be picky."

"Don't be so sure," she said.

Bergice looked on curiously.

"Do you know what Enochian is?" Alyssa said. "It is the ancient language spoken and written by Heralds. For centuries, people have tried to translate their tomes in order to access the secrets to their mysteries, but not one person has been successful. Even the most revered Garrison historians and scientists had their ambitions fail them. However, where they failed, I succeeded. Because the truth behind Enochian is that it cannot be mastered or studied by conventional means, but only inherited by a Herald!"

Bergice looked on silently, anticipating what was to come next.

"Alyssa?" Nick said.

"It's been so long since I've done this. I just hope it's enough. Yuriel, please lend me strength." Alyssa put her hands flatly together in a prayer and raised them to her lips, whispering in a different language. Nick couldn't understand a word she was saying, but it was unmistakably Enochian, the lost language of the angels! A glowing circle of light in the shape of star seal appeared beneath her. She reached her right arm into the air and the light shot into the sky, engulfing her. For a brief moment it looked as if she had disappeared in the brightness. As the light dissipated, she stood carrying a large silver flail, attached by a chain link to a golden ball of crescent spikes.

For the first time, Bergice looked genuinely surprised. "The *Morning Star*. The angelic weapon that belonged to the Herald of Justice. I have not seen it in well over a century. I wonder... why would Yuriel choose to bestow this power upon a mortal such as you?"

"He didn't. He gave it to Quinn Masters and to all females related by blood to inherit. Since I'm the last one, I thought I'd put it to some use," Alyssa said.

Simply astonishing. The lost angelic language of Enochian was never fully recovered after the Great War, yet she spoke it fluently enough to summon the weapons of angels. Not even the archangels were given the knowledge to access weapons crafted from Sanctuary. Nick had to give some credit to Peter; he kept her away from people for so long that old scriptures were her only friends, but at the same time he had given her greater powers beyond any knight in history. Perhaps not all was lost.

Bergice's eyes gleamed with delight. "I thought with the death of the Heralds, so died all of those with the knowledge of Enochian. Perhaps, if I took your life, then that accursed language will finally die."

"Why don't you just try!" Matt sprang forward, Alyssa followed quickly behind. As they approached him, they were synced with each other's steps in a flawless combat technique Nick had witnessed several times in close quarters training. However, it was the first time Nick got to see them use it in a life or death situation. Matt may have been intimidated before, but it didn't seem to faze his abilities. They dashed forward, with Alyssa lined up behind Matt until they were within striking distance. They exploded outwards, delivering their respective strikes from both Bergice's sides. However, their swift blows were easily evaded.

"Too slow. The reputable holy knights are sadly performing much less impressively than one would have presumed." Bergice grabbed them each by an arm and swung them in a circle, hurling them both in opposite directions. Alyssa rebounded hard off the ground and into one of the icy walls, while Matt was sent through a group of tall trees, catching every branch before crashing into a wall and hitting the snow headfirst.

Alyssa leapt back to her feet, shaking off the flakes of snow while watching for some sign of life from Matt. Sure enough he was back to his feet. His clothes were covered in leaves and a bit dirty, but he seemed fine. At once they moved to engage him, almost as if teleporting back to Bergice, who stood perfectly still. They were on his front and rear this time, trying to divide his attention, effectively cutting his reaction time in half. It was a standard combat technique when trying to gain an upper hand on a single opponent.

"Your recovery time is remarkable," Bergice, said amused. "Perhaps there's hope for you after all."

"It's going to take a lot more than that to stop two knights," Matt said.

"Then show me." Bergice motioned them over with his hand, goading them to attack.

They crisscrossed each other, flanking him on the left and right. Matt was able to latch onto to the ice demon and put him in a body hold. Alyssa appeared in close range, and with a quick couple of hand motions, she created a big ball of light in her palms. The Luxilight technique. It was strange however, that Bergice was completely at ease the entire time. It was almost as if he was expecting it. That was when Nick realized it, of course he knew—he *was* expecting it! But before Nick could warn his friends, it was too late.

"Take this!" Alyssa sent a large Luxilight blast into the ice demon. An immense explosion of light shone and for a few seconds, drenched the snow in another layer of white. It was so intensely bright, it forced Nick to close his eyes and shield his face with his hands to avoid being blinded. When it cleared, Alyssa stood staring into the sky at Bergice's lifeless body falling back down. They did it! A direct hit to an average demon would obliterate it from the face of the planet. Even if the ice demon did survive, there's no way he'd still be in one piece. But before Nick could cheer, he realized there was something wrong. It was too easy.

Bergice plummeted into the ground, his body making a perfect outline in the blanket of snow.

"That should do it," Matt said.

Alyssa and Matt ran to the spot where he had landed. She gasped and turned back to Nick. "He's not here."

Bergice was nowhere to be seen, which meant this fight was far from over. To the side, snow began piling up from the ground next to Alyssa, stacking and shaping itself into something vaguely reminiscent of a person. Unbelievable. Bergice was rebuilding himself with snow!

"Alyssa, watch out!" Nick yelled. "Behind you!"

Alyssa twirled around and swung her flail with all her might, but it was too late. Bergice swatted the *Morning Star* out of her hands and grabbed her by the throat, lifting her high above the ground.

Matt lunged at Bergice just as a pillar of ice shot from the demon's free arm, which collided with the knight and launched him several yards away. The force knocked Matt out cold. Bergice turned his attention back to Alyssa.

"Valiant effort, but surely you didn't believe your coveted Luxilight technique could do much more than annoy me did you?" Bergice asked condescendingly. "I have defeated armies of your knights by a mere swipe of my hand! Your purpose as a distraction has been fulfilled. You will detain me no further."

"Get your hands off me!" Alyssa gasped for air, her fingers clawed at his arm.

"As you wish."

Bergice slammed Alyssa headfirst into the ground, burying her body deep into the snow with only her legs left sticking out. Any regular person would have died instantly, since the force would have snapped their neck like a twig. Nick's heart sank into his chest.

Bergice had killed her. The damn demon murdered the only person he ever loved.

"ALYSSA!" Nick raced towards her. Bergice stepped back, almost courteously, and allowed him to pull her from the ground. He cradled her in his arms, her eyes were closed, but her breath was steady. He let a sigh of relief. She was still alive.

"She is very well trained. The impact would have crushed her skull if she didn't know how to absorb it at the exact moment," Bergice said.

"You're going to pay for that," Nick said, his other voiced echoed behind. He set her down gently and transformed his arms. "I'll tear you apart!"

He threw a blow that was easily caught. Bergice smiled dev-ilishly as he held him at bay.

"Your heart just isn't in it." Bergice tightened his grip on Nick's fist. Blood gushed out of his hand as the ice demon sank his sharp nails into the flesh. Nick roared. Trying to pull away was futile. So with all his might he delivered a kick that broke Bergice's grasp, and sent him flying.

"Hands off!" Nick said as Bergice's body slid across the snow and landed onto the surface of the frozen river. He then quickly lit fire underneath where Bergice landed, melting the ice and sinking him into the depths of the river.

That should keep him occupied for a few moments.

Alyssa opened her eyes, and reached out to him. "Nick... you're not supposed to be here," she said weakly.

Nick knelt beside her. "Don't be so stubborn. You and Matt tried your best, but it won't be enough when it comes to him." He took her cold hands into his. "It's me he wants. He'll do whatever it takes to get to me. I can't sit idly by while everyone around me gets hurt for my sake."

"Nick, please listen to me. This might be the last time we see each other. You're our only hope. I'm not saying this just because I love you, but because you are the key to saving this world. My grandpa saw it in you and I see it too. You have to live, for me."

Even in this dire situation, Nick couldn't fight back his joy. "You love me?"

"Yes, and that's why you need to get out of here."

Nick shook his head. "I'm sorry, but that's one thing I can't do."

"You wouldn't have gotten very far anyway," Bergice stood a few feet in front of Nick with his arms crossed. He looked perfectly fine. In fact, he looked even better than before. That kick would have crushed the ribs of anyone else, but all it did was slow him down for a few precious moments.

"Take it easy, Red." Nick maintained a smile as best he could. She hadn't noticed Bergice standing a few away and there was no need to alarm her. He set her head gently on the snow, and waited briefly for her to close her eyes. Rest well, he thought. It would all be over soon.

He stood and turned around to size himself up against the ice demon. The flames around his arms danced wildly. The pent-up rage was making itself known.

"Are you finished with your little love scene?" Bergice said.

"There are no known records of you at all in Garrisons because anyone who has ever laid eyes on you has died. But I think I finally understand. Like my rage, your greatest power is fear. You strike irrational fear into the hearts of your enemies, to disengage them and break them," Nick said, "I'm human, so I'm no different. However, my fear comes from something else, something rooted much deeper than anything you can pull from my mind."

"Tell me then, what do you fear?" Bergice said.

"I fear how badly this city will look when I drag your beaten carcass across it."

Bergice chuckled at first, and then his shoulders shook in a tiny fit of laughter. For a split second it appeared as if he would throw back his head and howl like a hyena. It was like he was sharing a private old joke.

"What is so damn funny?" Nick asked.

Bergice exhaled slowly, becoming serious again. Every ounce of emotion evaporated from his face. "This situation... I find it very nostalgic. I have an idea, let's make a wager. Lord Ozarael's orders were for me to kill anyone who found out about my presence here. However, since you prefer I leave your friends alone, how about a compromise? A fight to the death. Winner decides their fate."

"You've got to be joking," Nick said.

"From where I stand, you don't have much choice."

Nick had put his life on the line already. In this duel, the odds were definitely against him. But he was right, Nick didn't have a choice in the matter. Bergice was completely different from Astaroth or the Hellbeasts he had previously faced. His demeanor was calm, collected, as if he already knew the outcome of the battle. Nick on the other hand, was less than sure of himself.

Though he had become more comfortable with his abilities and progressed much faster than possible given the time frame, was it enough? Neither Matt nor Alyssa stood even a remote chance as a team, and one was a seasoned veteran while the other could wield angelic weapons. If he lost now, then he would lose everything. Everything he had learned and was trained for would be in vain. His best friend and girlfriend would die, and he would let everybody down.

The whole world depended on his success from spiraling into a cataclysm of chaos and destruction. Now wasn't the time to be gambling with millions of lives, but at the same time, Nick couldn't deny that he felt a strange pleasure about sheer magnitude of this situation. There was a certain thrill about rising up to this challenge. The burden of failing the world was miniscule in comparison to the satisfaction of winning this duel. That was what the blood lusting demon inside felt. He himself began to see this as the true test of fate. Maybe this was meant to happen. Like meeting Alyssa, perhaps meeting Bergice was fate's way of deciding if he was worthy of being a savior. He realized that if he wasn't ready to meet this obstacle head on now, then maybe he never could. Could destiny be changed? Now was the time to decide.

"Fine," Nick said, finally.

"Excellent. We will battle hand-to-hand. It is the basis of all combat!" Bergice said. "Now then, Prince Agrian, show me what you've learned!"

Nick called upon a giant ball of fire, which he hurled and followed after it, matching it in speed. He knew the amount of power behind that attack was enough to reduce a small city like Glenhaven into a flaming pile of rubble, but now wasn't the time to pull punches.

Closing in, he saw Bergice's lips move and suddenly a wall of ice appeared from thin air to his defense. A deafening crash. The collision turned his raging fireball into a black smokescreen. Nick emerged from the thick cloud that the two elements created and punched Bergice square in the chest, pushing him back. Bergice reacted by changing into ice. With a flick of his wrist, he summoned an icicle spear from the ground. Nick was surprised by the attack, but managed to catch it with both hands before it could pierce him. It took all his might to keep the spear at bay. He used his upper body strength to rip the giant spear from the ground and hurled it straight at Bergice, shattering him into pieces.

In seconds, Bergice rematerialized into his human form and delivered a kick. Nick quickly threw an arm to parry the blow. He reeled him in, charging his demon fist with an intense flame, and punched straight through him. The result melted a hole in Bergice's body. However, instead of collapsing into a puddle, the ice reformed over Nick's hand extinguishing the fire and created a paralyzing grip.

Nick tried to yank free, but he was held tightly in place. He could only watch as Bergice's icy fist shot straight at him. His head whipped back, the force was like no pain he ever experienced. He was dizzy, but managed to pull himself up. Nick wiped the blood from his mouth with a sleeve. Nick's vision was compromised by all the stars he was seeing. The beatings didn't stop there. A flurry of punches rattled his skull until he was sure he would pass out.

"I can't believe this is what I was waiting for." Bergice paused momentarily from striking him. Nick was badly bruised, only being held up by his arm frozen in place. "I expected so much more than this. Where is the spirit of the Inferno Bearer?"

"I'm just getting warmed up." Nick spat out some blood and with his free arm, blasted a stream of fire at Bergice's legs then, knocked him over with a quick leg swipe. He spun around and kicked Bergice away. Finally his hand was free!

He didn't stop there, he followed where he landed and grabbed him by the collar, holding him in place and delivering his retribution. Nick pummeled the ice demon in the face with the same ferocity as he did with Astaroth. He didn't stop until the sting of fatigue built up in his arms and by then all was left was a pile of snow.

"Your technique is unorthodox, to say the least," Bergice said, amused. He was standing behind Nick now, reformed once more. "But then again, you always had your own unique fluid style of fighting, brother."

"I told you not to call me that!" Nick shot back. Bergice's expression changed from playful to somber as if that remark had actually hurt him. How could it? Demons were emotionless beings.

"You really have no recollection, do you?" Bergice no longer seemed to be in the mood for banter. "Maybe this exhibition should come to a close." With a wave of his hand, the ice in the river rose. He manipulated the ice to shape itself stories tall, towering over the icy barricade around them as it formed into the shape of a giant monster. A sea serpent or some sort of dragon.

Whatever it was, it was not friendly.

The ethereal beast roared, blowing cold shards out of its mouth. The power of the roar pushed Nick back in the snow and covered him in a thin blanket of ice.

"Do you like my creation, Agrian?" Bergice said, proudly. "Pray you still have enough demon blood left in you to survive." He leapt high into the air; his serpent obediently lowered its head as he landed gracefully on top.

"Bergice!" Nick yelled.

"Brace yourself, Agrian!" Bergice shouted from high above. "If you cannot defeat me, then Ozarael is assuredly out of your reach!"

Nick shook off the ice and powered up his hands, his eyes burning with determination. This was it. The difference between their abilities would be revealed here. This would be the true test of rage versus fear.

"That's it, come and claim your reward!" Bergice yelled.

Nick ran across the frozen plane, and leaped into the air. As he soared, he threw his best fire blast into the ice serpent's head. The head vanquished into a thick cloud of white smoke. Nick squinted, trying to peer through the thick fog, but suddenly was engulfed by the mouth of the reformed beast. Before he could react, he was encased in a block of ice.

Nick thrashed to break free, but the ice block restricted all movement. The casing put pressure on his chest which made it difficult to breathe as well. He struggled violently against his crystalline prison, to no avail. He could feel himself losing consciousness. His eyes were drooping into slits, but before he passed out, a wave of air hit his face as the serpent spat him onto the snowy ground. The ice casing broke upon impact and Nick choked some air back into his lungs. His first instinct was to jump back to his feet, but his body would not budge. He was completely immobilized from head to toe.

Bergice strolled toward Nick, looming over him like a predator over a wounded animal. "Face it, you've lost, Agrian. Only the cold release of death awaits your companions."

Nick tried to speak, but his mouth was frozen shut.

"You're at my complete mercy," Bergice said quietly. "But despite our agreement I won't kill you. I won't even take you to Lord Ozarael. A death right now would be next to meaningless." He knelt beside him. "If you pledge your allegiance to Lord Ozarael, perhaps he will spare you. If you join us again you will see that our goals are far more aligned than that of your precious Garrison. Together we will rain chaos and destruction onto any of those who oppose us. Together we will unleash a new age of demons, where we can rule as we were meant to!"

"Over my dead body," Nick finally managed to utter once the feeling returned to his lips.

Bergice stood up and shook his head disappointment. "You don't realize it, but coming back with me will be better for everyone, including your beloved Quinn. You don't belong here with these filthy humans. You belong with us, your own kind."

Nick leaned his head forward a bit; his body was still stiff. "I never asked for any of this. What I am is my burden to bear, and I will use it because I need it to kill every single last one of you!"

Bergice's face hardened. "Those knights have brainwashed you far beyond logical reason, my brother. But perhaps the real monsters are those humans you hold so dear. Tell me, why do you give your allegiance to such a sad group? Have they accepted you for your true self?"

"They stand for something other than themselves. They fight for others—to protect people from danger. They serve a noble cause, something you know nothing about!" Nick said.

Bergice paused as he considered what Nick said. "That may be true for them, but can the same be said for you? I wonder… is that truly the force that drives you?" He circled Nick slowly. "Or is there something else perhaps that keeps the demon inside you from being unleashed?"

Nick didn't say anything now. He didn't want to give Bergice any more details or openings to get under his skin. Just then, Alyssa appeared behind Bergice. She raised her arm and swung the *Morning Star*. The spiked mace bashed Bergice in the face, caving it in and breaking it into fragments of ice.

"Speak of the devil," Bergice said as his head reformed.

"You underestimated us and so you failed to see the power of human will." Alyssa brought the flail down once more, only to have it deflected by Bergice's katana.

Nick tried to yell, but his voice was too hoarse and his cry came out as only a whisper.

Bergice dodged a kick. "The power of human will? The only thing humans have proven is their weakness. That is why you hide behind your shield of holiness and the reason for our existence to begin with! We were born from Lord Ozarael! If the first human could not find peace in solitude, how can you?"

Alyssa lunged at him with her mace, only to have her attack clash against his steel blade once more.

Bergice focused on Alyssa, his back turned to Nick, who was horrified by the new situation. "You have become quite bothersome, girl. To possess the abilities to manifest the power of angels in ways I never thought could be possible is quite a threat to our kind. I should kill you before you get the chance to grow."

"Leave her out of this," Nick growled. "This was supposed to be between you and me."

"She has insisted on becoming a thorn in our plans. I am only doing what is necessary." Bergice's katana was itching to strike, and Nick could only envision the worst possible outcome. If she continued to push Bergice, he would no doubt retaliate in the most vicious way.

Some life seeped back into Nick's body, but he still couldn't fully move. However, his voice had returned. "GET OUT OF HERE!" he screamed.

Bergice folded his arms, amused by Nick's attempt to thwart him. However, instead of running away during the distraction, she ran towards Nick.

"I'm not leaving your side, Nick," Alyssa said, much to his terror. She was falling into a trap. "If you go, then he has to take us both!"

"Forget about me!" Nick shouted again, but was no use.

"I'm sorry, I'm afraid that's impossible," Bergice said. "Agrian and I held a bit of a contest earlier. Unfortunately for him, he did not realize the severity of his decision. Now, he and the rest of you will be punished for his crimes."

"I won't give up, not on Nick," Alyssa said.

"Then shall we resume where we left off?" Bergice waited for her to strike. He was just toying with her now.

However much to Bergice's surprise, Alyssa threw Yuriel's *Morning Star* at his feet and bowed onto the icy floor before him.

"What kind of trickery is this?" Bergice asked.

"I don't stand a chance against you by myself. I knew that even before I made my first attack," Alyssa said.

"If you think I will give you pity, then you sorely miscalculated, girl."

She shook her head. "I know much about you and I know you have no ounce of compassion in your body. What I am requesting is to offer you a trade instead."

Bergice laughed. "What can a human hope to offer me? Besides, Agrian lost and forfeited the rights to your lives with it."

"You wouldn't want to kill me anyway," Alyssa said.

"And why not?"

"Through my veins flows the blood of Quinn Valentine. The binding power between her and Agrian has transcended life and death itself. That was her final wish. If you take me as your prisoner it will sever the struggle between both Nick and Agrian's conflicting souls. This is the key to bringing him back to evil. What I offer to you is the guarantee that the demons to win this war."

"If I killed you right now would that not achieve the same result?" Bergice said.

"I doubt Agrian would give his allegiance if you killed the love of his life. That would simply fuel his rage and hatred towards you, but of course you already knew that," Alyssa said.

Bergice looked both impressed and intrigued. Apparently not even the ice demon could resist her charm. "It would be worthwhile for me to hold onto the last remaining Valentine."

"Then do we have a deal?" Alyssa said.

"You realize the unspeakable pain the Crowned Princes will inflict upon you, with the only chance for your solace in death, yet you offer yourself so willingly. Do you not feel fear?"

"I have more faith in Nick than I do in fear of death." She palmed her hands on the ground and pressed her face between them. "It has been foretold. He is destined to be our savior!"

"How do you know I won't go back on my word?" Bergice said.

"You may be a demon, but I know you as a warrior with honor. You will not deny a knight their final request."

"No Alyssa!" Nick couldn't let her give up her life. It was the only reason he still had to fight.

Bergice chuckled. "I find your theatrics to be very amusing, girl. Very well, I will honor your request. Now, stand and face me."

She got to her feet. With a wave of Bergice's hand, ice encased her legs like makeshift shackles. He made a quick rotation of his hand and cut a chunk of ice on the floor below her, raising her up from the ground on a floating platform.

"Alyssa!" Nick called for her until his voice was raw, but he didn't care as long as there was even the slightest chance it could make a difference. Bergice turned to Nick, who lay stunned and motionless.

"This entire scenario reminds me of an old expression: 'Gods from the Machine.' Have you heard of it?" Bergice didn't wait for a response before he continued. "This saying hails from Fyria to describe what we are, and as you know the Fyrians are a superstitious people. They use this phrase when a sudden appearance of a supreme entity seemingly comes out of thin air to put an end to an otherwise impossibly complicated situation, right before being thrust into an even worse circumstance. Like a sudden rain washing away a raging forest fire only to bring about a flood. Or being lifted into the air by a strong draft right before your body is tossed into a crevice of spikes. 'Gods from the Machine' is an unexplainable and improbable disaster in the disguise of a miracle. The word 'machine' is as a way to illustrate this. It is a complete fabrication of your preconceived notion of traditional deities, like the Heralds. That is what we are Agrian, and what we were supposed to be. We are false gods that descended in order to bring ruin. Yet you act as if you belong to the mortal world, and challenge our beliefs for reasons I can't comprehend. I've waited years in the shadows for the day I could confront you and find out why you have chosen to walk the path of these humans. Then I found out it was all because of some girl.

"I was disappointed, to say the least, but now I see the irony of your choice. Losing your honor through combat is one thing, but letting a mortal sacrifice herself? The very mortal you swore an oath to protect. Your shame must be overwhelming.

I hope you find it in your abilities to redeem yourself before it is too late."

"I'm not through with you yet, Bergice!" Nick snarled through his gritted teeth.

"I'd rather you save the remainder of your strength and listen for a moment." Bergice pointed at Graves Tower. "I'm taking her to the underground laboratory below that tower. That is where Doctor Numerous resides and where the world will witness the completion of his new doomsday weapon. His plan will go off unhindered unless someone stops it by dawn. Save your beloved Quinn and stop Doctor Numerous before time runs out."

"What is Doctor Numerous planning?" Nick said.

"That is up to you to figure out, Agrian."

"I don't believe you."

"Of course not, but I know you'll try anyway. Remember, if you fail, then her fate is as good as sealed. She will be brought before Ozarael, and you'll never see her again." Bergice rose into the air, with Alyssa hovering on an ice block next to him. As he floated away into the sky, he left Nick with some final words. "We need to see whether or not Agrian still exists."

With that, he soared off with deafening speed in the direction of the tower. Alyssa remained standing on the hovering ice block as it moved the same way, slowly, as if Bergice was taunting him.

It was at that time Nick felt his legs functioning again. He sprang to his feet and jumped as high as he could into the air, but he caught nothing in his hands, and slammed facefirst into a pile of snow. He was too late. Alyssa was whisked away. They were long gone.

"ALYSSA!" Nick bellowed, slamming his fists into the snow creating a small fissure that shook the earth. "ALYSSA!" He punched the ground in his despair. His shoulders were heavy with sadness and he couldn't hold back the tears anymore. He kept on punching, unable to contain his frustration. He was a wreck now, sobbing loudly and yelling incoherently, but he didn't care. He fought to protect her—to protect everyone he cared about, but in the end it didn't matter at all. It wouldn't change the fact that he lost everything in one afternoon.

14

THE UNDERGROUND LABYRINTH

Without Bergice to influence the weather the temperature returned to normal. The ice had almost all melted by now, leaving the river overflowing its banks and giant puddles everywhere.

Nick heard a couple of splashes and turned to find his best friend, wobbling over. Matt was in terrible condition, as if almost to the brink of death. He was battered and bloody.

"What just happened? Why is he taking Alyssa to Graves Tower?"

"He took her…" Nick said quietly, grabbing fistfuls of slush harshly in his hands. "He took her, and they're going to kill her…"

"We have to get her back!" Matt said.

Nick didn't bother to wipe his eyes; the cold winds had already dried the tears to crust on his cheeks. He kept his back turned to Matt, afraid to see the disappointment. "It doesn't matter, we've already lost. There's nothing else we can do."

"What do you mean there's nothing we can do? You heard what he said. We have until dawn before the shield completely disappears! That only gives us a few hours to act!"

"Don't you get it?" Nick put his hands over his face, hiding in the agony he felt. "Even if we make it there, it wouldn't matter. We can't stop him. She's as good as dead." Hearing the words from his own mouth seemed to make the futility of their efforts more real.

Matt hobbled over and grabbed Nick by his shirt collar. "Snap out of it, Nick!" He shook him hard. "Stop feeling sorry for yourself and look at the bigger picture! Alyssa was taken, and you're just going to sit back and do nothing?"

"What else can I do? There's no one to help us. It's happening all over again…just like with Susan."

"That's why we got to take matters into our own hands!" Matt winced at the pain from his wounds and dropped Nick back onto his knees.

"If only Peter was here," Nick said.

"But he's not. None of them are. Gabriel, Lucius, and Bartholomew aren't coming. Everything is riding on us! If we don't try now, then she'll *definitely* die! Is that what you want? You live with regret over what happened to Susan, but now you have a chance to make sure it doesn't happen again! Are you just going to sit there and do nothing?" Matt said.

Was he really that weak? To let something stop him from saving the girl he was madly in love with, the girl he swore to protect? He remembered once telling her that he'd be with her no matter what, that nothing could ever stop them from being together. Was all that just a lie? No, he would be damned if he would wallow in his own self-pity. Not Nick Emberson. Not this time. Not ever again.

"You're right." Nick pulled himself to his feet. "Bergice may have won the battle, but this is far from over. We're going to get her back."

"That's sounds like the Nick I remember!" Matt winced at the pain again. "Help me get bandaged up and we'll be on our way."

"Right. And we need a plan. We may not have an army of archangels to help us, but we still have three knights on standby. Let's regroup and draw up the battle plans."

Back at the loft, the others were awaiting their return. Looks of confusion and fear were upon their faces as the party of three was now just two.

"What happened out there?" Garreth said.

"Where's Alyssa?" Daniel said.

Nick and Matt retold the story as best they could.

"I can't believe you let this happen!" Paul grabbed Nick and slammed him against the wall. "You idiotic demon! We let you go on your way for a few hours and now you've sentenced Peter's granddaughter to death!" He curled his hand into a fist, ready to punch him.

"I don't think fighting each other is going to solve anything right now. If Alyssa were here, she'd be angry for making a colossal waste of time," Garreth said. "And I'd appreciate it if you guys didn't fly off the handle so often. Things end up broken."

Nick pushed Paul away. "You think I wanted this to happen? I tried my best!" He pointed to Matt, who was now wrapped in bandages from the waist down. "*He* tried his best!

How were we supposed to know Bergice would show up? He was supposed to be in Fyria!"

Matt nodded furiously behind him. "It's true. The guy just came out of thin air and took us all down. We never had a chance. He made it look like child's play. Thanks to Alyssa, Nick isn't in the custody of the princes. At least this way, they don't hold all the cards."

"She sacrificed herself to save me…to save the both of us," Nick said sadly.

"A pointless gesture if you think about it." Paul glowered at Nick with the utmost contempt. "Because of you the only person I could remotely tolerate around here is in the clutches of a demon prince. All because you couldn't listen to simple orders!"

Nick couldn't get too mad by the insults because deep down he knew Paul was at least partially right. If he was half the demon he was meant to be, he'd have the strength to defeat Bergice and stop Doctor Numerous. Then they wouldn't be in this position. She would have been sitting with them, perhaps sharing a warm meal, instead of being taken away as a hostage. Now that Doctor Numerous had her in his clutches, who knew what the maniac planned on doing to her?

"Look, it's too late to change what has happened, but we can still help her somehow. We have to," Nick said. "Bergice said we had until dawn before they were transporting her back to Ozarael. They're waiting until the time of launch for some secret weapon that Doctor Numerous has been working on. He didn't give much detail to what it was, but he said she would be in the laboratory back at Garreth's tower. He's giving me a chance to save her."

"The word of a demon is worth nothing. We go there like you say, and I guarantee we'll be sealing ourselves in a concrete tomb," Paul said.

"It's an obvious trap, but at this point we don't have a choice," Matt said.

"No, Bergice isn't like that. He's…he's different than most demons," Nick said.

"Damn, so they must have discovered the secret underneath the building," Garreth sighed.

"What secret?" Daniel scratched his head.

"I had my tower constructed differently than other buildings in Hyperion. It has a research facility, a communications center, a training room, and a laboratory that is a small scaled replica of Fyria's Garrison."

"Even if you shrank a Garrison fifty times, there would be no room to house it within the confines of that tower of yours," Paul said.

"It's underneath the tower," Garreth said.

"I thought you hated the place. Why would you want any reminders of your past?" Matt said.

"Being a whitesmith was a significant part of my life. Building a miniature version of it was the only way to come to terms with my departure," Garreth said. "That was years ago. I have kept most of my old Garrison research there. Compiled through the years, it's more than enough information to give the Crowned Princes a definitive edge."

"Why would he choose Hyperion in particular? According to your research, Doctor Numerous had been seen in several cities, but he always returned to this one. What would be his reasoning?" Nick said.

"The Holy Shield is my guess," Garreth said. "That would explain why he would want to black out this city. As the central hub to all other shields, taking out this one would cause all the others to disappear."

"Then it's up to us to stop them as soon as we can," Daniel said.

"It is easier said than done. Now that they have Peter's granddaughter, they know we'll stop at nothing to save her. We're completely at their mercy," Paul said.

Daniel raised his hand. "Did you all forget there's an impenetrable layer of ice? Not even the fires of Agrian can melt through to the tower fast enough."

"That is why we can't take him head on. We use our training and knowledge to find another option. There has to be a way around this, as knights we're supposed to find solutions to every problem," Nick said. Matt looked at him and nodded with a knowing smile.

"What makes you think you're coming with us Cunningham?" Paul said.

Matt's face dropped. "Why not? You're not the boss of me, Paul!"

"Peter gave me authority in his absence. Do as I say or you'll give me no choice but to physically enforce it."

"Why don't you just try? I want to save her as much as you guys do! Besides, I have to pay Bergice back for what he did to me!" Matt said.

"I'm sorry Matt, but he's right. You can't come this time," Nick said.

"In your condition, you'll only end up only being a liability," Paul said. "And if you happen to get into trouble, I don't want to have to go saving you too. I don't want anything to detract me from our main priority."

"Unfortunately, I agree with them," Garreth said.

Daniel nodded as well.

"So that's the majority vote, huh? Fine then I'll stay behind." Matt folded his arms. "What are you all going to do about Bergice though? We were all powerless against him. Even when we did, no attack fazed him. He's like a walking machine of destruction."

"Unfortunately, a demon of that caliber is much too advanced for me," Paul said. "We resealed the shield so there should be minimal demon threats within the tower. We also outnumber him two to one. Assuming everyone here is competently trained, I see little room for error."

"So what, we rush the place, find and rescue her, and then move out as quickly as possible?" Nick asked.

"Precisely," Paul said. "I assume those instructions are easy enough to follow for you?"

Nick shot him a dirty look. "How can we do that if we can't even get in the building?"

"I agree that's no good." Garreth fixed his glasses. He was looking out the window and to his tower. "There are security cameras all over the first floor. It's much too risky."

"Prior to betraying us, Doctor Numerous was part of the Wisdom Unit, which meant he displayed a low combat ability. That compounded with the fact that he has aged quite a bit since he had any formal training means that he has gone over his peak," Paul said. "If there is a confrontation, I'm sure it can easily be dealt with it."

"Remember, he's also an Infernal now," Matt said. "Time is on his side. He must have changed significantly over the years to rise so quickly."

"I doubt it. He's just an alchemist," Paul said.

"None of that matters if there's no chance for you guys to get to him through that ice," Matt said.

"Fortunately, I already have a solution to that problem," Garreth said.

"What—have you got shovels for us dig our way through?" Paul retorted.

"No, there's a passage at the bottom of my building. I created it as an escape route in case of emergencies. We should be able to get in through the sewers," Garreth said.

"If they knew about your secret laboratory, then the sewers will be trapped too," Daniel said.

"No one but me knows about that passage," Garreth said.

"That's all well and good, but since Paul's plan is out the window, what do we actually do when we get inside?" Nick asked.

"Like I was saying, my company has a secret basement level, but I closed it down after I became too busy with managing the Holy Shield. Once we get access, we'll be at the entrance of the labyrinth," Garreth said.

"Labyrinth?" Paul said.

"I created it specifically as a defense mechanism against trespassers. Don't worry, I have memorized the pathways to get to the laboratory and according to what Bergice said, that is where Doctor Numerous is currently holding Alyssa," Garreth said.

"Very good. Now all we need is to better equip ourselves," Paul said. "Unfortunately we're not in Glenhaven and don't have access to personal belongings. However, I did prepare a small arsenal in the event a situation arose."

He went to the other room and came back lugging two giant cases. He opened the lids to reveal an assortment of tactical equipment and weapons.

Nick browsed through the collection for the upcoming mission and was finding it difficult to put any of it to use. Garreth sifted through the sizes to find an appropriate knight uniform.

Paul and Daniel had brought their own custom combat uniforms. The Garrison battle suits they had on bore a very similar design to Nick's own coat, but that was because he had based it on their template. Instead of being pure black like his, they were completely white, with silver trim and intricate gold shoulder pauldrons. They also wore standard leg straps and a belt with pouches and holsters to carry assorted weapons. Paul's suit was slightly different than the one Daniel was wearing in that it had a golden feather crest on the right breast of the jacket, symbolizing his experience. Nick ultimately decided to change into fresh clothes and replace his worn out boots.

By the time he got to the weapons rack Paul had brought, he felt completely lost. There were too many choices available, both extravagant and seemingly unnecessary. Battle axes, broadswords, whips, flails, knives, spears and just about any other melee weapon were represented. Most were too high of a risk to use effectively and quite bulky to take on a simple rescue mission.

"I know it's been a while for both of you, but choose equipment that bests suit this type of mission." Daniel stuffed some knives and holy water into his pouches. "Usually less is better, but I try to prepare for every situation."

"I'll stick with my katana. The walls of the labyrinth don't permit the use of using such colossal weapons," Garreth said.

Nick was compelled to grab one of each, but decided against it. He came to the conclusion that he didn't need a sword or gun or any weapon at all. Since he wasn't particularly well versed in any of them, trying to fight with them now would be a terrible decision. He realized he should stick to what he had spent years cultivating, and that was close combat with his hands. He also wanted to be able to fight freely when he transformed, and any other excess armor like greaves would be out of the question due to the flames he produced.

"I'll just use what Agrian was born to fight with." Nick made his hands into fists.

"Wait, what do we do if we cross paths with Bergice?" Daniel asked.

They stood silently around in a circle. They hadn't discussed in detail the possibility of that occurrence just yet. Nick hoped they wouldn't have to talk about the ice demon anymore. He did not want to admit it, but he was still rattled by the last encounter. Unlike Astaroth, whom he was able to decimate with some effort, Bergice was still a wildcard when it came to his true potential. However, he had already delivered him a humiliating defeat. Even with a fourth person, the chances of besting the ice demon in a fight were very low.

"There's nothing we can do to prepare for him. Combat varies with the times, but the strategy has always been the same. Breaking your opponent down is half physical and half mental. Our training is all we can rely on," Garreth said.

"I've heard stories about Bergice. His ability to read his enemies is incredible. He is a master at preying on the fears of his opponents through his presence alone," Paul said.

"All we can do is hope we don't run into him," Garreth said.

"What if we can't help it? What if Bergice gets hold of one of us and we can't escape?" Daniel said shakily. He was looking quite concerned; his voice was cracking.

Nick couldn't blame him. The young knight had never been sent into true battle. The only time he had a taste of demons was when he fought Nick and lost miserably. The idea of meeting another Crowned Prince in battle must have been especially nerve wracking.

"The chance we do meet Bergice means the possibility of death is imminent. However, this has always been the case for knights and demons. We will engage the demon and if death comes knocking at the door, then we will welcome him for we tried our best. This is why we were created and the reason we continue to fight. If any of you decide this is too much to handle, feel free to stay put. I could do without cowards on this mission," Paul said.

Garreth nodded. "I couldn't have said it better myself. Despite no longer being affiliated with any Garrison, I am still a knight."

Nick turned to Daniel. "Don't think so much, it's the only way to keep your fears from getting the best of you."

Daniel nodded and swallowed hard. "I'll be fine."

"Right now, Alyssa is our main priority. Once we save her, we rendezvous back to my place through the same route we took to get into the tower. As long as we work together, and quickly we should have more than sufficient time. However, if anything happens and it should take longer or we should happen to come across a hypothetical scenario, then I believe it should be every man for himself," Garreth said.

They all nodded.

"Then if everyone is settled, let's move out." Garreth had slung a brown twin corded rope over his shoulder.

Nick and the others followed and took the elevator of his loft to the ground level floor. Garreth folded back the Pailean rug to reveal a large manhole. He lifted the lid as Matt securely fastened the corded rope to a hook on one of the building support beams.

"Good luck, may the Heralds watch over you all," Matt said.

Garreth tossed the rope into the darkness and one by one they slid a hundred feet to the sewer floor. Nick lit his hands to form a makeshift lantern, which revealed the one-way tunnel. Soon they were on their way to the underground secret entrance.

As they trekked deeper, the water was significantly deeper than they'd expected, but Nick knew it was due to the melted snow that recently washed down the drain. The high level created resistance in their strides and slowed their movement, but thankfully they didn't have to go far. After sloshing around the slimy green water for some time, Daniel stopped dead in his tracks.

"What's wrong?" Garreth asked.

"Is it just me, or does the water level seem to be rising?" Daniel said.

He was right. The water was indeed very high now. Within seconds it had reached to his upper chest with no signs of dropping. To avoid extinguishing his flames he raised his arms over his head.

"They must know we're here," Paul said. "At this rate, they probably hope to drown us like dogs!"

Nick turned to Garreth. "How much further do we have? I can't keep this up when the water gets too high."

"We're almost there. Don't worry," Garreth said. Suddenly there was a crash and a tidal wave of rushing water thundered toward them.

"Not soon enough. Switch to Luxilight," Paul said.

Daniel and Garreth gathered light into their hands just as the wave hit. Nick closed his eyes and braced for the impact as the water washed away the flames from his arms, nearly sweeping him off his feet. Though the Garrison boots provided excellent grip on all surfaces, even slimy ones, it wasn't enough. He felt himself being carried by the current, flipping around in all directions. However, he swam furiously in the dark tunnel, until his head found the ceiling with a thud. A narrow gap of space between the top of the tunnel and the water left a space to breathe. As long as he kept himself afloat and his mouth facing upwards.

"Nick where are you?" Daniel called.

Nick faced the direction of the sound. Three orbs of light lit the murky sewer depths. They were using the Luxilight technique as a guiding signal! He swam against the unrelenting current toward the light and was eventually pulled through a manhole by Daniel. Nick gagged and spit out large amounts of dirty water, clearing his system. He glanced around the room and found nothing but a single ladder at the far end.

"Now aren't you glad we decided to travel by sewers?" Daniel said.

Nick ran his hands through his dripping wet hair. "Wonderful, considering I almost drowned."

"Well, at least this proves Bergice isn't around to influence the area anymore. The increased water level means he's far from here," Daniel said.

"Excellent, which means all we have to worry about is Doctor Numerous. Let's get going then, I'm not interested in standing around," Paul said.

"Just a second. There's something I have to tell you guys before we proceed," Garreth said. "We're at the entrance of the labyrinth. Once we venture into the next room, there's no turning back until we get Alyssa. So it is important that you all know that when I created the labyrinth, I also kept in mind that some people might stumble upon it. What I mean is that I've taken measures to protect my secrets."

"What are you saying?" Daniel said.

"Don't tell me, your maze is laced with deadly traps?" Paul said.

"The labyrinth is a trap in itself, but Doctor Numerous has been down here and found a way to bypass it right under my nose, so now I don't know what we have to expect. If he's made any changes I don't think they will be very pleasant. It's best for us to stick together at all times," Garreth said.

"Agreed," Nick said.

They ascended the ladder to the basement level. They stuck close together as they made their way down a long hall. In this part of building there were no fancy marble floors and beautiful decor, everything here was stone, a concrete labyrinth. Torches scattered along the top of the stone walls, mirroring each other on both sides and seemed to be duplicated over and over again down the endless pathway. The effect was jarring, and created a sense of confusion and isolation. They walked along the passage in pairs. All at once, the halls began to shake with the distinct echo of rocks sliding against each other in the distance.

"An earthquake?" Daniel said timidly. He crouched in a fetal position.

"Get up, you're embarrassing yourself." Paul jerked him up.

"Should we be worried by that?" Nick pushed himself against a wall.

"No, it is a defense mechanism I designed for the labyrinth. It is an automatic shuffle that activates every once in a while. The halls turn and slide in order to change paths and confuse people," Garreth said.

"You did a very good job," Daniel said.

"What would possess you into thinking this shambles of a fake Garrison would need this much security?" Paul said.

"Because this is where the Holy Shield generator is located," Garreth said.

"You're telling me the world's most powerful demon deterrent is housed here? You lie. The protective shield is projected through a series of satellites," Paul said.

"That is only partially true. Every major city in the world has a Holy Shield generator, but the central one remains here in Hyperion. The Holy Shield relays messages to satellites which then feed its power into smaller receptors in other countries around the world. I designed it this way to ensure that Hyperion remain the epicenter of the world," Garreth said.

"So now the reason for Doctor Numerous choosing to break in here doesn't seem so strange anymore. You don't think he plans to try and steal it?" Nick said.

"That was my guess exactly. Or it seems to me that he would want to destroy it in order to allow demons to roam freely through our cities," Paul said.

"It'll be much easier than going city to city and creating small leaks," Daniel said.

"Then this begs the question of why he hasn't done it yet," Garreth said.

They glanced at each other as if to find the answer, but each conclusion seemed to make less and less sense. Instead of dwelling on it, they followed Garreth along the corridor, which then split in the middle to three more hallways. They took the leftmost path. However the halls became too constrictive and unable to fit two full-grown men walking side by side anymore, forcing them to move down in a straight line.

"Did you hear that?" Garreth drew his katana. "Something is up ahead."

"It sounded like an animal. It could be another Hellbeast," Paul said.

"We can't fight like this, not if we're lined up like lambs to slaughter," Daniel said.

"I know my way, I'll check it out myself." Garreth rushed ahead.

"Daniel, you're the closest. Follow him just in case," Nick said. The baby-faced knight nodded and disappeared down the hall.

A few minutes passed and Paul turned to Nick. "How long has it been since we entered?"

After coming to the same realization, Nick bolted after Daniel with Paul following closely. By the time they made it back to the fork, it was too late. He had only a second to catch a glimpse of the young knight, just as the walls moved in and the maze shifted and cut them off. Now they were separated.

In an instant, they had lost their guide through the labyrinth as well as half their team.

15

A SPECTER'S RIDDLES

Nick tapped on the wall with his fist. The sounds echoed throughout the labyrinth. "The walls aren't very thick. I think I can break through."

"We can't just burst through like a couple of maniacs. It'll give away our position and we'll lose all tactical advantage. If Doctor Numerous gets wind of our location then the mission will be a complete failure," Paul said.

"What else can we do?" Nick said.

"I trust that Garreth and Daniel possess the minimal skills to survive without us for a while. The only thing we can do now is continue to push forward. We don't have a guide, but we'll make due," Paul said.

He took one of the torches that dimly lit the halls and walked forward with Nick close behind. They passed several hallways, keeping quiet and on constant alert to their surroundings.

After a series of twists and turns however, a question formed in Nick's mind. Now that they were alone it seemed the best time to ask. "Have you ever met Bergice in person?"

"No. If I did I doubt I would have lived to tell the tale. I've only heard stories about him. None of which were pleasant," Paul said.

"It was strange, he kept calling me brother...I can't put my finger on it, but I felt something there. It's like we had a connection, and for a brief moment I understood where he was coming from," Nick said.

"Peter didn't tell you anything about Bergice?"

Nick shook his head.

"Truth is, no one knows much about the Crowned Princes. How they operate is still a mystery. Any information worth knowing about them was recorded in books years ago by historians during their reign, but most of them have disappeared with the ages. As you know, you used to be the leader of the many legions of demons, but things changed when you decided to help out humanity. Bergice, was known as one of the demons with whom Agrian shared the closest bond. They were so close they considered each other brothers. However, interests were divided when you met Quinn, and your newfound love for the human race raised the conflict that sparked the Great War," Paul said.

Nick had always been told that his strength at peak level was phenomenal, but his encounter earlier seemed to prove otherwise. As for being almost like a brother to Bergice, is that why he let him go? Could there have been some lingering sentiments ? No, there couldn't have been. Otherwise, why would he lead him into an obvious trap and use Alyssa as a pawn? Bergice was no different from any demon he'd read or heard about thus far; he was only interested in trying to harm him.

"Your betrayal and threat to their plans is why you're the most hunted demon on their list," Paul said. "You possess much strength, so much that it was said that only the mightiest archangel at the time, Clarion the Silver Knight could match your true power."

Clarion the Silver Knight was one of the first people Nick was taught about when he joined the Garrison. Clarion served with Sir Marcus and played a pivotal role in saving the world. He was a legend among the holy knights and the Garrisons, revered in the pages of history and immortalized through stories for his great wisdom and strength.

"Then why couldn't I defeat him?" Nick asked.

Paul's eyebrows furrowed. "As the Lord of Fear, he has the uncanny ability to strike fear into the hearts of his enemies. Perhaps this is what caused you to falter."

Was that it? He'd definitely felt a connection with Bergice earlier, one that made him question his position as savior of the world. Despite how enraged he had become, there was no way he could have had a chance. Was he holding back subconsciously because of some sentiments he had in the past? If it was, he had to push those feelings out. He wouldn't make the same mistake twice. And he certainly wouldn't let the demon in the past control his chance for a future.

"I guess you're right. It won't happen next time."

"There's a demon buried inside you, which means you'll always be tempted to sway off the path of good. At the same time, you're also human and have the ability to make the choice. Demons and humans have never been able to coexist peacefully together, and I doubt it'll ever change. Agrian was the exception," Paul said.

Nick nodded. "But I—"

Paul stopped suddenly, alert now, his hand on his sword. "Did you hear that?"

"What is it?" Nick whispered. He had been so busy talking that he had momentarily forgotten about the mission. His ears perked, listening hard as he gazed down the dark hall.

"I hear something over there, coming out of the wall." Paul pointed to the right.

Sounds were definitely coming through the other side of the walls as well.

"Could it be Garreth and Daniel?" Nick said. A short pause, and then more muffled sounds—like a conversation on the other side.

Paul felt around the wall and then one opposite of it. "These walls are composed of different material. I think there's a hidden room behind it." He groped around the stones, pushing them individually. Something clicked. The wall was actually camouflaged panel! It slid to the side and revealed a closed door.

A tickle ran down Nick's spine. "Wait, I'm getting a similar feeling from right before I met Astaroth and Bergice. Whatever is behind the room isn't friendly."

"A new demon threat? It could be Doctor Numerous," Paul said.

It wasn't Bergice. No, the vibe was different, but at the same time it was familiar. It had to be another demon. It was hard to tell because the voices were faint, but some weird energy was emanating from that room. He had to satisfy his curiosity and find out what it was.

"I can't tell," Nick said.

"How can you be sure it's not Bergice?" Paul stared warily at the door.

"The 'presence' is different," Nick said.

"We have an obligation to deal with this situation now," Paul said.

Nick tiptoed to the door with Paul so close they kept bumping into each other. Paul twisted the knob on the door slowly. They glanced quickly around the area, paranoid at the thought of something suddenly popping out from the shadows.

Much to their surprise, the room was nothing special. It was a condensed version of the Garrison library. The room was decorated with bookcases and cabinets with few furniture pieces for sitting and lounging about. Papers were scattered around a large desk in the center of the room. A chair behind it had been flipped on its side. Strangely, there was nobody in sight. Perhaps the voices they heard were nothing more than a heightened paranoia. However, that did not explain why Nick felt that familiar tingling sensation in his body.

"I don't see anything out of the ordinary, aside from it being messy. Graves must have made this into a private study." Paul picked up a stack of papers, sifting through them. "Though he claims he hasn't been down here in ages, someone must have found this room and made no subtle attempt to hide that they were searching for a particular document."

"This looks like a good clue."

Nick grabbed the folder splayed open on the desk and flipped to the front page that held the words "Soul Eater Project" scrawled across the center. As he turned the pages he saw multiple graphs and images of the Dolere Flos and the blueprints of Graves Tower. There were even maps of the Glenhaven region. He checked the log dates—all of this had been planned and calculated six years ago.

"Nicholas, come take a look at this," Paul said. Nick looked up to see Paul holding vials of blue liquid.

"What is that?" Nick said.

"It's Doctor Numerous' plan. He's calling it 'Soul Eater.' Apparently he's run quite a few tests already." Paul showed Nick the test tubes that were each labeled "Soul Eater" with numerical numbers labeled next to them.

"What could this possibly be?" Nick held up a vial to look closely.

"How should I know? I'm a warrior, not a scientist," Paul said.

"It's been recorded in these files which date back about six years ago. Sound familiar?"

"That's around the same time Doctor Numerous went rogue and was banished from Fyria's Garrison," Paul said.

"Exactly."

Paul snatched the packet of papers that Nick was looking through and flashed it in front of Nick. Paul stuffed them into his coat pockets. "This may not mean anything to us right now, but if it's excerpts from this journal he's been keeping then it's bound to be worth something to someone else. Whatever this 'Soul Eater Project' is, it's been years in the making and we can't afford to let it fall into the wrong hands."

A small piece of paper fluttered to the ground in front of them. They looked up simultaneously to find a giant rat-like man with large red eyes gazing down at them, and hissing menacingly. It was wearing a white coat over his dark brown fur. It dashed at them with its fangs bared, ready to kill. It was the demon Nick sensed!

Nick and Paul jumped back as the rat dove at them. It missed and hit the floor, but the demon had managed to whip its tail after, narrowly hitting Paul, but catching Nick in the chest. Nick crashed backward into a bookshelf. The entire section of tumbled down upon him.

Paul pulled out his sword and swung viciously at the demon. His metal blade clashed with the demon's fangs, and they were locked in battle of strength. However, Paul possessed the superior might. He pushed the rat demon backwards, and struck its claws with the blade. The rodent's arm thudded to the ground.

The rat demon recoiled with a squeal and fell on the floor. It thrashed about, knocking down the rest of the bookshelves. It settled in a corner after a while, licking to its wound.

Paul took the opportunity to close in on the demon with his sword pointed at its throat. "Well, well what do we have here? Vermeek, I had thought a demon as pitiful as you would have been long dead by now."

"Paul Evans! I knew waiting for Lord Bergice to return was a foolish mistake!" Vermeek hissed.

Nick was back on his feet now. He went to stand next to Paul, blocking the exit to the room.

"What exactly are you doing here?" Paul said.

"Business that does not concern you humans!" Vermeek snarled.

"I took your arm just now, but I can take much more if you anger me." Paul stabbed the demon in the shoulder and twisted the blade, causing it to screech in pain.

"You can torture me all you like, but there's nothing you can do to me that I will make me betray Doctor Numerous! I will never talk!" Vermeek said.

"Is that so? Maybe you have forgotten what Luxilight feels like?" Paul charged a glowing ball of light in his palm.

"Wait a second, Paul. Let's not go overboard and end up killing our only source of information. He came to this room to gather the files pertaining to 'Soul Eater Project.' I doubt Doctor Numerous would be too thrilled if he finds that his previous research was destroyed," Nick said.

Nick swept the vials of test tubes onto the floor. They broke on impact. The blue contents seeped into a nearby drain. The demon scrunched against the wall, eyes wide. Through his feral visage, Nick could tell that it was angering him.

"I will not break so easily," Vermeek said.

"Fine. Paul, give me the files," Nick said.

Paul pulled the contents of the Soul Eater Project out of his pocket and slapped them into Nick's hand. Nick lit the opposite arm on fire and moved it dangerously close to the documents.

"Fire? Who are you?" Vermeek said.

"Stop trying to change the topic, Vermeek. No more games. I know you were keen on getting this information, so there's no use in trying to pretend. We're running low on time and I'm not a very patient man." Nick guided his fiery hand closer and closer to the files.

"Wait, stop!" Vermeek said at the last second. "I'll tell you everything you need to know."

"Good choice." Nick tossed the files back to Paul for safekeeping.

"How are you able to control fire like that? I've never seen a human capable of controlling the elements," Vermeek said.

"You're talking to Agrian, the Prince of Rage," Paul said.

Vermeek's eyes widened. "A Crowned Prince? You're just a boy!"

Nick stepped closer, staring darkly at the man. "It doesn't matter who I am, but what I need from you is information."

"I work for Doctor Numerous as his assistant, nothing more. I was never privy to any of the inner workings of his plans like Astaroth. What I do know is that he has long since completed the Soul Eater, and only requires the use of his special notes to put on the final touches."

"He's holding a friend of mine in the laboratory. Take us there and you are free to go. Do we have a deal?" Nick said.

"Lord Agrian, if you're trying to rescue the girl he has imprisoned then I suggest you give up. Even if you manage to get past the obstacle Doctor Numerous has placed, the odds of you surviving an encounter with an Infernal are very slim," Vermeek said.

"We'll take our chances, rat. Now what other obstacle has Numerous set to stop us? Was this maze not enough of a challenge?" Paul said.

Vermeek was nervously shaking on the floor and clutching the stub of his arm. "There's a powerful demon he's summoned at the end. Far more powerful than the average one of its type, it has an unrelenting thirst for blood."

"There is no demon alive that cannot be defeated by my blade," Paul said.

Vermeek shook his head. "Even a master knight like you cannot hope to defeat this demon alone, Paul Evans. It will require more than the brawn of the Garrison. That being said, I will accept your offer and take you to the girl."

"A demon's word means next to nothing," Paul said.

"This is our best choice. Having a guide would be better than wandering aimlessly around this labyrinth," Nick said.

Paul sighed. "You better hope you're right about this, Nicholas."

He grabbed Vermeek by the arm and yanked him to his feet. Paul wrapped his arm around the rodent and pressed the sharp edge of his blade to the demon's furry neck. They left with Paul slowly escorting the demon out. Once back into the labyrinth, he kicked Vermeek in the back, holding his sword so the tip of the blade rested on his coat.

"Walk. You're leading the way. If you try anything stupid, you die." Paul jabbed him in the back, careful not to actually impale him.

"A-as you wish," Vermeek said obediently. Nick felt a bit badly for the treating him so harshly, since the demon was already wounded, but it was the only way to ensure that it wouldn't try to escape.

The plan now was to use Vermeek as the access for the demon barrier that Doctor Numerous had said was impenetrable. And with Paul's already extensive knowledge on the blueprint of the area, it was absolutely failsafe, just as long as the rat man stayed true to his word. Also, having a hostage put them at a much needed advantage.

"You're lucky you're too pathetic to kill. If Nicholas wasn't so weak I would have slit your throat the moment you tried to speak," Paul said as they walked through the dark corridors.

"Contrary to your beliefs, Paul Evans, demons are far more crafty than you humans moonlighting as holy beings," Vermeek hissed. "Even with two full scale wars, we have survived total eradication, our resilience knows no bounds. One of our most powerful demons also hails from your Garrisons! You are the pathetic ones!"

They bickered between themselves as Nick trailed behind, keeping his attention elsewhere. He thought of Alyssa and how it would feel to hold her in his arms once more, to experience the warmth he had been craving. How were they treating her in the laboratory? Even if they managed to make it to the end, could he trust Bergice to keep his word? A thought struck Nick, and he interjected their argument with a new question.

"Vermeek, where has Bergice gone? He said he would to be here at the stroke of dawn for the project launch."

"When Doctor Numerous designed the Soul Eater, he did it with the intention of impressing the Crowned Princes. It succeeded in intriguing Lord Ozarael, but the demon king sent Lord Bergice as his extension to monitor the progress of experiment and report back the findings. I presume Lord Bergice has gone back to deliver the last report before it launches," Vermeek said.

"It feels like we've been down here for hours. How much farther till we reach the end?" Nick said.

"You'd better not be leading us in circles," Paul said.

"We are almost there," Vermeek promised.

"What exactly is Doctor Numerous' power as an Infernal?" Nick said. "There are four Infernals: Famine, Pestilence, War, and Death, but I haven't found a single clear answer."

"He is known as the Infernal of Pestilence. Though I cannot say what his abilities are because he refuses to display any of his powers, unless provoked in combat. The only hint of an Infernal's given powers is related to their namesake," Vermeek said.

"Pestilence? Nicholas, are you thinking what I'm thinking?" Paul said.

"The Dolere Flos. It explains why he would be obsessed with poison plants, but why would he need to grow so many for all these years? What do they have to do with the Soul Eater Project?"

Paul nodded. "Something tells me we'll find out soon enough. First thing's first, our task is dealing with the 'trap' he's laid out for us at the end of all of this."

"What type of demon are we facing?" Nick said.

"Have you ever heard of the Specter?" Vermeek said.

"A Specter?" Paul said suspiciously.

"They are demon guards. Highly resilient and very powerful. Doctor Numerous has placed one at the entrance of the lab and his experiments. The only way to bypass it would be to answer a riddle. It acts as a failsafe should any intruders stumble upon his research."

"I know what a Specter is," Paul said with mild annoyance, as if suggesting otherwise offended him. "But I didn't know Doctor Numerous had the ability to summon one."

"It is another ability reserved for the Infernals," Vermeek said.

"This is going to mean more trouble for us," Nick said.

"Are you up to it? I've never faced a Specter before without a group of at least ten men," Paul said.

"Maybe there are alternatives to brute force. Are you good at riddles?" Nick said.

Nick knew a little about Specters. They were different than most demons in that they were intangible creatures used by higher ranked demons to guard their valuables and prisons. These Specters were designed to ask difficult riddles that were impossible to solve without knowing the answer beforehand. If answered correctly, they would grant safe passage. However, an incorrect answer, then they would manifest themself physically and devour their prey as punishment.

"I am many things: a tactician, a genius combatant, but the one thing I am not is a riddle master," Paul said.

Nick and Paul followed Vermeek closely. After another series of twists and turns, he stopped in front of double doors at the end of the labyrinth. However here, Vermeek stood his ground.

"Why are you stopping now?" Paul demanded. "If you're trying to set us up…"

A set-up would be hard to spring on Nick as he was on full alert mode now.

"According to our agreement, this is as far as I will take you. After this room you will be at the entrance of the main laboratory. Up ahead and behind those doors is the girl you seek," Vermeek said.

"That was the deal," Nick said.

"However, I am also seeking Doctor Numerous. Perhaps, I will go with you the rest of the way," Vermeek said.

Behind the steel doors an incredibly foul stench hung in the air; it, attacked their senses. Nick twisted his face in disgust. Paul pinched his nose and cupped his hand over his mouth. Vermeek happily sucked the air up his nostrils.

Paul turned to Nick. "Ugh, what is that smell?"

"The refuse from the deceased left by the Specter," Vermeek said with delight.

The floor crunched as Nick walked past the tattered and discolored colors of former Garrison member uniforms. Curiosity took the better of him and he looked down to see the dead and rotten bodies of his allies. The odd floor feeling was due to being covered in their bones, and from the looks of it, they had been there for some time now.

"Our brethren…used as fodder for this monster." Paul said.

It was strange, but after the initial shock to his senses, the stench no longer affected him. In fact, now that Nick had time to let it settle in, it started to give off a distinct aroma. Perhaps it was the demon inside him acting as a buffer, dulling his innate human repulsion.

However, seeing dead people spread before him was another story. Memories from the Den of Pain came back to him, and he felt an intense despair like he had never before. It was earthshattering to know that these many fallen soldiers devoted their lives to protecting their homeland, and now they were lying in heaps underground like those hounds. Like dead dogs. They deserved better than this.

One particular corpse stood out, looking more recent than the others. The clothing wasn't like the others: it wore a red blazer, meant for a smaller framed body—a woman's. Nick could just barely make out the nametag that read "Abigail," otherwise known as Garreth's secretary. It was painful to see how an innocent woman was mutilated and killed for merely being at the wrong place at the wrong time. She, like the rest of them must have had feelings of pure terror permanently stuck on their faces right until the end. This Specter was much more dangerous than he thought, perhaps more so than Astaroth.

"The Specter did all this?" Nick murmured.

"Yes, my lord. Doctor Numerous insisted the Specter be properly nourished in order to be combat-ready for you," Vermeek said. "He had been using prisoners from both Glenhaven and Hyperion to quench the demon's blood thirst for years, priming the Specter with strength several times its original. With the way he's been preparing this particular Specter, I don't even think a force of fifty Garrison knights can defeat it!"

"This is troubling," Paul said.

"Let's hurry and get this over with," Nick said. Knowing there were bodies lying around them made standing there unbearably uncomfortable.

"Very well, now that my promise has been fulfilled I will be taking my reward!" Vermeek screeched. The rodent demon clawed at Paul, ripping his coat pocket and stealing the Soul Eater files.

"You—" Paul said. They chased the demon, but its speed on all three legs made it impossible for them to keep up.

They continued until they came across a giant red painted symbol on the floor. It was hard to tell by the sheer size, but the brush strokes and general look of it appeared to represent a demon seal, more specifically the Seal of Pestilence. There was something different about the seal this time. Instead of being black, it was red, the primary marker for a summoning. And inside the outline of a skull that was melting away, as if rotting.

"He got away…" Nick said.

"And now we're trapped behind this seal!" Paul stamped his foot. "I knew we shouldn't have trusted him!"

"How did this happen?" Nick said.

Paul lifted his foot with red slime covering the bottom of the boot. "The Seal of Pestilence is painted in red paint here. This has to be where it was summoned."

Nick took in a deep breath, and shook his head. "That's not paint."

White smog began to fill the room from the floor, seemingly from nowhere. It crept in slowly at first, before coming up together into a thick cloud before them. The large cloud swirled and fanned out, becoming a maelstrom that tossed the two of them to the wayside.

Nick staggered back to his feet. He stood wide-eyed as the cloud molded itself into a monstrous shape with giant arms coming out from a rotund body. After a few minutes, the smog dissipated to reveal its true form in the shape of a large, furry feline-like demon with two giant arms that reached around them like a cage. The arms had five long, sharp claws on its ends.

Where its face might be was a gaping mouth with rows of sharp teeth that seemed to run across its entire head. Nick half expected the demon to topple over with such heavy and disproportioned limbs, but the lower half of the creature floated in midair. It was indeed an apparition, but a frightful one to behold.

"IN ORDER TO PASS YOU MUST ANSWER MY RIDDLE. IF YOU CANNOT, THE CONSEQUENCES WILL BE YOUR DEATH. ARE YOU PREPARED?" the Specter boomed, the force of which almost knocked them over again. "THOSE WHO DISOBEY THE RULES SHALL PERISH!"

Nick turned to Paul then back to the apparition. "What is the riddle?"

"I am a greater good than the gods, a force more destructive than the evils of sin. I am what the wealthy desire, but the poor possess. To consume me would be death. What am I?" The Specter said.

"We only have one guess and that's it. It will devour us if we get it wrong," Nick said.

"You don't know answer?" Paul said.

"If only Gabriel was here with us," Nick said.

Paul closed his eyes and muttered to himself. Nick watched as the knight was trying to make connections here and there in his head. It was like witnessing a machine or a supercomputer make calculations, trying all the algorithms in order to come to a significant conclusion.

However, he couldn't rely on Paul to solve this riddle nor could he rely on Agrian's brute strength. He may have been a demon, but he was a human first and foremost and had a capable mind of his own. This was a chance to prove he was smart enough in his own right to perform in an area in which his demon side was lacking. Though he never regarded himself a genius of any sort, he wasn't about to lose in a battle of wits with a nebulous creature.

Nick broke down the riddle in literal form. Nick thought about a "good greater than the gods." The possibilities were very limited. The only gods he knew in history weren't really deities, but angels that ruled over in Sanctuary. They were the ones who created life, and in essence the demons. Demons were a "force more destructive than sin" and were the bane to the existence of people. In many ways these two were like mirrors of each other, like two sides of a coin, or black and white. Angels were the epitome of good and the demons were the greatest form of evil. There was nothing that could outmatch these two because nothing else could be so absolute.

However, what he could not grasp were the parallels between the rich and the destitute. How could a wealthy man desire something that only the poor would possess? What could be consumed but result in death? The only solution he had was the poisonous plant, Dolere Flos, but that was only because he had been dealing with it recently.

"I'm drawing a blank," Paul said finally. "I'm afraid the only solution we have is going to have to engage and kill this thing."

"Wait a second." Nick waved an arm to silence him.

The more he thought about the poor and the rich, the more he realized how closely related they were to good and evil. They were both also at opposite ends of the spectrum. The riddle was more or less repeating the most common truths that people knew, yet could not relate to. Humans themselves were gray and had many traits that could never put them in such simple categories, and that was the reason why Bergice could not fathom how Nick could betray them.

Bergice was a demon, and was bound by that due to his nature. He was created as an agent of fear and molded to be the exact opposite of the angels Ozarael detested. And that was when it finally dawned upon Nick, how simple the answer must be.

"Answer now, mortal," the Specter said.

"Nothing," Nick said.

Paul's jaw dropped. "Nicholas, you fool! Don't give up without at least even trying!"

"I didn't give up," Nick said. "That is my answer, Specter. Nothing."

The Specter made no antagonistic gesture or any move that indicated whether his answer was correct. Nick's thumping heart beat through his jacket as they waited. Maybe he was wrong, but even so it was the best he could do.

"YOU MAY PASS," the Specter finally said.

With that the hulking demon disappeared the same way it came, into a cloud of smoke that dissipated into thin air. The seal on the floor stopped glowing as well, a sign that the effects of the summoning had worn off. Left behind from the smoke was a green keycard.

Nick picked it up, shook the slime from it and saw that it was labeled "Plant Room." He turned to Paul. "This keycard was put inside the Specter as some kind of prize for beating it. Another ploy by Doctor Numerous?"

"It seems that way. The more time we spend playing as his pawns, the less time we have to stop him before he enacts his plan," Paul said.

Now that the Specter was gone, they were one step closer to saving Alyssa. They opened the door and entered to find two more doors with their purposes painted on in bolded, black letters. One was labeled "Plant Room" and the other was "Main

Laboratory." Nick could practically feel her in his arms once and again, and was primed and ready to finish this mission before Paul grabbed his shoulder.

"What are you doing? Alyssa is right through these doors!" Nick said.

"There is something hidden in this Plant Room, Nicholas. I can feel it," Paul said.

"I don't care! We're too close to get distracted now."

"I didn't think you were dumb enough to fall for another trap. Something isn't right with this. Somehow I don't think Doctor Numerous gave us as a keycard as a reward," Paul said.

"I know rats, and I know that rat lied to us. Vermeek knew much more than he led on. Why didn't he mention a plant room?"

"He was a lesser demon. A flunky. He probably wasn't given any information," Nick said.

"Look, Graves said he created the labyrinth to conceal his own private Garrison. Up to this point he made a pretty good imitation of all the rooms—except for this Plant Room. In all my years I've never heard of such a thing. For whatever reason, it must have been Doctor Numerous who designated this room for a purpose not related to the Garrison. Combined with the fact that this room also has keycard entry only suggests it is something of great importance—like that Soul Eater Project," Paul said.

Nick faced the main laboratory and then to the Plant Room. "I have a bad feeling about this."

"In most circumstances I would agree with you, but we can't pass up this opportunity especially if it is also possibly related to his plan. As knights we have an obligation to investigate strange occurrences and this one seems the strangest of them all. I think we should check it out."

"If only we had a clue that we weren't about to walk into another trap. For all we know it could be another decoy set up to slow us down. Another Specter could be waiting for us," Nick said.

"We'll never know unless we try."

Nick hated to admit it, but the longer they went back and forth on the issue the more curious he became as well. Bergice had already stated the doctor had a plan in store for them. If there was a chance to figuring it all out, it would be more beneficial to their cause to at least take a little glance.

"Fine, fine let's just hurry it up," he relented.

They slipped the keycard into the single slot panel and opened the double doors. As they stepped in, they must have triggered a motion sensor because the lights flickered on, illuminating the entire room from top to bottom. What they saw came as a complete surprise. The center of the room, a few yards away, was filled with rows and rows of plants. These plants were encased in a thick circular glass case, protecting them and preventing tampering of any kind, like a very expensive green house.

Aside from the plants, the entire room was grey and very plain, with the exception of the edges of the room where a metal grated walkway connected stairways to the upper levels. Nick peered through the thin slits onto the upper floors; stairs continued and led into a small, square room at the top.

Paul pressed his face against the glass. "Nicholas you got to take a look at this." He tapped on the glass.

Nick walked closer, and took one hard look. Suddenly everything became clear.

"It can't be!" he gasped.

16

THE SOUL EATER PROJECT

Nick walked closer and examined the plants through the thick glass. They were the same Dolere Flos plants from the Den of Pain, but there were more stored here in this facility than in that entire cave! Not to mention they were about twice the size of the ones he'd seen. It must have taken years to grow and collect this many. Why were they brought here?

"This must be why Astaroth's hideout was at the Den of Pain," Paul said.

"He's here. I feel his presence radiating at the top of this room."

"Bergice?"

Nick nodded. "But he's not alone. There's another demon with him."

"I thought he wasn't supposed to be here," Paul said.

"Well, I guess he changed his mind. If we keep quiet long enough maybe we can find out exactly what's been going on down here," Nick said.

As they ascended the stairs, they caught glimpses of more rows and rows of these plants on each of the subsequent levels. All were grown to a larger and unnatural size, almost three times the size of a mature plant.

At the final steps, Paul stopped abruptly and shoved Nick harshly against the wall. He pointed to his ears then at the room ahead, indicating he had heard something. He pantomimed again by putting his hand over his mouth in a message to not say a word. Nick nodded and leaned forward to get in better listening range to the voices right around the corner. One he could unmistakably identify as Bergice, his voice was too distinct to be anyone else. He was apparently reading aloud a list to someone else, and that person could only be…

"Doctor Numerous! Do I have your full attention?"

"Yes, Lord Bergice," he answered with a low voice.

Nick knelt as close as he could to the step and very slowly peeked around the corner.

"I thought I heard a noise."

Bergice was pacing back and forth with his katana bouncing against his leg. He had his back facing Nick. Kneeling in front of him was Doctor Numerous. Apparently their conversation wasn't very pleasant because the ice demon's posture was rigid, and the tone of his voice didn't sound pleased. On the floor next to them lay Vermeek, lifeless, his eyes open. Blood trickled from a gaping stab wound in his torso.

"Do not change the subject!" Bergice said.

"A thousand apologies, my lord. Vermeek must have lost the keycard on his way here." The way Doctor Numerous spoke suggested that he carried himself with eloquence and refinement, but of course, it was all a façade. There wasn't an ounce of nobility in his body. He was a traitor and beyond repentance for his crimes against the Garrison and a sin against nature for choosing to become a demon.

"A careless mistake that cost him his life. If any of our guests stumble onto that keycard and access this room, then this whole operation would be a failure, would it not?" Bergice said.

"Not at all, my lord. Even though Lord Agrian and Sir Evans managed to find a way out of the labyrinth, they should not survive their encounter against the Specter. Your ingenious plan to use Evans as the delivery boy proved valuable because now that files are back in our hands. And we have the access code to launch the Soul Eater," Doctor Numerous said.

"Graves thought he took all precautions to guard his belongings, but he couldn't fool me. Now make sure the calculations are correct and we shall proceed as planned."

"The latest test showed that the Soul Eater performed perfectly my lord."

"Excellent, now rise."

Doctor Numerous obeyed, and when he was standing tall in all his glory, Nick saw firsthand how truly imposing he was in person. He was at least a foot taller than Bergice, and wore a black lab coat over matching pants. The photos that were taken of him couldn't capture the true menacing physical features of this man. He massive shoulders and powerful arms that hung firmly at his sides, which showed the mark of years spent cultivating. Despite being an alchemist and having a genius intellect, he looked nothing like how the others described him. Perhaps the demon transformation turned the once-fragile knight into a beast at peak physical perfection.

"My lord, I must say it gives me great pleasure to have you here in time to witness the final installment of my master plan," Doctor Numerous said.

"Everything has been set? What of the broken sword?"

"We have retrieved Sir Marcus's fine steel just like you wanted. As long as we have it in our possession, it can no longer be used against us. My lord's brilliance knows no bounds!"

"Vigilance is expensive, but well worth the price, don't you agree?" Bergice said.

Paul and Nick shared a look of confusion. What did he mean by that? The sword of Sir Marcus would have been a great asset to their arsenal, but there were plenty of powerful historical weapons. Why such morbid fixation on this one?

"I have also captured those trespassers. Lord Agrian and Sir Evans will not have any more assistance," Doctor Numerous said.

"You've proven you could capture two measly knights, but what about Agrian and Evans? I told you I wanted them all when I returned, but you failed to deliver. As an Infernal this is unacceptable. Perhaps Ozarael was too quick to have given you this position."

"Capturing those two was no easy task in this ever-changing labyrinth, my lord. Besides, the one called Daniel is an aspiring archangel, and Graves is a long time veteran," Doctor Numerous said.

"Excuses. You and I both know that dealing with numbers should have been child's play for you. Had you been defeated in battle, it would be irredeemable. You have already allowed them to progress this far into this tower. Don't let them interfere with anything here or in the main laboratory, otherwise everything will be ruined," Bergice said coldly.

"I have studied Agrian's file extensively. I know everything about him and who he used to be. It will only be a matter time when he makes his first and final mistake. He cannot resist coming back for the girl. His love for her has rendered him stupid and impulsive. Having his fallen comrades as added incentive will surely fuel the flames of rage and make his capture quite easy," Doctor Numerous said.

"Don't underestimate him because of his love for the human. She is no ordinary girl. Make no mistake, the descendant of Quinn Valentine has made him stronger not weaker. I have already witnessed the difference personally," Bergice said.

"You've met Agrian? And he was able to escape from you?" Doctor Numerous said incredulously.

"He's a tricky opponent," Bergice said.

"Well, I still have to find out his results against the Specter. In either outcome I should be able to gauge the extent of his growth," Doctor Numerous said.

"And what would this comparison tell you?"

Doctor Numerous smirked. "Whether or not he can stop an Infernal. If they pass the Specter unscathed, then the powers that Lord Ozarael bestowed upon me should prove to be more than enough."

"Lord Ozarael is grateful for your assistance through the years. The success of this latest scheme will decide whether or not you are ready for the next step. Perhaps you will be rewarded with something you've desired for some time now?" Bergice said.

"You know exactly what I crave, my lord. I will not fail you or Lord Ozarael."

"You better hope, for your sake that you don't. And remember, I don't want you to get carried away with any of our prisoners. If I find so much as a missing hair on any of them, then the consequences will be dire."

Doctor Numerous nodded. "Of course, I just wished we could have gotten to the president in time. Having him as leverage would have been more useful." His expression changed to puzzlement. "I still can't understand how he was able to escape from you. At such an early stage in his development, Agrian barely had enough time to learn the full extent of his own fire abilities."

"Agrian is a fast learner. Even with the rudimentary training he received from that Garrison, he's developed into a brilliant tactician. He knows how to play to his strengths and exploit the weaknesses of others. The humans wouldn't stand a chance if he were to join us again. However, our encounter has shown me that he no longer desires to walk the path of his brethren. The Agrian I once knew is no more. Therefore he is no longer of any use to us, and is now a problem that you must dispose," Bergice said.

"Gods from the Machine...you want me to kill him? But what about Lord Ozarael?"

"What about him? I'm telling you plainly that Agrian must die and it must be by your hands. Consider this the only condition for your ascension. Killing Agrian is the only way to prove whether or not you are fit for a place among us. Unless you have any doubts this can be achieved?" Bergice said.

"Of course not my lord, but I don't want to suffer Lord Ozarael's wrath for killing the Inferno Bearer he despises."

Bergice drew his katana with lightning speed, and swung with the blade, stopping inches from Doctor Numerous' neck.

Nick winced a little at the sight, as he expected to see the alchemist's head sail in the air and blood soaking the walls in red.

"If you dare to question my judgment again you will personally incur my wrath, do I make myself clear?"

"Yes my lord," Doctor Numerous said timidly.

"Excellent." Bergice sheathed his katana. "Now then, make sure everything goes according to plan. I want Agrian dead and Hyperion to be leveled by sunrise so that the entire world may witness our might."

"That is a guarantee my lord," Doctor Numerous said. Nick heard the smile on his face as he spoke. Whatever incentive they were offering, it was enough to placate him. Funny, since he already achieved what he wanted, what else could be left?

"I have some other business to attend," Bergice said. Doctor Numerous bowed until he had left.

Alone now, Doctor Numerous went to the computer nearby and pushed a series of buttons that he read silently to himself. He chuckled aloud before tearing the pages into pieces and tossing them onto the floor before he promptly left the room through the door closest to him to the main laboratory. Unencumbered by any more guests, Nick and Paul moved into the room.

"Did you catch all of that?" Nick said.

Paul nodded. "I can't believe I was stupid enough to take the codes he needed to launch Soul Eater. And now we can't make sense of how to stop it!" He went to the keypad and typed frantically at the computer console, only to be denied access again and again. "Dammit! We need Graves for this!"

"Be careful, you don't want to—" Before Nick could finish the computer screen lit up and a loud, female generated voice came through the speakers.

Beep. Automatic sequence beginning. Beep.

A sound of whirring rang loudly and rotating blades lique-fied the plants in place, turning them into a thick, dark purple substance. Once the process was completed, the hatches holding them opened and sucked them through various interconnected pipelines and into one, singular large pipe that continued into the main laboratory in the room next to them.

"What's happening?" Paul said.

"The Soul Eater is making the final preparations for launch," Doctor Numerous' voice boomed over the loud speaker. "The glass tubing from this room connects to the main lab which has an automated mechanical projector that comes out from the surface every few hours in order to maintain the integrity of the Holy Shield. Normally, this device uses the special formula synthesized by Graves, which projects the invisible barrier that wards and protects citizens from the demons. However, I've replaced the formula with a combination of the Dolere Flos and other deadly chemicals of my own creation to form the Soul Eater! That's the substance you see being transported into the main laboratory. It has taken years to perfect the formula, but I've succeeded in creating the ultimate weapon! Once I launch it, the Soul Eater won't create a shield but unleash a poisonous gas, which will essentially kill everything it touches!"

"You've been planning this doomsday weapon for years now," Nick said.

"Yes. Hyperion is just the beginning. According to my cal-culations, I've perfected the plant and made the virus an odor-less gas that is virtually untraceable. I'm going to systematically kill entire populations and they won't even know until it is too late," the loudspeaker said.

"Can't we stop the launch from here?" Paul said.

"The activation counter has already been set. There's nothing you can do to stop it now. And even if you could evacuate the hundreds of millions of people that are soon going to be affected, there's no place in the world where you could hide them all. The radius covers enough to blanket the planet twice over! Now sit back and enjoy the show!"

Nick charged his arms and blew up the loudspeaker with a quick fireball. "That should shut him up."

Without another word Paul leapt forward and hacked at the clear pipe. Nick watched the sparks fly as the sword clanged against the glass with a ferocity he had never seen. It was of no avail however, as the glass was built to be much too durable. However despite the fruitlessness, he had continued to strike over and over again until he was huffing and puffing with fatigue.

"Dammit, how could I have let this happen?" Paul said. He was shaking with anger. "I'm going down as the knight who failed to prevent the world from the biggest genocide in history."

Nick couldn't help be feel a bit empathetic seeing Paul so downtrodden. Though they weren't exactly friends, he also carried the burden of being held in such high regard by his peers. He was hailed as a prodigy in battle and a warrior on the path of becoming the next archangel. His reputation was rightly earned, but none of that would matter if they were all killed.

"There might still be a way. The tubes feed into the next room, maybe if we tried to manually disable it from there," Nick said.

"It shall be no easy task. He's going to be waiting there for us and he's already beaten both Garreth and Daniel."

"It's a little too late to be scared," Nick said.

"I'm not afraid of battle…I'm afraid of failure."

"We'll find a way. But the first thing we have to do is make sure that this machine doesn't exist ever again. And since we're not exactly technological geniuses, that leaves only one clear solution." Nick charged another fireball and blew up the computer console.

Paul smirked. "I couldn't have done it better myself."

"We're going to rewrite history. Your legacy to this world isn't tied to the success of this mission. Your greatest accomplishment is going to be helping me save it," Nick said.

Paul glanced around the room, which was torn apart with tiny fires. "I suppose the plan to use the element of surprise is completely off the table."

Nick grinned. "To be honest, I'm glad he knows exactly where we are. I got a little tired of sneaking around. I hope you don't mind but lately I've developed a flair for making big entrances."

He walked to the door, the only remaining object untouched by the chaotic fire assault and kicked the door down with all his might. The door tore off the hinges along with the pieces of wall it was securely attached to and sailed in the air before hitting the floor with a hard clang.

He was disappointed to find that the one eyed doctor was nowhere in sight. In fact there were no demon guards at all. No Hellbeasts. No Specters. It was completely empty.

"Where is he?" Paul held out his sword.

This room was much more different than the Plant Room, taking on a more futuristic and cutting edge design. They followed the single glass pathway that was transferring the Soul Eater and it led them to an operating table at the bottom center with multiple computers and bookshelves, which housed the rest of the research. The table next to it had vials and containers for various liquids. All over the walls were little orbs that stuck out. They had a circle outline to them, which suggested they weren't there just for mere decoration and could move in and out of socket. The glass tubing feeding the purple poison continued until it stopped at center of the room and into what appeared to be the Soul Eater device.

The device was shaped like a large pod with cannon turret attached, and had a seat with controls connected to it for what appeared to be used to fire manually. Nick couldn't believe how close they were to it. How could one machine control the fate of the entire world?

"Let's destroy it now!" Paul rushed to the device with his sword drawn.

A crackle of static sounded just before Doctor Numerous's voice boomed through a microphone. "I wouldn't do that if I were you. You both did good work in creating a mess of my operation. And though you managed to get this far, I assure you it was all by design. Listen to my advice, and turn yourselves over quietly."

"So we could line up to die? No thanks," Nick said.

"I already defeated the other half of your party singlehandedly. What makes you think you two can do any better?"

Nick caught a glint of red laser sensors as Paul passed through them with his stride. Before he could open his mouth the sensors triggered long metallic arms that shot from the orbs on the wall towards them like snakes. The ends of the silver arms opened like clamps and they were coming straight at them.

"Paul!" Nick shouted.

Paul reacted quickly and sliced through the ones coming head on with ease, splitting it in two. It was then like watching a ballet, as the knight ducked and dodged through the ones that came after him from below and behind his peripherals, eventually making his way to the cockpit of the Soul Eater. He twirled his sword in the air, preparing the stab the system and ridding them of the threat once and for all. But it was too soon to celebrate as he was struck by a figure from above.

Doctor Numerous stood on the seat triumphantly, staring down at Paul, who was dazed and shocked by the sudden blow. The few seconds he let his guard down was enough for the tentacles to snare him.

"I offer my opponents the option to surrender or fight and they always choose the latter. I'm glad, as it makes things much more interesting," he said. He pressed the large button on the remote control he was holding.

The panels on the walls were actually prison cell compartments, which now slid open to unveil the others in captivity. Daniel and Paul, bruised and bloody, stood upright with shackles binding their hands and feet against the wall. Paul was lifted and bound to the wall beside them.

All three of them were lined up and mounted like trophies to commemorate Doctor Numerous' victories. It was a despicable scene, and the fact that they were being paraded around in their weakened conditions infuriated Nick even more. Although it was obvious this was his plan to elicit an emotional reaction out of him, Nick wasn't prepared to be this upset.

Unable to watch anymore and contain the force that was Agrian, he charged forward and transformed into his demon alter ego before he tore through the metal tentacles that flew at him, shredding them with ease. With his increased speed and dexterity he was able to move through much faster than Paul. He was driven by bloodlust, and wouldn't make the same mistake of dropping his guard for even a second.

He maintained his rhythm destroying every tentacle until the room was cleared and all the sockets in the walls were vacant of orbs. All that was left was the sound of static electricity from broken wires and the smell of smoldering metal.

Doctor Numerous clapped loudly. "Impressive, Agrian! Truly impressive."

"You'll have to do a lot better than that if you're planning on beating me," Nick walked towards him, ready to end this once and for all before Doctor Numerous quickly whipped out a remote control from his lab coat and waved it into the air.

"Did you honestly believe you could just walk in here and save her that easily?" Doctor Numerous said. "I have a contingency for every possible move you make before you even make it."

"What's that, another doomsday device?" Nick said.

"No, actually it's the game changer." Doctor Numerous pressed the button and a large, vertical steel bed rose from the floor. There standing, strapped by thick metallic bindings was Alyssa. She was unconscious and unmoving.

"Alyssa!" Nick yelled. His initial instinct was to rush out and attack the alchemist, but he refrained.

"Not another step!" Doctor Numerous said. "The girl is attached to this contraption designed for testing on people with a rather... unruly disposition. She has quite the powerful will and strength beyond what her stature suggests. Surprisingly, she struggled for a while before I had to discipline her."

"Discipline her?" Nick said through gritted teeth.

"Nothing permanent, I assure you. However, I can inject her with enough Soul Eater to annihilate a small village at one click of a button faster than you can ignite another fireball, so I suggest you stand down."

"How do I even know she's alive?" Nick said.

Doctor Numerous caressed Alyssa's face. Touching her so intimately made Agrian's urging in Nick's head go off the charts. "Rise and shine my delicate princess."

Alyssa awoke screaming at his sight, the sound of her cry seemed to excite the Doctor, as it infuriated Nick. His emotions swelled up inside, almost surfacing to the breaking point, but he had to remain as calm as possible.

"Where am I?" Alyssa screamed as the bright lights hit her face.

"Alyssa!" Nick yelled. It took her awhile before she could locate his voice.

"Nick, you're here!" Alyssa stared up at him, almost at the brink of tears. "He did…he did terrible things to me."

"Stay calm for now. I'll get you out of there soon," Nick said. Just hold on a bit longer, he thought. There's bound to be a way out of this.

"Now that you know she's alive, I urge you to stand down, otherwise I can easily change that," Doctor Numerous said.

Nick hesitated at first, but reverted back to his normal state and put his arms behind his back.

"I surrender."

Doctor Numerous smiled malevolently. "That's a good boy. However, since we're both demons, I don't think I can merely take your word for it. Turn around slowly and take a few steps backward."

Nick obeyed and suddenly he was enveloped in a circular cage composed solely of beams of light.

"What is this?"

"It's called a Light Prison. It's a demon cage that I synthesized with the express purpose of trapping you. Don't bother trying to escape. The cage is composed of high grade Orichalon, which creates a powerful imitation that is ten times stronger and more durable than Luxilight technique."

"You've thought of everything haven't you?" Nick said.

"Of course, I'm a genius."

17

AMBITIONS FOR ASCENSION

"Most demons are bloodthirsty warriors who live for the thrill of battle. However, as an Infernal you decided to use these built in trinkets and blackmail to beat us. I doubt your superiors would allow a demon in their ranks live with a victory that was hollow." Paul said.

"Superiors?" Doctor Numerous laughed brazenly. "Superior would suggest that you believe Bergice was better than me in some form or fashion. I outclass all the Crowned Princes in every way because I defeated all of you without even lifting a finger."

"You think too highly of yourself," Nick said.

"I disagree. In fact I did extensive research on you before and after your transformation. I learned all your techniques in combat and have a counter for every single one. There are no physical challenges you can provide me, so why bother with a contest? However, you are quite the slippery one, just like Bergice said. You were able to beat the Specter as well as my metal snare seekers, but it is of no consequence. Using that girl to force your hand worked just like I hoped. Did you think I was going to let you interfere with Soul Eater's launch? I'm no fool. I always have another plan just in case."

"You're insane if you go through with this!" Paul said. "Ending the population will do nothing. Once everyone is gone, the only thing the demons will rule is a pile of dust."

Doctor Numerous laughed menacingly. "I don't care because none of that matters. Only absolute power does! And since none of you are in any position to threaten my power, I suppose it wouldn't hurt to let you know the details of my true master plan. While the destruction of humanity serves no real purpose for me, it will guarantee my objectives are met. My dream will finally be achieved!"

"But to go this far…" Garreth breathed heavily and struggled ferociously against the steel bindings, which left deep imprints on his body. He looked terrible, bloodied opened wounds were all over him.

Doctor Numerous approached them, his hands behind his back casually as if he was about to take a tour around a zoo, watching all the caged animals.

"Unfortunately for you, Sir Garreth, it was the only way. From the beginning, I had been tasked by Lord Ozarael to stage the attack on Fyria for the sole purpose of removing all the soldiers from Glenhaven and in order to gain access to the precious supply of Orichalon. I veiled the assault with the threat of the Bergice, the Prince of Fear, whose reputation put everyone in a state of frenzied panic. And with the chaos drawing away their attention, I could pass through Heaven's Peak and procure a substantial amount of the Orichalon ore in order to create your holy cage. That was merely the first phase."

"So everything was just a smokescreen. You never had allegiance to them either, did you? You double crossing snake!" Paul said.

"I still don't understand where the Sword of Sir Marcus comes into play. Even if you could somehow resurrect its true power, it would be impossible for any demon to wield," Nick said. He remembered how badly he was burned before by merely touching the fragments.

"The holy sword serves no importance to me. However, Bergice was adamant that we retrieve it. I assumed it was for his personal trophy prize, considering their past conflicts. We had believed that this was virtually impossible, considering that it was already in the possession of the Garrison and heavily guarded by their strongest soldiers. Fortunately for us, your superiors were foolish enough to entrust such a sacred and prized weapon to a bunch of children. You carried it with you, bringing it to me without having so much as to lift a finger. You might as well have delivered it to me wrapped in a neat little package," Doctor Numerous said.

"Damn you!" Paul snarled.

He rushed forward with all his might, but the Doctor pushed a button on his remote and an electric jolt came from the tentacles, shocking him and causing him to scream and writhe in anguish. Nick could see the smoke coming from Paul's body as he crumpled to the floor.

"That's enough back talk from you boy," Doctor Numerous said.

"You have us now, why don't you just let Alyssa go?" Garreth snarled from the side.

"She will be useful as bargaining chip when the time comes and the great, Supreme Commander Peter finds out and comes with a full force of knights. Don't you see, my plan has no room for error. No matter what outcome, the Garrisons will take a severe loss. Whether or not you stop me is of little importance because the result will be the same! The fruits of my labor will award me as the next Crowned Prince!"

"You can say that because you're hiding safely on the other side of the cage. It's a pity how long it took for the Fyrians to root out such a weak coward among their ranks." Nick said.

"Coward you say? Need I remind you about a certain knight who died thanks to you?" Doctor Numerous said.

Nick became silent.

"I've studied your file very thoroughly, Agrian. Does the name Susan Stillwell mean anything to you? You don't have to answer because I already know about your sordid past and the shameful act revolving around her. You'll be eager to know that there's more to that story than meets the eye."

"What are you trying to say?" Nick said.

"That situation…I find it to be very nostalgic, or should I say ironic? Your records indicate that you were one of the young soldiers that participated in that infamous mission at that Fyrian village six years ago. It was known as one of the biggest tragedies in Glenhaven Garrison history. Susan Stillwell was among some of your best knights that fell that night, and it was all because of your inexperience and cowardice. After that you battled with insomnia and relied on an intense regimen of medication for years because you could never stop reliving the moments of horror as you witnessed her death. Throughout it all they never did catch the perpetrator responsible, did they?"

"All the demons that were involved died that night in the fire," Nick said.

"That was the logical conclusion they came to when the cavalry arrived afterwards. However, I have a different recollection of the events," Doctor Numerous said malevolently.

"What are you saying?" Nick said.

"The cries she made were heart wrenching, weren't they? She must have suffered right until she died," Doctor Numerous said.

The realization hit Nick harder than he could have imagined. "No…it—it can't be! You were there that night!"

"Yes, I was the one leading that raid, Agrian. I remember that night so vividly, almost as if it were just yesterday. I was cornered by her after she took my eye, on the brink of defeat and certain death until you showed up! You were calling out for her, calling out like a lost child for his mother. She dropped her guard down for that instant and it was over. I left her alive, but severely wounded before I blocked every exit and then I lit the entire complex on fire. I waited from afar on high ground and away from the scene, watching from until all I could hear was her bloodcurdling cries for help."

"I…I didn't know…"

"We shouldn't be fighting, Agrian. No, I should be thanking you. If it wasn't for your timely intervention I would have been the one that died that night and none of this would have ever occurred. Ironic how fate works isn't it?"

Nick felt nauseous. "All this time I could have saved her."

"Yes, but instead you sealed her fate! Because of your foolishness she now lays in a pile of ashes and soon you and the rest of the world will join her!"

"If you're too afraid to fight Nick, then why don't you try fighting me?" Garreth said.

Doctor Numerous laughed uproariously. "Did you think that you could goad *me* into one on one battle with you? You may not be at your full strength, but there's no chance I would risk my chances of success on foolish game of pride."

"Because you know he'll find a way out and beat you," Garreth said.

"Silence you insolent brat!" Doctor Numerous roared. A click of the button and a large jolt went into Garreth. His body convulsed violently before he also fell to his knees. "I will become more powerful than anything you could ever fathom!" he screamed.

"Stop it! Leave him alone!" Nick shouted as another jolt went through Daniels's body this time and he echoed Garreth's pain, writhing violently.

"I realize that these shocks would do little more than anger you, Agrian. So instead, all frustration I feel will result in a nasty surprise for your friends." Doctor Numerous waved a hand towards his captured friends. "And I'd hate for you them to die before you got to see the real show. It's going to be quite the spectacle."

"No!" Nick shouted.

Doctor Numerous laughed as he tossed the controller in the air in front of Daniel's face, taunting him before quickly swiping it back.

Nick's initial reaction was the same as the others, but in this situation he had to choose his words wisely. It was bad enough that they were all captured, but now everyone except for him had lost their strength and will to fight. He needed to find some kind of weakness to exploit. One thing he'd learned from Peter was to never go into a fight without at least a chance of success. He had to do something that was failsafe, something that he could use in case a direct attack was impossible. What he needed was some kind of opening, a way to figure out what to do before the Doctor got bored and decided to kill them. Problem with this was he couldn't see any discernible weaknesses from the Infernal. Suddenly overhead speakers crackled and the familiar female generated voice came on air.

Beep. Soul Eater at maximum capacity. Readying launch in approximately thirty minutes. Beep.

"Dawn is approaching. Soon it will all come to an end." Doctor Numerous' eye gleamed with delight. "Now all I have to do is wait for Bergice to return."

"Before you go through with this, can I ask you something?" Nick said.

"What would that be?"

"I know you once shared the dreams of becoming an archangel. What changed you?"

"Interesting question, Agrian," Doctor Numerous marched back until they were face to face. "Fate has delivered me a great favor by bringing me this far, and making me almost complete. We are so similar, yet our choices make us different. You chose to be weak and stand with mortals, while I elected to rise above them. That's the difference between you and me. I can never be satisfied until I am the strongest."

"We're not alike at all. I believe in justice and in humanity," Nick said. "I'd never stoop to your level."

"You are quite right, Agrian. Because unlike you I won't squander my newfound power. As you know I was once human too, but I gave that up when I swore my allegiance to Ozarael and revealed the secrets of the Garrison. I exchanged my humanity in order to receive powers beyond my wildest imagination—beyond the limits of any human. It was an easy trade."

"It was a stupid choice."

"It was the only way to escape a life of mediocrity. Since childhood, I knew I was given life in this forsaken world to become something greater than what had been offered to me. Unfortunately, my weaknesses as a human hindered that. Only as a demon, could I finally show the world my true capabilities."

"You could have done so much good in this world if you didn't turn," Nick said.

"Perhaps, but you are in the position to say that because you were born to be coveted and admired, where I was not. Years and years ago I was just a knight named Frank Barrett with prodigious skills as an alchemist. I was average in everything except for my ability to synthesize potions and spells, which was why I was forced to work as a teacher in the Fyria. I'd slave for days and days teaching kids how to become great knights worthy of becoming the next Clarion or Michael. However I was always filled with the shame of my own failure to become one. Days became months, and months years before I realized I was no longer happy with my own life. I hated living attached to my fate as a pitiful alchemist and I was determined to do more. But the more I trained, the more my goals slipped further and further away. I was becoming older and weaker in a world where new knights with talents and potential that far surpassed my own were thriving. I had almost given up." A grin came upon his face. "That's when fate stepped in.

"One day I came across the forbidden demon text known as the Book of Ozarael and was instantly captivated by his life and his teachings. It was an archive of demon rituals and spells he had created during his reign—it was black alchemy! I became obsessed with demons and I quickly learned that their powers could be attained!" Doctor Numerous threw his arms in the air, unable to contain his immense excitement. "Yes, it was then I devoted my life to becoming something better than I already was—a demon! I practiced black alchemy until I memorized every spell and incantation. But that wasn't enough. I needed to meet Ozarael myself.

"Then, one night I used my knowledge to paint a summoning seal on the floor and called upon Ozarael. Charismatic and intelligent, he promised a new world of possibilities in exchange for my soul. I gave it to him freely and in turn became a demon. I performed several tasks to prove my loyalty and quickly I became an Infernal. It was then I finally understood the importance of having true power. I was reborn. No longer was boring, weak Frank Barrett. I had become Doctor Numerous! Now I am among the ranks of gods. And soon I will ascend and be like you, a God from the Machine!"

"Being a demon is nothing to be proud of when you lose everything that makes you human." How a man could purposely choose to destroy his own humanity was beyond unthinkable to Nick. This man took everything he had for granted; it was infuriating to see someone so selfish.

"Your eyes are becoming a brilliant red. You must be truly teetering on the edge of reason. I can feel your hatred, your seething anger. How does it feel to be completely out of control? How does it feel to be completely at odds with the demon inside you?"

"Like a pain you won't ever be able to imagine," Nick said.

"You hate me, but if the positions were reversed, would you not have done the same? We are both split down the middle in terms of our loyalties. But our separate upbringings allowed us different advantages. You had some to help to embrace the inherent good that resides at your core, something that was impossible for a demon. Quinn brought out the light hidden inside darkness. I, on the other hand, was never that fortunate. I found solace in evil." Doctor Numerous rolled up his sleeves and pulled off his black rubber gloves. His arms were reptilian and scaly like Nick's, but they were black, and more jagged, a true representation of a demon's hand.

"Your arms!" Paul gasped.

Doctor Numerous gazed down with pride. "Strikingly familiar is it not? Though I cannot manipulate fire like you do, I promise I can wreak as much damage without it."

"What if this doesn't work? There are, and can only be, five Crowned Princes," Nick said.

"This is true. But Ozarael created Agrian and the other four the first time, which means it's certainly possible for him to do it again. In any case, a spot among them will require a vacancy before it can be filled."

At this point, Nick was certain he had lost. He was trapped without any way out. Then just as he had given up, her voice spoke from across the room.

"Nick, remember what I told you! Every angel needs two wings to fly!" Alyssa said.

Nick touched the necklace that Alyssa had made for him and suddenly it all became clear. Orichalon was the holy substance made to coat weapons and it was sent from Sanctuary to help humanity combat demons. Of course! The bars were similar to Luxilight and that technique became harmless when it came into contact with itself. Since he couldn't pass or touch it because his soul was occupied by a demon, perhaps he could do so with a fresh coat of Orichalon! However, he realized that even if he were to escape, Doctor Numerous still had Alyssa as leverage. What could he do?

"What are you babbling about, girl? The stress of torture must have caused you to suffer a mental breakdown," Doctor Numerous said.

"Doctor Numerous, you consider yourself an expert on torture, but what you put us through is nothing I haven't faced before. Electric currents? It's juvenile. Not to mention something I'd expect from an amateur," Alyssa said.

"Alyssa, what are you doing?" Garreth said.

"You're a failure at everything you try, which is why even if you kill Nick, you'll never take his spot!"

"Shut your woman up, Agrian. I don't want her to die before Bergice returns."

"The all-powerful Doctor Numerous can't even control a single prisoner, what a joke!" Alyssa said.

Doctor Numerous glared at her. "Very well, then perhaps punishment is in order." He pulled out his remote and sent a jolt to Alyssa's steel bed. She was in terrible pain, but refused to scream.

"Stop it, Alyssa!" Daniel cried.

"That's all you got? I've fought Hellbeasts with more bite than that!"

Another jolt at a longer duration, yet she still refused to scream. He kept a steady pace of electric shocks until smoke came from her body. Doctor Numerous' wrath was focused solely on her. The time to act was at hand.

Nick yanked off the necklace and crushed the stone into a fine powder which he rubbed all over his hands. He grabbed onto the bars, the coating idea worked as he expected and he was able to prevent any burns or bodily harm to himself. With all his might, he bent the light to make an opening large enough to crawl through. Once free from the prison, he transformed into his demon form and threw a well-placed fireball that destroyed the remote that Doctor Numerous was holding.

Doctor Numerous clutched his hand and spun around in awe. "How did you get out? No demon can escape my light prison!"

"A gift by my guardian angel." Nick set his arms ablaze. "Before I begin to beat you into the ground, I hope you for your sake you live up to your title."

Doctor Numerous laughed heartily. His eye turned crimson. "Now I will show you the power of an Infernal. I am called Doctor Numerous: for I am many."

18

THE MANY FORMS OF NUMEROUS

Doctor Numerous trembled violently, as if he was having convulsions. He grunted and groaned aloud, like he was possessed. Suddenly two identical copies of himself emerged at each side. So this was the unique ability the Infernal possessed—the man had the ability create perfect clones of himself!

Nick had no idea how to handle a situation such as this, as no training could have possibly prepared him.

"Shocked, Agrian?" the Doctor Numerous' said in unison. They all stood poised exactly the same way. "I am Pestilence of the Infernals, and like poison I will spread like a virus and devour you into oblivion," the doppelgangers said together.

"You monster!" Garreth shouted. "That explains how you could be in so many places at once!"

The Doctor Numerous in the center chuckled with superiority. "Yes, and with my abilities I was able to travel around the world and reside wherever I pleased. I kept everyone focused on this wild chase, making them believe they were hunting demons. What they didn't know was that I was biding my time, readying myself for the perfect opportunity to launch my greatest assault on humanity."

"What was that?" Nick said.

"My ultimate goal is ascension. To achieve that end, I would personally deliver millions to early graves in order to prove myself to the princes. But even my powers are limited. Even if I split myself into a million copies, as a single man I couldn't hope to stop the wrath from the Garrisons alone. It was then that I remembered the Tower of Graves in Hyperion. The conception of the Holy Shield. The birthplace of tranquility. The beacon of hope that allowed humans to live their lives without fear of demons. How perfect it would be that the ultimate symbol of protection suddenly became the greatest weapon of mass destruction. Unfortunately, the process took longer than expected because I was forced to keep the knights off my trail," Doctor Numerous said.

"Sorry to have interfered," Nick said.

"Minor obstacles since my plans fell into place regardless," Doctor Numerous said. "Now that you know, it's time to for you to die!"

"You're not going to have that chance!" Nick rushed towards him, his arms glowing more intensely with flames.

Doctor Numerous created more three more copies, making a total of six. He charged Nick; the copies following on his sides zigzagged between each other, making it impossible to tell which one was the real one. Nick threw two fireballs, destroying two copies, but as they exploded into black smoke, two more appeared to take their place.

"What—!"

The Doctor Numerous' laughter echoed throughout the chamber, as the room filled with more copies. "Try again!" they jeered.

Nick hurled bursts of fire relentlessly all around, but the copies multiplied faster than he could destroy them. It didn't seem like there would be an end. There had to be some method to stopping this madness, some key weakness that he did not see.

"Why don't you fight me one on one, you coward?" Nick shouted.

"As Pestilence, my powers are superior to yours, or any other demon," the entire group cackled. "You should be grateful you are among the privileged few that have been able to witness it!"

As more and more copies appeared, he was unwittingly being pushed until he felt his back up against the wall. From his sides, a few stragglers from the large group managed to lash out and grab his arms, forcing them into a lock and preventing him from blasting any further. Nick struggled to push them off, but the horde was too powerful in their numbers. There were close to a hundred of them now.

They forced him to submission on his knees. Several of the copies wore deranged looks on their faces, like a cannibalistic tribe ready to kill and devour him.

"For your insolence, I will show you true pain." The doppelganger closest punched Nick across the face and then in the stomach as the others held him down. Doctor Numerous repeated the combination a few more times, gratifying his sadistic appetite with the harsh blows. Blood formed on Nick's lips, but he couldn't retaliate. He was intrigued by the mad alchemist. His single eye was glowing red, the color of pure malevolence.

Doctor Numerous reminded Nick of himself when he had lost control the first time, when he was drunk with the rush of power and inconsolable rage. Like his first time fighting Daniel, he was out of control, bent on destroying him. However, Nick couldn't let himself dwell on this fact for long since his eyes were swelling, and his vision blurry. He had to think of something fast before he ended up as a bloody pulp...or dead.

A doppelganger grabbed a fistful of Nick's hair and pulled his battered face close, so close Nick could smell his warm, putrid breath on his skin.

"How does it feel to be at my complete mercy?" he asked condescendingly.

Nick spat blood in his face. "Does that answer your question?"

Doctor Numerous dropped his head and wiped his face, grunting with disgust. "Truly as revolting as I've heard. It's high time someone taught you manners."

Nick wanted to reply with something snarky, but his head was pounding so hard he could barely think.

"You've always been hailed for your famous fighting prowess." Doctor Numerous rolled up his sleeves. "Innovative and powerful is what Bergice told me to expect, but I've yet to see you display any of these qualities. I suppose he over-exaggerated."

The doppelganger kicked Nick hard in the chest, knocking the breath out his lungs. "Or is it because you continue to hold on to your ridiculous human attachments?" he said mockingly, and delivered another punch to Nick's face. "Love, friendship, and the rest of that stupidity you believe in has gotten you in this pathetic predicament, hasn't it?"

Nick glared at him; he felt the burning sensation in his eyes. The burning was growing intensely, eclipsing the pain. Agrian was primed and ready to break loose.

"And that girl, that lovely girl you came to save." Doctor Numerous leaned in close again, dropping his voice low that Nick was the only one who could hear him. "When she was brought here, she begged that your life be spared. Funny, isn't it? Delusional more like it. A girl in love with a demon? That's a recipe for disaster, wouldn't you say?"

Nick stared blankly at the floor. Doctor Numerous was trying to provoke him, to draw him into a frenzy. The mere mention of Alyssa in association with the threat of danger made his blood boil.

"Nothing left to say? No more witticisms? I didn't think so. But one thing's for sure, at least she won't have to be sacrificed this time. I'll do the honors myself. How I will enjoy hearing her scream for her life. Begging for mercy as I peel the skin off her lovely bones." Doctor Numerous slapped Nick across the cheek. "It's rather sad really, you have to witness the death of your lover twice in a lifetime."

"STOP!" Nick was fuming with so much rage that his body could barely contain it.

The Doctor Numerous doppelganger smirked. "Too much for your stomach to bear?"

"I'm done…" Nick said quietly.

"What? Speak up!" Doctor Numerous stroked his beard. "I can barely hear you!"

"I'm done," Nick said again as clearly as possible.

"Done? Why, we've only just begun! Don't tell me you're giving up so soon?"

"No, I mean I'm done playing with you. Starting now, you're finished."

Doctor Numerous waved his hand is dismissal. "You're delirious, the beating you've received must have affected your ability to think straight."

"Because I know something you don't know, something you've been dying to figure out. You've been waiting to see what I was truly capable of and when I went down so easily you assumed that I didn't have the power you were searching for, didn't you?"

"What are you getting at?"

Nick's comment seemed to pique a sincere interest from him.

"While you were you busy going on and on about your power, the fact remains that I've been holding back."

"You were holding back against *me*?" Doctor Numerous asked, as if it was the most ludicrous thing in the world.

"Yeah, and to be honest you didn't exactly exceed my expectations either." Nick shot him a smug grin.

"Y-You're bluffing. I've beaten you! You're finished!"

"All this time I've been keeping him inside of me, afraid I would end up a monster if I embraced evil with open arms." Nick gazed at his hands. "I didn't want to sell my soul just to have power. I didn't want to live life knowing that these hands would be forever stained with blood. Because I know no matter how many times I'd try to wash them, it would never fade away. I cursed the Heralds for making this my fate." He clenched them into fists. "But now I know why I was made this way. It wasn't because I was a part of some cruel joke by destiny. No, the world needs the Inferno Bearer to make amends to scum like you."

Nick yelled at the top of his lungs, the scream echoed throughout the chamber waking Garreth and Daniel. The power in his body intensified as he relinquished control over Agrian. In his mind, he visualized himself pushing away his own conscience in order to grasp his full potential. In order to reach this new plane of power, a tangible demon plateau that wasn't accessed through just simple rage. It was a rage with purpose.

Nick couldn't stop. He kept going, and the room kept shaking even more violently. The many Doctor Numerous clones struggled to keep from toppling over each other. The mechanical tentacles flew around like a can of worms tossed in the air. The heavy equipment launched to the other side of the room, smashing themselves into heaps of tangled metal. The entire laboratory was churning inside and out like a concentrated hurricane in this one spot.

"No! You're ruining everything!" Doctor Numerous roared, but his voice was rendered to almost a whisper, drowned by all the mayhem.

Nick let out a giant burst of fiery energy that was sent from all sides of him. The blast destroyed the doppelgangers in an instant, leaving clouds of black smoke as they each dissolved into piles of ash. Thankfully his friends were safe, as they were too far from the battle to receive any harm. However, the real Doctor Numerous wasn't so lucky. He was badly injured, trapped underneath a probe-like device and surrounded by broken test tubes and equipment.

"Finish him!" Paul shouted from afar. "Destroy that monster before he has a chance to retaliate!"

Nick was way ahead of him. He threw the smoldered metal pieces off the doctor with a single hand. It was over.

"To be defeated so easily…" Doctor Numerous muttered in disbelief. "I was too careless…."

Nick stared down at him, not saying a word. He grabbed the doctor by the throat and lifted him away from the scrap heap. "You had a backup plan for everything, but you didn't think I could fight back, did you?" He slammed the doctor against the wall. "Didn't you? Well that mistake is going to cost you, Cyclops. You should have done better research."

Suddenly the alarm blared and bright flashes of red from signal lights went going off like he had won the lottery. That female generated voice from earlier crackled through all the damaged sound boxes in the laboratory.

Beep. Launch sequence commencing. Beep.

"It's happening already?" Nick said.

"The Soul Eater had been programmed to launch before the moment you stepped into this room. I told you I had a contingency for everything. Even if you kill me, there's no way you can stop it. You missed your last chance. You'll regret that forever!" Doctor Numerous said.

Still holding Doctor Numerous, Nick turned to Garreth. "How much time do we have?"

"Ten minutes at most. It takes approximately ten minutes until the Soul Eater reaches the peak of the tower," Garreth said. "Hurry, you have to get to the top and disable it before it's too late!"

"How?" Nick cried.

"The G at the top has the manual override built into it. Destroy it, and you'll stop the Soul Eater!" Garreth said.

"You have more important things to worry about, Agrian. Like yourself!" Doctor Numerous pulled a dagger from his pocket and slashed at him. "This isn't over in the slightest!"

Nick leaned back, narrowly avoiding a serious cut to his throat. He heaved the man aside. Doctor Numerous landed on the floor and rolled back onto his feet. Then he began to shake violently as he did before. What was happening now? The alchemist was transforming. Nick watched on, mesmerized by how a simple man became a monstrosity.

His lab coat and undershirt tore from his body. His limbs grew larger in size, and then his bottom half. He took on the insect-like features of a scorpion. His arms retained their jagged demonic appearance, but his hands were replaced with razor sharp hooks. He grew a long, thick dark green tail with three blades fanned out on the end of the tip. Nick jumped back and distanced himself; the tail was swung around wildly as if it had a mind of its own. From a safer distance, he was able to get a better look at Doctor Numerous, who somehow managed to retain most of his humanoid characteristics.

His body was now covered in thick plated scales that seemed to emulate the image of a physically fit man. He retained his eye patch, but his beard was replaced with thick brown insect fur. His single eye was three times larger and completely red. His mouth was filled with razor sharp teeth and there were two long fangs that protruded at the top. The man was dangerous with doppelgangers before, but now he was in his full demon form.

A fast tail swipe nearly cleaved Nick's head clean off, but he managed to narrowly avoid it at the last second. Doctor Numerous knocked Nick backwards with his huge pincers, the force caused him to rebound into the rubble.

Nick was right back on his feet, and he charged his arms, summoning two fireballs, and threw them. They hit their mark, but Doctor Numerous merely shrugged them off. What happened? The destructive power of his flames had burned through him before. The alchemist's new body must have doubled as a shell that made him impervious to attacks.

Doctor Numerous laughed mockingly. There was a hissing sound in his voice now to fit his new appearance.

"Looks like you're tougher than you look," Nick said, his arms radiating a brilliant blaze. "But I am too."

He rushed forward, dodging the pincers and tail, and delivered a mighty fire-induced punch that knocked the demon off balance. Right after, he slid underneath him, grabbed Doctor Numerous' long tail and swung him towards the ceiling.

Nick dropped down then used the momentum to spring up and propel into a tackle that took him and the insect demon through into the first floor.

He got to his feet and darted to the elevator, frantically pressing the button and waiting for it to open. As the elevator descended, Doctor Numerous snapped out of his daze and charged forward, the sound of his feet clipped on the marble floor. Nick managed to slip into the elevator and close the door just as the demon reached him. A crash! Pincer dents formed on the inside. He hit the button for the highest floor and was shot up, well on his way to reach the Soul Eater.

He sat to catch his breath and collect his thoughts. Nick glanced through the glass elevator and saw the Soul Eater coming up also. At the top, right above Garreth's office appeared to be the location of the launch. He'd have only a few minutes to disassemble it, but he didn't have any other choice. It was a race against time and he was in the lead for now.

The rate of the elevator took a sudden nosedive as a heavy weight seemed to be sucking it down. Outside the Soul Eater was catching up. What was going on? A sharp tail slashed through the bottom of the elevator inches from his face. Through a small hole a single red eye peeked through. Doctor Numerous hissed at him. Nick's first instinct was to send a fiery blaze straight below him, but held back because a miscalculation could cause him to plummet to his own death.

A momentary pause. The tail stabbed through again, almost skewering him whole. This continued several times. Nick avoided each swipe as best he could, but the next time Doctor Numerous might not miss. The bladed tail retracted and sliced upward. Nick melted a hole in the ceiling, leapt through, and landed on top. The slashing tail had punctured the ceiling. Before it could rear back for another swipe at him, Nick latched on to it. He was swung side to side, banging the walls hard on the sides, the rugged metal screws scraping harshly against his skin. Still, he clutched on desperately until the elevator drew to a stop. He punched through the wall and tumbled in Garreth's office. A crash and he spun around just as Doctor Numerous tore down the elevator door. The insect demon whipped his tail. It wrapped around Nick's midsection and slammed him into a glass table.

He staggered to his feet, his backside was cut deep with shards of glass; fatigue weighed heavy on his body. He'd made it to the top in one piece, albeit with more blood loss than he originally wanted.

He glanced out the window to monitor the progress of the launch, but with the position of the room he couldn't see a thing. He had to stop Doctor Numerous before he could get outside onto tower roof and deactivate it. Unfortunately, no visible stairways or elevators led to the top. His situation looked even bleaker.

"Great. Now what?" Nick muttered. He had seemingly hit a dead end.

"AGRIAN!" Doctor Numerous hissed.

Nick spun around as the demon barged in, tail thrashing about, tearing most of the furnishings and anything else left of value. "There is nowhere left to run! The only way out now is through me or as a fifty story drop!"

"I wouldn't have it any other way."

Nick leapt at Doctor Numerous, but the alchemist's powerful tail darted at him like a spear thrown at lightning speed. Nick redirected the tail into the floor, wedging it deep. Trapped in a tiny room with nowhere to go, he had only one option left. He lit his fists and came in close to engage the alchemist in an old fashioned slugfest.

He pounded the insect demon's body relentlessly, blocking the large swinging pincers and keeping his focus on damaging Doctor Numerous' thick hide. If his fire couldn't pierce through, he hoped applying physical pressure would do the trick. No effect. The punches merely bounced off his rock hard body.

Even with Doctor Numerous pinned, Nick was at a complete disadvantage. The insect demon's sheer size and reach was enough to keep him at bay. He dodged and ducked the barrage of strikes, but time was not on his side. If he continued at this pace, they'd all still wind up dead. He needed a new strategy.

Then it dawned on him.

For a demon, Doctor Numerous retained many of his human characteristics. The inner layer between the scaly muscles had a softer tissue. If there was some way to puncture it, he could finally dish out some pain. Unfortunately, Nick's hands couldn't reach behind the thick armor plates. He glanced at the wriggling tail and it all came to him.

Nick slid underneath the insect demon and unplugged the tail from the floor. He ran circles around Doctor Numerous' legs, tripping him over and toppling him on his belly. Nick flipped him over, stood firmly on the demon's arms, and stabbed the thin opening between his pectorals.

Doctor Numerous screeched.

It worked! Nick dragged the tail like a knife to cut an outline in the demon's own chest. Nick shoved his hands in the newly formed crevice and tore the shell apart, revealing even more soft padding of skin underneath. Now it was time to go to work.

A flurry of strong fiery hits made contact on the newly exploited weak point. Doctor Numerous was no longer able to attack, forced instead to lie there like a worn-out punching bag. Nick finished his assault by tossing the demon in midair. When he dropped back down, Nick drop-kicked him against the wall, breaking the Pailean paintings Garreth had hung on the over the fireplace. The damage to the wall revealed a large flip switch.

On the floor, an unconscious Doctor Numerous had reverted back into his human state. As much as Nick and the demon inside wished to kill Doctor Numerous, his duty as a knight was to stop the launch. He hadn't realized until now how out of touch he'd become by letting go of his inhibitions. How apathetic fighting made him. How fast he could fall. Thankfully, he caught himself before going too far.

"Consider yourself under arrest." Nick knelt and put Orichalon-coated handcuffs on the demon. He stepped over the alchemist and flipped the switch. A portion of the wall and fireplace sank into the floor. A short spiral staircase rose up. He climbed to the top and pushed open the tall rose-colored door. He was at the very top of Graves Tower now, the thin air made him woozy. It was still cold and dark, but some light peeked over the edge of the mountain ridges in the distance. The blackout earlier made sure the giant G that was no longer lit, but that didn't stop the Soul Eater from rising up the building. Nick ran circles around the oversized letter but could not find the manual control box Garreth had mentioned.

Beep. Soul Eater launching. Beep.

The weapon was setting itself up, and humming loudly now as the Soul Eater formula was being prepared. Panicked, he raced around the G again searching desperately for the control box.

There it was! Within arms-length! He went to grab it, but was repelled by only a mere touch, the violent jolt of holy magic ran up his arm and he pulled back from the stinging pain. Judging by the throbbing and smoke coming from his burnt hands, this wasn't just Luxilight. No, it must be another layer of Holy Shield—a contingency only one as cautious Garreth could think of. Nick threw a series of fireballs at the box, but they ricocheted off the ethereal barrier, one almost striking him in the torso. His demon powers were useless now. The countdown began.

Ten...

Nine...

"Slag it!" He rushed to the G and rammed his arms against the shield. Immediately he felt the intense burning sensation of the holy magic trying to push him back. Damn his corrupt soul!

Eight...

Seven...

His arms were losing all feeling, but he had to reach it before it was too late—no matter how much pain it caused him!

Six...

Five...

His whole body was inside now, and as he was moving in closer and closer, every inch of his flesh felt like it was being stabbed by millions of needles.

Four...

"ARGHHH!" He had to close his eyes and bite down on his lower lip to keep from passing out.

Three...

He felt the box in his hands.

Two...

He ripped it out and crushed it with all his might.

Beep. Launch sequence canceled. Beep.

Nick collapsed onto the floor and allowed himself a couple moments for it to sink in. Complete silence. He did it. The world was safe. The shield was gone, but at least everyone else still lived. There was only one loose end left to tie. Doctor Numerous.

Doctor Numerous let out a braying cough, his hands on his throat, trying to regain his breath when Nick reentered to room.

"Did I do it?" Doctor Numerous croaked.

"It's over, Numerous. You're coming back with me to Glenhaven," Nick grabbed Doctor Numerous by his cuffed arms. As te pushed his captive towards the elevator, the ground began to rumble. He ran to the windows just as they all shattered simultaneously. A cold draft rushed into the room.

Nick barely had time to react to the flicker of silver that streaked through the air past him. It sliced through Doctor

Numerous' leg, cleaving it clean off just like what happened to Vermeek. Nick recognized the blade and spun around to see him standing there on fifty stories of ice, with a look of amusement upon his face.

"Bergice."

Doctor Numerous clutched the stub of his leg, blood gushing all over the carpet. He looked up at Bergice resentfully. "But…why?"

Bergice walked by Nick, pulled his katana from floor and sheathed it. "I was listening to your story throughout this entire operation, and I was rather shocked to learn of your motives."

"I-I was only after Agrian!" Doctor Numerous cried now on his back, his hands applying pressure to his wound. "Just as you had commanded!"

"I don't remember giving that order," Bergice said coolly.

"But you did!" Doctor Numerous yelled. "You told me I could become a Crowned Prince if I followed your orders!"

"We never really expected you to succeed," Bergice said. "When you went with my order without question I knew I'd made the right decision. I told you to assassinate one of my brethren and you obliged so willingly. Lord Ozarael and I were right to doubt your loyalty. We knew you never had any real allegiance towards us. Since the very beginning you were just a puppet."

Doctor Numerous's eye widened, like he had a sudden epiphany. "Y-you planned this from the very beginning!"

Bergice clapped his hands. "Impressive Doctor, I was beginning to think you would never figure it out. From the invasion of Fyria to the production of Soul Eater, those were just parts of a master plan by Lord Ozarael to divide the Garrisons enough so we had a chance to restart our uprising.

"We let you believe you could fool us by spurning your pathetic dreams. It allowed your own overconfidence and delusions of grandeur to be your undoing. To think, with just with one false promise planted in your greedy little head, we saw to it the Soul Eater was finished right on schedule so Agrian could stop it."

"I am your savior! I helped you all! Without me, this whole project would have been an utter failure!" Doctor Numerous screamed.

"No, if you had succeeded, this project would have been a failure. The Soul Eater Project was never about destruction of the shield or unleashing a plague. It was the catalyst to bringing Agrian back to life," Bergice said.

"What?" Doctor Numerous yelled.

"Now your usefulness has long outrun its course. You shall be terminated," Bergice said.

"Bergice. You snake! You traitor!" Doctor Numerous snarled.

"You're one to talk. I'd known for a long time of your hunger and lust for power. You humans are all the same, it's become so boringly predictable," Bergice said. "You should thank me for giving you a few extra years to live. Instead of outright killing you, I suggested to Lord Ozarael that you play the villainous role we needed in this operation in order to test Agrian's resolve and nurture his growth. And I must say you performed just like we hoped. For that, I've decided you still deserve some type of reward." Bergice touched his index finger to Doctor Numerous' forehead. "Savor your last breath, doctor. This will be painful."

From head to toe the alchemist was slowly being frozen solid. Nick had to watch as his worn out legs forbade him to move.

Once finished, Doctor Numerous looked statuesque enveloped in ice, with only the look of terror remaining on his face.

"I've made it my own personal objective to uncover and exterminate the vermin that seem to linger within our ranks." Bergice took a step by to admire his work. Then he laid his hand on the handle of his katana, got into an offensive stance and very quietly uttered a single word.

"Duck."

Nick hit the floor.

With one swift strike, Bergice drew his katana and with a spinning slash he tore off the top half of the building while simultaneously, blowing out every remaining window and shattering the frozen body into a million tiny pieces.

As Nick got back to his feet, they were now standing out in the open. They were free from the confines of the tower. The sun was rising, partially illuminating the city and he could see that the demons from the forests and caves were now running rampant around the streets of Hyperion. Everything the shield had once separated was now integrated. Evil and good were blended seamlessly together.

"Breathtaking, isn't it?" Bergice watched the Hellbeasts roam across the streets. "The wave of revolution is upon us. Now with the Holy Shield gone, we can finally reclaim what was stolen from us. Our birthright."

"So that was your plan all along. Doctor Numerous and the Soul Eater were just a test in order to make sure my growth was on schedule. I played right into your hands. You wanted me to destroy the Holy Shield," Nick said.

"Precisely. You can inform your superiors of what transpired here. Let them know this is Lord Ozarael's declaration of war."

"Is that it?"

Bergice said nothing, merely looked on with cold eyes.

"Answer me! Why did you help me? Agrian became exiled because I helped humanity the first time. Now he's come back because destiny foretold I was to bring the end to you all, yet you to let me live! What possible reason could you have to spare me?"

"It would be easy to kill you, since you've obviously exhausted your strength. However, I don't find taking advantage of your weakness a challenge worth undertaking. I am a warrior, Agrian. I thirst for a worthy battle."

"Won't Ozarael be disappointed when he realizes you failed to capture me?"

Bergice turned around, his face composed. "I see no failure. Lord Ozarael wanted the Holy Shield destroyed and I completed that task. He wanted the legendary sword *Vigilance* belonging to Zelios, the Herald of Bravery. I have already delivered it to him. He has also instructed me to eliminate Numerous, which I have done. I have no other obligations that need immediate attendance."

"You're not like the others, are you?" Nick said.

"We both fight for different things. You fight to stop us and I fight to save our kind. I do not resent you, Agrian, though the same can't be said for Lord Ozarael. You are the bane of his existence, and a traitor that must be killed.

"We had an agreement Agrian, and I always keep my word, especially in matters that puts one's honor at stake." Bergice's face showed no sign of emotions, but Nick had no doubt he was telling the truth. "Before I go, consider this to be the second and final time I grant you mercy, brother. The next time we meet it will be in very different circumstances. For that I expect you to be prepared. We all expect great things from you when the time comes."

As Bergice turned to leave, Nick was attempted to chase after him, to find out the truth behind his eerie message. However, as he tried to move, his knees buckled and shook. Below him an icicle of gargantuan proportions shot through the floor and sent him sailing off the top of the building. He tumbled fifty levels, his body too weak to grasp for anything except the air in front of him. The last thing he felt was a cold chill run down his spine.

19

A CHANGE IN PLANS

Nick woke in a bed in the Glenhaven Garrison infirmary, hooked to medical cords. He looked down and realized his clothes were gone and he was dressed in a thin, blue medical gown. Was this a dream? The last thing he remembered was plummeting off of the tower, which should have instantly killed him. But somehow he made it back in one piece. He turned to find Alyssa sleeping soundly in a chair next to him. She was dressed in fresh new clothing and had his black jacket draped over her like a blanket. He must have been here for some time. Nick sat up and was assaulted by pain in every cell, particularly his back.

He remembered fighting Doctor Numerous. He remembered Bergice's appearance. He remembered stopping the Soul Eater Project, but at the cost of their national security. With the destruction of the tower, the people no longer had a Holy Shield to protect them from the evils of the outside world. Now they would require the constant protection that could only be provided by the Garrisons. Even though he prevented genocide of epic proportions, Nick couldn't help but believe that maybe this was just the beginning of things to come. How long could the Garrisons maintain peace when chaos loomed over them, waiting to strike?

At this time, Alyssa let out a loud yawn and stretched her arms in the air. She blinked a few times and turned to him, her bright green eyes made even brighter as she smiled.

"Well look at you, you're finally awake."

"How did I end up in here?" Nick said.

"We found you in a puddle of water outside the entrance of the tower the morning the Holy Shield disappeared," Alyssa said.

Puddle? He must have landed on a soft patch of snow around the tower. That would have explained the chills he got before passing out.

"What about everyone else? How long have I been here?" Nick said.

"Everyone's fine. My grandpa's back. He's spent most of the time setting up the usual protocols after an invasion. It's been three days since we figured out the whole set-up in Fyria turned out to be a major pain in our sides, but thankfully there were zero casualties. Garreth and the others have been up all through the night, making transmissions and trying to keep the peace in neighboring cities."

"How did you all manage to escape?"

"Bergice freed us when you went to stop the Soul Eater. He said it was just a part of a bigger plan."

"I see. At least you're all safe." Nick felt at ease for the first time in weeks.

"I know what you mean. It's like the burden in my chest has been lifted."

"What about you?" Nick reached over and took her hand.

"I'm fine, thanks to you. You saved us all."

Just then Gabriel entered, clad in full armor, and holding his helm in his hands. Nick released Alyssa's hand.

"I was just coming in to check up on you, kid." Gabriel turned to Alyssa, "Pete wants to talk to you. He says it's very important so I suggest you go now."

"Right." Alyssa walked briskly past the archangel, turning to give Nick one last look before leaving.

"You look like you've seen better days," Gabriel said. "Paul filled us in on the details of what occurred in Hyperion. Doctor Numerous really did a number on you, didn't he? I have to admit, we were all surprised to hear how well you handled him."

"I'm lucky to be alive." Nick rubbed his sore shoulder.

Gabriel chuckled. "When you've been in this business long enough, you're always teetering between life and death. Besides, it could have been worse. If the Soul Eater had been launched, we wouldn't be sitting right here, would we?"

"Is there any way to bring the Holy Shield back?" Nick said.

Gabriel's face became solemn. "The destruction of Graves Towers has ensured that the shield is gone forever. Every Garrison in the world is in a state of frenzy, trying to set up their emergency defense measures. As for us, we're on lockdown until further notice."

"Then everything was my fault. I destroyed the machine. I took out the tower. This wouldn't have happened if I wasn't so reckless," Nick said.

"No one blames you for what happened. It was a no-win situation and you did what you had to do in order to save millions.

However, with the shield gone, Ozarael's put us on the defensive. Perhaps this was his intention all along," Gabriel said.

"It was, among other things. Bergice told me so."

"There has never been another demon in existence more powerful or cunning than Ozarael. He was able to cripple our strongest defensive measure without so much as even lifting a finger. We stopped him twice before, but that was before you were reborn. Now that you've defeated an Infernal, he'll be even more dangerous because he knows you're much closer to reaching him."

"Then he has to be stopped before an uprising can start!" Nick said.

"Start? War has already begun. Within hours of the shield's destruction, the Crowned Princes revealed themselves and brought their legions in an attempt to take over most of the major countries. Once the lockdown lifts, my troops and I will go to the frontlines to help the nearby cities."

"What about me?" Nick said.

"Get dressed and report to the library wing for your next mission," Gabriel said.

Nick waited for the archangel to leave before he got up. His legs were sore, as if he had just finished running a marathon. He walked around a bit, restoring feeling back into his feet. He washed his face at the nearby sink with cold water, waking his senses. Then, he grabbed fresh clothes that were neatly folded on the edge of his bed and quickly got dressed. He slipped on his signature jacket and was out the door.

Nick located an extremely packed library. Knights from the Wisdom Unit were grabbing books and research materials, grouping up and cramming last minute preparations before the lockdown was lifted. The room was so crowded that Nick almost missed Lucius pacing the middle of the room, looking perturbed, like he had received terrible news.

"Sir Lucius, I expected you to be talking about strategy with your squad," Nick said.

"They have their orders when situations like this arise. If years of preparation haven't given them a clear sense of how to operate efficiently without my guidance, then no amount of training now will be of any use now. You've made quite the impression on Ozarael with that victory over Doctor Numerous. I suspect, based on your performance, they've started the war earlier than expected. They must fear what is to come and that is good news for us," Lucius said.

"That's what Gabriel said too, but I'm not really sure I deserve all the praise. It's not like I did it alone."

"Don't worry, the others will receive credit where it is due," Lucius said. "Now Nick, what I have to tell you is going to contain sensitive information and I prefer we discuss it in a more private setting."

Nick obliged and followed him to one of the empty private studying rooms in the corner of the library. He took a seat and Lucius shut the door behind them.

"What's going on?"

It was unlikely that this was good news because Lucius looked forlorn, his charming and easy smile were nowhere to be found. He was worried as if he had seen something in Fyria that made him upset. Could this have to do with their false mission?

After a few minutes of silence, Nick grew increasingly anxious. Lucius wasn't even looking at him at this point, but through him, and towards the wall. Finally, he took a deep breath and pulled a manila folder from his coat and placed it on the table. His eyes were sympathetic.

"During your time in the infirmary we ran some tests and found something troubling. While it's true that connecting yourself to Agrian is pivotal in our campaign in the war against the demons, the tests have shown that unlocking the anger from Agrian can lead to adverse consequences for your body. The more times you tap into your powers the easier it will become to corrupt you. Your body will become used to the evil that eventually you will crave it—like a drug. Eventually there will be a point when feeding Agrian your rage will give him enough power to completely take over you."

"So what you're saying is that eventually it will turn me into a shell of my former self?"

"I'm afraid so. It's eating your soul. Even though Quinn Valentine has given Agrian a soul, having a demon housed within your body is still toxic to any human being. In fact, no human alive has ever been able to resist full corruption. And despite all the good you can do with your powers, it cannot be denied that Agrian has an agenda of his own."

"Then he wasn't lying. The Soul Eater Project really was about bringing me back."

"Who told you this?" Lucius said.

"Bergice. Right before he killed Doctor Numerous." Nick looked at his hands. "If it really is corrupting to me, how am I supposed to fight them without my powers?"

"Normally, in a situation like this, we use holy water to ward off demon possession. However, since it's attached to your soul it has could have an unpredictable response, and might kill both of you if we attempted such a procedure. For the time being we should take a new approach to this situation, perhaps rework your involvement in our plans."

"I'm already in too deep, Lucius. I'm not turning my back when they depend on me now more than ever!" Nick said.

"Of course not, but at this time it isn't wise to constantly throw you into dangerous missions because that will only speed up the inevitable. Instead, you should focus on nurturing your good side and give yourself a chance to remember what it is like to be regular Nick Emberson."

"Dammit, I'm a Garrison knight. I've proven I can handle it. I deserve to fight on the frontlines just as much as anyone else!" Nick was standing up from his seat now, hands firmly planted in the table.

"You won't stop taking on missions, but first you need to learn how to balance yourself mentally. We thought we could provide help, but even with all our research, the best insight we have on your demon situation is still vague! We need you to be fully prepared so you don't fly off the handle and do something outrageous every time some demon threatens Alyssa!"

"What's that supposed to mean?"

"I didn't want to be the one to talk to you about this, but we already know about the two of you," Lucius said.

"You guys already knew?" Nick felt slightly nauseous now, and slumped back into his seat. "What about the Supreme Commander?"

Lucius nodded. "Believe me, you didn't want to be there when Peter and the others came to the infirmary to find her sleeping next to your bed. I'm sure I don't have to tell you that he feels strongly about separating the both of you, but Nick, this is for your own good. Bergice knows of you relationship.

There's no doubt in my mind she'll be on the demon's radar. They'll be waiting for the opportunity to strike at her again. Is that what you want for her? She's already lived most of her life behind bars because of Peter's strict rules. Do you want to be the one responsible for taking her freedom again?"

Nick shook his head. "Of course not, but I can't see my life without her."

"Fate has already proven that you two have come together against impossible circumstances before. Perhaps, now is the time to see if love can truly thrive against all odds. I'm not Peter, and I'm not going to tell you what to do because that's for you to decide. However, I want you to think about what's best for both of you."

"Where does he plan on sending me?" Nick said finally.

"He wants you in Pailo. Sand country. Peter has a friend there who can help you with this. He's pulled a lot of strings to get her to agree to do this personal favor," Lucius said.

"A friend?"

"A former Garrison knight who became a demon sorceress, then reverted back to serving the side of justice. If anyone can help you control the demon within, it would be her," Lucius said. "According to Peter, she'll make you the best."

Nick took a breath. "So when would I get to come back?"

"I'm not going to lie, but you know as well I that the world is a mess right now. With everyone exposed, there are a lot of fires we have to put out. Every Garrison has their hands full. If I were to estimate, I'd say completion of your training will take about three years, at the earliest. But that's certainly a small price to pay when it will ensure that you will be in the best condition when you return."

"If we even have that luxury."

"I sense you disagree with this change in plans?" Lucius said.

"What, do you honestly think Ozarael is going to sit there and wait to *let* me beat him? By the time I'm done, who knows how many lives will have paid for it! I don't need more deaths on my conscience."

"Realize who you are talking to, Nick. I am an archangel and one of seven elite knights to hold that title in the world. As long as we stick by Peter's plan, there's no way it can fail. You'll see. Three years will go by faster than you can imagine, and believe me, the demons will bide their time and the war will still be here when you return," Lucius said.

"I don't have much choice then, do I?"

"I'm afraid not. Now then, Peter has prepared your vehicle for travel as well as most of the supplies you'll need along the way. You are expected to leave within the next few days after the lockdown ends. That should give you time to say your good-byes before you go."

"Lucius, what if I can't master Agrian?" Nick said.

"You can do anything you put your mind to, Nick. If there is anyone with the will to do it, it would be you. Besides, think of what will be waiting for you when you come home," Lucius said.

Nick wandered out, walking aimlessly around their stronghold until he found himself back in the hospital wing of their Garrison. The full force of their conversation had hit him, and he was feeling less than enthused about what the future had in store. He needed someone to help take his mind off of this. He needed to talk to Matt.

He went to look for his best friend in the infirmary wing. After talking to some of the medics, he was told that Matt had made a resounding recovery. He went to each one of their usual hangout spots until he eventually found him sitting with Joni and Daniel in the lounge among many other knights and soldiers. The soldiers around them were watching the screens that were covering the aftermath of the destruction in Hyperion.

Matt looked up as he walked towards him, and his face lit with a grin. He stood and clapped. Everyone to turn their attention to Nick. Once all eyes were on him the entire room erupted in a resounding applause, with several people whooping and cheering his name. Receiving praise from his peers was unfamiliar territory for him, and Nick didn't know how to react, except for smiling politely before taking his seat with his friends.

"What's going on?" he said.

"Everyone knows you beat an Infernal. No other knight with such little experience could ever say that they accomplished what you did," Matt said.

"We're just glad you're safe, and you can leave all that behind you," Joni said.

"I have some other problems."

"Where is Alyssa?" Daniel asked.

"That's what I wanted to tell you guys. I'm getting transferred to Pailo as soon as they lift the lockdown," Nick said.

"They're sending you away?" Daniel said.

Nick nodded.

"You saved millions from death. You're a hero! They should be throwing you a damn parade!" Matt said.

"Peter found out about me and Alyssa. I guess I should be glad he didn't banish me."

"Nick, I'm so sorry. But you know Peter and how protective he is of Alyssa. How else did you think he would react?" Joni said.

"Well, at least you're not the only one getting transferred," Daniel said. "After the Hyperion incident President Evans wanted Paul to go into hiding with him because of what's currently happening. But you know how stubborn Paul is, and he refused, so Peter made an agreement to send him to the Coros Garrison."

"Why Coros of all places?" Nick said.

"The Garrison there has seen the least action in recent years, so he'll be taking part in the war, but not to the extent that the others will. Leave it to Peter to find a compromise that actually works," Joni said.

"He must be furious. Paul Evans, the archangel apprentice forced to turn tail before the war even officially begins," Nick said.

"No kidding. I was there when the call was made and even though I hate the guy I understand how he feels. His dad wants him to be safe, but it's absolutely shameful to abandon Glenhaven because of this attack and Paul knows it," Matt said.

"Are the rest of you are staying here?" Nick said.

"Of course. Glenhaven Garrison needs to stay united. As the center of the world, we have to remain the shining example of all Garrisons and that means that we cannot fall," Joni said.

"And I'm going wherever Joni goes," Matt said.

"We've discussed everything in the Grand Hall, and we know that the Crowned Princes have planned a five-pronged assault in each of the major countries that facilitate the largest Garrisons. From the looks of things, it appears as if they plan to divide the countries among themselves," Daniel said.

"Every demon wants a piece of this little pie we live in," Matt said.

Just then a guard wielding a spear came in and tapped Nick on the shoulder. "Supreme Commander requests your presence, Nick."

Nick followed the guard to the entrance of Peter's office. He was ready to engage in the biggest screaming match of his life. He was prepared to tell the old man off for everything, and make him feel responsible for separating two people who were meant for each other. But when he opened the door and was ready to let his mouth run loose, he found that the old man wasn't alone. Another knight was in the room. And she was sobbing hysterically.

"There, there my dear," Peter said.

"Thank you, Supreme Commander." She wiped her face with a sleeve. She walked past Nick and out the door with her head down and without making eye contact.

"Nicholas, I thought you would have taken your time. I trust Lady Nancy's breakdown will be kept to yourself?"

"I hope everything is alright," Nick said.

"She was just expressing her thoughts about the incident in Hyperion. It was quite the terrible tragedy. Nancy had a younger brother who lived there, and he was killed by demons as he tried to flee during Astaroth's raid. He worked under the president as a part of his staff and was the only one in their family tree to have had the privilege to live a civilian life," Peter said.

"Why are you telling me this?" Nick was feeling both sorry and angry. It was as if Peter was purposely divulging other people's personal information in order to dissuade him or to soften the rage he had been feeling before his stumbled onto this scene.

"I'm telling you this because, of all people, you have experienced the loss of someone significant. Just like you, a person she cared about no longer lives because their life was stripped away by a demon," Peter said.

"And I made that demon pay for what he did."

"Doctor Numerous is one demon among thousands. Now that you've made a name for yourself, there's going to be backlash. Ozarael has issued a demand for Agrian's capture. Dead or alive," Peter said.

"If you think waving around the fact that Ozarael wants retribution is going to scare me away then you're wrong, Peter. I'm in love with Alyssa and she loves me and there's nothing you and this Garrison can do to stop us from being together."

Peter slammed his fist on the desk. "You don't get it do you? Casualties are building up behind us at every turn and all you can think about is yourself! I have nothing left in this world besides Alyssa, and I'll be damned if I let any harm befall her just because you've fallen in love! You promised you'd stay away from her, Nicholas! You promised!"

The old man rubbed his face and exhaled his frustration. "Nicholas, you're like a son to me, but if anything ever happened to Alyssa, well, I wouldn't want to stop looking at you that way. I can't make the choice for you because I know you were meant for each other. It was naïve of me to believe that separating you two I could somehow prevent the inevitable, but the truth is fate can't be tampered with by anyone. You found each other despite my best intentions and now it is too late."

Nick promised himself that he would be relentless in his stance, that nothing that came from Peter's mouth could change his mind. However, he hadn't anticipated this reaction. Watching the old man become such an emotional wreck for the sake of Alyssa was absolutely devastating. She was the only person left in his life who kept him going. If something ever happened to her, the weight of that loss would destroy him. Alyssa was to Peter was like Susan was to him, and going through a trauma like that was a pain he wouldn't wish upon his most hated enemy.

"It was fate that put us together, and I can wait forever to be with her. But Supreme Commander, there's something I need to know. If it wasn't for the fact that she was a demon target, would I have your blessing?"

"I can't think of another man more worthy," Peter said.

"Then I'll do it your way," Nick said, finally.

"Thank you."

"Though, I don't think she's going to take the news very well."

"She'll come around eventually," Peter said.

"I need to get a few things sorted and I'll be ready for dispatch."

"First things first. Before you head to Pailo, we need to take the proper precautions. I'm sure Lucius has informed you about the corruption, has he not? The only way to make sure you don't exert yourself too much and get out of control would be if I placed a Hand of Peace on you. Letting you run wild without a proper seal before was irresponsible on my part. I had assumed that controlling emotions would be very easy, but I never realized how difficult it could be until I heard the testimonies from your peers."

"What are you planning to do?" Nick said.

"We are going to tattoo a holy inscription on your back. It is a temporary solution until you gain full control and can be taken off once you've finished your training. Now follow me."

They took to the Peace Unit wing of the Garrison, and found an empty room with only a single operating table and Joni waiting for them with needle in hand.

Joni bowed. "Supreme Commander."

"At ease." Peter turned to Nick. "Lie on the table so she can apply the seal." He removed his shirt and did as told. Joni took a seat next to him, preparing the proper tools.

"The Hand of Peace is a seal with Orichalon-based ink. It will keep Agrian at bay and prevent your rage from further corrupting you," Peter said.

Nick felt the sting of the needle in his back and the Hand of Justice being applied deep into his skin. If he hadn't just barely survived death he might have screamed in pain, but the sensation of the tattoo being stitched to his body paled in comparison to the excruciating agony of walking through a Holy Shield.

"We have recruited Garreth back as a whitesmith in our Wisdom Unit and he has already begun research on the sword of Sir Marcus. During the process we learned that the material isn't merely a different type of Orichalon like we had originally assumed. It was formed from Sanctuary itself, an angelic weapon that survived natural destruction despite being broken for years. This is why it was able to hurt you in a ways you've never experienced before," Peter said.

"Was it passed along to him the same way Yuriel gave Alyssa his *Morning Star*?"

"Yes, a fact that Sir Marcus failed to reveal. The broken blade is called *Vigilance* and once belonged to Zelios, the Herald of Bravery."

"That's exactly what Bergice told me," Nick said.

"Keep your guard with you around him. Bergice may act noble, but a demon is still a demon, Nicholas. His only goal is to help Ozarael enslave humanity. Don't forget that," Peter said.

"Got it. Though, he has been truthful with everything he's told me so far. For what it's worth he was the one who told me that Ozarael wanted the weapons from the Heralds, but I can't see what good it would do."

"It wouldn't do much good at all. Don't worry about it too much, for now. Just focus on the mission at hand and we'll let the Wisdom Unit draw conclusions," Peter said.

"Done," Joni said. The whirring of her needle stopped and Nick slipped his shirt and jacket back on. The cotton blend shirt gave relief to his tender back, which was still slightly raw.

"Joni, I need your assistance," Peter said.

"Yes, Supreme Commander?" Joni said.

"I'm sending you to Pailo with Nicholas. During his training I need one of my best clerics there to monitor him, just in case anything should happen."

"Yes sir!"

"Nicholas, there's one last thing. Even though you will be training for a majority of the time, that doesn't mean you won't have the opportunity to put your skills into practice. A certain city in Pailo has become overrun by a rogue demon warlord who has designated himself their king. Dethrone him."

20

THE HARDEST GOODBYE

Nick was standing around in his empty room. In a few days he had packed everything except for the furnishings. It was funny how someone's entire life could fit into a single suitcase. As he stared at the blank walls, they appeared much smaller than he remembered.

The lockdown had been lifted and almost everyone had cleared out and gone to their stations in neighboring cities to provide aid and protection. There they would remain for as long as the war lasted. He wished that his friends could have been here to see him off, but perhaps this was for the best. It gutted him to think of how he'd feel saying goodbyes. Would he have broken down? How pathetic would it be to witness their supposed savior and hero bawling like a big baby? No, he would retain his stoic nature, but deep down he knew it would break his heart. For as much as he wanted to master Agrian, the most stinging pain was knowing he would be separated from Alyssa.

Even worse was the fact that he hadn't Alyssa about his relocation. He had come up with a hundred reasons for not telling her, but truthfully Nick just couldn't bring himself to do it.

As he grabbed his suitcase and left, a pang of sadness welled in his chest as the only place he'd ever known was no longer his home.

He decided to take a walk around the Garrison, a final trip down memory lane. His first stop was the battle coliseum where he stood in the middle of the field. He walked to the wall he put Daniel into and touched the newly formed surface where there was once a giant gaping hole. Then he made his way to the strategy room, the library, the infirmary, and finally the lounge, where he had a drink to himself as he watched the news on one of the screens. Several familiar knights moved around carrying lumber or hammering the walls as they were doing their part to rebuild the damaged areas of Hyperion.

The sounds of boots on the marble floor caused Nick to look up. Garreth stood before him in Garrison clothing with a drink in his hand. "I'm glad I found someone here who hasn't been shipped off yet." Garreth did a quick spin. "Not a sight for sore eyes, don't you think?"

Nick glanced at the gold patch on his arm. "Peter said you were back in the Wisdom Unit. I figured it was just a matter of time."

"I thought it would take some convincing, but he seemed to take my reenlistment pretty well. Things are still rocky, but we're on good terms." Garreth took a seat next to Nick. "Because of what we accomplished, I'm already back on active duty."

"Congratulations."

"What about you? I'm sure Peter has plans for our newest Garrison hero," Garreth sipped his drink.

"I'm going to Pailo."

Garreth nearly spit out his soda. "Pailo? Of all places, Peter's sending you clear across the world?"

"Things got complicated…and well, it's already set in his mind."

It took a minute for Garreth to process, but then his face grew somber and he shared an empathetic look. "If it makes you feel any better, I know she's the type of girl to wait for someone she cared about until the end of time itself. I wouldn't be too worried about it. It's not like any other guy stands a chance."

Nick nodded. "I appreciate hearing that Garreth, especially from you."

"No problem. Have you seen Daniel? I was supposed to meet him in the training field before we left, but I can't seem to find him," Garreth said.

Nick shrugged. "I thought everyone had already left."

"Apparently not everyone," Matt said.

Nick turned to find his best friend standing there with his goofy grin on his face. "Surprised to see me?"

"Matt, what are you doing here? I thought you'd be in Hyperion," Nick said.

Matt pulled up the chair next to Garreth and sat down. "That's where they wanted to send me, but I figured, slag it. If you and Joni are going a mission, then I wanted in too. So I talked to Pete, and convinced him to let me go with you guys. It's our little trio, just like old times."

Nick smiled. "This is the best news I've heard all day."

"I'm going to take a wild guess and say that you still haven't told Alyssa about this arrangement," Matt said.

Nick shook his head.

"You tried breaking up with her once and it nearly killed you. Do you really think you can do it again?" Matt said.

"I don't know."

"I've known Alyssa for years and I think telling her flat-out would be the best thing you could do. It wouldn't be fair to her for you to just up and walk away without at least saying goodbye," Garreth said.

For the remainder of the conversation Nick sat in silence, caught up in his own thoughts. He let Matt and Garreth converse with each other, half listening to their talk about upcoming missions, the future of their lives, and what would happen if they lost the war.

That's what it came down to the most: winning or losing. This all depended on Nick and whether or not he could rise to that challenge. The combined efforts of the Garrisons were strong enough to beat the Crowned Princes twice before, but a third time? He didn't want to be selfish, but maybe they could do it again without him. Surely it could be possible, but tempting fate could also lead to adverse consequences. He had almost died several times already; he didn't want his life cut short now. Not when he finally had a life to return back to.

He imagined a world where he could walk hand in hand with Alyssa in broad daylight, a world where he had Peter's approval. It would be entirely possible in a perfect world. But as of now, things were far from perfect. Trying to mend this fragmented world would require him to fulfill his end of the bargain to the bitter end. He would have to stop the demon threat as fate intended.

After a while, they said their goodbyes and went their separate ways. Garreth had to go to his post and Matt to make the final preparations for their flight. Nick promised Matt he would meet him and Joni after his conversation with Alyssa. As he paced around outside the room she was currently staying in, he ran through the entire conversation in his head until he was sure he was ready.

He knocked on her door. She opened it, wearing a bright smile on her face. Alyssa leapt into his arms, embracing him in a warm hug. In that instant, he nearly forgot everything except her.

"I knew my grandpa couldn't scare you off, even though I'm sure he tried his best," Alyssa said. "I heard he threatened to send you clear across the country just to split us apart. How crazy is that?"

"He has his reasons. At first I was outraged, but when he and Lucius explained the situation to me it seemed to be the most logical decision," Nick said.

Alyssa's smile faded. "Don't tell me you're considering it?"

"I already agreed."

"What!"

"I've been thinking about it a lot, and it's the only option I have left. I can't let what happened with Doctor Numerous ever happen again," Nick said.

"If I didn't get captured then we wouldn't be in this situation. I'm more trouble than I'm worth."

Nick put his arm on her shoulder, turning her to face him. "Don't say that, don't ever say that! I did what I had to because I couldn't imagine a world without you. Even if it was fate that brought us together." He put his hand over her heart. "It was because of this that we're still standing here. Your love saved me. It saved us both."

"Then I guess you storming Hyperion and saving my life and almost dying in the process just pales in comparison doesn't it?" Alyssa said sarcastically.

"That's right."

"How can you say that?"

"Because it's true. Don't you see? You saved me first. And I'm not talking about what happened with Bergice. When the whole world gave up on me, when I lost my reason to fight, all I had to do was think of you. You give me the strength to be what I am, Alyssa. Without you, I would have never been able to fight back. I wouldn't have the heart to do any this."

"You're just saying that."

"I'm not. That's what Bergice meant to do too. He was testing me, trying to see if I lived up to the reputation."

"And you did. You beat Doctor Numerous."

"At what cost? Having Agrian inside me is turning me into the very thing I swore to destroy. It will continue eating up whatever is left of my soul. If I keep it up, soon there'll be nothing left. I think that's what Bergice wanted from the beginning. And now that they know how much you mean to me, it'll be even easier to exploit me because they know that you're my only weakness," Nick said.

"You told me you weren't going to let the world split us apart. You said we would always be together!"

"That hasn't changed."

"Yes it has! You're going to the other side of the world! Nick, you can't be serious. It's crazy—no, it's just a stupid ploy to drive us apart. Without the protection of the Garrison, what are you going to do? "

Nick shook his head. "No, I can't keep on relying on Peter. I hate to admit it, but I am too weak right now. The longer I stay behind these walls, the weaker I'll become. After talking to him I know for sure my presence here would only lead them to you. Trust me when I say that this is for the best thing for both of us."

"Then take me with you. There's nothing for me here either," Alyssa said, on the verge of tears.

"What about your grandfather? What about everybody else?" Nick placed his hands on her shoulders. "You're the second in command to the Glenhaven Garrison. With everything in chaos they need you right here, right now."

"I can't stay if it means losing you," Alyssa said.

"We can never truly be apart. That was our promise, right?" Nick took hold of the angel feather dangling around her neck. "Even if the world fell to pieces around us there wouldn't be anything to stop me from coming back to you. Nothing could."

Tears were streaming down her cheeks now. Nick mustered all his strength to keep from crying. His heart ached as well as his body, but he wrapped his arms around her nonetheless, feeling her warmth and smelling her sweet fragrance. He'd carry the memories of her. He closed his eyes, praying, wishing that there could be another way. But there wasn't. Not this time.

"I can't believe this is happening," she whispered. Nick didn't want to leave things like this. He didn't want her memory of their last conversation with him to be filled with so much sadness.

He tilted her chin up and gazed into her eyes. Those green eyes he loved so much. "I haven't even left yet, and I already miss that perfect smile of yours. I don't want to leave without seeing that one last time. Smile for me, please?"

Alyssa tried her best to resist, but after such an intense gaze, she could no longer hold it in and laughed through the tears.

"It's not fair. You always do that. You always say the cheesiest things at the worst times."

Nick smiled. "Just promise me to keep that smile when I'm gone. It looks good on you."

All he could do was to grab this moment and kiss her deeply. For those few moments everything stood still and they were the only two people left in the world. Nothing else mattered. No demons, no war.

As he let go, Alyssa wiped her tears with her sleeve. "You better come back fast, Emberson." She took off her necklace and draped it on him. "So we'll never be apart."

He kissed her one last time on the forehead. "I'll be back before you can even begin to miss me, you'll see."

"That's not true," she whispered.

Nick heard her as he walked off, but didn't dare to look back because he was afraid it would stop him. He made his way to the hangar and got into the last remaining plane. It was a small four-seater painted in the Garrison colors. Matt was already inside, playing with toggles and buttons in the pilot seat. Joni sat in the back, reading over the mission brief.

"I wonder how things will be when I'm gone," Nick said. "I don't want things to change without me."

"It doesn't have to be that way. The one thing that life guarantees is uncertainty. We don't know what's going to happen next. Fate works in mysterious ways and all we can do is wait to see what each day has in store for us and make the most of it. I think every person struggles to deal with situations out of their control at one point or another. So I think the only question you have to ask yourself is: are you ready for what's next?" Matt said.

Nick pulled the seatbelt over his chest. The hangar doors opened and the bright rays of the sun poured onto them. The vast blue sky seemed to go on and on into the unknown. There were infinite possibilities, with no clear-cut path. It was daunting, the uncertainty that came with so much freedom. However, the warmth he felt made his initial fears and doubts disappear, and suddenly he was filled with hope.

"Let's find out," he said.

The plane shot straight toward the high sun, into the endless ball of fire.

End of Book One

AUTHOR BIOGRAPHY

Andrew Ly lives in Orange County as an entrepreneur.

He has a degree in Communications from Cal State University Fullerton. Though he is an avid writer, *Gods From the Machine* is his first published novel.

His author website can be found at andrewjly.com

Follow him on Twitter! His username is @andrewjly

www.ingramcontent.com/pod-product-compliance
Lightning Source LLC
Chambersburg PA
CBHW020227180626
46810CB00006B/2071